THE HUNT

Rose is the one that got away. She was the prey in a human trophy hunt run by an elite organisation known only as the Trail. She paid the worst possible price. Every moment since, she has been planning her revenge. And now her time has come . . . Chris returns from his morning run to find his wife and children missing and a stranger in his kitchen. He's told to run. If he's caught and killed, his family go free. If he escapes, they die. Rose is the only one who can help him — but for her, Chris is bait. And the Trail have not forgotten the woman who tried to outwit them. The Trail want Rose. The hunters want Chris's corpse. Rose wants revenge, and Chris just wants his family back. The hunt is on . . .

T. J. LEBBON

THE HUNT

Complete and Unabridged

CHARNWOOD
Leicester

First published in Great Britain in 2015 by
Avon
A division of HarperCollins*Publishers*
London

First Charnwood Edition
published 2017
by arrangement with
HarperCollins*Publishers*
London

A catalogue record for this book is available from the British Library.

ISBN 978–1–4448–3429–1

Published by
F. A. Thorpe (Publishing)
Anstey, Leicestershire

Set by Words & Graphics Ltd.
Anstey, Leicestershire
Printed and bound in Great Britain by
T. J. International Ltd., Padstow, Cornwall

This book is printed on acid-free paper

For Dan the Man

'Come what may, bad fortune is to be conquered by endurance.'
Virgil

'Run when you can, walk if you have to, crawl if you must; just never give up.'
Dean Karnazes

1

tiger

When he wanted to run faster, Chris Sheen imagined being chased by a tiger. Sleek, stealthy, powerful, it pounded silently along the trail behind him, tail swishing at the clasping brambles and eyes focused on his back. He didn't risk a glance over his shoulder. There was no time for that. If he did his pace would slow, and maybe he'd trip over a tree root or a rock protruding from the uneven path. He'd go sprawling and the big cat would be upon him. All they'd find would be his GPS watch and perhaps one of his running shoes, bloodied and torn and still containing a foot.

He giggled. Sweat ran into his eyes and down his back. Mud was splattered up his legs from the newly ploughed field he'd run across a couple of miles back. Blood pulsed, his heart thudded fast and even, and he had never felt so good.

He loved running with the dawn. Out of the house while it was still dark, leaving Terri and the girls sleeping, he was through one small woodland and already running down towards the canal towpath by the time the sun set the hills alight. Sometimes he saw someone else on the canal, walking their dog or cycling to work, but more often than not he was on his own. This

1

morning he'd seen a buzzard in a field, sitting on a recent kill and staring around as if daring anyone to try for it. Once on the towpath a heron had taken off close by, startling him with its sheer size. He heard a woodpecker at work somewhere, scared ducks into the water with their ducklings, and he'd caught a brief glimpse of a kingfisher's neon beauty. This early morning world felt like his alone, and he revelled in it.

Now, close to the end of his run, the giggles came in again. It was a familiar feeling. The endorphins were flowing, his heart hammering, and it felt so bloody great to be alive that sometimes he whooped out loud, running through the woods towards home. He ran with assurance and style, flowing across the uneven ground and watching ahead for potential trip hazards. Spider web strands broke across his face, but he didn't mind. Once, he'd arrived home to find Terri in the kitchen, sleep-ruffled and clasping a warm mug of tea, and when he'd hugged her — ignoring her protestations at his sweat-soaked clothing and cold hands — she'd screeched at the sight of a spider crawling in his hair.

He leaped a stream, slipped, found his footing and ran on. He knew this was a good run, he could feel it, but when he glanced at his watch he saw that he was well on course for a personal best. It was one of his regular routes — through a small woodland on the other side of the village, along a country lane, up a steep hill to a local folly, back down a rocky trail to the canal towpath, then under several bridges until he entered the larger woodland that led back home. Twelve miles, and his best time so far was one hour fifty minutes. Not bad for cross country, and pretty good for a middle-aged former fat bastard. But today he was set to smash that record by five minutes.

It was almost eight o'clock, and he'd still be home in time to make sandwiches for Gemma and Megs to take to school.

He emerged from the woods and headed across the large field behind the village hall. He waved at an old man walking his dog, vaulted the fence instead of passing through the kissing gate, and crossed the village hall car park.

Half a mile now, and he put on a burst of speed to finish at a sprint. It felt so bloody good. When he'd hit forty he'd been thirty pounds overweight and unfit, but then everything had changed. A comment one day from Terri — *I love you cuddly* — had started a snowball effect of worry about his weight, unhappiness at his appearance, and concern for his kids. He wanted to see them grow up. He wanted to take his grandkids for long walks. Four years later he was fitter than he'd ever been, leaner, stronger. He'd tucked his first two marathons under his belt, and the year before he'd completed his first Ironman, with plans for more. The Chris of four years ago wouldn't recognise the Chris of today, and he couldn't deny a little smugness at that thought.

'Morning, Carol!' he shouted across the road. Their friend was dragging rubbish bags up her driveway, still wearing her dressing gown.

'Nutter!' she called back, waving. She was wildly overweight and never walked anywhere, even drove to the village shop. Chris was fond of her, but knew who the real nutter was.

There was a strange car parked at the end of his street, a suited man in the driver's seat talking into a Bluetooth headset. He caught Chris's eye then looked away, still talking. Smooth-looking bastard. Salesman, maybe. Chris hoped the guy didn't knock at his door, but the 'No Cold Callers' sign didn't deter most. He was an architect, he worked from his home studio, and nothing annoyed him more than people disturbing him to try to sell him things on his doorstep.

Their house came into view. One more injection of power, swing those arms forward and back, watch the style, land on mid-foot and sweep forward, and . . . hit the watch.

Chris looked at his time and muttered a delighted 'Yes!' Terri wouldn't really care that he'd beaten his best time by almost six minutes. He'd tell her anyway.

Their bedroom curtains were still drawn. That was weird, because Terri had to leave for work in less than half an hour. Maybe she'd missed the alarm, although the girls foraging downstairs for breakfast and arguing over what to watch on TV should have woken her.

Panting heavily, already feeling the burn settling into his muscles, he plucked the front door key from his pocket and slipped it into the lock. He needed a pint of water and a bowl of cereal and fruit. But for another few seconds he breathed in the peace and quiet, readying himself for the pre-school chaos inside.

As he pushed the door open he already knew that something was different. *No, not different,* he thought. *Wrong. Something's wrong.*

'Terri?' he called, closing the door behind him. 'Gemma? Megs?' Nothing. No angry voices as his daughters bickered. No tired admonishments as Terri tried to get ready for work while the girls dressed for school. No sound of the shower running or perfumed scents on the air. The TV in the living room was muted, there was no music from upstairs, and the alarm on Terri's phone beside the bed must have been turned off. One of the joys of going out early was that he didn't have to wake up to One Direction singing one of their bland songs. Though Terri said she liked waking to blandness: it meant the day could only get better.

And there was something else. Something he couldn't quite place, apart from the unnatural silence, the stillness.

'Terri?' Four steps and he could look into the living room. The TV was off. There was no breakfast stuff scattered around. Usually the girls left their bowls for someone else to clear up, and lately he and Terri had been leaving them until after school, making the girls clear away their mess from the morning. Sometimes, anyway. More often than not he'd pick them up during the day, on his way through from his studio to the kitchen to throw a salad together for lunch. After today's run he'd probably treat himself to something more substantial, maybe some cheese on toast or a bacon bagel with . . .

One of Terri's slippers was on the floor by the doorway into their large kitchen-diner. Just one of them, lying abandoned on its side. So she'd been downstairs, at least.

'Hello?' No answer. They were hiding from him, of course, waiting to pounce when he climbed the stairs. But that certainty couldn't prevent the stab of fear that pierced his chest and ran cold down his spine as he started up. *It's not like Terri*, he thought. *Me, yeah, I'll jump out of cupboards and lark around, scare the kids. But not her.* 'Okay, I'm sweating more than usual, and the first person I find gets a really big hug.'

No giggles. No sounds of girls struggling further beneath beds or into wardrobes. The boiler ticked as it heated water, and that was all. The only noise in this usually bustling family home.

Chris ran up the last few stairs and checked the girls' bedrooms. They were empty, messy as usual, clothes strewn about. Gemma was almost fifteen now, and amongst the books and DVD cases were make-up packaging and teen magazines. Megs was nine. She had more stuffed toys than was probably necessary, and Chris waded into her room, shifting them aside with his muddy trainers. *Terri'll kill me for not taking them off*, he thought, but right then he didn't care. Something was wrong, and every time he breathed . . .

He could smell coffee. It had been rich on the air when he'd opened the front door, and it was only now that he acknowledged the scent. Terri hated coffee. And she'd never have made some

6

ready for him because she knew he liked it hot, fresh, and brewed by his own hand.

He darted along the landing to their room. Empty, bedclothes dragged down onto the floor. Terri's phone was on the carpet beside the bed. As if it had been knocked from the bedside table.

'Terri!' Chris shouted, shocked at the note of panic in his voice. For an endless moment he didn't know which way to turn, what to do. Grab her phone and call the police? And tell them what? Go back downstairs, then, check out the kitchen-diner where they were probably hiding, or maybe just sitting down having a quiet breakfast. Maybe he'd been so pumped up when he'd come in that he hadn't heard them answer, and now they'd be frowning at each other with jam on their lips, Terri rolling her eyes and the girls laughing as their dad staggered into the kitchen, a sweat-soaked wreck who'd almost run himself into the ground.

Yeah.

But when he glanced into the large family bathroom and saw the shower curtain on the floor, its plastic hooks strewn across the tiles along with scattered pot pourri, bath dry but for the splash of blood across one side and the smear across the wall beside the shower head, he knew that everything had changed.

His vision and senses became focused, sharpened by fear for his family and the surrealness of this moment. He saw things he might not have otherwise noticed. The bathroom window was closed, and Terri always opened it first thing in the morning. Megs' sleep teddy

— the one cuddly toy she couldn't get into bed without — was propped behind the bathroom door on the laundry basket. The shower power supply was on but the curtain, splayed across the floor with one end up on the toilet seat, was dry.

Blood.

Gemma tried shaving her legs, cut herself. Terri panicked, took her to hospital. But that just didn't add up. She'd have taken her phone, and he always took his mobile when he went for a run, *always*! He frantically dug it from his waist bag and checked, but there were no missed calls, no emails.

Breathing heavier now, he smelled coffee again.

He ran downstairs, trying to blink away the image of blood. Splashed on the bath. Smeared on the wall, as if someone had it on their hand, reaching for purchase as they fell from the bath (or were pulled, maybe they were *pulled*) and took the shower curtain with them.

He ran past the still-empty living room and barged the kitchen door aside. It struck the door stop and bounced back at him, and he shoved it open again, blocking it with his foot, not making any sense of what he saw, because what he'd expected to see was his family sitting at the small table eating breakfast, Gemma perhaps with a bandage on her hand and looking sorry for herself.

Coffee. Terri hated coffee.

There was a man leaning casually against a kitchen cupboard beside the back door. The door was ajar, a small fingerprint of blood on the

8

UPVC jamb. The man was holding a mug, the one from a Yorkie Easter egg that Chris's mum still insisted on buying him every Easter, much to his secret delight. The man watched Chris while taking another long sip of coffee. He raised his eyebrows in greeting.

'Who are you?' Chris asked.

The man lowered the mug and swallowed. 'Good coffee. Ethiopian. You ever been there?'

'No, I . . . who *are* you?'

The stranger put the mug on the worktop beside him and picked up a phone. He wore a nice polo shirt, chinos, well-polished boots. He reminded Chris of the guy he'd seen sitting in the car at the end of the street, and that connection suddenly seemed all too real.

'Where are my family? What are you doing here?' Chris's attention kept flitting to the open back door, that dab of blood. He was filled with a sudden, utter dread. His legs felt weak. His bladder relaxed.

The man looked at his watch, glanced at the phone screen, and sighed. 'Stay in the house. Don't go out. Don't call the police, or your wife and children will be executed. I'll be in touch.' Then he turned and opened the back door.

'Wait!' Chris said, darting across the kitchen for the man, reaching, fingertips brushing the fine cotton of his polo shirt before the intruder turned fluidly and stood, motionless. He stared at Chris, his eyes empty, face blank and terrifying.

'I'll be in touch,' he said again. He exuded danger in waves. Chris took one step back, and the man left and closed the back door behind him.

Terrified, shaking, alone, Chris waited for whatever might come next.

2

chosen

Rose screamed herself awake, sprang upright on the uncomfortable bed and pressed one hand against her chest, feeling her thundering heart and assuring herself that she was still alive. Sweat had dampened her vest and underclothes. She'd kicked the blanket off during the night. The musty confines of the caravan were sliced by sheets of dawn sunlight shining through broken blinds, and birds sang cheerfully outside, as if her husband and three children had never been tied up and slaughtered in some dark, dank basement.

The familiar flood of reality rushed in, and Rose groaned at the awfulness of it all. Sometimes in sleep there was escape, and occasionally in dreams she enjoyed some form of vicarious peace. But not this past night. The memory of what she had found was so vivid and fresh that it was like discovering the scene all over again. Four years had passed, but most nights she found her dead family afresh.

Already the nightmare was dissipating, leaving brash images scorched into her memory. Adam, his eyes as wide and empty as the vicious gash in his throat. And her three children — Molly, Isaac, Alex — lying dead where she had not been able to protect them, hold them, whisper

11

motherly words into their ears. She always remembered that, however hard she tried to forget.

She used the cramped toilet and dressed quickly, pausing now and then to glance from the windows. New habits persisted. It was dangerous to ever believe herself safe.

Outside, all was peaceful. The field where her caravan was parked remained empty right now — the farmer said he would be introducing some sheep in the next few weeks — and the grass was long, shimmering slightly in the morning breeze, jewelled with dew. The windows gave her good views in each direction, and she'd be able to see anyone approaching. Down the sloping field was the farm, still and silent this early in the morning. East lay the orchard, fruit-heavy trees dipping low limbs across the landscape. And to the north, a family of foxes played close to the hedge bordering the field and a woodland beyond, young cubs leaping, rolling, snapping at each other like puppies. She was always pleased to see them. If someone was close by, the foxes wouldn't be anywhere in sight.

Rose went through her morning exercise routine. One hundred press-ups, sit-ups and crunches, along with chin-ups, planks, and squats. Her body had grown lithe and lean. The exertion kick-fired her metabolism and got her blood pumping, and the distraction steered her away from her horrible dreams. For a time, at least.

After eating a breakfast of fruit and yoghurt she pulled the pistol from beneath the mattress

12

and tucked it into her belt.

She brewed coffee and switched on her laptop. The caravan was small and basic but suited her needs perfectly. She'd bought a new fridge and decent bedding, but the van's outside was as mouldy and worn-looking as when she'd first seen it. Five hundred pounds and it was hers. The farmer took a chunk of cash from her each week for ground rent and silence, and he was happy to ask no questions. That was fine. She never stayed in one place for more than a few weeks.

Drinking strong coffee, humming quietly, she started scanning her usual news sites. But the memory of her nightmare was strong. She closed her eyes and breathed in coffee fumes, because every time she thought of her family the grief was rich, deep, and sometimes crippling. She dreaded forgetting them, though sometimes remembering was almost too much.

But her dreams and memories fed her fury. She knew that her current existence was a form of self-imposed limbo, and everything she did now would lead to an eventual resolution. Perhaps then she could lay her nightmares to rest, and true grieving could begin.

There was no news that drew her attention today. The usual political infighting, celebrity inconsequentialities, faraway conflicts. She looked for murders or unexplained deaths. She sought news on kidnappings and shootings, unidentified bodies found strangely mutilated in city or countryside. Anything that might lead to the Trail.

As usual, nothing.

But something felt different today. Her nightmare clung on, and even though she had found nothing obvious on the net, perhaps today was the day to check again.

Rose gulped down the rest of her coffee in one and then opened a new browsing window.

She didn't like doing this too often. She accessed the net via a proxy server in London, had a rolling defence protocol that would lock her out at the first sign of being tracked, used no identifying markers or traceable elements, yet she knew that they had far more expertise at their disposal than her. Rose liked to amuse herself by thinking about some of the online contacts she'd made and how much stuff she had access to that would give the heads of the CIA and MI5 panic attacks. But accessing the Trail's own network was like dipping her toe into a river of alligators. It was only so long before she was noticed and they came for her.

She would only allow that to happen on her own terms.

She slipped by several firewalls and surfed communications she could not yet decipher. It was pretty standard traffic that she'd seen before, so she withdrew and re-entered under another address, creating an avatar that would easily be mistaken as a particularly intrusive trollbot, if anyone noticed it at all. Most trollbots' aims were to spread viruses or collect information. Hers was simply to observe. She'd given it a variety of source links which flickered and rolled every three seconds — a sex-drug site; a Nigerian billionaire with money to get out of the country; a guaranteed tip to increase cock size. She hoped that, draped in the paraphernalia of a million other trolls, hers was all but invisible.

While her laptop worked, she made more coffee. It was her one vice, and had been for three years.

For almost a year after escaping the Trail and finding Adam and her children murdered, she'd drowned herself deep in London's underworld. Her first thought had been to go to the police, but even then the shadow of the Trail remained over her, and the promises of harm they had levelled against her extended family and friends had felt even more real. They had proven themselves sickeningly brutal.

Then came the revelation that she was wanted for her family's slaying. In a way, that was the worst abuse of all — the way they had framed her, made a mockery of her love and grief. A madness had taken her. A blazing fury and a smothering grief. It was incomprehensible how quickly she had changed from a family woman with a good job and a nice house to . . . someone else. And so she had cut her hair, dyed what was left, and submerged herself in the chaos of the capital. It was ironic that she went to so much effort disguising herself when in truth she was already lost.

Those shadowy places were more about the people than the locations — lost, dispossessed, cast adrift by society, or fallen by the wayside of their own volition. No one had seemed interested in her, and she had taken notice of no one. Occasionally she worried about being recognised, though in truth grief had changed her more than a haircut and new clothes ever could. She was a hollow person, and her body projected that physically. Sunken cheeks, stick-like limbs, deep eyes like pools of dark ink.

London had been an ideal place to hide, and to drink. Every day, every night, alcohol absorbed and obsessed her, becoming her whole world. When the memories threatened to surface she drank some more to smother them, and if she ever approached sobriety, another bottle of cheap vodka swept her away again. Abandoned buildings and squats had provided places for her to sleep, and if in a drunken haze she lost her way, there were always the shadowy spaces beneath bridges or in rubbish-strewn alleyways. She was one woman in a city whose lifeblood was anonymity, and time and place lost all meaning. The moment of change when she'd found her family was a deep, wide chasm in her life. Sometimes she stood on the edge and tried to look back, but it was too far to see clearly. So she remained on the other side, wallowing in the guilt of survival and letting alcohol smother her across this new, barren land.

Seeing a member of the Trail had changed everything.

Rose had stumbled into the woman outside the Apollo Theatre one rainy, cold November evening. She'd been wandering through Soho searching for one of her familiar sleeping places, a deserted, boarded-up pub accessed through a broken back window. Many of the dispossessed knew that place. It stank of piss and booze, echoed with drug-fuelled mumblings and occasional cries of wretchedness, pleasure or pain. But that night Rose's befuddled sense of direction had failed her, and she'd emerged into the bright lights and bustle of Shaftesbury Avenue.

The lights had been blinding. Disorientated, she'd turned to make her way back into the shadows. People had parted to let her by, protecting themselves with space and muttered words of distaste. All but this woman. Rose had walked right into her, and many times since she'd wondered whether it had been orchestrated. Had the woman recognised her in that instant and engineered their collision? Had she been looking for her?

The last time Rose had seen her, she'd been standing beside a Range Rover somewhere in London's Docklands smiling broadly as a man told Rose to run.

As the heat of recognition grew quickly in Rose's mind, she saw that it had already settled in the woman's eyes. *Grin*, Rose thought, because that's how she had thought of the woman since that first meeting, in nightmares and booze-fuelled fantasies of revenge. *Grin, you're Grin, and I'll wipe that name from your face.*

Grin was smartly dressed, short and thin, strong. Her auburn hair was cut in an attractive bob, her skin smooth and relatively unlined even though she was perhaps fifty years old. She looked *nice*, like anyone's mother. But Rose knew her secret.

Grin had smiled and reached slowly, casually

into her raincoat pocket.

Rose still had no idea how she had reacted so quickly. Her hand snapped out, fingers closing around the object in Grin's hand, snatching, and then she ran. Losing herself in those rainswept streets had been easy, and the shouts and pursuit she'd expected never came.

The phone had worked for seven minutes before its connection was cancelled. In that time, she had hidden away and managed to scratch two numbers into her arm with a shard of broken glass.

Then she had ditched the phone in a trash-filled alley and fled. She'd somehow gathered herself, suffering a terrible couple of days of relative sobriety. She'd retrieved the necessary documentation and money she'd once hidden, at the time barely believing she would ever use it again. Italy was somewhere Adam had always wanted to visit with their kids, and it had seemed far enough away from London, remote enough, to lose herself once again.

That chance meeting in a city of millions had allowed the dormant seed of an idea to sprout. Revenge. And later, in the Italian heat, alcohol hiding her once more, she'd traced and retraced those healing scars on her forearm. Numbers that might lead to something else, like a code to discovery.

But even in Italy she had not been able to drag herself from the depths. She'd tried again and again, spending a day sobering up, but quickly following those brief moments of sick reality with long periods of even heavier drinking and deeper oblivion. She so wanted to find some way back. She dreamed of Grin's face opening beneath her pounding fists, a heavy rock, a wielded knife. But even approaching reality allowed the true, awful memories to flood back in.

She had been unable to find the strength to handle that. Not until Holt.

The laptop chimed.

Rose poured a new mug of strong coffee and sat down at the small table. Lifting the mug to her lips, she paused and stared down at the screen.

One of the inboxes she monitored had received a new email. It was only the fifth time in three years that such a mail had been sent and received. It was still marked in bold. Unread.

'They've chosen another one.' She sat back for a moment, stunned, chilled even through the rush of warm coffee. She knew that if she opened this email and read it, and they discovered it had been seen and read, everything might fall apart. The Trail would abandon their systems and networks and build again from the ground up, and she would lose everything she'd been working on, and hoping for, since bringing herself back to the world.

But the content of this email *was* everything. She could open it, screen-grab it, and mark it as unread again in a matter of moments.

She did not hesitate for a second before risking it all.

3

fifty minutes

Don't call the police, or your wife and children will be executed.

Chris stood motionless for a while, leaning against the sink and staring across the kitchen at the pinboard beside the fridge. There were photos on there, tickets for a show they were going to see in a few weeks, a couple of forms to fill out for a trip Gemma was going on with Scouts. Some discount coupons for the local cinema. A few of Terri's hair bobbles tied together.

Had the man really said that?

Chris closed his eyes and the world swam. He remembered the words coming from the man's mouth — how they'd sounded, the shape of his lips, the dreadful meaning — yet he still doubted.

He took in a few deep breaths and smelled the coffee. *His* coffee, that the intruder had brewed.

He took the phone from his pocket and placed it on the worktop. As he stared at it, it rang.

Grabbing the phone, dropping it, watching it hit the floor and break, case going one way and phone the other, Chris let out a hopeless cry. He went to his knees and picked it up — still ringing, not broken — and stroked the screen to unlock.

That voice again, cool and calm and inviting no discussion. 'Fifty minutes. Be ready.' Chris stood again, holding the phone in both hands. *Fifty minutes. Be ready.* Fifty minutes until what?

The back door was closed now, but he could still see the bloody smear drying on the jamb.

Everything but his family suddenly felt so distant. His work, their friends, his hobbies, all so far away from what was happening here and now. This was so surreal that his mind had picked him up and shifted him back a pace, making acceptance of the unbelievable situation easier. He'd felt something like this before. When his father had died three years earlier, there had been none of the disbelief and hysteria he'd been prepared for all his life. A distance had fallen around him, allowing him to cope with the situation and only starting to lift as grief eroded it away. It was a defence mechanism of sorts — perhaps purely natural, or maybe engineered by modern society and family needs — and for a while he'd felt an incredible guilt. But then his mother had told him that everyone deals with bereavement and grief in a very different way, and unnecessary guilt had no place in his heart. He'd loved her more than ever for that. He still did.

He dreaded the idea of her having to grieve again.

Chris looked down at his phone. *Don't call the police or your wife and children will be executed.* The words hung in the air around him as if taking on substance. Everywhere he looked he heard them. He stared at the screen display,

21

thinking, trying to work through the situation. Clicking on the timer, he set it at forty-eight minutes and pressed *start*.

Several minutes had passed since the man left. Standing in the kitchen, uncertain, he edged towards the back door, lifting the wooden blind aside to look out into the back garden. Maybe he should follow. Or call the police. That was his natural instinct, *anyone's* first instinct when something terrible like this happened. And how would they know? He should call them, tell them about the intruder and his missing family, and by the time they arrived . . .

He looked at the time on his phone. Forty-four minutes and counting.

Something moved in the garden. Chris squinted and looked again, scanning left to right across the well-maintained lawn, colourful borders, and the kids' stuff scattered here and there. Megs loved to play in the inflatable pool when it was warm enough. She said she wanted to swim the Atlantic when she was older.

'Shit,' he whispered, starting to shake. Fear gripped him. Terror at what was happening to his family, and confusion about why.

Movement again, and this time he saw the cigarette smoke rising from beyond the garden's rear hedge before it dispersed to the breeze. There was a narrow, private path behind there serving the several houses that shared this side of their street, and no reason at all for anyone to be standing there.

Placing his hand on the door handle he pushed it down, slowly, and opened the door.

A pale shape appeared behind the garden gate. Chris couldn't see much from this far away, and the gaps between the gate's slatted wood were only an inch across. But the smoking person was watching him.

He slammed the door again and retreated into the kitchen. 'Fuck, fuck, this isn't happening,' he muttered, pacing back and forth. He was chilled from the sweaty running clothes he still wore. He should change, get warm, get ready for . . .

. . . for the countdown to zero? Was he really just going to wait here like the intruder had told him?

Bollocks to that.

He held the menu button on his phone and said, 'Call Nick.' The phone called his elder brother, ring tone buzzing again, again, until passing on to answer phone. Chris hung up, pressed again and said, 'Call Angie.' She had five kids, an irregular boyfriend, and debt up to her ears, but his youngest sister was always a rock amongst stormy seas. It rang three times before she answered.

'Chris.'

'Angie, it's me, something's happened, something awful, and I need you to — '

'I can't talk right now.'

'What? Something's happened to Terri and the kids and you have to do something for me, but quietly, carefully. I need you to call the police.'

Silence. He could hear Angie breathing.

'Angie?'

'I can't talk right now.' Her voice broke, just slightly. Then there was the sound of fumbling before the call was disconnected.

Chris stared at the phone again, trying to make sense of his sister's words. Angie having a bad day? She had a lot of them, but she'd never been like that to him, ever. He'd pulled himself out of the land of lives his siblings lived, made a career for himself, made money. But they were still all the same really. They still loved each other. 'Angie,' he said, and the image came to him of her sitting alone in her kitchen, staring at the phone and shaking, while a stranger stood beside her own back door.

Chris snorted, shook his head. Pressed the button again. 'Call Jake.' He'd know what to do. Chris's best friend was a gruff bloke and could be a bit of a dick sometimes — his delightful ex-wife could attest to that — but he valued their friendship, and they were always there for each other. It was picked up after two rings.

'Jake, thank God. You've got to help me, mate, I'm in some scary deep shit here.'

'Get the fuck out of my life,' Jake said, and then he hung up.

Chris blinked at his phone. He tried to retain Jake's tone, the sound of his voice, but his words scorched away any ability to recall. Had he really just heard that from his best friend?

'This is . . . ' Chris started, and he laughed. Once, loud, an unbelieving outburst. But there was nothing at all to laugh at here. The bloody dab on the door was testament to that. 'What do I do?' Chris whispered. 'Just what?'

Filling the kettle, turning it on, he was moving on auto-pilot as he tried to think things through.

24

He glanced at his phone timer again. Less than thirty minutes to go.

He clicked on the Facebook app and entered his password. *Account temporarily suspended.*

'What?' he whispered. 'You're kidding.'

He exited Facebook and opened his email account. It usually went straight to his inbox, but instead it came up with his password entry. His heart fluttered. Didn't matter, that happened sometimes, once every few weeks he had to enter it again. Security measures, he supposed.

But even as he tapped in his password he felt the weight of dread.

Password not recognised. Please enter again. Be aware that password is case sensitive.

He entered it again, carefully, but already knowing what would happen.

Forgotten password?

How the fuck? How could they have done this? Maybe it was him, typing with clumsy, scared fingers . . .

. . . But no. It wasn't him at all.

The kettle boiled and Chris poured water into a mug with one hand. The other hovered over the phone, thumb stroking the 'phone' symbol, finger hovering over the 9.

It's a joke. A prank. A scam, scumbags scaring me to try and get some cash out of me. Or a reality TV show. Or . . . Anything but what it seemed. It had to be. Because things like this didn't happen in real life.

He tapped 9 . . . 9 . . .

The piercing electronic whistle was almost unbearable, screeching through the house from his phone, the small flatscreen TV on the kitchen worktop, and whining in from the living room where the big plasma TV had burst into life. Chris juggled the phone and almost dropped it, face screwed up against the sudden, unexpected sound. He pressed his right shoulder and left hand to his ears, still clasping the phone in his right hand and looking at the screen. Ready to hit the last 9 that would move events on apace and, perhaps, reveal more of what was really going on.

The keypad on his phone's screen had been replaced by something else. Winded, stunned, he barely even noticed that the deafening sound had ceased.

He thought it was a photo, but then he saw Megs nuzzle her head against Terri's leg, and Gemma stretched her tied legs and shuffled to change position.

'Oh no . . . ' he breathed. His throat was dry, voice hardly registering.

Terri was sitting on a bench in what looked to be the inside of a dirty van. The walls were rough and spotted with rust patches. A naked light flickered somewhere out of sight. His wife was tied to the bench with ropes around her legs and waist. She was blindfolded, and wearing loose jogging bottoms and a tee shirt. Megs was kneeling beside her, also blindfolded, sobbing softly. Gemma was tied up on the floor on Terri's other side.

There was a dark stain across the right shoulder of Gemma's school shirt. It seemed to match the patches on the walls, as if the truck also bled.

26

'No,' Chris said again, louder. 'Terri. Terri! Girls?' But they couldn't hear.

The image changed quickly, turning as whoever held the camera or phone on the other end switched it around to face themselves. It was a woman. Fiftyish, attractive, but with cold eyes. She smiled broadly, but only with her mouth.

She held up a gun.

'One 9 away from this,' she said, waving it back and forth and pointing it out of sight at his blindfolded family. 'Last chance. Next time we won't warn you again.'

'What do you want?' Chris shouted. 'Just tell me, I'll do anything, let them go and — '

'You're probably ranting and raving a bit right now,' the woman continued. She had a nice voice, calming, controlled. She could have been a school teacher. 'I can't hear you. But I know you can hear me. So calm down.' She looked aside at her watch. 'Twenty-three minutes. Be ready.' She smiled again, then the picture flickered off. His phone went dead.

'Ready for what?' Chris shouted. He raised his hand to hurl the phone at the wall, but held back at the last instant. 'For what?' He looked around for cameras, microphones, evidence of things in his home being tampered with. His home. They'd come in here, invaded his space, taken away his family . . .

He couldn't shake the image of his girls tied up like that. Megs crying and nestling against her mum. Gemma, bloodied, struggling and stretching, probably doing her best to release herself from her bindings. And Terri, sitting there

27

looking far calmer than she must feel. At that moment he would have given absolutely anything to have them back safe and sound. His safety, his sanity, his life, without a moment's hesitation he'd have handed them all over.

'I don't have much money,' he said. 'Twenty grand saved, a bit more, but I can't just get it. It'll take five working days. Is that what you want? It must be. Money' He frowned, thinking that through and really not understanding it at all. They lived in a nice house, but nothing special. Two cars, both over three years old. His architect's firm was reasonably successful, but he was the sole employee, turnover around seventy grand each year. Nice, but nothing spectacular. Nothing that would attract the attention of the sort of people who could do this.

Take his family, threaten his siblings and friends. Carry guns. Use his own tech against him.

He put his phone screen-down on the kitchen worktop and paced the kitchen again. He was sweating again now, chilled from his long run. He'd always had something of a vivid imagination, and now and then he'd written ideas down with the intention of one day writing a book. Terri had been encouraging, but it had never gone much beyond a few pages of notes and several tentative first chapters. Once, out on a long run, he'd imagined the end of the world. Running the barely used public footpaths across the top of a local range of hills, he'd lost himself for a few miles daydreaming about what would happen if he got home from the run and

28

everything had changed. His family, friends, neighbours, associates, all gone. Turn on the TV . . . white noise. Nothing on the radio. Leave home and everything is normal, return two hours later and find he's the only man left alive.

Now, that had happened. His whole world had changed, and unless he did precisely as instructed, they would end it. He didn't know what they wanted. But in less than twenty minutes he would find out.

Chris couldn't keep still. He walked back and forth, looking down at his phone every few seconds and waiting for it to make a noise. If the Black Sabbath song 'Paranoid' rang out it would be Jake calling him back to offer help. A whistle would be an email. A double-ping would be a text, perhaps from one of his siblings if they had a chance to secretly get in touch, tell him they were with him, they were doing their best. He picked it up and turned it over, checking the screen anyway in case he hadn't heard. But there were no messages, emails, or missed calls.

He didn't want to call his elderly mother. Not after what Angie had said, and Jake. He didn't want to know.

Landline, he thought. *I could contact the police that way.* But that would be stupid. Whatever their reasons for doing this, they'd planned it in detail. They'd have the landline covered. Bugged, perhaps, if what he saw in movies was true. It was far too risky.

He paused by the chopping board and leaned back against the kitchen units. Eighteen minutes.

He made himself a drink. Tea, lots of sugar. As

29

a teenager he'd always laughed at his parents whenever their first reaction to a crisis was to make tea, but as he'd grown older he'd come to recognise its calming properties. It wasn't anything chemical, he thought, nor was it the warmth. It was distraction. Waiting for the water to boil, stirring the tea bag, adding the milk, watching the tea darken, all these took time. But he couldn't distract himself from this.

He glanced up and saw the knife block. Six knives, all of them sharp. Terri had spent over a hundred quid on them, and he'd expressed his doubt that they were worth the money. But they were good knives that had kept their keenness over time.

Without pausing to scare himself out of it, he grabbed a medium-sized knife and slipped it into the waist of his running trousers, dropping his sweaty shirt over the handle with one hand as he picked up his mug with the other.

He turned and breathed across the hot tea, steam filming his eyes and warming his skin. The knife was cold against his hip. *And just what the fuck am I going to do with that?* he thought, trying to imagine himself plunging it into someone's stomach. He almost puked.

'I'm ready,' he said. 'No need to hang about.' The phone said fourteen minutes.

Slowly, he sipped at the hot tea and managed to convince himself that everything would be fine. If they'd planned to harm him or his family they'd have done so by now. They wanted something of him, though he couldn't imagine what. He'd made no enemies in life that he

30

could think of. He'd always been fair in business. He and Terri led a boringly normal life in many ways — loyal to each other, adoring of their children. He vented any need for excitement through his running, triathlons, mountain racing. *There are worse mid-life crises,* Terri said to him sometimes when he signed up for another extreme race.

Chris closed his eyes and breathed in the tea fumes, but found nothing approaching calmness. He felt like crying at the memory of seeing his family like that, taken somewhere unknown, bound and gagged. It had been a woman guarding them, but he couldn't help imagining how vulnerable they were to the men involved in this, too. Terri in what she called her comfy clothing, unconsciously attractive. Gemma, awkward and pretty, just developing into womanhood. Little Megs.

He opened his eyes, furious, and swigged at his tea. On the fridge door facing him, held on by magnets, were several drawings by Megs, a few money-off coupons for their local super-market, and a twenty-pound note. Gemma had been due to go to the cinema with her friends that evening.

He heard a knock from somewhere beyond the kitchen door.

Holding his breath, Chris put the mug down slowly, mouth slightly open, listening hard. The heating was off now, though the boiler was still warming the water. But he hadn't recognised the sound.

It came once more, definitely an impact of

31

some sort. His phone showed nothing so he turned it face-down again. Taking the knife from his belt and holding it down by his side, he walked through into the corridor beyond the kitchen door. Ahead of him the front door was still closed, and there was no sign of movement elsewhere.

Studio, he thought. To his right a shorter corridor led beneath the staircase to another door, beyond which their converted garage had become his business studio. It was a good size, with computer station, an old-fashioned drawing board, walls lined with pictures displaying his designs, and an informal area for clients with leather sofa and coffee machine. Nothing extravagant, but comfortable. And now there was someone there.

He thought about edging through the door, moving cautiously, carefully. But that's what they expected of him.

And he was angry.

Gripping the knife hard by his side he surged forward, shoved the door open and stepped quickly into the studio.

Something tripped him, he fell, one hand out to break his fall, the other twisted painfully as the knife was stripped from his grasp. He struck the timber flooring and tried to roll. A weight bore down on him, trapping him on his side with one arm crushed beneath his body, the other pressed between him and the person attacking him.

Chris kicked and writhed. A hand clamped down hard across his mouth. Another held his own knife against his throat.

He strained his neck and looked up into the woman's face. She looked hard, unflustered, and totally in control.

'I'm here to help,' she whispered. 'If you want to live past the next twenty-four hours and see your family again, do everything I say' She sat up and slowly took her hand from his mouth.

'Who . . . ?' he asked.

'I'm the one that got away. My name's Rose.'

4

just begun

She crept to the door into his studio and crouched beside it, peering out beneath the stairwell and into the hallway. Chris respected poise, economy of motion, litheness, but there was something else about the way this woman moved that disturbed him. Something inhuman. She moved like an animal, and like an animal she seemed ready to strike. She held the knife she'd taken from him as an extension of her arm, aimed forward, ready to slice and stab. Her movements were soundless, and he searched for her shadow. He was happy to find it.

'What are you going to . . . ?' he began, and she was back to him between blinks, hand pressed against his mouth once again, eyes wide, head shaking once. She didn't need to speak. The threat was palpable, radiating from her in powerful waves, even though she made no hint that she wished to hurt him.

She went to the door again and crept out, until she could look both ways along the hallway — left to the kitchen, right towards the front door. Then she came back and crouched in the doorway. She wore black jeans, a casual jacket with bulging pockets, walking boots. Her dark hair was tied in a ponytail, businesslike, impossible to tell its length. She might have been attractive, once.

34

'Who are you?' he asked.

'I told you. Rose.'

'But what . . . ?'

'Shut up.' She held up one hand, head cocked, not looking at him. 'There's no time now.'

Chris glanced at his phone. The timer said nine minutes.

'Just listen,' she said. 'I'm here to help. I only found out they were going for you yesterday morning. But it was long enough to plan and prepare. They'll be coming in to get you soon, and then we'll be leaving. You understand?'

'No,' Chris said. 'My wife. My girls.'

'We'll get to them.' She tried to smile. It was a sickly expression.

'Where are they?' he asked.

'Not sure.' An economy of words, and they explained nothing.

'Why are they doing this?'

'You're an easy target.'

He was shivering again. His clothing was soaked with sweat, his body now trying to cool down. 'I need to go to the police.'

'No!' she said, looking back at him again. 'You can't even *try* to do that, or they'll just kill your family and move on.'

'You're not one of them?'

She glared at him. 'Are you stupid?'

'No, not stupid. I'm normal. I'm just a normal person doing normal things, and now my family are — '

The front door opened. Chris heard the familiar sound of the handle depressing, the catch sliding, and then the sigh as the door's

35

draught-proofing seal broke. It was so recognisable that Chris muttered, 'Terri?' before the door slammed and heavy footsteps marched along the tiled hallway.

'We're early!' a voice called. Chris recognised it as belonging to the man from earlier, the same man who'd threatened to have his wife and children executed if he called the police. 'Sorry for the delay. Traffic's terrible.' The man chuckled to himself, completely confident and in command.

Chris frowned at Rose and raised his hands, but she turned her back on him and flowed forwards, through the studio door, beneath the staircase and towards the hallway. *But if you go that way you'll end up* — Chris thought, and then every thought was sliced off by what happened next.

'So, where are you hiding?' the man asked.

Chris saw him appear past Rose, framed through the doorway beneath the staircase. Rose stood from her crouch. The man's eyes went wide and he reacted immediately, left arm coming up in a defensive gesture while his right hand delved into his jacket. But he had been too confident of Chris's confusion and fear, too sure of himself.

The sound the knife made when it stuck in his neck was horrible. He seemed to growl, and blood bubbled at his throat, splashing the air and pattering down on the hall tiles. He took his hand from within his jacket and Rose knocked something aside —

— *a gun, has he really got a gun?* —

— sending it clattering out of sight.

Rose grabbed the man's polo shirt collar with

36

her left hand and held him steady as she tugged with her right hand, once, twice, hefty jerks of her arm and shoulder pulling the knife out through his throat. His eyes remained wide, tongue squirming in his mouth as he started to slump.

Rose staggered backwards into Chris's studio, dragging the dying man with her. His blood was flowing. Not just dripping, but gushing from the dreadful wound, splashing on the floor and sending Rose slipping, shoving the man aside as she fell onto her back. Even as she hit the floor she hardly made a noise, but was up again in a second, kneeling on the man's back and grabbing him by the hair, pulling, his head moving back much too far as the wound gaped and he bled out.

Chris closed his eyes, but the sight could not be unseen.

'Don't faint,' she said.

The man was still making wet, coughing noises, feet scraping slowly at the floor as he tried to propel himself out of his killer's grasp.

Chris turned away and stared at his drawing desk. There were plans of a new house sitting there right now, his client's list of suggested amendments pinned above it. The client was a sixty-year-old man, someone who'd seen the world and made good money, and who now was settling down for retirement with his gorgeous forty-something wife. A good man. Great stories. *I wonder if he's ever seen anything like this*, Chris thought, and then he realised that Rose was hissing at him.

'*Now*, for fuck's sake! We don't have long!'

'What?' He turned, propping himself on his desk so that he didn't slump to the floor. There was so much blood. Could there really be so much inside a human body? He'd bought that rug with Terri on holiday in Egypt, and now it was ruined.

'I said go through there.' She nodded through the door at the hallway, where blood was spattered on the floor and sprayed in one artful arc across the apple-white wall. 'Stand facing the front door. When they come in, just wait there and let them come to you.'

'No,' Chris said, shaking his head. 'I can't just stand there and let them attack me.'

'They're not going to attack you! They want to take you. Do as I say or I'm out of here now, and I'll leave you with this.' She stood and kicked the corpse's head at her feet. It moved too loosely on the neck, and Chris had a crazy, shocking image of it rolling across the floor, grinning up at him as the mouth gasped for air.

'Okay,' he said. He didn't know who she was, why she'd arrived, how she'd even got in without them seeing. But right then, he didn't want her to go. Not because he thought she could protect him, but because she had answers. She knew what was going on. 'But my family . . . ' He nodded down at the body.

'What's started can't be stopped,' she said. She seemed excited, pumped, displaying emotion for the first time. 'No going back now, Chris.'

'You know my name.'

She rolled her eyes and shoved him towards

38

the door into the hall. But not too hard. It would have been easy to slip on so much blood.

He could smell it as he walked, a rich, warm odour. His feet splashed in it. Pausing at the door, he thought about removing his running shoes to prevent walking blood through the house. But he giggled instead, an hysterical outburst that burned at his eyes and filled his throat. He reached for the door frame, and even before Rose whispered from behind him he was composing himself, taking deep breaths through his mouth.

'Hurry!' She was closer than he thought, following him silently. He could almost feel her breath on the back of his neck. *She can help me*, he thought, but at the same time he realised that helping was not part of her agenda. She was here for something else.

Chris stepped into the hallway and turned to look along at the front door, and there were already shadows moving beyond the frosted glass.

'One step back,' Rose said. 'And don't look at me. I'm not here. I'm a shadow. Got it?'

He nodded, mouth suddenly too dry to speak.

'If you give me away, we're both dead. And then your family — '

'I get it!' he said. From the corner of his eye he saw Rose relax beneath the staircase, almost melting into the shadows there. She was motionless and silent. *She's not there*, he thought, taking in deep breaths once again. *The dead guy's not there. I'm here on my own, just waiting*.

39

For what, he was about to find out.

The front door opened. A man entered, and Chris recognised him from the car he'd seen parked along the street. He was tall, heavily built, the sort of man Terri might call a 'honey' while smiling at Chris and squeezing his hand. His sweet wife, always reassuring him that he was the one and only. He carried an Adidas kit bag slung over one shoulder.

A woman crowded in behind him. Black, much shorter, thin, wearing heavy-framed glasses and a casual sports jacket that might have cost a week's income from Chris's company, she was laughing as if at a joke. They seemed so casual with what they were doing. So confident.

They both saw Chris standing there and barely paid him any attention. Honey shrugged the bag from his shoulder. Glasses shut the door behind her, still chuckling and shaking her head. The joke must have been really funny.

'Where's Ed?' Honey asked. When he looked at Chris his smile remained, but his voice was ice-cold, his manner suddenly threatening. He could break Chris across one knee while still smoothing his hair with his other hand.

But Rose? Chris wasn't sure about her.

'Making coffee,' Chris said, pleased at his answer. Honey nodded, and Glasses rolled her eyes. It seemed Chris wasn't the only one with a caffeine habit.

Honey dropped the bag and kicked it along the hall. 'Right, there's stuff in there you need to . . . ' His voice trailed off. He'd watched the bag sliding, looked beyond it, and seen the dark

40

spatters of blood speckling the tiles by Chris's feet.

The sudden silence was heavy and loaded, and behind him Glasses was already tugging something bulky from her jacket.

'He says do you want sugar?' Chris said, and Honey looked up at him, frowning.

'Huh?'

Rose flowed from the shadows beneath the stairs, shouldering Chris against the wall and throwing the bloodied knife underarm. It struck Honey in the chest. He grunted, swiping at the knife with his right hand. The blade dropped and clattered to the floor, and a bloom of blood spread across his shirt.

'You,' Honey said. Behind him, Glasses raised the object she'd pulled from her jacket.

Rose shot her once in the face. The glass behind her shattered and she fell against the door, her spectacles sliding down her nose and resting on the ruin of her right cheek.

The gunshot was incredibly loud and made the second shot sound much more muffled. Honey staggered back a step, stood on Glasses' hand where she was sprawled against the closed door, and then moved forward in a sudden lurch. There was a hole in his chest, another spot of blood rapidly growing close to where the knife had wounded him.

'You!' He shouted this time, and Chris barely heard. His hearing had been blasted away by the gunshots, and now a heavy, high whine seemed to ricochet inside his head.

Rose crouched and fired again, raising the gun

up at a forty-five-degree angle and then falling to one side as Honey slouched on top of her. His outstretched hand clawed down Chris's chest where he was pressed to the wall.

Chris saw the exit wounds on the man's back, ragged tears in his jacket. He was dead when he hit the floor.

Rose pulled her leg from beneath the body and stood, pointing the gun back and forth between Glasses and Honey.

Chris was slowly shaking his head. It felt heavy, and when Rose spoke to him it was like hearing a voice underwater. *Daddy smells of poo*, Megs had said to him last time they went swimming, both of them dropping beneath the surface at the deep end and seeing if they could understand each other.

' . . . out of here now!' Rose said from a distance. She stood on the dead man like he wasn't a human being at all — and shoved Chris back against the wall. 'Really. Now! We have minutes, so we've got to go!'

'You killed them,' Chris said. His voice was incredibly loud inside his own head, as if he was the only real thing here. Perhaps that was it. Rose and the corpses were only nightmares.

She grabbed the Adidas bag at Chris's feet and pushed it against his chest, then knelt and started going through the dead man's pockets.

Chris watched. He couldn't think of anything else to do. She was efficient and quick, and in moments she had a set of car keys and a phone in her left hand. In her right, she still carried her gun.

'Will there be more of them?' he asked, looking at the damaged, blood-spattered front door.

'Plenty,' she said. And then she grinned with delight. 'I've only just begun.'

5

three

I've only just begun. But in truth she had started all this years ago.

She'd spent a long time imagining what it would be like to exact some sort of revenge. At night, in between nightmares about her family's final moments, and during the day when she strove to better prepare herself for what was to come, she would dream: pointing a gun and pulling the trigger; running them down with a car; tying them up and setting them on fire; slashing out with a knife. So many ways to kill those of the Trail who had killed everything about her, and sometimes she lost herself for hours picturing their deaths.

And they had recognised her. That had been a surprise, although she supposed that they were always looking for her.

But in truth it was nothing like she'd expected. She had felt not one sliver of regret when she killed, but neither had she felt a flush of satisfaction, nor the much sought-after contentment she had been expecting. Their blood still stained her hands and clothing, but it was as if she had watched someone else do the killing.

She put her hand to her mouth and tasted blood.

'Are there more outside?' That Chris Sheen

wasn't a gibbering wreck was something she could only be grateful for. But perhaps his reaction was a skewed echo of her own. She didn't feel shocked or even pleased, maybe because her mind might be shielding her from events.

She wished it wouldn't. Now that her revenge had begun, she wanted to experience every joyous moment.

'Not here, not right now,' she said. 'Shut up and follow me.'

'But my family will — '

'Shut up!' She pressed her finger against his lips. He flinched from the stickiness of their blood. 'Follow . . . me.'

She looked at the phone she'd taken from the first dead man. The home screen was a picture of two little children, and she stared at their faces, frozen, swallowed away into memory. Her own children had been that young, and would never be older. *He has a family. He has kids.* How some-one like him could have been anything like her, Rose could not conceive. She shook her head to dislodge the confusion. It was useless to her, and she was determined to keep her mind in the moment. She'd spent too long living in the past, and the future she so desired was here and now. This was everything she had been waiting for.

Chris touched her shoulder. She blinked rapidly for a second or two, then nodded at him.

'Quick,' she said. 'And quiet.' She headed back into the study and crossed to the French doors. She'd come in that way, and it would be quieter to leave that way, too. She picked up the loaded backpack she'd left just inside the door, slung it

45

over her shoulder, then rested her hand on the door handle.

Neighbours would have likely heard the gunshots, but most of them would have no idea what they were. A car backfiring, someone hammering, a TV turned up too loud; for people living in Cardiff, and especially in nice neighbourhoods like this, the first thought at such a sound would never be, *Gun!* That would change when the bodies were found.

But as she slipped from the doors and looked across the front garden, Rose realised that things might not be so simple. When she'd shot the woman, the glass in the front door had shattered. And now across the street there were several people gathered around a car, examining a hole in one of its side windows.

They'd still not immediately think of guns and bullets. Their minds wouldn't work that way. But it meant that she and Chris didn't have long.

He followed behind her, close and quiet. That was good. She needed him more than he needed her, but she'd never tell him that.

As they approached the open gates at the end of the short driveway, she pressed the button on the key fob. A little way along the street, a white BMW's lights flashed twice.

A couple of the people examining the damaged car looked up. One of them smiled and raised his hand to Chris, then his expression fell a little when he saw Rose.

'Morning!' Rose said. 'Lovely morning.'

'Yes, lovely,' the man said uncertainly.

'Don't look at him or say a word,' she

whispered. She led Chris along the pavement to the BMW, climbed into the driver's seat, dropped the backpack in the passenger footwell, and watched him get in beside her. He still had the kit bag clasped to his chest. Taking the gun from her pocket, she placed it between her legs on the seat. Then she checked the phone again.

'They've seen my front door,' Chris said.

'Doesn't matter.' She scrolled through the contacts list. There were only half a dozen names registered. She smiled when she saw the photos beside two names. And then she saw other faces, knew them, hated them all over again. 'Here they are,' she said.

'Who?'

'The Trail.'

'What's that?'

She glanced across at Chris, sitting confused and scared and still shocked numb beside her. He didn't need to know, not yet. Not until they got away from here and were closing on their destination.

Her destination. Because from this moment forward, she was taking charge.

She started the car and pulled away, making a three-point turn so that they didn't have to pass Chris's neighbours. Heading off along his street, she saw parents starting to leave home with kids. The school run. She missed that. She missed *everything*. For a moment her mind drifted again, flitting back to memories she could do nothing to temper and which seemed to become richer over time. Sometimes they were more real than her reality.

Your memories will be your downfall, Holt had said to her in Italy. *You let the past distract you so much that it blurs your present.* But memories were all she had left, and she never tried too hard to lose them.

'How many people have you killed?' Chris asked.

'Three.' Their dying expressions already felt familiar.

The phone in the door pocket beside her trilled. She didn't answer. As soon as it rang off she knew that the alarm would be raised. *They're starting to panic,* she thought. *I can feel that. I can sense it.* And she could. She knew the Trail so well — had lived and breathed them for the past three years — that their thoughts were hers, their emotions and actions so tied into her existence that she might as well have been monitoring their individual heartbeats, their pulses.

They wouldn't yet know she was here or who she was. But soon.

'Where are we going? You need to let me out, now. Let me go.' Chris's voice shimmered with panic. 'You leave, I won't say anything. Got to *get out!*' He tried the door handle, but she'd clicked on the central locking.

Rose checked ahead. They'd pulled onto a small commercial street with a few shops on both sides, and the road was wide, not too busy.

'Stop the car!' He grabbed for the steering wheel. Rose nodded across at Chris's window, eyes going wide. When he looked, she launched a fast, accurate punch at his temple. His head

48

jerked sideways and struck the window, and he emitted a long, low groan, slumping in his seat. His eyelids fluttered.

She'd learned the theory, but had never done that before.

Rose checked the mirrors and looked ahead. No one had seen. And if someone did notice him now, he was sleeping on his way to work, that was all.

She could imagine the heat of the Trail's networks buzzing with consternation. The phone rang again.

This time she answered.

6

please

Gemma had no idea why they hadn't blind-folded her as well. Maybe they needed a witness to what was happening, needed one of them to see just how serious this woman was. Or perhaps they just assumed she'd be no trouble.

Right then, they were correct. She was so scared, she seriously doubted she could even stand.

'Please,' Megs said.

'Will you shut her up?' the woman muttered. She'd said the same thing a dozen times, tone of voice hardly changing, but Gemma felt the air charging. Danger hung heavy. Violence sim-mered.

'Megs, you need to keep quiet,' their mother said.

Gemma's heart hammered, vision blurred. She had never been so terrified, and she wished she could hold her little sister and make her feel better. The comfort would go both ways. But Megs was tied in a kneeling position next to their mum's right leg, and Gemma herself was also tied, next to her mother's left leg and with thin, strong ropes holding her against the van's wooden seat. Her mother was on the seat, the two of them on the floor, all so close but with little comfort to be had.

50

'Please,' Megs said. She must have said it a hundred times, so many that the word had lost meaning.

'Come on, Megs,' Gemma said again. 'It'll all be fine, it's just a game or something, a reality TV show. We'll be famous!' It was difficult sounding so positive and in control when she was so scared, but Gemma had always been protective of her little sister.

The windows in the van's rear doors were covered with plywood boards, and a small, naked bulb provided the only light inside. It swung on a loose wire, light and shadows dancing around the vehicle's interior. The space revealed was battered and well-used, the walls scabbed with rust, floor dirty, scratches and dents scarring the exposed metal bodywork.

'If you just untie her, she'll calm down a bit,' Gemma said.

'Really?' the woman asked, raising an eyebrow. While they were being taken from the house, Gemma had heard her called Vey. The strange name only added to Gemma's fear. Who called anyone Vey?

Were they going to be killed?

'Where's my dad?' That he wasn't here with them terrified Gemma. He'd always said that she had a vivid imagination, and she imagined him arriving home from his run and finding the house empty, meeting someone left behind to kill him. Her dad, in his sweaty, tight running kit that she often took the mickey out of, opening the door and being met with a fist or a gun.

The unreality of things hit her. That helped.

51

'You just keep still and quiet. Be a good little girl.'

Gemma couldn't remember the last time she'd been called a little girl. She was fifteen in six weeks, and already almost as tall as her mum. She hadn't been a little girl for a while. *Vey doesn't know how to talk to kids so doesn't have any*, she thought, and she filed that in her memory bank. She called it 'the box', and imagined it as a concertina file like the one Mum and Dad used to store their household bills and other stuff. She closed her eyes briefly to open it and slip in this new piece of information. She didn't bother with alphabetical order, just filed it in one of the cardboard folds.

The van bumped gently over a series of sleeping policemen. *We're still in the town*, Gemma thought. She'd seen a film once where someone had been kidnapped, thrown into a car boot, and then tracked where they were being taken by listening to noises from outside, counting turns, making a mental map of the route they were taking. It was ridiculous, and she'd lost her way after the first couple of turns. But the box was still mostly empty. Every scrap of stuff she put in there might help her.

And concentrating on that might distract her from the terror that threatened to smother her.

She had just stepped into the shower when they came. A shout from downstairs, a scream from Megs, and then the door to the bathroom had swung open and the tall man entered. 'Get dressed,' he'd said, not even glancing her up and down.

52

Through her shock, Gemma had plucked a bowl of pot pourri from the small shelf beside the bath and flung it at the man. He'd caught it casually and thrown it back at her, dried flowers and bulbs showering the bathroom. The bowl had smashed on the tiled wall, and one heavy shard sliced across her shoulder. One foot had tangled in the curtain and she'd tripped from the shower, reaching out for balance but failing, tearing the curtain from its rings, falling to the floor with a heavy thud that vented the air from her lungs and winded her.

And something had happened. Her panic had dispersed, drawn back by the feel of warm blood cooling on her skin as her shoulder wound bled. There were smears across the shower tiles. *Dad'll see that*, she'd thought, already starting to think ahead.

'Please let us go,' she said, knowing they would not.

'Please,' Megs said.

Vey pressed her lips tightly together and sighed. She still held the gun. She'd shown it to the phone earlier, the screen too far away to see clearly. Gemma thought Vey had been talking to her dad, although what she'd said was confusing. Something about one 9 away, and twenty-three minutes.

She flexed her right shoulder a few times. Her school shirt had stuck to the dried blood, and rolling her shoulder opened the wound again.

And then Gemma saw a long nail on the van's bare metal floor. It had rolled into a joint between segments, and was now covered with a

53

scattering of dirty sawdust.

She looked away quickly, down at her feet curled under her. Her legs were going numb. Looking anywhere but at the nail, she flexed her muscles, trying to keep numbness at bay. The time might soon come when she'd have to move quickly.

7

the hills

He dreamed of his family. Their voices accompanied him up and out of unconsciousness, and they were with him when he opened his eyes. His wife was beside him, Megs and Gemma were in the back seat, bickering softly over who was winning their game of Legs. They often played it when they were travelling, counting pub sign legs on their own sides of the car. The Duke of York had two legs, the White Horse four, and so on. Gemma made up pub names like 'The World's Longest Millipede' and 'The Herd of Spiders', but she always let Megs win in the end. He tried to turn to speak to Terri but there was something wrong with his head, his neck. He opened his mouth to speak, but the pain was too much. It throbbed and pulsed within him like a living thing, too big for the inside of his head, rolling and turning and pushing with its many legs, its horse's spider's millipede's legs.

Where are we? he wanted to ask. *What's happening?* But as he closed his eyes again, wishing away the pain, he remembered.

He looked. Hedgerows flashed by. The woman, Rose, sat in the driver's seat, glancing over at him. Her expression betrayed nothing.

'Sleep,' she said. 'Rest. You'll need it.'

Where . . . he tried to mouth, but even moving

his jaw sent spasms of pain through his skull. He closed his eyes. The car's motion was lulling, and the dreams welcomed him again.

★ ★ ★

It seemed like moments before he woke again, but it must have been longer.

'Nearly there,' a voice said. He thought it was Terri, but then Rose tapped his arm. She had blood under her fingernails. 'Here. Take these, and drink this. Need to have your wits about you. They're close, so we haven't got long.'

The truth crashed in again with a flood of sensory memories — the splash of spilled blood, the warm tang of gun smoke, the fear on his family's faces in the back of that van. A freezing terror so deep inside that he could never hope to reach it.

He tried opening his eyes again, squinting at the liquid fire pouring in and swamping his mind. Each jolt and bump of the car on poorly maintained roads was amplified a thousand-fold and punched through his head. But pain was nothing. A transitory thing, barely remembered and beyond description. Several years ago he'd been on several pain management workshops when a twisted back had put him out of action for weeks. There, past a sheen of new-agey trappings, he'd learned a powerful truth — that pain was all in the mind.

He opened his eyes and sat up fully, groaning out loud against the hammering inside his skull.

'You hit me.'

'Sorry.' Rose, the murderer, was driving with the gun nestled between her legs. He took the water bottle she offered, and then the small foil pack of pills. They were strong pain-killers. He popped three from the pack, held them on his tongue, and took a swig from the bottle. It tasted strange, vaguely bitter. An electrolyte drink. He used them when he went on very long runs, replacing electrolytes in his body to balance those lost through excessive sweating. This was an endurance athlete's drink, not a murderer's.

He squinted at the bottle. It was full.

'How long . . . ?'

'Couple of hours. You were in and out, so I gave you a mild sedative. Needed time to drive, didn't want you distracting me, jumping from the car, something stupid like that.'

'My family,' Chris said. The memory of what he'd seen of them on the phone screen hurt more than any physical pain could, and there was no way of ignoring an agony like that. He didn't *want* to ignore it.

'The best way you can serve them is by doing what I tell you.'

'You sound just like *them*.'

'I'm *nothing* like them!' She did not shout, but still her voice was loud.

'Where are we?'

'Almost there.'

'Almost where? Why can't you answer me straight?'

Rose sighed and stared ahead, concentrating on driving.

Feeling sick and light-headed, Chris looked

57

around, waiting for her to speak, hoping she would. There was no way he could force her to say anything. He could only hope that her promise of keeping him alive, and everything else she was doing, would help and not hinder him and his family. She knew what was going on, and the only way she'd tell him was if she wanted to. *And how will that benefit her?* he wondered. Because it was painfully obvious that everything she was doing was for herself.

They were in the mountains. Chris knew these places. The vista was wild, windswept, undulating, with still lakes hidden in deep valleys and sheer mountains looming over them. Streams carved glimmering routes down mountain-sides. Grasses, ferns, heathers, and scrubby trees painted the landscape green and purple, and here and there forested areas huddled across mountainous foothills. Snow speckled the higher peaks. Sheer rock faces hung grey and forbidding, and even though sunlight touched them, the mountains remained cool and aloof. It was a mythical land where the true wildness of nature existed close to the surface, unhindered by considerations of civilisation. Even the road they followed was barely allowed here, twisting and turning through the rough terrain. Drystone walling lined the road on both sides, and here and there were lay-bys for parking, and rough tracks leading up into the hills.

The land was huge, the sky even larger. Humans were small here, stripped to the bare essentials of existence, the trappings of their lives made inconsequential by the scope and scale of where they were. Nature was in command.

Chris loved landscapes like this. He lived for the few times each year when he could get away for a weekend, with or without his family, and run and hike through the mountains. He was not a believer in anything divine, but being somewhere like this invoked the closest he ever felt to a spiritual experience. Once, running across the foothills of Ben Nevis, he had realised that he was an animal, just like any other. It was a sobering, thrilling experience. He had always remembered that time, and dwelling on it made him calm, and sane, and able to face the trivialities of business and human existence with renewed strength.

He thought he recognised this place, and a glimpse of a bilingual road sign confirmed his suspicions. They were heading into the Welsh mountains.

But nothing about this was right.

'I'm just an architect,' he said. 'I live a good life. Nice, comfortable, uninspiring. Boring, some of my friends tell me. But I like my work, love doing sports with my girls. My wife and I get on well, still, after a long time together. We've got our differences, but who hasn't? We're happy.' He nodded, blinking away tears. 'This isn't my world. I know stuff like this happens, and it scares me because of my girls. It terrifies me that people like them . . . and you . . . exist. I see it on the news sometimes, you know, 'Young girl kidnapped, raped and murdered', and sometimes the terror just makes everything seem so hopeless.'

'That's because you can't protect your family,' Rose said softly.

'Yes. Yes! Terri and I do everything we can for our kids, but you can't allow for evil.'

'I'm not evil,' she said. 'My family was very much like yours.'

'Was?' Chris could hear something in her voice that betrayed that, perhaps, he was getting to her. Maybe she was starting to feel something. Even when she was tugging her knife through the remains of that man's throat — an image he would never, ever be able to shake, try though he might — her face had barely changed.

'They're dead,' Rose said. 'The Trail killed them all. My husband and three children.'

'No,' Chris breathed, thinking of his own family trussed and blindfolded. 'It was a woman in the van with them. She might have children of her own, how could she — '

Rose laughed, bitter and harsh. 'Oh, don't for a second think of them as human.'

'What do you mean?'

'They're not people. Not normal. They're monsters. Now shut up, we're almost there, and I need to listen.' She powered down both front windows in the car and tilted her head.

'For what?'

'Helicopter. I think we've got the lead on them, but we'll have to stop soon.'

'I have no idea what you're doing,' Chris said. He sounded pathetic, pleading, but Rose did not react. Whatever she said about them — the Trail, whoever they were — seemed to apply to her as well.

'Rucksack in the back. Take what's useful from the bag they gave you, too.'

'What's — '

'Shut the fuck up!' she snapped, glaring at him for a second then looking ahead again.

Chris reached into the back seat and snagged the rucksack resting there. It was a good one, a forty-litre day sack that he might well have chosen for himself. Several access zips, a waterproof cover in the base, small hip pockets on the waist strap. A whistle and compass built into the shoulder straps. Hydration bladder. It was heavy, and he grunted as he lifted it over into his lap.

For a moment he considered slamming the bag against Rose. He could knock her head against the doorpost, grab the wheel, steer them off the road and into a stone wall. While she struggled he could grab the gun from between her knees and press it into her stomach, and then everything would change. Then he would be in charge, and all the answers he sought would come tumbling from her mouth.

Except . . . he wasn't sure they would. She would only tell him what she wanted him to know, gun or no gun. She was like no one he knew — one of them, those people he knew existed but whom he had always hoped he would never have to meet. Violent, brutal, a sharp edge in a life he'd strived to make so smooth. And he had never touched a gun in his life.

She glanced at him, as if reading his mind. Then she frowned and leaned to the side, concentrating on the road but listening for something else.

'They're close,' she said. 'We don't have long.

I'll be leaving you soon.'

'And going where?'

'Check the bag.'

'Do you know where my family is?'

Rose shook her head.

'You do. You know.'

'I don't know! But as long as you're going along with things, they'll be safe. They'll stay alive.' Rose was looking up and around as she drove, trying to spot the helicopter only she could hear.

'Yours didn't.'

'That's because I didn't play ball'

'So what do I have to do?' Chris asked. He opened the rucksack and looked inside, knocked sideways for a moment by finding everything so familiar. New running trousers, base layers, weatherproof jacket, survival kit, energy gels, GPS watch, penknife, some energy bars, freeze-dried food packets. And a phone. 'What the hell . . . ?'

'There,' Rose said. 'We don't have long.' She changed down a gear and pressed on the gas, powering them up the steep, winding road that headed for a low ridge between two monolithic peaks. Chris leaned forward and looked up and ahead of them, and after a few moments he saw the shadow of a helicopter moving against the mountains across the valley. It looked so small against that vast landscape, but he could tell it was larger than a private chopper. Military, perhaps.

'Rose, please. Please help me. Tell me what's going on.'

'You're going to get out of the car and start running. I'm going to lead them off. That'll give you a head start.'

'But why?'

'Because they'll be hunting you.'

'What?'

'This is a hunt. You're the prey.'

He shook his head, trying to make sense of anything she was saying. That distance he'd felt back at the house — drawing him back from events, allowing him to react without going mad — suddenly seemed shakier than ever, and fear flooded in once more. His head still throbbed. A cool, sharp pain pulsed across his temple where Rose had hit him, and just thinking of that assault made him feel sick. He'd never been attacked like that before. He felt sick.

'The Trail provide people for rich clients to hunt.'

'What, like chase down? Catch?'

'Kill'

Chris shook his head. He couldn't take it in. *Kill?*

'It's a trophy hunt,' Rose went on. 'Like with lions and elephant in Africa, except this is with people. You're the target. There'll be some fat rich fucks in that helicopter who've paid millions each to hunt and kill you. The Trail set it up, provide everything they need — training, weapons, backup and support. They ensure there're no repercussions. Except I've changed their plans a little. This one was supposed to take place in Cardiff Bay and the docklands. The Trail would have steered you here and there, made sure you did all the right things. It's set up, completely, and when they felt the time was right and everything was safe, they'd have engineered the kill. Cleared up the mess, sent everyone home. Big money.'

'Big money. Money? You're doing this for . . . ?'

'I'm doing this because I escaped my hunt, and because of that the Trail murdered my family. And now I'm going to kill them. All of them. See? Understand?'

'I can't escape,' Chris said softly.

'No. But you can run. They know that, which is why they chose you. But by bringing you up here, into the wild, I've done you a favour. You have an advantage over the rich fat fucks now, and whatever the Trail had set up in Cardiff is useless to them. It'll all last much longer.'

'But my wife. My girls.'

'Are safe while you're still on the run.'

Chris closed his eyes and tried to take it all in. It was impossible to digest, too huge to contemplate. Too unbelievable.

'It's a joke,' he said. He even managed a small laugh. 'A wind-up. Reality TV, or something. Derren Brown's hypnotised me.'

Rose said nothing. He saw the dried blood on her hands, remembered what she had done. That had all been real. Nothing like that could be faked, not without movie trickery. He'd been there to smell the blood, hear it hitting the ground, see the ragged mess of the man's throat, see the impact of bullets.

'It's real,' he muttered. Rose glanced across at him, then pointed.

'There,' she said. 'By that spur of rock on the ridge. That's where you get out. Hide for a bit, get ready. You'll know when to head off.'

'How?'

'When they get there.' She slammed on the brakes, turned to him. He thought perhaps she'd hand him the gun, but she didn't. Maybe that would make things too easy for him.

'You don't give a shit about me,' Chris said, and a glimmer of something passed across Rose's face, an expression he could not identify. Then she smiled, and for the first time it seemed almost genuine.

'There's a phone in the rucksack. It has my number, only mine. I'll do my best to look after you. But I'm going to be busy, and you have to look after yourself, too.'

He could hear the helicopter now, rapidly coming closer. He stared at Rose. She wasn't about to change her mind. Nothing was going to change, and Chris knew that he had to take action.

'What happens to my family if they kill me?'

'Usually they're let go if the hunt's successful.'

'Usually? How many times — '

'Out,' Rose said. She touched the gun.

'What, or you'll shoot me?' But he could see that she was getting edgy now, hand resting on the gear stick, foot caressing the gas pedal. Itching to go.

Chris opened the door and stood from the car, hanging on to the metal for a moment as dizziness threatened to drop him. He slung the rucksack over one shoulder, and Rose threw the

Adidas bag out at his feet. He was hoping she'd say something else to reassure him, or to help. But even before he could close the door the car skidded away, raking his legs with shards of gravel as it tailspun back onto the road and up towards the ridge. He saw her silhouette lean over and slam his door shut.

Chris stood there swaying in the midday sun, cooled by the mountain breeze. He had never felt so far away, and so alone.

The helicopter appeared to the north, higher up against one of the mountains, describing a gentle descent towards the ridge where the road disappeared. He couldn't see the BMW right then, but he knew that Rose was accelerating up towards that ridge, too. They might just reach it at the same time. He wondered what would happen then.

Hunt, he thought. *That's ridiculous. That's crazy.*

Then the helicopter changed course, its shadow flitting and leaping down the mountain's craggy side like some wild animal.

Coming right for him.

8

holt

Of course, he only wanted to fuck her.

She couldn't imagine why any man would show interest in her otherwise. She was a physical mess, an alcoholic, dirty, her hair now long again and knotted, clothes unkempt and worn through in several places. When she did look up from her feet it was to search for the next drink. She only saw as far as the morning after, and never took much notice of how hard that would be. She was a failure, a wreck, a hollow woman with a dead family and nothing left to live for. Existing was now simply a habit.

There was before, a beautiful utopia of love and friendship, joy and pleasure, and a contented pride in everything her children did, every single day. And then there was after, a smoke- and booze-filled miasma of crippling, unbelievable grief. In between was the unbridgeable gap of her pursuit and their murder.

How could anyone be attracted to what she had become?

But he sat next to her at the small corner table all the same. He didn't speak for a long time, just continued to drink from a smoked glass. He topped up from a bottle in his bag, and she liked that. His expression when he tipped the bottle against his glass made her smile. Smiling was an

67

unfamiliar expression, and it made her facial muscles ache.

The bar had seen better days, but worse days too. Apart from the regular clientele — her, a grizzly bear-sized African man with one arm, a couple of old women who looked like vultures and must have been sisters — it sometimes entertained more adventurous tourists on their way back from a trek in the Italian mountains, or perhaps some local workers looking to expand their horizons across the area. She'd seen several fights here, one randy couple having a drunken, clumsy screw out by the basic bathroom, and four alleged Mafia men playing cards. The barman made his own wine, and offered it for sale only to people he knew would appreciate it. Rose drank at least a bottle each night. She supposed the joint had its charm.

'Drink?' he asked.

'Single malt.'

'But of course.' He sounded French. That surprised her, though she wasn't sure why. Maybe because she'd expect a Frenchman to have more class. He called to the barman and ordered her drink, and the same for himself. When the two glasses arrived he tipped his into hers and slid the glass in front of her.

'My name's Holt,' he said.

'Jane Doe.'

'I thought I recognised you.'

She drank her double in one, then dribbled half back into her glass, keen to give the appearance of making it last. Stupid, really. He'd been watching her drink for half an hour, and she'd managed three in that time. He topped up his own glass from his bottle once more, and she paid close attention for the first time. And frowned. The fluid didn't have that vaguely oil-like consistency of a spirit, not even vodka, and it was completely clear.

'You're drinking water?'

'Please don't tell anyone,' Holt said. 'My reputation won't survive. And Celso will eject me from his bar.'

She snorted laughter and took another drink. She couldn't tell whether it was really single malt, but she didn't give a fuck. It burned on the way down. That was all that mattered.

He might have been one of them. They'd found her at last and he'd come out here to deliver the killer blow. She'd been expecting it, and fear of the Trail had no bearing on why she continued to hide. It was life she was trying to elude, not them. And right then she didn't care if he *was* Trail. The difference between death and this excuse of an existence was negligible.

'You mutter when you're drunk,' he said.

'I do not.'

'You might think you don't, but you do. You ramble. You're just too drunk to even notice, or remember when you eventually surface.'

'I never surface. There's nothing to surface to. I just drink, sleep, wake, repeat.'

'Well, if you want to do anything about what happened, that's the first thing we have to change.'

He tipped his glass back and drained his water, and Rose stared at him open-mouthed.

69

'How much do I say?' she whispered.

'You talk to your dead family,' Holt said.

Rose dropped her glass and sobbed, so violently that Holt must have thought she was having a fit or a stroke. She pressed her hands to her face and squeezed, trying to hold in all the memories of her dear dead loved ones, afraid that they'd be gone forever if she let them go.

Holt's arm rested hesitantly around her shoulders. There was no pressure there, nothing other than a desire to comfort. No one had shown her such kindness since . . .

Since she had run. Escaped. Since she'd fled normality, left the world, and let herself be consumed by the stark underside of life. There was no kindness this far down.

She rested her head against his shoulder and started to cry. That was when he told her the rest about what she mumbled in her drunken stupors — the sorrow, the guilt, the fury.

Lowering his voice he whispered close to her ear, 'You tell Adam how much you want to kill them all.'

Rose's crying paused, a dammed flow burning as it readied to burst through again.

'I can help,' Holt said. 'I know all about killing.'

9

trail

He was still wearing his running kit from that morning. It had dried during his journey here in the car, and he could smell the odour of his early run. When he'd sweated that out, everything had still been normal.

For a moment he considered waiting where he was, rucksack and bag at his feet while he waved his arms over his head, motioning the helicopter to land on the widened area of road. He'd talk with them. Negotiate. Offer them money, or whatever else they wanted, so long as they released his wife and the girls. They must have made a mistake, anyway, and picked on the wrong family. He'd swear silence.

Then he remembered the woman's cold, calm smile in the van as she'd waved a gun towards his blindfolded loved ones. And he knew that Rose had left him with very little choice.

Shrugging on the rucksack, slinging the holdall over one shoulder, he jogged across the lay-by and leaped the ditch beside the road. It only took a couple of seconds to see where he should be headed; an outcropping a few hundred feet up the hillside, a worn gully leading up to it, stream splashing down over rocks and past scrubby trees. Most of the way he'd be hidden from sight from the helicopter, so long as he stayed low. He'd worn his black running tights and a black technical tee shirt that morning, so it could have been worse. On a road run it would have been hi-viz gear all the way.

As he ran, that sense of unreality gave him pause several times, and he stopped and snorted disbelief. But he could hear the helicopter growing closer, rotor sounds *whup-whupping* across the valley and echoing from the mountains.

Don't stop, he thought. *Run fast, keep low. Not far, then I can see what's going on. Hide, watch, figure out how fucking mad Rose is.* Was she in with them in some weird way? An *agent provocateur* whose job it was to guide and steer him, as she'd said they would have done to him in the city?

But there were those people she'd killed. Though he had never witnessed a death in real life — the only body he'd ever seen was his father's laid out in the hospital's chapel of rest — he knew for sure that such brutality, such violence, could not have been faked. And in her eyes and voice afterwards, the truth of her revenge.

She was mad, but right then he'd be mad to ignore everything she had told him. He had to assume it was the truth until he could prove otherwise.

He slid down into the gully, one hand out to keep balance. The ground here was covered with short, stumpy grass, with frequent tufts of a hardy purple heather and a more ragged low-level shrub. There was sheep shit everywhere. Clumps of wool clung to plants, and down in the gully he found the scattered remains of a dead animal — a stripped spine, ribs, leg bones, and a sad skull with scraps of skin still attached.

The stream was barely a trickle. In the wetter months this would be a torrent, but now it was easy to climb its course, moving from rock to bank and back again. He kept his head down, using his hands as well as his feet when the incline grew steeper. He didn't worry about his feet getting wet, but knew he might suffer later. Wet socks often resulted in blisters.

Glancing up frequently, Chris made sure he was heading towards the rocky outcropping he'd noticed. He'd become quite proficient at judging distances across landscapes such as this, and knew that features could often appear much closer than they really were. He'd scouted this one well. The helicopter was much louder now, approaching the wider area of road where Rose had dropped him off.

He only hoped it could not land anywhere else. He hoped that they wanted a hunt, and not just a quick kill, otherwise they could simply shoot at him from the air. He hoped he was faster than them, fitter, better prepared for confronting the changeable elements these mountains could throw at the unwary.

Chris was also painfully aware that he knew nothing. This was ridiculous, unbelievable, and everything here was new.

Breathing hard now, he moved slowly and methodically, resisting the temptation to leap and run up the gully formed by the stream. He'd soon wear himself out that way. Walking uphill, pushing down on his knees when not using his hands for support, would be as quick as trying to run. Gravity might only be a theory, but it was an insistent one.

The stream ran down directly through the rock feature he was aiming for, finding its way amongst the jumble of massive boulders that might have been there for ten million years. As he approached them he paused, pressed low to the ground and turned on his side so that he could look back down the way he'd come. The road already seemed a surprising distance below him, and the helicopter was just appearing from behind a fold in the land. It was close to the road, stirring up a storm of dust and dried plants as it dipped lower.

He'd never been interested in aircraft, not even as a kid. And with two little girls there wasn't much call for toy soldiers and Airfix models. But he reckoned this was similar to the helicopters used to ferry workmen back and forth to oil rigs in the North Sea, a passenger craft with enough room for a dozen people, as well as equipment and luggage. Still dwarfed by the landscape, it took up most of the road as it touched down.

Chris scrambled the last twenty feet out of the gully and into the jumble of rocks, ensuring that he was properly out of sight. He was sweating already. Some of that was fear. He panted hard, catching his breath, and made sure he had a clear view between rocks down to the road.

The helicopter's rotors kept spinning, though the motor's tone lowered.

He tracked the route of the road as best he

could up towards the ridge, and there at the top
. . . was that a car? He wasn't sure. It was too far
to see, and from this angle the sun shone into his
eyes. But he hoped that was Rose up there,
paused to see what was happening.

She could have stayed with him. Rose and her
gun, her knowledge of what was going on,
everything she knew about these people and
what they wanted . . . she could have stayed and
helped him.

But she was using him, a lump of meat as
meaningless to her as he was to these rich
hunters she'd told him about. Her only aim was
revenge against the people who'd murdered her
family. To the hunters he was quarry, to her he
was bait. It amounted to the same thing.

'Fucking hell,' he whispered, shaking, shivers
passing down his back and tingling his balls. He
still couldn't quite believe it. People would pay
to hunt *people?* Though he'd always regarded
himself as a long-term optimist, he was also
aware that in a society of millions there were bad
eggs, twisted people with perverted desires.
Whether sick or evil, or occupying the wide
spectrum in between, these were realities that he
did his best to ignore. They were the people he
hoped never to meet, and who he was happy
leaving alone in their own skewed realities. But
he'd always known that such bad eggs sometimes
crossed over into the gentle masses. It was one of
his greatest fears.

Today he had met them, and his world had
changed. Rose was one. A bad egg, whatever the
cause of her badness.

And now, these others. The helicopter was filled with them. Rich people who might present a respectable facade for all but one day of the year, and today they wanted Chris Sheen dead by their hand.

He dropped the bag and rucksack from his shoulders and opened the rucksack, rooting around for the phone he'd seen before. His hand delved deep, moving other objects aside until he found the familiar shape of a smartphone.

He unlocked the screen. There was no service. 'Shit. Shit!' He stood, making sure he was still hidden by the rocks, holding the phone up towards the sky as if willing contact. He turned it this way and that, never taking his eyes from the top left corner. *No service.*

Later. He would call the police later.

Slipping the phone into the small, zipped back pocket of his running trousers, he crouched down again and opened the holdall. It contained a new pair of road-running shoes, useless to him up here. A woollen sweater that would hold water and become too heavy. A pack of sandwiches past their sell-by date and speckled with mould. There were spare socks and underwear which he slipped into the rucksack, but most of what the Trail had packed for him was useless. Of course. If what Rose had told him was true, they'd expected a chase through the city. Their aim would have been to make the hunt more exciting, not to give him anything useful.

He shoved the Adidas bag down between two rocks.

His shivering persisted. It was a warm September day, but in these mountains there was always a cool breeze drifting across the shadowed slopes. And after his sudden burst of activity, hunkering down motionless meant he was rapidly cooling. *Got to keep moving*, he thought. *If I have to start again quickly, got to keep warm*. So as he watched the helicopter he stretched his legs, massaged his muscles, kept the blood flowing.

The aircraft's big side door opened and people started to climb out. From this distance it was difficult to make out much detail. But Chris could see that they wore camouflage clothing, carried rucksacks, and he was quite certain that the objects slung on their shoulders were guns of some sort, not walking sticks.

His blood ran cold, stomach tingled. *Like real hunters*, he thought.

Two people exited, three, and the fourth tripped and fell from the aircraft, sprawling in the dust. The others stood around and watched, not one of them going to help. The fallen figure stood and brushed themselves down. A fifth person jumped down from the helicopter, and the five stood around, seemingly aimless. At an unseen signal they hurried to the roadside, then slipped down into the ditch. There they waited. Someone shouted at them from the helicopter, gesticulating from the shadowy interior. *Don't want them to be seen dressed like that, with guns. Too close to the road*. But Chris realised he hadn't seen a single vehicle since Rose had left him standing there, and he wondered just where they were. He had been running in Snowdonia several times, but he couldn't immediately recognise any of these peaks. He guessed they were more remote, in places where casual holidaymakers might not visit.

Three of the five seemed to be overweight. Either that, or their clothing was thick and bulky. He couldn't tell for sure, but he thought they were all men. One had already stripped off his camouflage jacket and tied it around his waist. He seemed to be wearing a black bandana around his head. A real Rambo character. One of the fitter-looking ones was tall and blond, standing apart from the others and shielding his eyes to stare up at the mountains.

Chris wished he had binoculars. He delved into the rucksack again, realising he hadn't checked every pocket. But though he felt around inside, he didn't find any.

It was as if Rose had given him not quite enough to survive, and on purpose.

She wants me to lead them on, survive just long enough for her to do her thing. He wished he didn't think that, but he could not deny the logic of the idea. She wanted to kill the people she called the Trail; those who organised the hunt, not the hunters themselves. And to do so the hunt had to continue, and she had to draw them in. If he escaped too quickly and his family were killed, her own venture might be over.

Until this happened to some other poor bastard.

But he had his own reason to lead on the hunt and not escape. She knew that, and if what she had told him about her own murdered family was true, she knew it better than him. If he escaped, his family would die.

'I need to stay alive. But I can't escape.' It was impossible. He could see no good ending to this, and he felt like curling up and crying it all away. *Man up*, Terri would have said, laughing ironically because over the past few years, when his love of the outdoors had led to new, more extreme adventures, he'd become what she sometimes called 'gnarly'. *You're just a bit dangerous*, she'd sometimes say to him, and he could tell that she liked that.

'Harden the fuck up,' he said.

He looked down the hillside again, and three of the five hunters had vanished. In the few seconds that he'd spent looking through the rucksack and feeling sorry for himself, they must have spread out and started up the mountain-side, secreting themselves behind scattered rocks and clumps of vegetation. He squinted and scanned close to the road, but he could only see two. Rambo was advancing slowly up the slope, making no effort to hide. Close behind him came another man, fat and already struggling.

The helicopter started powering up. Something glinted from its interior, the sun glaring from glass, and Chris realised that they were looking for him. They must have spotted him as they were descending, and now one of the bastards from the Trail was trying to give the hunters a head start. He crouched down further, realising that the sudden movement was the worst thing he could have done.

He didn't hear the shouted instructions, because they were too far away. But looking between rocks, he could see the shape in the helicopter pointing directly up at his position.

As the aircraft doors closed and it lifted away in a violent storm of dust, something smacked from a rock thirty feet to his left. It took him a moment to realise it had been a bullet.

Shouldering the rucksack, Chris hunkered down and crawled back into the rocks, keeping low, climbing one boulder and dropping behind another. Down the slope the helicopter soon rose into view against the mountain opposite. It looked so small and harmless, but he dreaded it coming towards him. It could act as spotter, hovering above him wherever he went and however fast he ran, and it would draw the five hunters towards him like moths to flame.

Maybe he could run faster than them, move across the terrain quicker. But with the helicopter above there was no escape.

That's exactly what they want, he thought. Yet again the hopelessness of the situation smashed in. Any chance he had of saving his family involved becoming a trophy kill for one of those people behind him.

He wondered what it would feel like to be shot. Would there be pain? Would he know he was going to die? He wasn't sure which he'd prefer — an injury that killed him slowly, awareness leaking away as darkness came. Or a sudden head shot, bringing death before he knew it.

The sound of the helicopter changed. He

paused, crawled across a low slab of rock and risked a look across the valley. The aircraft was rising, following the line of the road back up towards the ridge where it disappeared. And the car he thought he'd seen up there — the BMW Rose had taken from the Trail people she had killed in his house — was gone.

More gunshots rang out. They whip-cracked across the valley, and though he listened hard, he did not hear any bullet impacts. They were already shooting blind, flushed with the initial excitement of the hunt.

He clipped the rucksack tight. In the hip pockets he found a handful of energy gels, and he tore one open and gulped down the sweet contents, placing the empty wrapper back in the pocket. Then he took a moment to examine the steep mountainside above him. If he climbed he would be slow, and an easy target if any of them happened to be a good shot. But if he moved along the slope to the south, he could just make out a slope of jumbled rocks and boulders that led up to a shoulder of the mountain. That's where he would aim for. There would be cover there, and once up on the ridge he'd be able to make a better judgement about where he was and where he should go.

Heart thumping, feeling strong and yet terrified, Chris started to run.

10

vet

'I was a vet,' she said. 'We lived near Chelmsford,
nice little village, friendly community. We had
good friends. Adam was a landscape gardener.
The kids loved the countryside. I treated
animals, put them down, made them better. It
didn't feel like I was making a difference, not in
the scheme of things. But for every sad owner's
face I saw, there were a dozen happy ones.
Sometimes it's the pets that make a person's life
worthwhile. A little old lady with a scratchy cat, a
young boy with his dog. You can tell a lot about
people by their pets.' She turned to Holt where
he sat by her window, ever-present bottle of
water in his hand. 'You ever had any pets?'

'No. But I am a vet.'

Rose snorted, then sniffed back a shuddering
sob. Jesus fucking Christ on a bike, how she'd
kill for a drink.

She'd pleaded with him at first, told him how
the way to come down was by reducing her
intake day by day. But Holt had shaken his head.
He wasn't the sort of man you argued with, or
who did things by half. She'd only known him
for three days but she recognised that already.
Short, slight, bespectacled, hair greying, dark
skin weathered and leathery and so lined she
couldn't tell wrinkles from scars, he projected

the look of a bookworm, not a mercenary. But he had such stories.

She'd only heard a few of them so far, but he held the weight of many more. A red history, heavy with death.

That was in the Comoros, on an island called Anjouan. A man called Badak had already killed three families. He shot the men and women to death, then raped the children and hacked them to pieces with a machete. His men feared him as a demon. I tracked them for three days, shot two of his men from a distance. The others fled. A day later I caught Badak in a snare, tied him to a tree, sliced him from throat to cock, and stuck a lizard inside him. I filmed the whole thing and let the people see.

The stories were like a dark star within him, the black hole of his endless, terrible experiences drawing her with a dreadful gravity. They promised experience. He promised help. At last, she perceived a route out of the spiral she had descended into.

She saw a way to hit back.

'Why are you helping me?' she asked.

'Am I helping you?'

Rose nodded. She was sweating in the steamy hotel room, shaking with alcohol withdrawal. Every time she closed her eyes she saw her family as she had found them. With a drink inside her, at least they were sometimes still alive.

But yes, he was helping her. For the first time in almost a year the future, however bleak, seemed further away than the next drink. She had cast aside initial doubts and suspicions, trying not to worry about just how she had bumped into him, how someone like him happened to find her. She'd even asked him. His response had been that, sometimes, people like them washed up on the same shores.

So she had assigned their meeting to coincidence. And he had made such promises.

'At first I thought you just wanted to fuck me,' she said.

'Is that what most men want of you?'

'Hah!' She shivered, drew a hand over the sweat beading her brow. 'Only if they're desperate. And I've never let them. Not once.'

Holt shrugged and stared from the window. Rose couldn't even remember the name of the little town where they had met, but here in Sorrento it was scorchingly hot, the streets bedlam, and the smells of delicious cooking and rank sewage wafted through the curtains with each breath of sea air. Her mouth watered and her stomach rolled. Four miles east of them people lived in cheap, chaotic housing, while in the harbour's à la carte restaurants holidaymakers spent a local's daily earnings on a plate of imported meat. A site of such contradictions seemed a perfect place to hide.

'It's been a long time since I had a cause,' he said, turning to face her. He was very still when he spoke, only his mouth and eyes moving. Every movement was spare and necessary. 'Sometimes my causes were convenient because they paid well. That's the definition of soldier of fortune, I suppose. On occasion, just now and then, I

84

believed in something. But what you tell me happened to you . . . ' He sighed. 'It's the children. Not you. Not your husband. Don't care what one adult does to another, because it's the adults who run the world. We can make our own choices, mostly. But when the children are hurt, that's when I become sad. And angry.'

The children, she thought. Less clouded by alcohol than she had been for a long time, yet shaken by the burning need she still felt for blessed oblivion, her memories were becoming richer by the hour. Molly, stabbed behind the ear and left sitting up as if still waiting for her mummy. Isaac, lying in his own blood. Alex, one little hand still clasped in his father's and his face a mask of dried blood. There were flies on them. They'd been there for so long by the time she found them that time had moved on, and nature had moved in.

'You have children?' she asked.

Holt stared from the window, silent. It was as if she'd never asked the question at all. Maybe he'd had children and they were gone, but she could not ask him that. She knew how that would burn.

'I'm ready to learn from you,' she said. 'Everything you know. All of it. And I'll pay you, somehow, one day.'

Holt turned to her again and his face creased into a smile. He had a beautiful smile. 'I have almost three million dollars in a bank account in the Seychelles.'

She raised her eyebrows.

Holt shrugged gently. 'What's a man like me

85

to do with beaches and blue seas?'

'How long will it take?' Rose asked.

'What?'

'To train me?'

He laughed as if the very idea was faintly ridiculous. Then he looked at her, really looked at her for the first time, and she had never been scrutinised like that before. It was so thorough that he must have seen into her, to those imprinted memories that she had never been able to escape. She was naked beneath his glare, stripped of clothing and skin, flesh and bones. He saw to the heart of her, and then he seemed to relax in his chair a little, drinking some more water as he looked from the open window once more. He stared out at the view across the city rooftops to the sea beyond. He seemed hesitant.

'Holt,' she said.

'Yes,' he said softly, as if answering a silent question of his own. Then he turned. 'Yes. I'll tell you some things that will help. A few tricks. How to fire a gun, how to fight, how to watch. Some knife work, some fist work. It helps that you're already away from the world. And you have violence in you already, Rose. I see where it simmers. I'd say you're halfway there.'

86

11

ambush

As soon as they dropped off the hunters, Rose knew that the Trail would come for her.

She drove as hard as she could up the mountain road, and when the helicopter passed overhead and continued down the valley, she slammed on the brakes. Gun nursed in her lap, she used the remote wing mirror control to track the aircraft's progress. It was not slowing or turning. Of course not, not yet. It had its cargo of rich arseholes to disgorge first.

Part of her wished that she'd stayed with that poor bastard Chris Sheen. She could have run with him into the hills, and by nightfall she could have killed at least half of the hunters, if not more. But mere blood was no revenge, even if it was the blood of those who'd murder someone for nothing more than the sick thrill. And it wasn't the hunters she wanted, but those who'd sent them on their way.

The ones in the helicopter, for a start.

She hoped that Adam would be proud of the action she was taking. He'd understand, she was certain of that, because they'd once had the conversation that many couples have after a glass or two of wine, when life is good: *If anyone hurt you or the kids, I'd happily kill them,* he'd said. They'd laughed about it, imagining all manner of action-hero scenarios, and although she hadn't verbalised it at the time, she'd always thought the same. So yes, she believed that Adam would approve.

Her children, though? Rose doubted they'd even recognise her any more. That made her so terribly sad. It felt like a betrayal, but as a mother she knew that sometimes a parent had to do what was right for their children, however cruel or harsh it might seem.

'I'm still a mother,' she whispered, and no voices rose in dissent. 'That's why I'm doing this. I'm looking after my children.'

She drove on, alert to movement or the flicker of reflected sunlight. It was possible that the Trail had placed other members to ambush her as she escaped the scene of the drop-off. With a sniper hidden on a hillside close to the road in both directions, whichever way she went she'd have to pass them. Even an average shooter would be able to put a bullet through her windscreen.

But she hoped they'd not had enough time to arrange anything. The whole hunt for Chris had been set to take place in the city south of here, so her enforced change of location, and her killing of three of their members, must have caused them a massive headache. Perhaps they'd take her sudden appearance as an unexpected bonus. But they'd be out of sorts, confused, and fucking angry. And that's just how she wanted them, because the angry made mistakes.

She scanned the wild hillsides as she powered up the winding road towards where it passed over the ridge between two mountains. She'd already scouted out the place where she'd wait for them, on one of her several trips up here over the past few months. It had always been her own intended hunting ground for them when the time was right, and with good reason. She'd been here on holiday with Adam, before they were married, when their romance was a dangerous, passionate, exciting adventure, rather than the comfortable friendship it had become. When the kids had come along they'd allowed themselves to turn into parents rather than lovers, although the bond of love was still strong. But when they'd holidayed here together their love had been untamed, as tempestuous and unpredictable as the landscape and climate.

They'd hiked for six days, wild camping, bathing in streams, sleeping in a small tent and making love under the stars, buying food from farms and small village shops, and by day two they'd both known that they would be with each other for the rest of their lives.

Adam had been right, at least.

Keeping one eye on her mirrors, Rose drove the car up towards the ridge. She'd already noted the lack of other traffic. That could simply be down to the remoteness of this place, or it could be that the Trail had set up roadblocks. They'd not want anyone happening across their weekend warriors tumbling from the helicopter in combat gear and bearing rifles.

The dead man's phone on the seat beside her started to ring. She ignored it. She'd considered ditching it, but there seemed little point. They'd be able to track it easily, but she had no intention of hiding from them. Not yet, at least. It rang off and went to voicemail. She'd speak to them on her own terms and no one else's.

The road opened up on the left into a gravelled parking bay, and she slammed on the brakes and skidded the car around ninety degrees. From that angle she could look back down the valley, and the car's nose was also pointing at the road, ready to go at a moment's notice.

This is it, she thought. *I'm in the thick of it now*. She almost laughed, because already she was more visible than Holt had told her to ever be. The Trail knew who she was, where she was and what she was driving. Holt would have snorted in disgust.

But Rose wasn't a mercenary. She wasn't even a killer, not like him. Not cold-blooded, someone happy to end a life for a perchecque. Holt had always known that, really, but he'd chosen to ignore it. He had helped prepare her hands for blood. She knew that somewhere in there, unspoken and not acknowledged by either of them, he'd fallen a little bit in love with her.

This moment was when everything could go wrong. She was exposed and vulnerable here, and though the Trail didn't exactly have the upper hand, the field was more level than she would have preferred.

She liked being hidden away below the radar, unknown, unseen, the shadow of a ghost.

But this part was always going to be this way.

She could see the helicopter further down the valley, sitting on a wide parking bay beside the road. Clouds of dust were whipped up by the rotors, swirling, dancing and spreading in complex and beautiful patterns. Through the dust she could just see the clumsy figures of the hunters, disembarked and already moving off onto the landscape. She glanced at the outcropping of rocks where Chris should have hidden. Beyond and above was wild country — his sort of territory, a place he was well used to. She only hoped he didn't fuck up and get himself shot too soon.

A flash of memory jarred her. They came like this sometimes, especially if her mind was active, the thought of grief and revenge hot.

She was sitting on a rock on a mountainside, the view laid out before her beyond breathtaking. Adam was beside her. They'd been sharing a flagon of farmhouse cider that they'd bought from a local farmer — potent and cutting, quite vile, but it gave them a warm buzz that drew them even closer together. There were no roads, no houses, nothing manmade in sight. They were intruders here, and if Rose concentrated she could distance herself completely, be part of the landscape and understand just how wild this place really was.

She blinked and the memory faded, leaving behind the taste of foul cider on her tongue.

'I hope you're as good as I think,' she muttered. If Chris got himself shot straight away, everything was fucked. And now she had revealed to the Trail that she was still alive.

They would not stop looking for her until they'd avenged their dead.

'Come on then,' she muttered. She picked up

the gun, and when she blinked she saw the Trail woman's head snapping back when she'd shot her in the face. 'Head shot,' she muttered, thinking of Holt, smiling.

The helicopter lifted off. Rose tensed. When the aircraft turned and headed back up the valley towards her, she shoved the BMW into gear and roared over the brow of the ridge.

The road snaking down the other side followed the natural lines of the hillside, old stone walls protecting drivers from a steep drop on the left. The wall was holed in a few places, and Rose wondered at those stories. But not too much.

She'd already planned where she was going to make her first stand, and it took only thirty seconds to get there.

She stopped the car hard against the stone wall on the left, rock scraping against metal. Leaving the engine on, counting silently in her head, she grabbed the phone and gun, opened the door and dashed across the road, slamming the door behind her. She wanted them to think she was still in the car. That way, they'd come closer.

It would take them a minute to reach her, maybe less. She could already hear the distant thud of rotors echoing from the barren mountainsides.

The trees grew close to the road here, leading up a narrow gorge that widened into a deeper ravine in the hillside further up. She'd chosen this location because it would be impossible to land the helicopter — the road was too narrow, with looming rock bluffs threatening to catch the rotor blades, and the hillside was steep and rocky both below the road, and above, where the gorge cut into the mountain.

They'd have to hover closer to see what she was doing.

She climbed a rotten wooden fence and then moved in amongst the trees. It was cool in there, calm and quiet, and a startled sheep scurried away up the slope.

Rose hoped she'd thought this through correctly. She wondered what Holt would have thought of her plan, and for a moment she wished she were back there with him, haunting the hot bars and bustling streets of Sorrento like the ghost of the man he was meant to be, or had once been.

But she'd spent her time with him almost three years ago. It was time to be herself again.

Her breath came fast and nervous. What if they *could* land? Would the trees shield her as well as she hoped? What if they slipped down ropes from the helicopter and surrounded her? She hadn't planned this enough. Hadn't considered every possibility, every permutation.

She closed her eyes and controlled her breathing, and thought of something Holt had said. *Once you're in play, don't worry about maybes.*

The sound of the helicopter suddenly changed and grew louder as it crossed the ridge and drifted down towards the car. She could see it through the trees, hanging out over the valley and slowing as it drew level with the idling

93

vehicle, three hundred feet out. She kept completely still. They were watching, and they'd be checking the area around the BMW as well as the vehicle itself.

'Come in closer,' she said. 'Come on. Come and see.'

The helicopter's side door slid open. The sun was beyond, so the aircraft's interior was in shadow. Still she felt watched. She slowly lowered herself down until she was lying on the loamy ground, mostly sheltered behind a tree trunk. The gun was clasped in her right hand, her index finger resting across the trigger guard. She'd only touch the trigger if she was going to use it.

'Come on . . .'

If the helicopter came close enough, she'd stand and open fire. It wasn't much of a plan, but it was all she had. Her blood was up, her need to avenge nowhere near sated by the three dead people in Chris's house. They were only the start.

And she had yet to meet Grin.

Holt had told her that to down a helicopter you should always aim for the tail rotor. The chance of hitting the pilot was remote, and the windscreen would often deflect a bullet off-target. The possibility of loosing off shots at the bodywork and hitting something vital was also small. But shoot at the tail rotor, and it would only take one good or lucky shot to shatter one of the blades and send the aircraft into a deadly spin.

One good shot. She had fifteen bullets, and

three spare magazines.

'Come on.'

The aircraft drifted a little. A puff of smoke bloomed in its dark doorway, one of the BMW's side windows shattered, and a shot rang out.

Rose didn't move. It was too far out, and tempted though she was to stand and start shooting, she'd mess up her only chance.

Another puff of smoke, another impact on the car. Several more followed, the shots sounding distant and lost amidst the broad landscape, the wide sky.

'Come closer, come *on!*' she said, frustrated.

But the Trail weren't stupid.

The helicopter tilted away and flew off down the valley. Its whipping rotors *thud-thudded* from the mountainside, and soon it was far enough away for her to hear the sound of the idling car engine again.

Rose stood, let out a held breath, and leaned against the tree. A warm breeze brought the smell of heather. A red kite circled high up, still searching for a kill. But she didn't feel disappointed. She'd known it was a long shot, in more ways than one.

Losing them now only meant that they'd be there for her to kill further down the line.

12

rage

'Piss stop,' Vey said. The van ground to a halt and the handbrake clattered on.

Gemma glanced up at her mum's blindfolded face, then whispered across to Megs.

'Hey, Megs, we're going to stretch our legs.'

'Not you,' Vey said.

'What? But I need to go.'

'Then go.'

Gemma felt a rush of anger, blooming at the centre of her and radiating out to tingle her numb limbs. It had first manifested an hour before. Burning through the cool distance she'd cocooned herself within, the rage had surged to the fore when Vey laughed at her mother.

'We don't have much money,' her mother had said, voice low and calm.

'Don't worry, I have,' Vey had said, laughing past the grin that drew a wrinkled mask across her face.

Gemma had felt the rage beginning to grow then, and she welcomed it back now.

'You really want us to wet ourselves?'

Vey didn't even look at them.

The van's rear doors opened. Gemma squinted against the light flooding in and saw Vey jump to the ground outside. A shadow filled the opening. A man stood watching them. It was

96

the tall man from the house; she'd heard Vey call him Tom. She'd filed his name away, but as she slid it into the box she'd grown cold. *They won't tell us their real names, will they? They'd only risk doing that if* . . . But she would not allow herself to complete that thought. To do so would be to let the fear back in.

'I need to go toilet,' Megs said.

'Me too,' Gemma said, glaring at the man. Her eyes were growing accustomed to the light.

'You can hang on,' he said.

'I *can't*!' Megs said. Gemma hated hearing her sister sounding so scared and upset, but she didn't shift her attention from the man. She was striving to see something in his eyes beyond cold, calm indifference.

'Let my children go,' her mum said. 'Whatever this is, please just leave them by the side of the road, and take me instead.'

'Mummy!' Megs said. She was crying behind her blindfold, and every time her shoulders shook, Gemma could see her grimacing in pain.

The man did not even respond.

'At least untie us from the bench,' Gemma said. 'Please.'

'Starting to sound like your sister,' Vey said, reappearing beside the man and climbing back into the van. 'Please please please!' Her mocking of Megs was almost too much.

'Fuck you,' Gemma whispered. Behind her she heard her mother's sharp intake of breath, and Megs' sobs shuddered into a shocked giggle. Inside, Gemma smiled.

But Vey and the man seemed unfazed. Without

another word he slammed the doors, and Vey settled once more in her seat across from them, nursing the gun in her lap.

As the van started moving again, crunching across gravel and then onto a smooth road surface, the acidic tang of urine filled the confined space.

Megs started sobbing once more and said, 'Sorry, Mummy, I'm sorry.'

'It's not your fault, honey, don't worry, it's not your fault.' Gemma glared at Vey and forced her own bladder to let go.

13

scree

Chris did what he knew best. He ran.

The aimless, random shooting soon died down when the helicopter left. His pursuers must have realised that they were alone then, and the initial buzz gave way to thoughts of pursuit and conserving ammunition. Crouched down, Chris paused to watch the helicopter head north up towards the ridge into the next valley. The car was no longer where he'd seen it parked up there, and Rose was long gone.

They would be after her. She'd killed three of their number, and now that their clients were on their own expedition hunting him, the Trail would be attending to more personal matters.

He hoped that Rose knew what she was doing. She'd seemed efficient and calm in the house, and very certain about her actions. But there had been aspects to her and the things she said that made him realise that this wasn't her world at all. Perhaps once, she had been just like him.

He used the rocky outcropping as cover for as long as he could, climbing diagonally up the mountainside and keeping the spur between him and those chasing him. Moving quickly and confidently, he tried to keep to sheep trails where the ground below was easier to make out. Ferns grew almost to his thighs, and clumps of heather

99

clung around boulders tumbled down the hillside in a time before any human had ever set foot here.

Chris usually loved the indifference of nature. Whether he walked across this mountain or not, his presence would have no effect whatsoever on its journey through time. Today, that indifference was more cutting than ever. For an instant it felt smothering, and the unfairness of what was happening threatened to drive him down, its weight unbearable. But he maintained his pace, looked to the horizon, and focussed on where he was going.

He moved at a pace that he knew he could comfortably maintain for two or three hours. His runs in the hills often lasted that long, sometimes longer. True, he had never run with a target on his back before, and that gave him added impetus. But he would also have to be cautious that the threat did not make him push too hard. He knew his body well — what he could and could not do, the aches and pains, the signs of dehydration and exhaustion — and he had to keep listening.

He was also not used to running with such a weight on his back. Sometimes he'd take a small backpack, especially on longer jaunts, usually containing a water bladder, waterproof, phone, and a few snacks. But the pack he carried now was at least three times as heavy as those he'd usually take. He had to factor that in. It was just one more thing to think about.

When the slope was manageable he ran, watching the ground several steps ahead so that his pace was not staggered by unexpected rocks or potential trip hazards. He jumped any hole or rock that might have slowed him, landing softly on the ball of his foot and driving forward, using his momentum to take him on beyond the danger without allowing a jarring impact to risk injury.

The backpack was snug to his back and shoulders. He could hear the swish of fluid in there, and was pleased that he had a decent amount of water. There were energy bars and gels, and dried meals, too. But other than the out-of-date, mouldy sandwiches he'd taken from the holdall the Trail man had given him, he had no real food.

That was something to worry about later.

At a steeper part of the hillside he had to slow down, pausing in a depression in the ground to view the lie of the land. To reach the high ridge he was aiming for he'd have to climb past the ferns and up a rocky slope, and it was probably steep enough to have to use his hands to grasp at the ground and haul upwards. Not exactly a technical climb, more a scramble. But it would slow him down.

He stood up straight and looked back along the slope, shielding his eyes from the sun. At first there was no movement other than the gentle swish and sway of occasional plants in the breeze. Then he saw a flicker way along the slope and a little down from him. The camouflage clothing made it difficult to make out, but the spike of a weapon gave the hunter away. Further back and down, a flash of white. Another hunter

101

had already stripped off their jacket to reveal a white tee shirt underneath. Good. He'd be able to keep better track of them.

At least they were a good distance away. Chris had no idea about guns, but he guessed that even if they had the best rifles money could buy, they'd have to be a crack shot to even get close to him at this range.

But he didn't know that for sure. It was a gamble. He'd have to gamble a lot if he was going to get out of this.

Thinking about guns, the sniping abilities of those chasing him, the distance he was putting between them . . . this was all so ridiculous. He looked around for a moment, breathing heavily, hands on hips as he searched for whoever was playing the big joke on him. Maybe he really *had* been hypnotised, let loose in a TV reality show. Maybe his family were in on it. But there was no Rose, and none of his family looking down. It was real. He knew that, even as he continued working through the disbelief, because he could remember the blood and gunfire in his house, and the emptiness when he'd returned home to find the stranger drinking his coffee.

He had to shrug off the unreality, shake the conviction that this was a trick, a joke, something bad that could only ever happen to other people. This was real.

'I'll just wait for them to get here, talk them down,' he said. They were normal people chasing him across the hillside. Not soldiers or killers, not if Rose was to be believed. Rich, but ordinary people, probably with jobs and families, pets, health worries and favourite songs. He'd just wait. Talk to them. They'd all realise together how stupid this was.

He raised his face to the sky and closed his eyes, and a gunshot echoed across the valley.

He ducked down. He'd not heard the bullet — no whistle, no impact, no ricochet like they showed in the movies — but wasn't even sure that he would. That far away, wouldn't he feel the impact before he even heard the shot? He thought so. Which meant that this one had already missed him when he'd heard the report.

It also meant that they'd seen him.

Carefully, he lifted himself up again, looking past a jagged spine of rock and across the hillside. A flock of small birds took flight, darting and singing in the mid-afternoon sunlight. He envied them their easy escape.

The movement was easier to spot now, because the men were running faster. They'd seen him. Any pretence at caution, at stalking, was gone. He had to move.

Straight up the slope was too steep, and it ended in an almost vertical scramble that would slow him down far too much. He could go down into the valley, but that would give them the high ground. Maybe he'd reach the road before they moved down and across the hillside to cut him off, maybe not. It was too risky. He had to keep to his original plan — up the steep slope at an angle towards the ridge, then down into the new valley on the other side. He'd take advantage of every second he was out of their sight to get as far away as he could.

But not too far, he thought, and Rose's voice finished the sentence: *because if they lose you, you lose everything*.

He considered taking a few seconds to check again in the rucksack, but unless there was a machine gun in there it would be wasted time. So he moved instead, ducking low and following a natural depression in the land, kicking through a pile of old bones and tangled wool. Fresh sheep shit rolled beneath his trainers, and several creatures startled him as they fled. If the hunters had half an ounce of sense about them they'd see that, and note the direction he was taking.

He switched directly uphill for a couple of minutes, crawling as low as he could on hands and knees. He tried his best to avoid the sparse fern plant stems, following a line of moss-covered rocks for a time, then dropping down into another dip carved by a dried-up stream. He used this to move uphill faster. His heart hammered, breath came deep and fast, and he was soaked with sweat once more. No time to stop for a drink; that would have to wait. The bladder was full, but Rose had not fed the drink hose out through the opening in the rucksack. He'd have to stop to take a drink.

But he couldn't allow dehydration to get a hold on him. He might have a long way to run, and he had to consider his nutrition as seriously as his route across the rugged landscape. That was another advantage he hoped he had over these men — the knowledge and abilities required to survive a long chase in the mountains.

104

Climbing from the small ravine, he looked back downhill. But the fold in the land he had just climbed blocked his view. He didn't like not being able to see how close they were, but it also meant that they couldn't see him.

It was maybe a hundred metres to the ridge line, up a steep slope with plenty of opportunities for cover. He could creep as slowly and as carefully as possible. Or he could run.

Something punched at him — the memory of his wife and kids in that van, its impact like a solid fist to his chest that purged a cooling flush through his veins. He felt light-headed and weak. *This isn't me!* Once, when he and Terri were courting, they'd been in a pub in their local town. They were childhood sweethearts, and they grew together through their teens with all the emotional and physical upheaval that accompanied the process. It was still a time when going out and drinking together was a novelty, and an older, bigger man had stumbled into Terri. She'd fallen against a shelf filled with empty glasses and a dozen had shattered on the floor. She'd been lucky not to gash her arm open.

But instead of leaving it there, the drunk had started ranting at her, spittle speckling his beard, arms waving. Chris had stepped in and punched him in the face, and he'd gone down in a heap.

Applause through the pub, a sickening sense of dread in him, and a look of terror in Terri's eyes. It was the first and last fight of his adult life.

He didn't do violence. He hated conflict and confrontation, so much so that as an adult he'd avoided it all his life. Terri made all the phone calls to haggle with insurance companies or negotiate the price for a new car. Sometimes he was called a wimp. Some friends said that he'd never have a bad word to say about anyone, whether they deserved it or not.

This was not him.

He started uphill. Cutting across the hillside to make the going less steep, he pushed with his feet and grasped with his hands, aiming for solid rock rather than stones that might be loose. His trail-running shoes with their plastic nibs clasped onto the ground, and he used each solid footfall to propel himself upward. His calves burned, knees throbbed. He soon started breathing heavily again, but settled into a decent rhythm. Chris knew the effort he could expend to maintain movement over a good distance, and he kept to that now. A shot, a shout, and he would have to move faster.

He closed on the ridge, skirting around a dip in the hillside, visible only because of the thinner spread of ferns. Perhaps his pursuers wouldn't notice that, they might fall in and break a bone, call for help or extraction. He assumed they'd have constant contact with the Trail.

He pressed flat to the sloping ground and rolled onto his side, looking back and down. He could still see his pursuers, struggling uphill towards him. They were already spreading out, the two in the lead — one of them the fit-looking Blondie — seeming to work together, three others strung out behind them. At the rear came the big Rambo character, stripped off to his white undershirt. They were too far away to make out their expressions, but he hoped they were hurting.

Just as he started climbing again he heard something. He paused, opening his mouth and breathing out slowly as he listened for the sound of engines. There, in the distance back to the north. The helicopter appeared low over the ridge and followed the road down into the valley.

What did that mean? Had they found and killed Rose? He clasped at the phone in his small back pocket, but it would waste time to call her now. And whether she was alive or dead, her fate had no effect on his immediate situation.

The hunters had also paused to watch the helicopter, and as it drifted off way down the valley two of them waved. Chris laughed. They were like kids on a hike waving as their parents drove away and left them to it.

He only hoped the helicopter really was leaving them to their own devices.

He moved off again, faster than before. The ridge was close, maybe thirty metres away. He had no idea what lay beyond — a gentle slope into the next valley, a tangled descent of fallen boulders and difficult climbs, a sheer drop. Whatever, he would have to make the most of it.

Thirsty, scared, heart thumping, sweat flowing, he gained the ridge and crouched down, running quickly across its highest point. He'd seen the movies, read the thrillers. He knew that he'd offer them a silhouette to shoot at.

Sure enough, the first distant cracks echoed up to him. A bullet ricocheted way downhill

107

from him, and another buzzed past to his left. He didn't know how close it had been, but for him to hear it he guessed pretty close. Luck? Or was at least one of them a decent shot? He didn't know, and had no desire to wait to find out. He ran until he was below the ridge line, then paused.

The view was staggering. To the east and south, craggy mountains spiked at the air, a shoulder of ridges and ravines connecting them. The valley before him wound generally south-west, and to the west was the mountain he was working his way around, its summit speckled with the remnants of snowfields. It was wild country. There were no roads visible. The landscape was barren and appeared unfarmed, though he could make out a few irregular lines of random rubble-walling drawn here and there. Occasional huddles of sheep crumbed the wide expanses of open moorland. The sky above was huge, smudged here and there with high clouds but generally warm and blue. He needed sun cream. He should search his rucksack for a hat.

But all of that was later. Because now he had a chance to put some real distance between him and his pursuers.

Ahead of him, the whole slope was a field of scree.

If Chris was careful, this was where he could get far enough ahead of them to pause and take stock. Scree running wasn't easy. It was dangerous, unpredictable, and it took not only a steady concentration, but a willingness to let go. Tense up, be too cautious, and the scree would have you. It wasn't running, but falling with style.

Tensing and then relaxing his shoulders, shaking his hands down by his sides, he focussed only on the next few minutes. He'd make a diagonal descent, hopefully gaining the other side of the scree field halfway down the slope. From there, he'd make his way into deep cover.

He started a slow, even run. The first few metres were on solid slabs of rock, and he plotted his course almost without thinking, stepping from one rock to another, looking ahead, gliding over the ground. When he hit the scree, everything started moving. The loose shale beneath his feet slipped like cracked ice, disturbed by his footfalls and plucked from its precarious state by gravity. It flowed, and Chris allowed himself to be carried with it. Arms loose by his sides, shoulders relaxed, he maintained balance through his core and hips. Each sweeping step was three metres long, then five, as whole spreads of scree started pouring downhill. Dust rose around and behind him, but he was already moving too fast for it to affect his eyes or throat. By the time the grey clouds billowed, he was past.

He grinned. He couldn't help himself — despite everything that was happening, all that he'd already seen, this simple act pumped adrenalin around his body and set his senses on fire. This was what he lived for, and how he'd continue to live.

He took long, high steps, going with the flow instead of fighting it. He aimed for the other side of the scree field, allowing himself to be carried downhill as well because to fight it would be to risk injury. The scree carried him, and his quick, long steps kept him on its rapidly shifting surface. Any hesitation or forced pause might allow his legs to sink deeper, and then would come the broken bones.

Even before he reached the far edge of the scree, he'd decided that he would wait to see what happened.

The noise filled his ears. If they'd already made it to the ridge and were shooting at him, he'd never know. But he was moving quickly, and the dust clouds behind him would offer some element of protection. Down the slope from him, great sheets of shale poured downward into the valley, whispering and then roaring across the stones beneath. For a moment he thought of going that way — down, instead of across — knowing that he could make it to the valley floor quickly. But once down there he'd have nowhere left to go, and he was sure he'd lose an advantage. He knew the hills, and he had the experience and energy to run them.

As he closed on the far edge of the scree, he started taking shorter, more calculated steps. At last the ground beneath him stopped moving, and instead he moved across the ground, darting for the shelter afforded by a tumble of rocks, and the trees that had grown amongst them. It was an ideal hiding place — shadowy, uneven, and with a stream tinkling down from the mountain-side.

Crouching in the shadows of low trees, Chris

settled and looked back up the slope. He had to squint, but he was pretty sure none of the hunters had made the ridge yet. That was good, it gave him time to have a drink and check the rucksack contents in detail.

There were two full water bottles, as well as the water bladder. He took a drink from one, and it was already warm. Then he fed the bladder's water feed pipe through the hole and clipped it to the rucksack's left shoulder strap.

Beneath the energy bars and gels he found a pack of flapjacks, some mixed fruit and nuts, two bagels with jam and peanut butter. That was a relief. It was good energy food, the sort he'd have chosen himself, although there wasn't much of it. There was a map and compass, but that was useless if he couldn't work out where he was to begin with. A head torch. The penknife had a three-inch blade, fork, spoon, and other implements he'd never need. The clothing was good quality outdoor wear.

He had maybe a day's worth of supplies.

Tugging the phone from his back pocket, he activated the small screen and checked it again. There was no signal, and when he scrolled through the contacts there was only one number listed, unnamed. *Rose*. Even if he did have a signal, he guessed the phone was locked in some way so that he couldn't use it to call anyone else.

Rose was using him as much as they were. He'd thought that from the beginning, when she'd saved him by slaughtering three people in his own home. And now? The police would be swarming all over his house — his neighbours had seen him with Rose, and seen the bullet hole in the car window. It would be a major crime scene, screened off from the rest of the street and all over the national news. *Architect and family missing, leaving two men and a woman brutally murdered in their home.*

'I'm a wanted man,' he whispered. But even if he did desire to give himself up to police, he couldn't. To do so would be to doom his family to the same fate that Rose's husband and three children had suffered.

At least, that's what she'd told him. Could he believe a single word she said?

Movement on the ridge caught his eye, and he quickly packed the rucksack again, tucking one of the water bottles into the outside net pocket.

The first of the hunters was up there, shielding his eyes and scanning the scree slope below. Two others soon joined him. If any of them had an ounce of sense they'd see the disturbed pattern in the shale, the settling dust, and know which way Chris had come.

They were still too far away for him to make out their faces, but he could see by their stance and gesticulating arms that they were arguing.

'Come on. Chase me.'

The first man — the tall, thin blond one — started across the scree slope. A shorter, fatter man followed. The third waited, obviously having decided to take a rest while the other two caught up.

'Come on, Blondie,' Chris said. And he smiled, because it was already obvious that these bastards didn't know what they were doing.

Blondie took small, hesitant steps, and when the scree started to slip beneath him he fell into the hill, reaching out to hold himself upright. He paused until the movement ceased, then slung his rifle across his back and started crab-walking across the slope.

Behind him, the fatter man was taking high, short steps, and Chris could see that his momentum was already getting the better of him. The ground started to shift, and the more he tried to slow down, the faster he moved. He might have cried out for help, but his voice was lost in the mountain's amused whisper of loose stone. Accelerating into a clumsy run, heading straight downhill instead of across, he made the mistake Chris was waiting for. As he jammed both feet together in an effort to halt, the hundreds of tonnes of shale around him kept moving.

This time his voice was audible as he cried out in agony. One or both of his ankles had gone, perhaps his shins too. He fell forward so that his head was aiming downhill, and the way his arm folded Chris thought his wrist might have snapped as well.

Blondie paused in his crab-walk and looked back and down at his companion. They both grew still, and the roar of the sliding shale slowly lessened to a loaded stillness.

'Help!' the fat man shouted. His voice was high, almost comical. 'Help me, I think I've broken my — '

'Fucking idiot,' Blondie shouted.

The other two men had arrived up on the

ridge. Rambo had now removed his shirt as well, and even from this far away Chris could see rolls of flab and his heavy gut hanging over his waist. Good. He wouldn't be able to keep this pace for much longer.

'Help!' the injured man called again.

'Help him!' Blondie shouted up at the ridge. Then he started moving again, taking slow, careful sidesteps. Whenever the scree whispered itself into motion, he paused until it subsided. Not the easiest or most efficient way to cross, but it would work. Leaving his injured companion behind, Blondie was continuing the hunt.

That's the one I'll have to watch. He's learning already. And he doesn't give a shit.

Chris was relieved that Blondie was not moving faster. But he'd have to move quickly to put distance between them.

14

lemons

Holt nursed her through the nightmares. Previously, fed by alcohol and the vagueness of a brain slowly losing its way, those bad dreams had been unfocussed, surreal visions, hanging with her when she awoke but never revealing themselves fully.

Sobering up and becoming part of the world once more, the nightmares hit her full and hard.

Holt was always there when she awoke. His hand clasped hers, as if pulling her up from the depths of nightmare, and she'd haul him down and hug him tight. She stank of piss and sweat and fear, but he never drew away. She knew he'd smelled it all before. There was nothing sexual, nothing provocative in their contact or her need for him. And ironically, the more snippets of his history she learned — the killing, the chaos, the life constructed of blood and war — the more she trusted his motivations. If he wanted her he could take her almost without blinking. This was all about being human.

And then one time the nightmare never came, and she found herself in dreams. There was a vague awareness that was dreaming, though she was not steering or dictating, but that didn't make it any less wonderful. Adam and her beautiful children were there, and they were holidaying in a place they'd never been. She and Adam had loved the countryside from an early age, and now the five of them were camping in the Rockies. The scenery was spellbinding, humbling, life-affirming, and Molly, Isaac and Alex were all just a little older than she had ever known them. *This is what might have been*, she thought, and rather than sadness she felt contentment. They would have come here together and had a wonderful time. There would have been love and affection, adventure and wonder. A dream was all she could hope for, but it was something.

When she awoke, Holt was sitting in his usual place by the window. He'd nodded off in the chair, and the breeze brushed the light curtain back and forth across his arm. He seemed not to notice. His shirt had rucked up when he'd shifted, and she saw the angular black glimmer of a gun in his belt. It was the first time she'd seen him with his guard down.

Rose sat up quietly, and the movement woke him up. He stared right at her, expressionless.

'Right,' he said. 'You look better.'

'I feel . . . ' She shook her head. She didn't know *how* she felt. Better? Sober? Not even nearly. She guessed that she'd never shake the taste for drink, but she *could* build a defence against it. Knowing that sobriety might occasionally give her such dreams would be a good start.

Holt stood, stretched, all creaking bones and groaning muscles. 'Come on,' he said. He grabbed a black holdall from behind the small sofa against the room's far wall.

'Where?'

He took a gun from the bag. It was small, squat, ugly, and Rose felt a flush of queasiness when she saw him check it over. Then he held it out to her.

'Time to start learning,' he said.

The sickness evaporated. Excitement rose in its place.

★   ★   ★

It was the first time they'd left Sorrento since he'd taken her there, however long before. She'd lost count of the days, each one fading into the next, periods of darkness marked as much by her disturbed sleeping pattern as the rise and fall of the sun. Holt had arranged for food to be delivered to their room, and several times they'd changed hotels. They were the sorts of places rarely included in tourist brochures, and while clean and comfortable, they'd never win awards.

They were never disturbed.

After three hours in the car — it was an old taxi, though she couldn't imagine Holt ever working that job — he drove them up an old track that led into the mountains. Twenty minutes later they stopped in front of a long, low structure, weeds growing in its gutters, windows boarded up, firmly locked doors protecting an empty interior.

Holt did not have a key, but that did not slow him down.

She didn't ask him what the old building was or how he knew they'd be safe using the gun inside. It was probably best she didn't know.

He set up a few old beer cans on a wooden bench and fired a few shots at them. Four out of five found their target.

'Your turn,' he said. He loaded the gun for her and told her where to stand.

The weapon was heavier than she'd expected. He stood behind her and showed her where to place her feet, how to bend her knees slightly, how to clasp her right hand around the gun and cup it in her left hand. He explained about safety catches and grips, then stood back.

Rose rested her finger on the trigger.

'Squeeze, don't pull,' he said. 'It'll kick a bit.'

She squeezed. It kicked. A splinter leapt from the wooden wall behind the cans on the bench. The gunshot was incredibly loud, but after the first two her ears were numbed and the explosions seemed more distant. Her hearing hummed as Holt changed magazines for her, and this time he held her arms for longer, chin resting on her left shoulder as he drifted the gun slightly left and right to help her aim.

The fourth shot found its mark and a can flipped back into the wall.

Rose smiled. A flush of success lit her. She looked back at Holt and he was nodding slowly.

'Well done. You killed a can.'

Her smile dropped, and she turned back to the range.

'Never go for a head shot,' he said behind her. 'Always shoot at their centre of mass, that way you're less likely to miss. And even if your aim's a bit off, a bullet to the shoulder or hip will incapacitate them for long enough for you to move in and make the kill.'

She blinked past her hands and the gun, looking at the old tins left standing. She waited for Holt to say more, but he had fallen silent once again. He was watching her, perhaps assessing how she reacted to his comment, and the realisation that this was all about killing people. Not tin cans.

Rose closed her eyes briefly, and when she looked again she imagined Grin standing in front of her. She aimed at her right eye and squeezed the trigger. A can bounced from the wail, blasted into two parts.

'Head shot,' she whispered. If Holt heard, he did not comment.

★ ★ ★

They spent another hour shooting, then sat in the shade outside and passed a water bottle back and forth.

'But sometimes the hard bit is getting them where you can kill them,' he said. 'Aiming the gun, pulling the trigger, seeing what you've done to the person . . . that's all in here.' He tapped his head. 'Morals, desires. The need for revenge. That's something for you to handle and settle with yourself, and live with forever, and I can't help you with that. But there are also practicalities.'

Rose took the bottle from him and drank a healthy slug of water. 'I can do it,' she said. 'They're not people. Not in my eyes.'

119

'So these Trail characters, you think they'll come to you? Stand quietly while you point the gun, not fight back while you're hesitating, battling with yourself — '

'There'll be no battle. I get them where I want them, then I'll kill them.'

'Hmmm,' Holt said. He didn't quite laugh, held back a smile.

'You doubt me?' Rose asked.

'It's not my place to doubt you. I barely even know you. I'm just saying that the ability to kill someone isn't just in your desire and willingness to pull the trigger. It's in the planning. Lot of people forget about that. They get so tangled up in the why that they forget the how.'

Rose drank again, looking out across the harsh landscape. Heat haze feigned a lake in the distance, nestled within the rolling hills. Lemon trees hustled in strict lines, the crops covering mile after mile. In rockier places, hardy trees and low shrubs clung to pockets of soil. Evolution had given them the ability to survive in this hot place, and she too was evolving. She was nowhere near the woman she had been, though she retained a residue of that wife and mother inside, and she always would. That was essential.

But now she was growing towards someone and something else.

Rose was surprised to find that she was shivering, even in the heat. Whenever she blinked, dark visions haunted the place behind her eyes. She knew who and what they were, but she didn't want to look.

'Shit, I could do with a drink.'

'Of course you could!' Holt said, laughing. 'You think anything is that easy?'

'Don't know. You tell me. You're the one who takes a water bottle into bars.'

'Touché.' He laughed and drained his bottle. He held it up to the sun and stared at it, like a drunk considering another empty glass. 'I haven't had a drink in seventeen years,' he said.

'Congratulations.'

'And nine months, and probably a few days.'

'And still counting.'

'It's just a thing, now. A part of me. Occasionally I want a drink so much it hurts, but that only lasts a moment or two, and those moments are fewer and farther between. Being an ex-alcoholic is as much part of me now as being French, or being someone who . . . ' He tapped the gun in his belt.

'Why did you stop?' It was a loaded question, and once out there she realised how intensely personal she was being. The air between them was suddenly uncomfortable, the silence fragile and sharp.

'Because when I was drunk, I couldn't shoot straight.' He stood, groaning and holding his knees like a much older man. She could see how fit and gnarly he was, and she thought the constant moaning and holding of joints was partly a facade. Maybe he didn't even realise he was doing it any more. Projecting weakness would put a potential enemy at ease. And it made her wonder how much else of what she saw was not the genuine Holt.

Standing, he lifted his shirt and showed her his

left side. His flank was scarred and knotted, skin folded and hard.

'And one time, I missed.'

Rose nodded slowly. It was all about control. A younger man, a drunk, he had survived purely through chance. Now he balanced every move he made. He kept hold of fate by the tail.

'So what else can you teach me?'

'Let's take it easy,' he said. 'One thing at a time.'

Rose went to object, but he silenced her with a look. Holt could do that. Sometimes he carried his whole violent history in one glance.

'What?' he asked. 'Got somewhere better to be?'

★ ★ ★

Sometimes she found Holt looking at her strangely. He never attempted to hide the expression, but neither did he explain it. It was enigmatic, a sort of worried confusion, as if he was trying to make a difficult decision. She tried to put her own explanation in place — he was falling for her, he wanted them to screw, he was starting to have second thoughts about what he was doing. None of them seemed to fit. Maybe it was hesitation or doubt she saw in his eyes.

He'd raise an eyebrow and wave away her concern, then talk about something else.

She only discovered what that look meant much later, long after she believed she would never see him again.

15

broken bones

Rose had never been a runner. When she was married — a wife, a mother, someone who still had a part to play in the normal world — she'd sometimes gone to Zumba with friends, and she and Adam had taken it in turns to walk their family dog. But she'd always left the more extreme, energetic activities to others. Adam had played football. Their children had gone swimming and biking, and Molly had been a ballet dancer since she was five. Rose had always said that being a mother kept her fit.

She'd always known that she was fooling herself, and there had been frequent vows to increase her exercise. Like many late-thirties couples, she and Adam had been the proud owners of an exercise bike that acted more as a clothes horse, a rowing machine that was gathering cobwebs in their garage, and she'd bought an expensive pair of running shoes that had served well when she was gardening or walking the dog. The will was there, but so were all the other time-consuming things that went to make up a life. She'd complained that she'd never had time, but in truth she had never made it.

After her family's massacre, losing time had come easy to her. The drink, the city, the

London stench and chatter of tourists and anonymity, days and weeks drifted by without her differentiating day from night, season from season. And then she'd seen Grin, and fled, and Holt had found her.

Now she wished to hell he'd taught her more. His reply when she talked about fitness and strength had always been, *I can't build your muscles or force you to run.* And so she hadn't.

After abandoning the BMW where she'd dropped Chris off only twenty minutes before, she had started working her way uphill. And she was suffering. She'd brought her gun, and given Chris everything she thought he might need to survive out on the hills, but she'd neglected to look after herself. Even as she reached the huddle of rocks where she'd told him to hide she was already gasping for water, sweating, and on the verge of passing out.

Good planning, Rose! she thought. *Fucking idiot.*

She moved on quickly. He'd have run away from the hunters, up towards the ridge she could see in the distance. She listened for the sounds of the helicopter returning. The gun was heavy in her waistband, her phone tucked in the front jeans pocket. She was sweating. The jeans were chafing.

Remembering the dead people in Chris's house made the pain, the discomfort from sweat, and the thirst seem inconsequential.

She had shocked herself. She'd dreamed for years of pulling the trigger and seeing one or more of them die at her own hand. Holt had warned her that there was no saying how she might react. He'd known the hardest of killers crumble, and seen the meekest of people turn into heartless, soulless murderers.

'Do you think about life?' he'd asked.

'I used to,' she'd replied.

'Every death is a story,' Holt had said. 'Every life halted is the end of every part of that story. You're turning something living into something dead. Destroying a miracle.' He'd surprised her with the use of that word. He'd claimed no religious beliefs, yet he'd used a term that surpassed science. 'Life is something we can't explain. And you'll be stopping it.'

'They're not alive,' had been her reply. 'Not in any way I can understand.'

Ending three lives, she had barely blinked. Perhaps her reaction would be delayed. Maybe because she hadn't yet had a chance to pause and consider what she'd done, the full implications of her actions were yet to impress upon her. But she could think of slashing the man's throat open with the knife, shooting the other two at point-blank range, and there was not a flicker of remorse inside. For all she knew, those three had been present at her family's death. They might even have done the killing.

She was happy with that lack of remorse. It made what might come next easier.

Chris and the hunters had a good head start, but she knew that she'd catch up with them. She had to. The men who paid for such a service were usually rich and, if not actually fat, then unfit. She'd found that out, as well as a lot more, during the years she had spent researching and snooping on the Trail. She'd never tried to understand them, because she'd known from the beginning that was way beyond her, and she didn't *want* to understand. But she had attempted to know them.

Normally middle-aged or older, wealthy and successful, usually married with children, owners of their own companies or high-up executives in multi-national corporations. On occasion, a politician or a military man. She'd discovered some oddities — a younger, less wealthy man who somehow found his way into this sordid, sick world, and once, a woman. Rose had been shocked at that, because she'd discovered that the woman was a mother.

There had come a time when she'd considered exposing them all. But though she had some elements of proof, exposure might rob her of the chance for vengeance. Remaining covert, hidden away out of the Trail's sight until she was ready, had been her priority.

There would come a time, though, when everyone who had been involved in a hunt would come to regret the choices they had made. She had kept good records, and was careful about where they resided.

Closing on the ridge, she heard a distant rumble. She paused with her head tilted to one side, trying to ease her panting, one hand cupped behind her ear. It was a long, low whisper, like a strong breeze but somehow more solid, more textured. She ducked down and lay flat against the ground, ferns hanging above her

126

offering scant cover. Helicopter? She didn't think so. They'd still be making their plans for her, and she'd gambled that they would not yet want to corrupt the hunt with a hunt of their own. So far it seemed she was right.

The noise died down and a lonely silence fell across the valley once more.

Don't worry about it, bunny, Adam said.

Rose frowned, shook her head. He'd spoken to her before since he'd been murdered, but only when she was rising from a drunken slumber into a consuming hangover. She'd usually silenced him again with more booze. She hadn't heard his voice in some time.

'Not now, baby,' she said. 'I don't need that right now.' Silence. She sighed and started climbing again.

★ ★ ★

By the time she reached the ridge half an hour later she'd heard that gentle, rumbling whisper two more times.

On the other side of the ridge, splayed down the hillside into the wide valley beyond, was a wide scree slope.

'Hey!'

She ducked, hand reaching for her gun, looking around to try to locate the source of the shout.

'Hey, down here!'

Halfway across the slope and a couple of hundred metres down, two men waited on the hillside. They were hunters, both wearing camouflage gear and small rucksacks, and she could make out the stark black lines of their rifles on the ground beside them. One of them was sitting, the other seemed to be crouched across the slope, lying at an awkward angle.

Rose thought quickly. They hadn't been panicked by her appearance, so they probably didn't know about her. And why would they? The Trail wouldn't want to advertise that they had encountered a problem, and that one of their past targets — the only one who had ever got away, as far as she could tell — had returned. It would make them look bad, and that was something they could not afford. They'd probably found a way to explain the sudden change of venue. Maybe they'd suggested it was added excitement, an extra element to the hunt.

She smiled. Perhaps this was when her own haphazard plan — no plan at all, really, just an intention to kill as many Trail members as she could, even though she didn't know *exactly* how many were involved in this hunt — began to take on a more manageable form.

'I'll be down now!' she shouted.

The sitting man stood, and she was pleased to see that he left his gun lying there. 'Edge down slowly, and don't fight it when the shale shifts,' he shouted.

Rose held up one hand. Yeah, right, easy for him to say. This was why she had brought Chris up here, because he seemed to know stuff like this. Like the hunters, she was just muddling through.

Several hair-raising minutes later, she was

crouched ten feet from the two men. And in those minutes she had pulled on a disguise. It was more mental than physical, though she tried to exude control and confidence, and did her best to present an aura of professionalism.

'What happened?' she asked.

'Max broke his ankles and a wrist,' the man said. He was average height and build, maybe fifty, with manicured nails and a haircut and shave that probably cost an average family's weekly wage. He spoke like he didn't give a shit.

'Clumsy,' Rose said.

'Yeah, well, you pricks send us where we're not expecting to go and — '

'Hey, hey, who're you calling pricks?' Rose said. *They do think I'm Trail. Of course they do. Why else would I be running around up here with a gun in my belt?*

'Just get me out of here!' Max was pale and sweating in pain, propped awkwardly on his right side and in imminent danger of rolling downhill. His left foot drooped at an odd angle, and his left hand rested on his ample stomach.

'You know there's a recovery fee?' Rose asked.

'What? After all I've paid you?' He was furious, but trying not to move because the pain was so great.

'Which one are you?' Rose asked the well-groomed man.

'Patrick McMahon.'

'Right, Mr McMahon. My guess is that you're keen to — '

'Hell, yes. You'll stay with him? You'll make sure he's taken care of? I mean, you're all right here?' His voice trailed off as if realising the foolishness of what he'd asked.

'Of course she's all right,' Max said. 'She's one of them! Dickhead. Anyway. Thanks for staying.'

'No problem. Dickhead.' Patrick looked down at the injured fat man, then rolled his eyes at Rose.

She forced a smile. *He'll have a wife, maybe kids. Big house, several cars. The name's familiar . . . actor, TV guy, writer? Maybe just a well-known businessman. But today, he wants to kill Chris and cut his balls off as a trophy.* Her smile turned into something else, a forced grin that hurt her face. Patrick's face dropped as he backed away, then he snatched up his gun and was moving carefully across the scree, taking longer steps as it shifted beneath him. He didn't look back.

She could have shot him from there. She rested her hand on the gun in her belt.

'So are you going to call the helicopter back?'

Rose watched Patrick a moment longer, then squatted down next to Max.

He stank. He was shaking, even though the afternoon up here was pleasantly warm. A breeze whispered across the mountainside, flicking hair into her eyes. She reached out to touch his ankle, then held back. It was so tempting . . . but if he screamed in pain, Patrick might decide to come back and help.

'So when the fuck are you going to . . . ?'

'Just give me a minute,' Rose said, pretending to look him over. In reality she was watching the other hunter gain more solid ground. He didn't

130

even look back before disappearing across the mountainside, hidden by tumbled rocks and a fold in the land that sprouted a few stark trees. His movements looked clumsy and desperate. He was keen to catch up, and she couldn't understand how someone could be so eager to kill.

Not without a good reason.

'You don't look like one of them,' Max said.

'What do you mean?'

He shrugged, and the movement must have shifted broken bone against bone. The shrug froze and he winced, so hard that his fat face wrinkled into something resembling a bulldog.

'Can you move at all?' she asked.

'No . . . ' he croaked through that twisted-up face. He was paler than ever, and she thought he might puke.

She hadn't expected this. The thought of what she'd do to the hunters was a possible part of her vague plan — hurting them might be a way to lure in the Trail — but she hadn't expected one to present himself to her on a plate like this.

'So, the others . . . ' she said, trailing off.

'Huh?'

'You know, Patrick, and . . . ' She waved her hand as if trying to recall.

'I don't know their names. Why the hell would I know their names? So are you lot going to get me to hospital, or what?'

'Yeah, sure,' she said. 'Let me use your satphone.'

'You don't have one?'

'Crap reception,' she said, hoping it would

131

silence him for a bit, at least. He'd already removed his small backpack, and she sat a few feet from him and rifled through it. She kept one eye on him, one on his gun. It looked like an expensive weapon. Of course it was. Rich people wouldn't want to kill with a crappy piece of kit.

Max groaned, rocking backward and forward slightly on his one good arm.

He had water, food, ammunition, and a satphone. Its screen was locked, but when she unlocked it a single number was outlined.

Rose took in a deep breath, closed her eyes, thought things through. This was a gift, and she had to use it well.

'I'm going to ease you onto your back,' she said.

'No, don't move me, it'll hurt — '

'I've got to check you over! Listen, I had medical training in the army, I can't just leave you lying there in case . . . ' She trailed off and looked at his feet.

'What?' he asked.

'Okay, quick and easy,' she said, hoping she'd injected just the right amount of seriousness into her voice.

'What's wrong?'

'Just let me see.' She eased herself in front of him and prepared to push him onto his back, glancing again at his left foot.

'What is it?' he asked again.

She pushed against his left arm and chest, rolling him onto his back and freeing his good arm.

He groaned, reaching for her, hand fisted. It

132

was a clumsy blow that barely nudged her, but she leaned over him and pinned him to the ground by his shoulders.

'You ever want to walk again?' she asked.

Max nodded.

'Here.' She handed him the satphone. 'Call and tell them what's happened while I deal with you.'

She turned away, mind racing, pretending to look at his wounded ankles but listening, waiting for his reaction.

The satphone beeped.

Rose hovered one hand above the wounded man's legs. She winced at the stink of him. He was a pissing, moaning nobody, a wretch, and while he probably had more money than she'd ever see or even dream of, it made him a monster. She wondered why he'd become what he was, but really she didn't want or need to know. She wouldn't question him or plead with him.

She'd simply use him.

'Hey, yeah, it's Max Lyons, you've gotta help me. I've fallen and broken my ankles, and I can't . . . What? Yeah, already.'

A pause.

'No I'm not alone, one of — '

Rose tweaked his ankle. Max shouted, dropping the phone and slapping his arm down onto the shale. She picked it up and handed it to him again, turning away and leaning over his legs again.

'Sorry, yeah. Yeah? Okay, I'm about a mile down the valley from . . . oh, okay.'

She knew that they'd be able to track onto his satphone signal. She'd have liked to know how long they'd take to get here, but there was no way she could ask.

'Thanks,' Max said. 'Thank you.' The whiny gratitude in his voice almost made her want to puke. The phone beeped as he disconnected, and she nudged his ankle again.

While the man cried and moaned, Rose pocketed the satphone, shouldered his rucksack, and picked up his rifle. She was nowhere near as experienced with a weapon like this as she was with the pistol, but Holt had taken her shooting once with a much older rifle, a Carcano from World War Two with adapted scope. He'd pronounced her a natural. She checked the safety, scanned down the mountain through the scope, and then slung it over her shoulder.

Then she looked down at Max.

'People like you came after me, once,' she said. 'For all I know it *was* you.'

'Wh . . . what?'

'And because I escaped, they killed my husband, daughter, and two sons. Molly danced. Alex liked *Diary of a Wimpy Kid*. Isaac was obsessed with space and astronauts. And my husband . . . ' She trailed off.

Max only frowned up at her. Perhaps it was the pain making his brain slow, but she saw pure confusion as he tried to compute what was happening.

'They made my husband watch as they killed my children with knives. Have you ever seen anything like that?' She pursed her lips. 'Yeah.

Actually, I expect you have. You're the kind of sicko who watches those terrorist decapitations on the internet.' A flicker of his eyes told her that she was right. 'Imagine someone doing that to your children.'

His eyes went wide. 'What are you going to . . . ?'

'Do to you?'

Max glanced at his rifle over her shoulder, looked around at the barren, deserted landscape. There was no one, nothing.

'I can't have you making a noise when they come, warning them.'

'I won't, I won't say a word!'

She turned away, looked down into the valley, and tried to pretend he wasn't squirming on the ground behind her. She had to get to cover soon, but for a moment she tried to remember being here with Adam. Drinking in the wilderness, the remoteness, and feeling safe because they were with each other. But this time her dead husband did not speak to her.

Maybe because she was wrong. He'd *never* approve of what she had become, and what she was about to do.

'Whoever you are, I'm sorry about your family, it wasn't me, this is my first time and I only did it for . . . Just because I wanted something different, and . . .'

She could tell that he was crying. Probably snotting and foaming, pain and fear and self-pity making him the true, non-man he'd always known he was. Maybe he'd believed that hunting and killing someone would make him more of a man than he'd ever been.

They had to get close. Rose couldn't risk them being warned by Max. Or seeing blood.

'Please, I won't say a word when they come, I'll keep quiet and not mention you and when they take me away I won't say a word.'

'I know,' she said softly. She pulled the gun from her belt, turned, pressed the barrel up between his legs, aimed into his body, and pulled the trigger.

The shot was muffled by his fat thighs. He jerked, screeched, his eyes opening wide. Then he started to shiver uncontrollably, both hands — the good one, and the broken one — clawing at his abdomen.

Rose stood and circled him slowly, looking for an exit wound and signs of blood. His crotch and inner legs were darkening, but if they saw that they'd just assume that he'd pissed himself.

She found that she was breathing light and shallow, and her vision began to swim. *Murderer*, she thought, trying to apply the name to herself. But while it fit, it didn't inspire any emotion. She was dispassionate. They had made her this way.

'Adam,' she whispered. Nothing.

She walked away from the dying man, striding carefully across the shifting shale towards the cover of rocks and trees.

16

plan

Chris needed a plan.

He sometimes did his best thinking in the hills. The conscious part of him was always concentrating on the terrain, making sure he didn't turn an ankle or stray from whichever route or path he intended following. But the subconscious part of him found freedom in the wild, and while he ran or cycled he would often think things through. Problems with a current project, disagreements with Terri, his own aims and ambitions. Sometimes he took longer expeditions as a chance to really step back from where he was in life and analyse, make sure he was truly happy. Difficult, long runs removed him from the world and allowed him to view his life almost dispassionately. The fact that he was always pleased with what he found — eager to get home and see Terri, play with his girls, and return to work in his studio once again — meant that things were at peace.

Not everyone had that chance to take a step back, or took it if they did, and he pitied them.

From the moment he'd returned home from his morning run and seen the stranger in the kitchen, drinking his coffee and leaning against the worktop as if he owned it, Chris had barely had a chance to think.

137

But now he felt in control for the first time that day.

To his right — by the time and position of the sun he judged it as west — the ridge he'd just crossed veered up towards the summit of a tall, craggy mountain. Its pinnacle was hidden by hazy cloud, and from this angle he did not recognise it. To the east was another range of hills, and between the two was a deep, steep-sided valley. There were no visible roads following the valley floor, although he could make out several vague farmer's tracks criss-crossing the lower slopes of the opposing mountainsides. A few uneven lines showed where rubble walls had been built in the past and then fallen into disrepair. There even seemed to be fewer sheep speckling the hillsides here, as if this valley, these mountains, were too remote even for them.

It was a harsh, unforgiving landscape. People died out here. Every year walkers got lost and died of hypothermia, and casual climbers took on routes that exceeded their abilities and fell to their deaths. Snowdon and its surrounding areas claimed several souls each year. A famous mountain, popular with tourists and weekend walkers, its many dangers were hidden beneath a veil of familiarity and a tame veneer. Even with a hundred people drinking tea and eating cake in its summit café, someone unprepared could be bleeding their life away on its harsh slopes.

Chris was more than prepared. This was his world.

There were now four men hunting him. The fat bastard who'd fallen and broken bones on the scree was out of it. Maybe he'd be rescued, or maybe he'd stay there all night. Chris didn't care. With his family being held gagged and at gunpoint, he'd be happy if the scumbag froze to death.

Of the remaining four, it was Blondie who posed most danger. He'd continued even when a companion was injured, his ultimate aim driving him onwards. *I'm his ultimate aim*, Chris thought, and the nape of his neck tingled. He must always remember the target on his back.

The Rambo character was overweight and looked unfit. He might not be able to keep up for too long. Of the other two he had yet to form an opinion. But it seemed certain that he was not dealing with people like him. As the hours went by, the idea of trying to negotiate with these men seemed more and more foolish. There was obviously a lot of money involved in this; these were rich dicks looking for a forbidden thrill.

But he still needed a plan. So as he kept a good, easy pace across the wild mountainside, he thought things through.

Running blind, on and on, would only end one way — with him lying dead on a mountainside. Maybe they'd take their trophy and then leave what was left of him there to rot. It could be weeks or months until he was found. Or, if they bothered to hide him away well enough, it might be many years. He'd become the skeleton of a mountain runner ill prepared for the environment that had probably killed him. Would his family be alive to receive the eventual, tragic news?

He couldn't think that far ahead.

If he slowed down and let one of them shoot him, perhaps he'd save his family. Or perhaps not. It was a chilling thought. If a madman went on a shooting spree in Sainsbury's, Chris would have instinctively leaped in front of his family to protect them, or gone at the gunman. But that wasn't the same as intentionally being shot to death. It was dying taking action, not resigning himself to inaction.

He wasn't sure he could do that.

His heart was beating fast, but not through exertion. It was stress, pure and simple. He didn't know what to do next, and not knowing felt like a noose tightening around his throat.

Even if he did manage to contact the police somehow, they'd view it as a call from their most wanted man. Three people slaughtered in his house, his family missing . . .

His story was unbelievable.

'Fucking hell!' he hissed as he ran. His thighs were aching, feet hot, back wet with sweat, but he was used to this; he liked the sense of physical exertion. What he was not used to was not being in control.

He'd pushed hard since the scree slope, choosing a difficult route uphill that involved some scrambling, working his way around giant boulders, and climbing a couple of short, steep cliffs. Nothing too dangerous — nothing that his pursuers wouldn't at least attempt — but he'd hopefully put some distance between him and Blondie. He'd looked back many times, but though he'd seen no sign of pursuit, it was a difficult landscape to read. Dips and slopes, ridges of rock, folds in the land meant that someone could be within twenty feet of him and he might not see them.

But if Blondie had moved as fast as him, he wouldn't last until sunset.

Chris settled beside a spur of rock. He was positioned so that anyone more than fifty feet away wouldn't see him, and if one of the hunters approached the way he'd come, he would see them first. A quick drop down the rock's sheer side, and then there was a steep descent that he could escape down. He'd be close to them, but a rapidly moving target. He hoped they weren't that good a shot.

He finished one of the two bottles of water. It was warm and unsatisfying, but it would quench his thirst for a while. He'd need to refill the bottle as soon as possible, and the water bladder was also half empty. Without purification tablets he risked picking up a bug, but he'd drunk from mountain streams before without any ill effect. Just another risk in a day that was filled with them.

He gobbled down an energy bar, too. They tasted pretty grim, but they were heavy on carbs and sugars and would get straight to his muscles.

Plucking the phone from his pocket, he pressed the dial button. As he held it to his ear he kept glancing around, rucksack back on, squatting on his feet instead of sitting, ready to spring into motion at the first sign of movement.

'Already?' Rose asked.

'Sorry,' Chris said. 'Forgive me having some questions for you.'

'Make them quick.'

'Where are you? What are you doing?'

'Waiting,' Rose said. 'So ask.'

'What am I supposed to do?'

'What you're doing.'

A buzzard family was circling the grassy plain of the valley down below. Two adults and an infant. They were almost level with him, drifting on thermals and never once needing to flap their wings.

'I'm running.'

'Good. Stay alive, stay ahead. But not too far.'

'Stay just in their sights, yeah?'

'If they lose you for too long, think you've escaped, the hunt might be over.'

'And then?'

Rose did not reply. He imagined her sitting on a hillside somewhere, phone pressed to her ear, gun in her other hand. She'd be weighing everything she said carefully. He was her pawn, not her partner.

'Just where are you?' he asked again.

'I told you. Waiting.'

He lifted himself up a little, looked around, and gave the finger to his surroundings. He listened for any reaction at all down the phone but there was nothing.

'I don't have any way out of this, do I?' he asked.

'Just do as I tell you and I'll help.'

'You're only helping yourself!'

'Don't shout. It's quiet up here, noises carry. Weird. I don't like it.'

'I do.'

'Yeah, I know. Your social media's full of this kind of shit. That's why I brought you here.'

'Where are they holding my family?' Chris asked. It was the only question that really mattered, and the only destination that made sense. If he found his way to civilisation and called the police, his arrest would likely prompt his family's murder. He squeezed his eyes shut, trying not to consider that, but doing so only let him see more of their despair. Terri, tied up and gagged and trying to be strong. His poor young daughters, wondering why he hadn't been there to protect them. He'd told them he always would.

'No idea,' Rose replied.

'I don't believe you.'

'Whatever.' She was cold, distant.

'Where were they keeping your family when they killed them all?' She didn't respond. That was what he wanted. To shock, upset her.

'Not far from home,' she said softly, after a while.

'Then mine will be in Cardiff,' he said.

'Don't know.'

'It makes no sense going further with them. Tied up in a van like that, the further you travel, the more chance of being found out.'

'Listen, these people are serious! I know about them, you've no idea some of the things I've found out. *No idea*. They're professionals.'

'Then Cardiff makes even more sense.' *An old house with a basement, maybe. Somewhere people are used to seeing activity. Or maybe one of the new apartments in Cardiff Bay, there are*

143

so many down there.

'Don't think of going there.'

'Why not?'

'Because they'll never let you get that far. If they think you're getting too close the Trail will intrude on the hunt, kill you, kill your family, then disappear.'

Chris frowned, scanned the rocks around him, looked down the slope and back at the hazy mountaintop. 'You're not concerned about my family at all, are you? Or me?'

'That's right.' Cold again, emotionless.

'Fuck you, Rose.' Fury coursed through him. 'Your family's already dead!'

'And there's no saying that yours . . . ' She trailed off.

'What?'

'I've got to go.' And she disconnected.

Chris tried calling her number again, but after two rings it was unavailable. He stared at the phone as if he could will her to call back. Dialled in '999', pressed the call button, heard nothing but a single tone.

He felt like crying. He felt like screaming. But at least after that call he was not so aimless.

Cardiff, and home. It was more of a plan than he'd had before.

17

change

'I never thought I could change so much,' Rose said.

'You were completely changed the moment it happened.' Holt was driving them up into the forested mountains to the east of Sorrento. He drove a Range Rover this time, at least ten years old and with almost two hundred thousand miles on the clock. It smelled as if it had been used to transport animal dung for the last forty thousand of those miles, and the whole driver's side of the interior was greyed with a fine layer of cigarette ash. Holt smoked foul-smelling tobacco, rollie hanging from one corner of his mouth as he drove. His fine, greying hair flickered in the warm breeze.

Rose thought about what he'd said for a while, leaning back in the seat with her arm resting on the opened window-sill. She looked out across the landscape and thought about never coming here with Adam. Italy had been on their list of things to do. They'd actually had a real list, scribbled in the back of the small notebook he'd often carried with him, and sometimes he would whip the book out and they'd add something more, another dream. Top of the list, the first thing written down, was 'Have kids', and after each birth he'd ceremoniously lined the sentence through. Some of the other entries had been ticked off. Many more remained unfulfilled. It was the first time she'd thought of that notebook since the murders. She hated the idea that it might now be in an evidence box somewhere, contents pored over by investigators searching for a marriage problem that had never existed. *How could she have done it?* she imagined people asking. *How could she kill her own children?*

But beyond such thoughts lay madness, and she'd pulled herself too far through to submit to that now.

'No,' she said. 'I don't think so. Not straight away. I lost myself pretty quickly, but I was just trying to hide from what had happened. Deep down I was still the old Rose, just hanging on. Avoiding looking back. I only really started to change when I came here.'

'And met me?' he asked. She already recognised that tone; he was being playful, though most people would have had trouble detecting any trace of humour.

'Yeah,' she said. But Rose knew she had to be careful, because of that way he sometimes looked at her. Though she was learning from him and able to bear looking into the future once more, she also had to remember that she hardly knew him at all. Perhaps he was contemplating all the lives he could have lived if things had been different. Maybe some of them were with her.

She'd only once asked him about his own family past, and the expression on his face as he'd turned away dissuaded her from ever asking again. She wasn't sure whether it was grief or regret. Whichever, it had scarred him badly.

'That's me,' he said. 'The changing man.'

'But for the best,' she said. She'd been sober for almost a month, and though the hankering still sometimes bit in with glass-like teeth, she felt that she'd finally started to emerge from the other side. 'You brought me through, and you're helping me move on.'

'By helping you sober up?'

'Yeah. And teaching me to kill.'

Holt chuckled, a grating sound that was as close as he came to a laugh. It sounded like an old engine dying down. 'Rose, I've told you before, I can't teach anyone to kill. I can show you how to follow someone in a crowded street, how to pick a lock, how to avoid being seen, the ranges and capabilities of various weapons. I can tell you how to hold a gun and pull the trigger. But killing someone is something you have to teach yourself.'

'That part will be easy,' she said. 'You're showing me how to get there.'

Holt drove with one hand and rolled a fresh cigarette with the other. It looked casual, but as with everything she watched him do, Rose knew there was a measured assurance about his actions. His movements were spare but efficient. He turned from the winding mountain road and started down a lane leading into a heavily overgrown ravine. The track was barely visible and looked unused, with plants sprouting from cracked earth and several small rockslides that the Range Rover negotiated with care. The landscape had become more hostile and beautiful the further east they'd driven, and now they were surrounded by steep slopes and deep forests. True wilderness.

'How many people have you killed?' she asked. The question just fell out, hanging in the air between them. Ash drifted from his cigarette to swirl across the car.

'Fifteen,' he said without hesitation. 'Close, so I could see them die. Most of them with a gun, three with a knife. One with a broken wine bottle. Others?' He shrugged. 'At a distance, remotely, with bombs and machine guns? Many more.'

Rose blinked a few times, trying to compute what he'd said. So many dead at his hand, and here she was willingly riding into the wild countryside with him. And still she struggled to understand the way he sometimes looked at her — not lustfully, but with an indecision that seemed so unlike him.

But she was not afraid. Because Holt had already changed her so much, and if something went wrong she knew she would do her best to fight back. He had made her life mean something once more, and the last thing she believed he wanted was to take it.

They drove on in silence for a while longer, then he parked in the shadow of a cliff and killed the engine. The sudden silence was calming, and Holt sighed and sat back in his seat, tipping his hat over his eyes.

'And now?'

'I've been driving for three hours, and I'm not

as young as I used to be. Now, siesta.'

Leaving Holt fidgeting to get comfortable, Rose jumped from the Range Rover, leaving the door open and looking at their surroundings. The deep, narrow valley was a wild place with no signs of humanity. The trees grew thick down here, but higher up she could see sparser slopes, sun-baked and desolate. A scatter of lizards scampered away into cracks and dark places in the ravine wall, and nearby were signs of a dried-up stream. When the rains came this place would flood.

Rose sat in the shadows and waited, watching the Frenchman snooze in the vehicle.

Killing is something you have to teach yourself, he'd said. Maybe that was true. But Holt would help her make the grade.

★   ★   ★

They spent three days parked and camped down in the ravine. He taught her the basics of how to follow someone across such a landscape, staying far enough back to remain hidden, but close enough to not lose your quarry. It was hot, hard, thirsty work, but he didn't let up. He made Rose carry four litres of water with her when they left their camp in the morning, and she only had more water upon returning after sundown. Four litres felt heavy when they set out, but it was nowhere near enough.

Sometimes he stalked, sometimes he instructed her to stalk him. He talked about footprints and how to tell whether they were left accidentally or

149

on purpose. He told her how to spot movement from a distance with the sun in your eyes. They triangulated sun flashes from uncovered equipment, and sounds from a radio he left tucked behind some rocks.

Once, when Rose had spent three hours tracking Holt towards a small clump of trees and bushes on a steep slope, he leaped from cover and fired his pistol at her. Dirt flicked up around her feet and scratched at her face and eyes, the blasts thumped at her ears, shock sent a cool flush through her that she thought might still her heart. Furious, she stood her ground as he advanced, ready to shout and rage at him. But when he was almost close enough to touch, he raised the gun again and fired it past her right ear.

Rose shouted and went down, hands pressed to the side of her head. On her knees, she looked around as sound slowly began to hiss back in from a hot distance. Holt's mouth was moving but she heard only a distant mumble, like listening to him four rooms away through closed doors. A low whistling grew in her ears, and then a hum that would last for days.

'Bastard!' she said, and Holt raised an eyebrow.

'We have to work on that,' he said. 'Get flustered in a gunfight and you'll come second. Let's eat.'

* * *

She was with Holt for seventy-three days. She'd lost track, but he had been keeping count. And

150

he never once tried to touch her. She wasn't sure what she would have done if he had. She was scared of him, she respected him, and however much she learnt and thought she had changed, he was someone from a very different world from hers. But she was not attracted to him, and she could not imagine ever being with another man now that Adam was gone.

It wasn't the thought of betrayal that chilled, but simply that her life was on hold.

She felt that very keenly. While she was in Italy, learning things she had never imagined, everything else was frozen. Adam and her children were only just dead, no matter how much time had passed. The outside world moved on but nothing changed.

Slowly, the old Rose was eroded while the new Rose built herself up again with new talents, both deadly and subtle. But her deeper, inner self remained — a woman in love, a wife, and a mother in deep mourning. She would not lose her hold on that.

Ten weeks, he told her, was not a very long time. But he also added that with someone like him, it was worth a lifetime of study on her own. The internet might give her a thousand pieces of advice on breaking and entering a target's property, but Holt was able to show her how it could be done silently, quickly, and with a gun still clasped in one hand. She could buy all manner of surveillance equipment online, but he demonstrated how to track a vehicle with a pair of runner's GPS watches and a smartphone.

Close to the end of her time with him, the

things he was showing her took a subtle change, the emphasis shifted. At the time it didn't seem strange, but looking back on it she remembered a particular point when he seemed to make that decision. He left her one morning after showing her knife skills, and when he returned that afternoon he brought a pack containing forging paraphernalia. From then, they went from fighting and killing to more covert activities. He seemed to turn even more serious, if that was possible. He'd taught her to kill, now he was coaching her in how to stay alive. How to hide.

They talked a lot about staying below the radar, off the grid. It was easier than she had ever imagined. In her life before, she'd believed that everyone was a number, and to shed that number was almost an impossibility. But Holt told her that he'd existed for the past fifteen years without showing up on any databases, and with no trace of his identity stored or recorded anywhere.

'What happened fifteen years ago?' she asked, but Holt ignored the question.

Travelling with false documents, spotting and avoiding CCTV cameras, filtering money from existing bank accounts, making landline calls that did not leave a trace, dealing with mobile phones without leaving an electronic trail . . . Holt schooled her on all this and more.

Killing someone silently and instantly with an eating fork. High-speed driving techniques. How best to clean blood spots out of clothing, and how to dispose of soiled clothing if the bloodstains were too heavy.

Sometimes as the sun went down, they talked about music and movies.

★ ★ ★

When the final day came, she was not surprised. She knew from before breakfasting together that this was it. They drove out into the hills, and on the way Holt started summarising aspects of what he'd been telling her.

She listened for a while before saying, 'I know you're leaving.'

'Something like this is never finished,' he said. 'You can always keep learning. *I'm* still learning. Sometimes, you just have to accept that you know enough.'

'And I know enough?'

'You're an attentive pupil' He smiled across at her. Then the smile dropped and he returned his attention to the road ahead.

'There's still so much I don't know,' Rose said. She suddenly felt afraid, and alone, even though for now he was still with her. Maybe she'd secretly been hoping he always would be.

'There's a woman in Switzerland who will give you false documents, for a price. I'll put you in touch with her. If she knows you come from me, the price should be fairer. And I know a guy in Germany, I'll give you his address, he can help you with some computer stuff. A real whizz. He once emptied one of the CIA's covert bank accounts and donated sixteen billion dollars to a donkey sanctuary in Spain.'

'Lucky donkeys.'

153

'Dirty money.' He emitted that dry, clanking chuckle, then his face dropped a little. 'I've done all I can for you, and more.'

'Holt, thank you. I'll see you — '

'No, you won't. Not after this. After this, I'll be disappearing as well.'

'Aren't you already disappeared?'

'Not enough.' It was a strange comment, and he did not elaborate.

They reached a small lay-by and Holt pulled off, killing the engine and looking at the view. This landscape was wide, wild and harsh, peppered with white farm buildings and small villages.

'Give me an hour,' Holt said. 'Then find me.'

They left the vehicle, he laced up his trainers, and Rose watched him jog away from the road and into the hills.

For the whole hour before she went after him, she wondered whether this was his way of saying goodbye.

★ ★ ★

Their final evening together was spent at a tourist restaurant in Sorrento.

Rose had found him after a couple of hours, and she realised that he hadn't taken the day seriously. He'd done little to cover his tracks, and he had been sat waiting for her on a large boulder beside a fast-moving stream. On their way back to his vehicle they had been like friends taking a nice walk in the hills.

The restaurant was bustling with couples and

154

families. They took a table near the back by the doors to the kitchen, and Holt sat facing the entrance.

'Sparkling water or still?' he asked.

'You know how to show a woman a good time.' Rose laughed, and he joined in. She didn't think she'd ever heard his laughter so full and deep, as if he was forcing it to blank out a sadness.

It was a relaxed evening with flowing conversation, and as normal a time as she'd ever had with Holt. Knowing that their time together was almost at an end lifted the pressure of having to teach and learn. Now they were simply enjoying each other's company.

In that enjoyment, lay guilt. And it was not long before Rose felt the ghosts of her family crowding around her, memories dank and heavy. She started telling stories about her children, and as she saw them running and rolling and playing, and heard their laughter, she began to cry. She looked down and tried to hide her tears, but Holt scolded her.

'Never stop crying. I haven't.'

Rose dabbed at her eyes and looked around. She had no wish to bring attention to herself. He'd given her plenty of advice about remaining innocuous, all but invisible in plain sight, and here she was making a scene. But Holt didn't seem to care. His gaze was distant, and she knew that now was her last chance.

'Holt, your past. What happened to make you . . .'

'Make me the monster I am today?'

155

'No. The man you are.'

He sighed heavily and held up his glass of water, swilling it around as if it were the finest red. She'd never seen any sign of his erstwhile alcoholism, but now she could see the glimmering need in his eyes.

'My wife left me,' he said. 'She found out what I did. What I am. She took my daughter. I haven't seen her in almost fifteen years. My little girl will be an adult now.'

'You could find them!'

'Of course I could,' he said. 'Her leaving me and taking my Carrie isn't what makes me sad. It's the fact that they're better off without me.'

'Holt — '

'Coffee? I need coffee.'

They stared at each other, wallowing for a while in each other's loss. Then the waiter arrived and the moment was broken, and as he left Holt started rolling a cigarette. Rose knew that this meant he was ready to leave. And this time, from this restaurant, he would be leaving alone.

They drank their coffee. Then he stood, kissed her warmly on the cheek, and bid her goodnight. She watched him weaving his way between tables, passing couples enjoying a romantic meal, and she was amazed at how many people did not look at him. He moved like a ghost. She wondered what he had been like in his previous life, and what had made him change. He'd really told her nothing at all.

After sitting there a little while longer she realised that he'd left her with the bill. For all

156

that he did for her, it was the only payment Holt ever took.

With a chill, Rose realised that she was now more alone than she had ever been before.

18

her world

Rose slipped the phone into her jacket pocket and hunkered down between the rocks, still and silent. She'd left the dead man's rifle with him, hoping it would make the scene seem more real. She already thought that had been a bad mistake. She was at least a hundred metres away from the corpse — way beyond an effective pistol shot — but she didn't want to risk being seen or heard. Someone used to spotting from a helicopter might see the slightest movement out of place. And up here in the mountains, a breeze could carry the sound of a cough or tumbled stone a long way.

Even though she heard the helicopter approaching, there was no saying it hadn't already dropped off some of its passengers.

She listened intently, looking at the expanse of sky visible above the mountainside. Its rotors and engine were muffled and blurred, echoing from distant slopes and peaks. It was coming in from behind the mountain. There was nowhere to land on this slope, and she hoped that it would swing down the mountainside and hover, dropping a rope ladder for the hunter's rescuers to climb down and attend him.

Hopefully, they wouldn't see that he was dead until they were on their way down. He might have fainted. The wet patch on his crotch might be where he'd fouled himself.

By then she'd have rushed closer, spare magazines for her weapon at hand. And she'd keep shooting at the tail rotor until the bastards crashed.

She was moving moment by moment, taking opportunities as they arose and doing with them what she could. Holt would not have approved of such randomness — he was an advocate of caution and preparedness. But he'd also said that in combat situations, every plan would deviate at some point. If you were lucky it would be far into the engagement, when the bulk of the work was done. If you were unlucky, the plan would be screwed from the first moment.

Rose had prevented any plan fuck-ups by not really having a plan at all.

Arriving at Chris's house that morning she'd thought, *I'm going to get as many as I can.* You couldn't scheme against the Trail, because even after so long she knew so little about them. You couldn't second-guess or assume. They might be determined to play this compromised hunt through to the end, or they might kill Chris's family at any moment and then vanish, disbanding the entire network of their UK cell and building it again afresh. What kept her going was the idea that she would kill as many of them as she could before that happened.

Including Grin. *Especially* Grin, that bitch. From Chris's description, Rose was certain it was her holding his family at gunpoint. She knew some of the others from the negligible

159

information she'd managed to find, but she felt that she was intimately familiar with Grin's sick, stinking soul.

As she thought about the bitch, she touched her right thigh. They had that much in common.

The helicopter did not appear, and the sound of its engines did not change. The landscape muddled the echoes, muffling them, and Rose wondered what she'd actually heard. A hard breeze whistling between rocks somewhere across the slope? A distant car engine, echo gathered and bounced from one valley to the next?

She moved position slightly, shifting from behind shielding rocks to a shallow depression from which she could see more sky. The dead hunter was a dark hump across the shale. Looking at him, she searched for a feeling of regret or shame. But there was nothing.

She saw movement up on the ridge. Crouched down, she expected the hulking shadow of the helicopter to burst into view, its rotors whipping at the sky and raising a storm as it emerged from behind the shielding hulk of the mountain. But the movement was small, resolving into three people edging down towards the shale slope.

They'd topped the ridge much higher up than Rose, so high that the air around them was still hazy with low cloud. They moved slowly but confidently, spread out so as not to offer a huddled target to anyone taking a shot at them.

Me, she thought. *They're worried about me.* They'd have seen the abandoned car by now, know that she was still somewhere up here in the

160

mountains. And when they got close enough to see that the injured hunter was actually on his own — and closer still before they realised that he was dead — they'd know that she was responsible.

She had to think quickly. Two of them carried rifles over their shoulders. They were dressed casually — jeans, tee shirts, loose jackets — nowhere near prepared for a prolonged stay in the mountains. Which meant that the helicopter had landed somewhere up there, and they fully expected to return to it soon.

She'd never kill three of them. One perhaps, but even that was not guaranteed. They carried rifles, and once she'd let off her first few shots, they'd be at an advantage. Their range, accuracy and killing power would be much greater than hers, and she had only the element of surprise on her side.

Maybe she should have taken the dead bastard's rifle after all. But she'd hoped that seeing his weapon still with him would ease any suspicions they might have.

Moving back into the depression, then away from the shale slope and across the mountainside, Rose climbed carefully uphill, always maintaining cover between her and them. It meant that she was moving blind — if they'd caught sight of her, if they had suspicions, they could move across the shale slope and be upon her before she saw them. But it was a small gamble loaded in her favour.

They'd check out their injured client first.

She came to a spur of rock, twelve feet high,

161

easy to climb, but she'd be dangerously exposed while doing so. Hesitation and doubt had no place here. She started climbing, pausing as she rose above the surrounding cover and glancing back across the hillside. She could see the dead man and much of the shale slope, but the spur still hid the upper parts of the mountainside. If the men were descending, they still hadn't come far.

Climbing on, trying to move fluidly so as not to perform any sudden movements, Rose soon reached the head of the spur. She rolled onto the rough heathers growing there and paused on her stomach, face pressed to the ground.

Now she could see them. One was leaping quickly from rock to rock down the other side of the spread of scree, the other two were trying to crawl down the scree slope on their behinds. Good. They weren't used to the mountains, didn't know what they were doing. It gave her a flush of optimism for her and, curiously, for Chris as well. She'd not entered into this believing that she would help him in any way — she intended striking as hard as she could at the Trail, then melting away to face them another day, leaving Chris to his fate — but maybe that was misjudged. Perhaps she and Chris really could help each other.

She wondered which Trail members had come. She knew more about them than they could have believed possible, but even that was negligible. But she was too far away to identify them.

The first man had drawn level with the dead hunter beyond the scree, and now he stood shielding his eyes and calling.

'Mister Lyons!' His voice carried across the hillside.

Rose pushed herself backwards across the heather, glancing to her left. She'd be hidden from view in a few metres.

'Hey! Max! You okay?'

Not long until they found out. Rose moved faster, slipping behind a thicket of sparse shrubs. She didn't wait to see them approach the man, check him over, find that he was dead, because she knew what their first reaction would be.

They'd climb quickly back up to the helicopter. And they knew exactly where it was.

She made sure the pistol was tight in her belt and started to climb, pulling with her hands, pushing with her feet. Where the slope levelled a little she pushed on her knees, and where it grew steeper or more technical she used her hands again, grabbing rocks and pulling. She kept a careful eye on where she was in relation to the mountaintop, and also on the scree. If she could see the slope of loose stone, then they could see her.

Five minutes passed, ten. They'd have realised by now that their hunter was a corpse, and she hoped they wouldn't overreact. If they did, Chris's family would be dead in moments and then the hunt would be off. The other hunters would be gathered in, and then the Trail would come in force to make the kill themselves.

But there was so much money involved, she was confident that they wouldn't yet abandon something that had taken so long to set up.

She reached the ridge a few minutes later. She'd emerged from cover and had to ascend a rocky slope, darting from boulder to boulder and doing her best to not be seen. She could see way down the scree slope now, and the three men were still visible around the dead man. One stood cradling his rifle and keeping watch while the other two did something. She was too far away to see what.

The ridge was wider this high up, and exposed to the elements. A strong breeze blew from the north, carrying stinging raindrops that impacted her face and hands. She leaned into the wind, crouching, and pushed on.

As the slope behind her disappeared from view, she took one last look. The Trail men had lifted the body and were trying to drag him uphill. One still stood guard, scanning the mountainside all around. Making sure she wasn't seen, Rose crouched lower and hurried from view.

Dragging the body across the scree slope then all the way back up here would take them at least half an hour. Time was on her side.

She was looking for somewhere flat, a convenient site for the helicopter to touch down. It should have been easy to spot the helicopter, but she scanned the ridge leading up the mountain and what she could see of the slopes beyond, and there was nothing.

Had it lifted off again? She hadn't heard it, but she could not be sure. Sounds were distorted up here, confused by the wind, echoes, and the deceptive distances. She moved across the ridge closer to the drop down the other side. If she looked carefully, if she had binoculars and a better sense of direction and distance, she might be able to see the place beside the road where this had begun. But mist drifted in swathes, and the rain was increasing.

She moved up the ridge, jogging now to try to warm up.

Should have looked after yourself, Adam said.

'Yeah, right, I've always been great at that.' She laughed, the sound surprisingly loud. A few minutes later she had to climb a steeper jumble of rocks, careful not to slip on the wet surface and snap an ankle. How ironic that would be. They'd come back up here eventually, find her crawling for cover with pistol in hand, and take their time to shoot her from a distance. 'Fuck that,' she muttered. 'Swallow a bullet first.'

Fuck that, bunny! Adam said. *You've got too much to live for.*

She coughed a laugh, ducked down, looked around to make sure no one had heard her. Sounds carried.

'Let me do my thing, baby,' she said. 'You rest and just let me . . . '

She topped the rise of tumbled boulders, many larger than a family car, and there was the helicopter. The slope beyond opened into a wider shoulder between mountains a little higher up, a rock-scattered escarpment that had a few flatter, windswept areas. The wind blew hazy sheets of rain and mist across the ridge, wavering clouds that brought the helicopter in and out of focus.

Rose moved quickly, scrambling further up the

slope so that she could approach it from above. They would not have left it unguarded, but if she was too cautious, too slow, she wouldn't have time to get away.

And that's what she wanted. Once those three Trail members were trapped up here in the mountains, her own hunt would begin.

The dead man's satphone in her pocket crackled.

She dropped to the ground, snatched it out and switched it off, lying flat and searching for signs of movement around the grounded aircraft. A waft of smoke was plucked from the helicopter's open cabin door. Whoever they'd left behind was sitting inside, smoking and sheltering from the elements.

The satphone might have been one of the other hunters calling back to see if Max was all right, but she doubted it. They weren't friends, or companions. More likely it was one of the Trail. They'd have found the bullet wound, figured out some of what had happened, and were trying to contact her.

She almost returned their call, but it wasn't the time. Not quite.

Circling around, keeping to cover as much as she could, she started approaching the helicopter from uphill, closing on its tail end. Holding the pistol in one hand she kept the other held out for balance, scouting the ground before her.

Another gust of wind blew a sheen of rain across the escarpment, and Rose took advantage to move rapidly closer. Close up, the helicopter was even larger than she'd thought, and the smell of fuel and heat hung in the air. Even above the breeze she heard the ticking of cooling metal. She took a deep breath, readying herself for confrontation.

After one more glance around to make sure there was no one else, she emerged from behind the machine and walked confidently towards the doors, staying wide. She held the pistol down against her leg. Surprise would give her a couple of seconds' advantage, and looking like she belonged there would confuse the pilot.

A woman was sitting up in the helicopter's main cabin, legs dangling out the door. She wore a flight suit and smoked a cigarette, and when she saw Rose her eyes went wide. She made no sudden movements, other than glancing quickly around the escarpment. She looked at the gun in Rose's right hand.

'I'm just the pilot,' she said.

Rose hadn't expected a woman. It should have made no difference — she knew that some Trail members were women, including Grin — but for some reason it threw her. Perhaps some deeper, motherly part of her, a base instinct stronger than learning and experience could touch, still doubted that a woman could really be so brutal.

As Rose wondered how to handle this, the pilot rolled to her right and pulled something out of the flight suit's pocket.

Rose knelt and lifted her pistol, squeezing the trigger in the same movement, right knee slamming against rock, gunshot thundering in her ears, and she felt an ice-cold kiss across her right arm.

The pilot grunted and flipped onto her stomach, kicking with her feet to enter the shadowy cabin. Rose cupped her right hand with her left, winced as the cool pain turned blazing hot, and fired two more times.

Both shots found their mark. The woman jerked on her stomach and then lay still, legs hanging out of the cabin, right foot twitching slightly as her nerves danced towards death.

Rose stood and approached the aircraft, senses alight, ready. If anyone else was inside they'd have entered the fight by now, but she had to make sure. She moved quickly, crouching behind the woman to search inside the cabin. No one.

She climbed in, lurching forward into the cockpit. Both seats were empty.

Her arm was blazing hot and leaking blood, she needed to tend her wound, the Trail men might have heard the shots and would rush back, leaving the hunter's corpse to retrieve later . . .

Time crunched. A faint lightened her muscles and turned her stomach, and Rose bit her lip, hard. The taste of blood did nothing to distract from her injured arm. It was screaming at her, pain surging in close waves that broke even higher whenever she moved. She stood, swayed, grasped on to something to stop herself falling.

I've felt worse! she thought, remembering those glorious, agonising moments of childbirth, and berating herself for being so weak. She glanced at the torn jacket hanging beneath her tricep. It was already dark and heavy with blood, speckles dripping onto her thigh and the floor. But it would have to wait.

She gave herself two minutes. Then she'd have to be away, and with her injury she couldn't count on moving as fast as she'd like. It was doubtful that any of the men could fly the helicopter as well, but she couldn't take that chance. She had to put the aircraft out of action, gather anything that might be of use, and get the hell away.

It was her first time inside a helicopter. She scanned the cockpit, bemused at the spread of buttons and dials, looking for something to rip out or smash or cut. But there was no time for subtlety.

She swapped the pistol to her left hand and fired five shots into the instrument panel. Sparks sizzled and jumped from one impact point, but she had no idea whether any bullet had made a difference.

Then realisation struck, and she cursed herself again. Only recently she'd been ready to bring the helicopter down as it flew, so now she knew how to *keep* it down.

Moving back through the cabin, she saw a first aid box pinned to the wall by several straps. She pulled it free and held it beneath her left arm. There was also a rifle leaning casually against one of the main cabin's side seating. She slung it over her left shoulder. There were boxes of food strapped to the cabin's rear wall, probably supplies to be dropped to the hunters. She wondered what was in there — proper food, probably, not the energy stuff she'd sent out with Chris. Caviar. Champagne. She laughed, a manic guffaw.

169

No time. Every second she remained here was a second closer to being shot again, and she had her wound to tend as soon as she was away. Maybe she'd faint. That would be more of a waste than being caught with a broken ankle.

Stop thinking and start doing! Adam said.

She searched the pilot's body, grabbed her dropped pistol, and jumped to the ground.

Her knees went and she fell onto her front, narrowly missing smacking her nose into rock. Vision swam. Blood ran hot. Wind breathed stinging rain across the back of her head.

Rose lifted herself and stood, wincing against the pain and willing the faint away. It was *only* pain, that was all, something to embrace and analyse, but not to let her down.

Aiming at the tail rotor, she fired the last few shots in the magazine. One blade snapped off completely, spinning away in the wind. Another slumped and hung by a twisted thread.

Got to make sure, she thought. She pulled the pilot's pistol and emptied it into the engine compartment. One impact thudded heavy, and fuel started to pour from the hole.

She walked away from the helicopter and another dead Trail bastard. Then she ran. Even if they *could* fix the damage she'd done it would take them some time. And now their blood would be up, their anger raging, their need for vengeance a hot, tactile thing.

Welcome to her world.

19

nail

Vey and Tom came at them with knives, and Gemma really wasn't sure whether she had any energy or feeling left.

Ever since the piss stop she'd been working her hands, shoulders, buttocks and legs, trying to keep the blood flowing and numbness at bay. She tensed, terrified but determined to fight back if she had the chance, defend herself and her family to the last. But they were only cutting their bindings.

Sitting in cooling, soaked underwear and school trousers was very uncomfortable, and even though it was warm in the van, Gemma had found herself shivering. Several times she glanced at the nail on the van floor. It was maybe four inches long, speckled with rust. It must have been there for a while.

She kept it in mind. In the box, in fact, although in a part of it hidden away from everything else. The nail was kept in the box's false bottom, because for now Gemma didn't even want to think about it herself. Maybe Vey could read her mind. Maybe she'd already seen her looking at it, knew what she had planned, and was just letting her continue thinking that she was a clever girl. A clever little girl.

'Where are we?' her mum asked as Tom sliced

at the binds around her legs and waist. There was an edge of panic to her voice. Megs was sobbing again, and Gemma's heart hammered.

'Can't you take the blindfolds off?' she asked. Vey was kneeling in front of Megs, tugging the girl forward so that she could cut the ropes behind her. She paid no notice at all to the girl's cries. She seemed not to hear.

'Yeah, why not,' Tom said. He ripped their mother's blindfold off, and Vey did the same to Megs. They both squeezed their eyes shut.

Outside the open back doors, Gemma saw a gravelled parking area and the high wall of a building, one edge of a window just in view. A flower pot sat beneath the window with the drooping remnants of summer blooms. The air smelled sweet.

'Everything's fine, girls,' her mother said. 'We'll be fine, this'll all be over soon.'

But Gemma saw something that chilled her to the core — a small, wry smile on Vey's lips.

As Tom helped her mother stand and step from the van, Megs followed, sparing a terrified glance for Gemma.

'Hey, sis,' Gemma said. Megs hated being called sis, but now she smiled, her eyes red-rimmed and sore.

Vey squeezed Gemma's cut shoulder and pulled her forward so that she could slice the ropes tying her to the seat. Gemma cried out, even though it didn't hurt that much, because she wanted the woman to think she was growing weaker, more scared, less inclined than ever to cause any trouble.

'I know kids like you,' the woman said,

pressing her face close to Gemma's. Her breath stank, stale and redolent of old meat and cigarettes. 'You think you know everything because your tits are getting bigger and boys are looking at you. You think you're indestructible and the world's laid out for you to pick over. But don't give me any trouble. Because I've killed little girls tougher than you.'

Fear bit in, sharp and stinging. Gemma tensed her wounded shoulder against Vey's hand, and the pain fended off the fear and seeded that hot bloom of rage once again.

'I'm not a little girl,' she whispered.

Vey laughed, then stood and let go.

Gemma forced a soft cry and fell forward, rolling onto her back. She let her legs splay out helplessly across the van's floor.

'Up!' Vey said. 'Come on, shift it. Got some food inside for you, but only if you do as you're told.'

I've killed little girls tougher than you.

Hands still tied behind her back, Gemma's flexing fingers found the nail at last. She probed at its tip and the head lifted from the seam in the metal floor.

Vey jumped from the van and reached back in, grasping Gemma's shirt collar, pulling her upright, dragging her to sit in the doorway. 'Wait there for a bit, your legs have gone numb.'

Gemma swung her legs back and forth, pretending to wince at pins and needles that weren't there, while she tucked the nail into the back of her trousers.

Whoever these people were, she had taken her first step in rebelling against them.

173

20

swim

Chris sometimes wore a tee shirt bearing the slogan, *I Do Not Bonk*. It had attracted many amused and confused stares because, to most, 'bonk' was another word for screw. Strange to profess that. But to endurance athletes, bonking was the process of crashing during a race, energy levels at a minimum, glycogen stores depleted, muscles quivering their last. He knew how not to bonk.

He'd never been in a race where bonking would mean a bullet in the back of his head.

After his conversation with Rose he started running again, heading across the curving waist of a high mountain. The horizon he aimed for was always close, comprised of ragged rock formations or sometimes gentler slopes of small boulders and scree. He could not see what was around the next rocky spur or small ridge line, but he was confident that he would take it in his stride.

He'd been running for around four hours. The longest foot race he'd ever run had been an ultra-marathon, almost forty miles across a picturesque but challenging course in the Lake District. It had taken in a circuit of Coniston Water with a bow-shaped route out into neighbouring hills and back again for added excitement. It had taken him almost ten hours, which had put him in the bottom half of the finishers' list. But he'd only been racing himself and the elements, and simply finishing had been a massive achievement.

Compared to that, his exertion so far today had been merely a warm-up.

But so much was different. There were no water and nutrition stops. No way-marked course, no marshals to show the way, no St John's Ambulance in attendance in case of injuries or exhaustion. And no family at the end to cheer him home.

He felt like curling up into a ball and crying. He felt like raging, raving, finding someone to punch and kick. The unfairness of everything clamped around him, constricting his lungs and smothering him. Terri had always told him he was good at doomsdaying. He'd once been in a minor road accident with a hard-looking man who later turned out to be part of a local crime family, known for violence and intimidation. The man had refused to swap insurance details and Chris had very pointedly written down his vehicle licence number. The man had stared Chris out, then driven away.

A friend of Terri's had recognised the description, told them with whom Chris had had a run-in, and from there his mind had worked overtime. *What if I report him and he comes here? What if he threatens us? What if he follows me home from work, or follows you and the kids one evening when you're out for a walk? One phone call could lead to all that. They'll firebomb the house. Run us off the road.*

Terri had told Chris that the worst did not always happen.

Chris never did call the police, and he paid for the damage to his car himself.

It had been unfair, out of his control, and he'd had many sleepless nights over such a minor event.

The injustice of his situation now screamed at him with every blink, every footfall on rock or shale or mountain grass. And he was doomsdaying. *What if . . . ? What if . . . ?*

It was all out of his control. The Trail had set this up. The hunters were here to kill him to satisfy some perverted primeval urge. Rose was using him to exact her own vengeance, perform her own killing spree.

All he could do was run, filled with dread that any moment might be his family's last.

He'd finished the second bottle of water, the bladder was almost empty, and he was keeping his eyes open for a mountain stream to replenish his supplies. He'd also eaten the bagel, stale sandwiches, and a second energy bar. There were several more left, and a handful of gels, but he knew that he'd need some more proper food soon.

But he should forget about food. He'd find none up here, not unless he came across some hill walkers or extreme sports enthusiasts running or climbing. If that did happen, he wasn't sure what he'd do.

Maybe it would be best for them if he avoided them.

It was almost six in the evening. Sunset would be around nine, and up here in the mountains darkness fell very quickly. The sun dipped below a mountain or ridge and that was it — shadows fell, and any further movement and navigation, even with a head torch, became very dangerous. He'd heard of many people who'd died in the Welsh mountains simply from walking over a cliff, falling into a ravine, or taking the wrong turning at a navigation point. There were probably bodies still up here, merging back into the wild landscape to form part of its future, and becoming a part of its history.

He would not be one of those. He only hoped the hunters did not have night vision equipment.

The thought almost stopped him in his tracks. Of course they'd have such equipment. It would be part of the whole package, wouldn't it? These weren't the sorts of people who'd want a 'one shot' type hunt, man against man. They'd paid fuck knows how much so they could hunt and kill another human being, and using an automatic rifle packed with a decent scope, perhaps carrying tracking hardware of some sort, and possessing night vision binoculars, would make them feel even more talented. More 'special forces'. They'd probably been having wet dreams about this for weeks or months, and now they were in the game they'd be eager for the kill.

Blondie was keen. Driven enough to leave a badly injured man behind in dangerous surroundings, he already had Chris in his sights.

He'd seen them jumping and tumbling from

the helicopter, and most of the five had looked like overweight, inexperienced buffoons. But that didn't mean the Trail hadn't equipped them with the best kit money could buy.

Come dusk, he would either have to find somewhere to spend the few hours of total darkness, or risk moving by moon- and starlight. The sky was relatively clear right now, but that didn't mean that clouds might not come in later. This high up, the air could turn hazy without warning. More than once he'd been caught out on a mountain run when cloud descended, relying on good navigation to get him where he wanted to go.

And that was another problem. He still hadn't figured out exactly where he was. He was doing his best to spot obvious landmarks for when he had time to sit and analyse the map, but for now heading south was his only priority.

The mountainside levelled into a relatively flat, easy area to cross, and he took the opportunity to assess his condition. His feet felt comfortable in his trail shoes. There were no hot-spots that might indicate the beginnings of a blister. His calves, shins and thighs felt strong, no niggling pains. His knees were stiff and warm, but he was used to that. Sometimes when he complained of stiff knees, Terri would gleefully diagnose old age. He could feel the impacts of his footfalls up through his hips, and he was used to that, too. Nothing new. His arms hung loose, he kept his back straight and shoulders back, leading with his chest. He was maintaining his running style, which was important both to preserve energy and be most efficient, and to prevent injury. Fit as he was, a turned ankle would be an ironic end to this race. He'd never appeared as a Did Not Finish on a race results list, and he wasn't about to start now.

He tried to ignore the fact that he'd already run twelve miles that morning, and his body was also succeeding in disregarding those miles. It concerned him that stopping for a few hours during darkness might mean that he'd stiffen up. Maybe he'd walk. Maybe something else would happen. He could attempt to plan, but there was no saying where he'd be in ten minutes' time, let alone three hours.

The close horizon could be hiding anything.

Above him, the mountain was slowly obscured by hazy cloud, and he could feel rain spots pattering against his scalp. Below, the valley was still swimming in sunshine, cloud shadows drifting like huge sea creatures. There were still no roads or buildings. He was happy with the route he was taking, and just ahead the hillside rose into a spine of jagged rock.

It was an ideal point to climb and take a look back, and when he did he saw movement. Two shapes, far back across the landscape. Too far away for him to identify, they were following roughly the route he'd taken.

Chris crouched down, then grew still. *They need to know they're coming the right way,* he thought. *Need to know they haven't lost me. As long as the hunt is on, Terri and the girls are safe.*

He climbed across the rocks until he was in

179

sunlight once more, then rooted around in his rucksack for something to use. The penknife should do. He opened several blades and implements, then held it up and moved it back and forth, trying to gauge the right angle to catch sunlight and send a flickering reflection their way. It needed them to be looking ahead, searching for him, and if they were already growing tired they might only be staring at their feet.

'Come on, Blondie,' he muttered. He was the one man who would not give up. Chris waved the penknife again, twisting and turning his wrist and hand until —

A gunshot, so distant that it was barely a cough across the landscape.

He ducked down, realising that the bullet would already have struck or passed him by. He had no idea of ranges, but figured that a hunting rifle wouldn't be able to shoot accurately over such a distance. A sniper's rifle, perhaps. Specialist stuff used by the military. There was no saying *what* they might be armed with. He was in the dark.

Now that he'd been seen, he couldn't risk a lucky shot hitting him.

He started climbing again, and there was no more gunfire. Glancing back a couple of times he could see the two following him, and he caught hints of more movement further back along the slope. Seeing him had caused an excited reaction from one of them, but now they were preserving their ammunition as they tried to catch up.

He couldn't afford to let them draw any closer. Once over this rugged spine of rock he'd assess the landscape beyond, then pick his route further south. Whatever mountain range he was in extended to the far horizon in that direction. Chris welcomed that.

But slipping over the head of the knife-edge ridge, picking his way carefully down the other side, he feared that he'd made a fatal mistake.

He should have checked over this side first before attracting their attention.

The lake was perhaps three hundred metres across. Half of it was still bathed by sunlight, reflecting the sky like a highly polished mirror. The other half was an inky, unbroken black. It was wide. To his right, sheer cliffs edged the body of water. To his left, a stark, steep ridge curved around from the promontory he stood upon, encasing the lake and shielding it from the gentle drop into the valley beyond. He could see at least two small streams tinkling into the lake from higher up the mountainside, and there would be points of egress for the water, too. Attractive streams cascading down the hillside, providing waterfalls where the adventurous could shower and gaze in wonder at mini-rainbows.

'Shit!' He should have looked! If he climbed back over the rocks to head down towards the valley, he'd be instantly in view, especially now that he'd so usefully given away his position. Heading directly up the mountain to skirt the lake involved technical climbing that he wasn't experienced in or prepared for. Left from where he stood now was a precarious, exposed scramble. He might make it around the rugged wall skirting the lake, and over into the valley, before they arrived where he stood now. But he had his doubts.

Doubts he could not afford.

The lake's surface was alive with countless tiny splashes where heavy raindrops landed. It actually looked quite welcoming, but he knew that it would be cold, deep, dangerous. In all the triathlons he'd entered, the swimming had always been his weak link, especially open water.

Some people feared heights, and that was also a monkey on Chris's back. But he was even more scared of depths.

'Oh, shitting hell,' he muttered as he scrambled down the slope towards the lake's edge. He tried to gauge the distance again to the other side. He'd guessed three hundred metres, though it was quite difficult to judge as there was nothing to measure against. A rock he was looking at over there could be the size of a man or a car. He threw a stone as far as he could, watched the ripples, observed how long they took to spread across the lake. Maybe a little less than three hundred metres. Fully clothed, carrying the rucksack, he reckoned he could swim the distance in eight or nine minutes. If he set off as soon as possible, that would be plenty long enough to reach the other side before his pursuers climbed the ridge behind him.

He shrugged off the rucksack and tipped it up. He'd spotted the sealable plastic bag earlier, and now he silently thanked Rose for her foresight.

He threw everything into the bag — phone, GPS watch, map and compass, clothing and nutrition — sealed it, tied it to make doubly sure, and shoved it back inside the rucksack.

The lake was a good landmark. When he was across on the other side and away, having put time between him and his hunters, if not distance, he would make time to look at the map.

He shrugged the rucksack on again, made sure the straps were tight, and stood at the lake's edge. Its bed sloped steeply down from where he stood — he could see the bottom, and the water was startlingly clear — and from experience, he knew there was only one way to get into a cold lake.

He jumped.

His feet hit bottom, slipped on the slick rocks, and he went under immediately, cold stealing his breath. He kicked and his feet found only water. He closed his eyes and kicked for the surface, or where he thought the surface to be. The cold was deep in his chest, stilling his heart, probing fingers from his core to his extremities. A pulsing pain started behind his forehead, forcing against his eyes. As he opened his mouth to groan he took in a mouthful of freezing water.

He broke the surface gasping, spitting water and kicking his feet to stay afloat. *Come on Chris!* He'd done this before many times, on early season triathlons when the water was still cold, and on previous adventures in the mountains. He liked nothing more than finding a secluded pool or lake in the hills and taking a plunge, usually clothed, sometimes not. He'd only been caught out once, emerging from a lake naked, cold and exhilarated. An old couple had been walking their dog and they'd paused to stare. Then they'd waved and laughed, the dog barking at his pale nude self as they'd gone on their way.

Treading water, he let the initial hyperventilation subside, acclimatising as best he could. His clothing weighed him down and the rucksack felt five times heavier. In a race he'd be wearing a wetsuit; it buoyed him up and helped his weak swimming, and over the last couple of years he'd learned to ease his fears of what lay beneath.

He'd found that looking helped. Some lakes were so cloudy that he could not even see his own feet, while others — old quarries, or manmade lakes — often had visibility reaching down twenty feet or more. Either way, knowing what was beneath him seemed to calm his fears.

He couldn't do that now. He had no goggles, and no time. He had to start swimming.

Aiming for the other side of the lake, he kicked hard and pulled a few powerful strokes to get himself moving. He breathed bilaterally — breathe left, stroke, stroke, breathe right — spitting out any remaining breath and water before gasping in another lungful of air. His swimming had advanced hugely in the past couple of years. Two years before he could not swim four lengths of a pool without having to stop, exhausted, muscles burning and chest heaving. Now he could comfortably swim four thousand metres, and while he was not particularly fast, he was consistent. But he still sometimes had brief, inexplicable moments of blind panic. When he spoke to Terri about them she told him he was being silly, but he insisted that they were a healthy reaction to being in the water. Humans weren't meant to swim, and occasionally his animal self reminded him of that.

But not now. Swimming fully clothed and carrying a heavy backpack was already way beyond his comfort zone, and he could not afford a moment's doubt. His life, and his family's, relied upon him crossing this lake.

He quickly found his usual comfortable rhythm. It was strange swimming without goggles, but he opened his eyes whenever he turned his head to breathe, and the blurred sunlight kept him in touch with the world. He didn't usually kick hard when swimming — saving his legs for the bike and run phases of a triathlon — and he did the same now, using a light kick merely to keep his legs and feet up close to the surface. He relied on his arm stroke to propel him across the lake. It was a pleasant feeling, and one that he had only recently grown used to. On long swims, feeling himself glide, hanging on to the water and pulling himself forward, he often went into a contemplative state almost akin to hypnosis. Biking and running were his other loves, and with both of them it was necessary to pay attention to what was going on around him. Look at the trail or road before him, watch out for traffic or other bikes or runners, check his bike, concentrate on his running form. Swimming, he seemed to retreat into himself.

Perhaps it was an unconscious attempt to keep the fear at bay.

His hands cut through the water, smooth and

controlled. He reached for the opposite shore, grabbed the water and pulled, drawing himself forward, rolling as his opposite hand cut in, reached, grabbed. The roll was more jarring than usual, and he had to control it to make sure he didn't tip over too far. The rucksack was waterlogged and heavy, slipping from left to right on his back as he swam. The straps cut into his shoulders.

What if it pulled him down? What if he couldn't unlock the straps and the weight grabbed him, drawing him deep into colder, darker waters?

He gasped and sucked in water on his next breath. Coughed it back out beneath the surface, breathed to the other side, then tried to find his rhythm again, exhaling smoothly through his mouth.

Something touched his leg. He kicked hard to draw away and it happened again, a gentle, slick stroke from his knee down towards his foot.

He should have taken his shoes off and put them in his rucksack. What if he lost one?

He kicked again, tensing his toes to clasp on to his shoes.

Whatever had touched him was gone; a spread of long weeds left behind, an eel or fish swimming away.

What if there was a pike in here? They'd been known to bite off fingers. It could be circling him, trying to assess this stranger in its environment and wondering whether any part of him would make a tasty morsel.

Calm the hell down! Chris thought, and he

made a conscious effort to slow his flailing stroke, concentrating on his style and rhythm once again. He sighted after a breath and judged that he was at least halfway across, closing on the opposite shore just where he'd intended. At least he was swimming straight.

The rucksack slipped further to the left, dragging him beneath the water as he tried breathing to the right. He took in a mouthful of water, gagged, coughed it out, splashed as he tried to surface. The fear was instant and yet illogical — he was so close to the surface that his next breath would come in mere seconds. But he kicked and splashed, and opened his mouth underwater to shout out in instinctive fear. Took in more water. There was something slick in there this time, a shred of weed or perhaps a small fish, and he opened his mouth wider as he vomited it back out.

He surfaced at last, treading water as he caught his breath and tried to calm himself. Nothing touched him. There was no fish in his mouth, and the depths below him were innocent.

'Fuck's sake!' he shouted. His voice echoed back to him, but there was something strange about the echo. He couldn't place it. Odd. 'Hey!' he shouted, and once again the echoes came . . . but longer.

Saying more words.

He spun around in the water and looked back the way he'd come. At first he didn't see the movement because he was still in a part of the lake touched by sunlight, and it dazzled where it reflected from the frantic waves he was making.

Then he saw the figure silhouetted up on the ridge line he'd descended from so recently, and he couldn't believe the man had made it there so fast.

Blondie. It had to be. And he was pointing, and shouting.

Why share the kill? Chris thought, and the idea suddenly struck him hard, chilling, disbelieving.

Chris kicked himself around and started swimming again. He thrashed with his legs, kicking from the hip to provide maximum power, and heaved hard with his hands and forearms, grasping the water as far ahead as he could, shoving back at his hip. *It all comes down to how well I can swim,* he thought, and the fear was replaced with a strange, detached calm.

You've suddenly become a can-do guy, his wife had said to him a year or so ago. She'd been referring to his mid-life transformation from a fat, relatively unhealthy man to someone fit, lean, and capable. He'd learned to swim when he never thought he could, done other things that he'd never have believed possible for most people, let alone himself. His negativity had given way to a can-do attitude.

And he could do this.

He was Terri's can-do guy, and he would never let her down.

He swam hard. Pausing to look back would waste time, slow him down, and give Blondie a motionless target. He thought of zig-zagging, but at swimming pace it would have little effect. His best bet was to put as much distance between

188

him and his pursuer before —

The sound was strange, like a rapid, bubbling hiss. Water in his ears.

It came again, just when he was turning to the left to breathe, and this time he saw the water splashing up a few metres away.

He was within range.

What will it feel like? Will I even feel it in such cold water? Will I know I'm about to die . . . ?

The opposite shore was getting much closer. What he'd do when he got there was something to worry about when it happened. It looked rocky, ragged, and hopefully there'd be places to hide as he dashed from rock to rock, climbing the slope towards whatever might lie beyond.

That bubbling hiss came again, much closer this time.

Chris took action without even thinking about it, taking a deep breath, pointing his head down and kicking his legs up, pulling with his arms and descending below the surface. It was frighteningly easy, as his clothes and rucksack pulled him down. He levelled out and kicked hard, breast-stroking towards what he hoped was the shore. He tried not to exhale too much — a trail of bubbles would show Blondie just where to aim his next shot.

After close on a minute he rose quickly to the surface, exhaled, drew in a huge shuddering breath, checked his direction, and submerged again.

Something struck him in the back.

It was like a hard punch or kick, similar to many he'd felt at the tumultuous start of many open water triathlons.

Shot! he thought, *I've been shot!* But he could still lock and pull, so he stayed underwater and surged on. Those cold-water impacts often felt like nothing, the cold absorbing some of the pain or damage for a while. He didn't want to dwell on that. If the bullet had injured him, he'd know it soon enough.

He jigged to the right a little, kicked hard, held his breath for as long as he could, then surfaced again. This time there was no shot, and he risked a moment to look back the way he'd come.

All four hunters were descending the rocky slope. Even the fat one was there, lumbering downhill as if nothing and no one could stop him. *Fall and break your ankle,* Chris thought, but it seemed that his willing power wasn't strong enough. Blondie was still in the lead, thinking that getting closer was better than commanding the high ground. Was he really that stupid? The closer he came to the water's edge, the more difficult the angle.

Chris turned and started swimming hard for shore. This time he heard the gunshots, and they came from more than one rifle.

Maybe he'd made the wrong choice. He could have climbed and scrambled around the lake, at least then he'd have had some cover when they started shooting. Now he was exposed. And when he reached the lake's edge and tried to climb out, they'd have a clearer shot at him.

But three hundred metres was a long way.

He drew close to the shore, and his dragging feet knocked against the lake bed.

Water splashed close to his right shoulder. Another bullet crashed from the rocky slope above the lake and ahead of him, scattering rock splinters across his head and into the water.

The lake edge was shallower here, and he stood, swaying a little unsteadily —

— *From the swim? Hope so. Hope it's not blood loss from a wound I can't even feel yet* —

— then starting up towards a spread of boulders. The rocks beneath his feet were slick and he slipped sideways, trying to regain his balance but falling. He landed hard and started crawling, grabbing the slippery rocks and pulling, pushing with his feet.

More gunfire. Bullets whistled and ricocheted. He stood, gasping and shouting incoherently, and ran half a dozen endless steps to a pile of rocks. He fell behind them and scurried deeper, peering through a narrow gap and back across the lake.

Safe at last, he thought, almost laughing at the futility of it all.

He was in the shadow of the mountain here, the hunters on the other side in bright sunshine, and it illuminated their frustration. Blondie paced back and forth at the lake's edge, and for a minute Chris thought he was actually going to leap in and start swimming. The Rambo character was hunkered down catching his breath, and the other fat man was lying on his back on a flat rock. The fourth man, short, thin and bald, seemed to be taking photographs with his mobile phone.

A warm, glowing pain spread across his back. Chris shrugged off the rucksack, reached back

191

and grasped at his shirt, squeezing it, then checking his hand. No blood. It didn't *feel* that bad — more like he'd been punched hard rather than shot.

But he'd never *been* shot. Had no idea what it felt like.

There was a bullet hole in the rucksack, high up and to the right. He flipped it over and checked the mesh section that pressed against his back. There was no corresponding exit hole, and he breathed a sigh of relief.

Then he hurriedly opened the rucksack and peered inside.

The plastic bag was holed and torn in several places, and still awash.

'Shit!' He tipped the bag and emptied its contents on the ground between his knees. The penknife was bent, several tools projecting at fractured angles where the bullet had struck and fragmented. The map was holed but probably salvageable, printed as it was on showerproof paper. The water bottles looked okay. A couple of gels had bitten the dust, and the GPS display screen was blank. Water swilled inside.

The phone screen was black.

Bloody perfect.

But it could have been so much worse.

He shoved everything back into the rucksack and shouldered it again. It was time to leave. Once he got up the slope and disappeared over the top, he'd have an hour or so until they managed to edge their way around the lake. By then the light would be fading, and he'd have to come up with a plan to see him through the night.

No more gunshots cracked out as he started to climb. He risked a look over his shoulder, and back across the lake the four men were watching him. Blondie stood by the water, rifle held in both hands across his stomach. The other three were sitting close together, passing something back and forth. They drank from it. A bottle of whiskey, perhaps, otherwise there'd have been no need to share.

Good. Alcohol would dehydrate them, slow them down.

Chris gave them the finger. He couldn't help it, did it instinctively, knew that if he'd thought about it for even a second he'd have held back . . . but it felt good, and it meant that he could smile. The smile gave him a moment of optimism in a darkening world.

Blondie shouted in rage, his voice lost in the vast wilderness, and started shooting at Chris again.

Bullets whistled and whipped. Chris hid behind rocks. It was only for thirty seconds, but every wasted bullet was one less that could hit him.

His trail shoes squelched as he started moving again. He was cold, and as he moved his soaked outfit brought on the shivers. He needed a change of clothing — the spare running trousers in the rucksack were soaked — something warm to wear on top, and some decent food.

Failing that, somewhere to dry his kit might be a distant second best.

As he topped the next rise, he paused to look back down at the lake. The hunters were scampering around it to his left, pale spots far away and below, and it was difficult to imagine that they meant him harm. He experienced a rush of wellbeing completely at odds with his situation — he could fly ahead of them forever, confident on his feet, fitter than he had ever been, and slowly they would tire and crumple and die into these hills. His tiredness was negated by adrenalin, any pain he felt was weakness leaving his body. He would triumph.

'This can only end well,' he said, as if to imbue the landscape with his positivity. The wide, darkening skies remained silent, and the mountains stared back in mute mockery.

Fuck them, Chris thought, suddenly feeling very small. Running again, that brief moment of optimism faded with every footstep.

The mountain slope ahead gave way to a wall of almost sheer cliffs, craggy edifices that he would not dream of tackling. That left him with a choice — veer left and head down a series of slopes into the wide valley bottom; or turn right, negotiate a difficult scramble uphill, and enter the inhospitable mountaintop domain above the cliffs, where even now a heavy mist obscured his view.

Making things easy for him would do the same for the bastards chasing him.

He chose right.

An hour later he donned the yellow shower-proof jacket from his rucksack, soaked though it still was. He waited until he was sure the hunters had seen him before entering the cool mists.

21

no ties

The more Rose had discovered about the Trail, the more she knew that she needed help.

She returned to Italy just once. She went looking for Holt, ready to present everything she'd learned to him. He was retired, she knew that. A rich man with nothing to spend his money on. A haunted soul. Someone with a red history that she had no doubt was much deeper, darker and more traumatic than the few hints he'd given her, and which he'd likely never reveal. But she thought he might help because of the children.

That's why he'd taken time to instruct her, so he'd said. And with the Trail still active there would always be more children in danger.

Her second time entering Italy was as a different person. Not only had her name changed — she travelled under one of several *noms de plume* she had assumed for instances such as this, supplied to her by Holt's contact in Switzerland — but she was also a colder, wiser woman, with a wider horizon and dark stains on her soul that she could never have imagined before. The first time she'd come to Italy she had been a grieving, confused drunk seeking oblivion. This time her quest was for the most violent revenge.

Holt was no longer in Sorrento. She visited many of the locations they had frequented the year before — restaurants and bars, parks and beaches, abandoned buildings, seafront walks, and places so far out in the wilds that they did not have a name. She spoke to barmen and hoteliers whom she'd believed had known him, but came up blank. Either they were very good actors or, more likely, he was even better at remaining unknown than she had suspected.

Her fifth day there she spent outside a busy harbour café, watching tourists living their safe, trouble-free lives, and blending into the background. She was becoming good at that. The café was one of the few places to which Holt had returned several times when the two of them were together, and though she'd never asked, she had come to believe that the small, innocuous place meant something special to him.

There was no sign of Holt. If he *was* in Sorrento, he had seen her and preferred not to make himself known. And that made her hope that he wasn't there at all.

It had always been a long shot, because he'd passed that strange comment about not being quite lost enough. But at the back of her mind was the idea that he was always keeping an eye on her. Nothing had suggested this to her, other than her own troubled thoughts, yet she grasped on to the notion. She could not accept the concept that, to Holt, she had been just another lost cause.

That evening she returned to experience the café's night-time atmosphere. She dressed in different clothing, wore her hair up instead of down, and sat at a table she'd never used before. On the waiter's second visit to her table, she started asking him about Holt. She never mentioned him by name, instead painting the image of a mythical, shadowy figure, The Frenchman, a haunter of shadows. The man walked briskly away, and moments later someone else approached her. Uninvited, he sat in the table's spare chair. He and the waiter must have been twins, and they both wore the same leathery mask of bad times.

'You're looking for The Frenchman?' he asked in excellent English.

Rose nodded.

'Why?'

'I owe him money,' she said.

'Give it to me, I'll pass it on to him.' The man smiled, but it was ugly.

Rose stared him in the eye and finished her coffee.

The man's smile dropped. He returned to the bar where his waiter brother was waiting. They whispered to each other, glancing over at her. The music and chatter in the café receded as she focused on them, her heartbeat increased, and the idea of soon seeing Holt again suddenly made her both nervous and excited. She was afraid of him, but he was the only friend she had in the world.

The waiter nodded, then scribbled something on his pad, tore off the sheet and left it on the bar. He caught her eye to make sure she'd seen, then picked up a tray and went to serve someone.

Rose stood and approached the bar. The other man stood to one side, pointedly ignoring her. When she was three feet away and could see that the paper was blank, she felt the waiter's solid grip on her arm.

The two men dragged her out through the café's back door.

'No one asks about The Frenchman,' the owner whispered, and then he turned away.

Maybe this is what I wanted, Rose thought, letting them haul her through the kitchen and out past storage shelving heaped with packed food and bags of grains and spices. *Maybe danger is the only thing that will bring Holt.* She let herself be taken, feigning weakness, crying out when she thought they might expect it of her.

After the first slap fell across her cheek from one twin, and the first punch from the other rocked her jaw, she stood up straight, spat blood, and held up her hand.

The two men froze, wide-eyed and afraid. Rose was glad she couldn't see what they saw. *It must be in my eyes*, she thought, remembering those times that Holt had looked at her in such a way. Still, she believed that he'd never given her the full weight of his dreadful history.

Rose was still gathering the mass of her own, and she relished her complete control of that moment.

She punched the waiter in the nose with the heel of her hand, swinging her shoulder and putting her whole weight behind it. Bone crumpled, and he slumped to the ground with barely a whimper.

His brother tried to run back into the café, but she tripped him and then kicked him between the legs, dropping her other knee hard onto the side of his face as he curled up in agony.

The coolness was there. Holt said he'd seen it in her, knew what it meant — that she was ready to be shown things and willing to change — but this was the first time Rose had really experienced it in herself. It was a calm distance that seemed to slow down time, an awareness that located her limbs, her body, her strengths. And it was a remoteness from everything that had once made her human. She still cared when bad things happened to good people, so much so that her empathy was sometimes stifling and smothering.

But she could have cheerfully slit those men's throats.

Instead, she left along the dark alley, emerging into a bustling street rich with the scents of cooking food and the sea. The coolness remained, and in its embrace she saw how innocent everyone was. She alone walked with the knowledge of how cruel the world could be. It hung like a bubble of corruption about her.

★ ★ ★

She remained in Sorrento for two more days, and it was only when she grudgingly decided to end her search that Holt called.

She'd been moving hotels each night she was there. But when she'd given up any hope of finding Holt, and instead stayed merely to soak up more of the local atmosphere, she didn't bother changing hotels. Two nights in one place would not matter. It was out of the way, a small private business run by an energetic family who did their best to make her feel at home. The sort of establishment used by experienced travellers, rather than the larger, more glossy hotels booked by package tour firms. It was nice. She might have come here with Adam, if they ever had a long weekend away without the kids.

The phone beside her bed rang on that final morning. Even as she answered, coughing away the familiar dregs of bad dreams, still breathing in their dark clouds, she knew who it would be.

'Clumsy,' Holt said.

'What's clumsy?'

'Staying there for two nights. People will get used to seeing you. You'll be remembered. Especially someone like you.'

'Like me?'

'Attractive white woman travelling on her own.'

'Still such a smooth talker,' she said, smiling, because he so was not.

Holt only sighed.

'I'm sorry,' she said. There were a thousand questions — *Where are you? How did you know I was looking? How long have you been watching me?* — but none of them were worth asking. He'd tell her if he wanted to. 'I know you didn't want me to come back. But . . . '

'I won't help you,' he said.

'How do you know I haven't already finished?' she asked. 'Come here flushed with victory ready

200

to drag you off into the sunset?'

'And live happily ever after?'

'Maybe.'

He sighed again. *He knows everything,* she thought. She'd always believed that. What he didn't know via whatever contacts or methods he had, he seemed able to pluck from her thoughts. He had wisdom. Maybe it came with years, but more likely it was a product of the life he had always led. He lived on a different plane to most people, his perception insulated against the interference of modern life.

She sat up and took a long swig of water from the bottle beside the bed. Outside, mopeds buzzed along the narrow street, and the city muttered and rumbled as it came to life. She kept the phone pressed to her ear, but Holt did not talk. He was waiting for her to say why she'd come, what she wanted of him, how desperate things might be. Waiting to say no again.

'I have to tell you,' she said. 'But . . . not like this.'

'We've already said our goodbyes,' he said.

'Can't we meet?'

'I'm not in Italy any more.'

That shocked her. It was foolish, but for some reason she'd believed that he was calling from somewhere close. Perhaps even the next room; she thought that would be his style. Her heart sank a little, realising she didn't know him at all, and was not going to see him again.

'But tell me anyway,' he said.

So she did.

‘It didn't take me long to gather together everything I knew about them. There wasn't much *to* gather. Seventeen days working my way around the same place I'd seen Grin, and finally I saw her again. Clumsy of her, and I had to hold back from attacking her there and then. The impulse was there. And after everything you'd taught me . . . I could have murdered her in the street and walked away without anyone knowing.

‘But I followed her instead. She was fucking someone, that was the only reason she'd appeared there again. I was even kind enough to let her have her night there, then I went to the guy's flat. He wasn't one of them. If he was, he wouldn't have talked so easily. He didn't know her name, said they'd met on an internet chat room for people looking for casual sex. That was only the third time he'd seen her, and he said she hardly ever spoke, only told him what to do to her. He thought it was just her kink, and he got off on it. He was terrified of me. Maybe he thought that was *my* kink. I had no reason to hate him, but I did. He'd been . . . *inside* her. Inside the woman who'd murdered my family, pleasuring her, making her feel good.’

‘Did you kill him?’ Holt asked. The question didn't shock her as much as it should.

‘No. But I promised that if he spoke of me, I'd hunt down and kill his entire family.’

‘He knew you were serious.’ It was a statement, not a question. Holt knew he didn't even have to ask.

Rose thought of the kiss of the blade, the parting of skin, and the man's gurgled cry as he'd pressed the pouting wound on his thigh together.

'He gave me enough to work on. The last part of Grin's car number plate, a tattoo on her thigh, her accent. I did some work. It was a hire car rented through a third party, but the third party had a place in Camden, small empty office, stinking of rat piss. Just a registered address, but there was a cupboard filled with junked laptops. They didn't know how to wipe their data histories very well. I got part of a credit card number from there, traced that to an address in Sheffield. Old couple. They talked soon enough, all it took was a threat. I have no idea if Grin was even a relative of theirs — daughter, niece, granddaughter — but pretty soon I had an address in Edinburgh.'

'Sounds like a loose trail,' Holt said. He'd schooled her on tracking people this way, and how some people not wishing to be found would often leave false clues and pointers to throw pursuers off their scent. He called them loose trails because they were baggy, too filled with clues, too obvious.

'That's what I thought, but it was all I had. So I went to Edinburgh anyway, expecting to find nothing.'

'And?'

'It was an empty house. I watched for a while, and there was a young kid paid to go in twice each day, turn lights on and off, clear mail from behind the front door. I got in on the third night

203

and had a good sniff around. The mail was all junk stuff, nothing with a name. Everything was clean, dusted, pretty much pristine. But in one of the upstairs rooms there was a small case under the bed. It was filled with weapons and other stuff, survival equipment, false documents, few grand in cash. And a letter to Margaret Vey. On the surface it was a chatty one-pager about a holiday the writer had been on, but there was something strange about it. It was familiar, but impersonal. Like . . . an instruction manual. I didn't take anything, and left the way I'd come in.

'Margaret Vey. I had a name. But she didn't exist. I used some of the contacts you gave me — Isaac, MonoMan, and the woman at GCHQ. While they were doing their work, I did everything I could. HMRC, National Health, insurance and investment filing systems, passport office, criminal databases. Nothing. She was nobody.'

'False name?'

'Of course. But people use false names to get things, and hers didn't lead anywhere.'

'So what then?' Holt sounded interested. He wanted to know how Rose had found out what she had about the Trail, how she'd infiltrated so far. Enough to know when they had initiated another hunt. His interest was good, and she needed to nurture that. She didn't believe for a minute that she knew him any better than he wanted her to, but the excitement he felt at things like this had always been obvious. He lived off the grid, and that quiet zone beneath the radar was his playground.

'I remembered the tattoo the guy had described, and the accent. Went to Bolton, visited the studios there, showed them a sketch of the design I said I wanted — a snake coiled around a rat. No joy. But then I remembered the numbers I'd got from her phone the first time I'd seen her. Scratched into my arm. One of them was still visible, just, and it had a Bolton area code, so I tried it. And it was a tattoo artist who did home visits. I met him, talked about the design, and when I got the reaction I was looking for, I asked the guy about the woman while he was working on me.'

'You got the same tattoo?'

'Sure. Same place.' Rose touched her inner thigh. She didn't think about it too often, and when she did she felt only a blankness. It had been necessary, that was all.

'So what did he tell you?'

'Only her home address, where he'd been summoned to do the tattoo.'

Holt caught his breath. Rose smiled. It was rare to garner such a reaction from him.

'And?' he asked.

'I used it well. I kept my distance, but over the next few weeks I'd managed to intercept some of her mail, bug her phone line, hack into her broadband. I was as quiet as I could be. Any sign that someone else was riding her broadband, any hint that her mail had been opened and resealed, and that would have been it. The temptation to kill her was huge. But I was getting a good deal of intel, and as each new element fell into place,

205

a bigger picture was building. And it was terrifying. It was . . . ' Rose shook her head, wiping a bead of sweat from her temple. Street noises from outside seemed so distant, as if they came from another world. Her world was here, in this room, in her mind, balancing across the phone line to wherever Holt now was. A dark world of people who didn't exist, and whose reason for living was to provide kill sport for others.

'There are plenty of people who know how to live like that,' Holt said, and she knew he meant himself. For a moment she didn't want to shoot him down; he'd done too much for her, given more of himself than perhaps he'd intended. But even Holt didn't compare.

'No, Holt,' she said. 'It's more than that. It's like they were never born. I have a few names that probably aren't theirs. I have some grainy images, blown up from pictures taken from a distance. But apart from that, these people might as well not exist. They've got no past. Their present is nebulous. They move and interact without being seen, communicate through the white noise of a billion voices. They're less than ghosts. Barely rumours. First thing I'll do when I kill one is check them for a navel.'

Holt remained silent for a while. She could hear him breathing, thinking. She'd often tried to imagine what it was like inside his head, but even with every dark thing she saw in her future, she didn't think she'd ever get close.

'I'm sure they can bleed,' he said.

'I'm going to find out.' She didn't want to ask.

206

Had no way of pleading with him, not after everything he'd already done for her. But truth was, she was *scared*. They could make themselves disappear, and so they could do that to anyone else. She wasn't afraid of dying; she was already dead inside, the resurrected corpse of the rounded human being she'd once been. What inspired terror in her was the thought of never avenging her family.

The Trail had to pay, and for that she needed —

'I can't help you,' Holt said.

'Can't or won't?'

'Same thing.'

'But why?' She tried to keep the whine from her voice, wasn't sure she'd succeeded.

'I have my reasons. And believe me when I say, you need to do it on your own. This is your time, Rose.' He hung up.

'Holt!' She tried to call him back. His number didn't register, and she spent twenty long minutes contacting the local phone service provider. She was disconnected three times and passed along to another person, and in the end she was given her own number as the source of the call.

Rose threw the phone across the room, pleased when it smashed. She hoped he was trying to call her back, feeling sorry, and getting desperate and frantic when he couldn't actually reach her.

But she knew that wasn't the case. Wherever he was now, Holt was sitting back with his feet up, drinking water, and probably not even thinking about her at all. To move, exist, and survive beneath the grid, there could be no ties.

She was on her own, and she had some killing to do.

22

clean

In pain, confused and excited, Rose had to prioritise, without emotion and with the killing of as many Trail as possible as her one and only aim.

She could hide close to the helicopter and open up on them as they approached. She might get one, maybe even two, before she was killed. Or she could flee, take time to fix her wound, pursue Chris and those hunting him, and draw the three Trail men after her.

Surviving this had never been her priority. But now that she was on the ground, and she accepted that some of the Trail would go on living if she died in these mountains, surviving suddenly seemed more attractive. Her present was a place of pain and killing, but the future was once again a landscape she wished to explore.

So for a while, she ran.

★ ★ ★

'Got veins,' she said as she started cutting away the sleeve of her jacket. It's what Adam had used to say if he cut himself gardening, or washing up, or clumsily trying to do some household DIY. He didn't like wasting time doing stuff he didn't enjoy, always said he'd rather spend time with his family than painting a wall, putting up a shelf, digging a flower bed. And sometimes Rose used to think that his injuries were self-inflicted. But his dislike of blood had been real, and she'd come to accept that her husband was simply clumsy.

Got veins, he'd say, holding up a red-dripping hand for her to look at, turning away because he didn't want to see. Once, when he'd come off his bike, he'd walked two miles home and let her peel the torn Lycra from his leg instead of checking it out himself. That had been a trip to the hospital and eight butterfly stitches, and he'd still not once looked. Not until it was all covered up.

She saw him with his throat slashed open.

'Got veins,' she whispered again. She peeled the cut portion of sleeve down past her elbow and pulled the remaining sleeve up onto her shoulder, revealing the wound. It was worse than she'd expected. She knew that bullet wounds were almost never neat — hundreds of rounds fired into pigs' carcasses with Holt had shown her that. This one had entered just beneath her elbow, torn diagonally across her tricep, and exited beneath her armpit. An exit wound was good news. There was no telling whether any material from her jacket had been pulled into the wounds by the bullet, but she had to assume it had been. Even though the bullet had passed through, the risk of infection was large, especially considering the angled depth of the wound.

Dizziness threatened. Rose looked away, bit

her lip. *It's not me*, she thought. *It's someone else, not my arm, not my blood leaking away.* She had to be objective and dispassionate about this if she was to fix it and move on.

She looked again. The fleshy underside of her arm was swollen and full, and already turning a dark purple. Blood was pooling in there, forcing up against the skin. At least the swelling was closing the entry hole. She couldn't see the exit hole, but feeling with her left hand, her fingertips brushed against the tear in her skin.

She leaned forward, head between her knees, trying not to tip sideways even though she was sitting down. She was groaning without realising, so she bit her lip again. Tasted blood. *Got big, big veins, Adam.*

She had to clean and bind the wound. A hefty dose of painkillers should see her through the rest of the day and night, and she suspected all this would be over by then. After that she could retreat to a doctor she knew, pay him the last of her money and get him to sort her out. Or more likely, there'd be other, more fatal wounds to add to this one.

'Come on, Rose,' she whispered. 'Kick up the arse. No time to fuck around. Do it and move on.'

Come on, Rose, Adam said, agreeing.

Sitting up straight, she looked around to make sure no one was stalking towards her. A cooling breeze lifted her hair. She was maybe a mile across the slopes from the helicopter. Once the Trail men reached the aircraft they'd be there for a while, assessing the damage, trying to see what

211

they could fix and decide what the next course of action would be. Following and killing her, she knew. But she had a good head start, and they couldn't know for sure which way she'd come.

It would be dark soon. They'd likely have night vision tech, GPS devices, other stuff. Darkness would be their friend and her enemy.

She set to work on her wound. The first aid kit from the helicopter contained two packs of saline. She ripped one open with her teeth, lifted her arm and squeezed the sachet into the entrance wound. As the salt-water sluiced through the hole in her arm she couldn't help crying out, burying her face against her left shoulder to try to drown out the sound. But she remained conscious. It wasn't the most effective way of cleaning the injury, but it was the best she could do right then. She considered using the second sachet but decided to retain it for later.

Antiseptic sprays were next, aimed into entrance and exit wounds as best she could. Her damaged arm was shaking now as she held it up, strained and torn muscles quivering, and each movement drove the agony deeper.

She needed stitches. There was a needle and thread in the first aid kit, packed and sterile, but she wasn't sure she could do it. The entry wound would be easy enough to reach, but the exit was beneath her arm, out of sight even if she could twist her arm around without passing out from the pain. Stitching only one rip was pointless. Instead, she shook a small pack of clotting powder and, without giving herself a chance to think about it too much, scattered some of it directly into the bullet wound.

She pressed hard on the hole. Surroundings receded. Pain ruled. Her arm and shoulder were the centre of her world, the throbbing sun of pain around which she orbited. She wasn't sure how much time had passed, but when she was able she twisted around and poured a good amount of powder into the exit wound.

More agony. She leaned back and lay on the ground, looking up into the dark blue sky at the clouds that drifted there, uncaring of the drama down below. The world went on. That was something she'd found difficult to accept after her family were slaughtered — that even people she'd once been close to still woke in the morning, had breakfast, went to work, watched TV, argued, loved, ate, pissed, slept. Some people still cared, but the deaths of her family really had affected no one more deeply than her. And she'd had no chance to share the grief, having to hide away to avoid repercussions, from the law or the Trail. The idea that her friends, parents, and Adam's siblings would now think of her as a killer had struck a coldness in her heart that never went away.

The isolation had pushed her away from the world, accelerating her withdrawal into a place darker and deeper than anyone knew. She'd lived there alone; her own new world, drenched in cheap alcohol fumes and awash with nightmares.

'Now you can watch,' she whispered to the sky. The clouds, the air, the hillsides and lakes could see what she was doing and bear witness to her revenge. Blood was spilled in the mountains. She was creating a fresh new world for herself.

You're strong, bunny, Adam said. *Come on. Since when did a gunshot kill anyone?*

She gasped a strained laugh. Hearing his voice, imagining his dark humour, suddenly brought him so close that she could almost smell his breath.

'Hurts,' she whispered. She sat up and went about binding the wound. It was still bleeding, but the clotting powder was slowly doing its work and would hopefully prevent any more drastic blood loss. She wrapped the bandages tight, pinned them closed. After swallowing several painkillers — enough to hopefully calm the white-hot flames, not too much to dull her senses — she stood and kicked around the mess at her feet. She wanted them to find the discarded packets and know the way she'd come. She wanted them to follow.

She pulled out the satphone she'd taken from the dead helicopter pilot. The screen was dark, but one press of the central button and it illuminated again. It displayed a full-terrain image of the surrounding area, and at the top left corner throbbed a gentle blue glow. Rose frowned, looked closer, turned the phone so that the map display also shifted. She nodded. Of course. They wouldn't trust the outcome of a hunt like this to overweight desk jockeys.

Made things a lot easier for her.

She checked the rifle. Only four rounds. She had two magazines for her pistol. She should have searched for more ammunition at the

214

helicopter, but what she had would suffice. Shouldering the rifle, pocketing the handgun, she set off again across the mountain.

23

night vision

Chris frequently enjoyed running at night, either through their local woods, along the canal towpath, or in hills if he felt more daring. He loved it. During the winter months it meant he could fit his training in at convenient times that did not impact his family too much, but there was something more fundamental. It felt wild, dangerous, and tapped into his primal urge to run.

He always used a head torch, its powerful beam stretching far enough ahead to pick out terrain. A second torch attached to his belt cast a complementing beam, meaning that shadows gave texture to the landscape and showed him potential trip hazards. Beyond the light, the darkness was deeper. He only went to places he knew well, so that he didn't have the added complication of navigating as well as running. He liked the sense of isolation it gave him, the only sounds his heavy breathing and smooth footfalls. He enjoyed the feeling of speed as the illuminated ground passed by beneath him. He loved it when eyes were reflected back at him from fields, hedgerows and woodlands — cattle, cats, foxes, badgers, and other creatures that quickly vanished. There was nothing quite like running at night.

Now, he hated it. He was cold and miserable, tired and afraid. Dusk had not quite fallen, but the heavy mist cut out much of the remaining light. He had a head torch that he didn't dare use — they would see it from a distance and home in, rifles at the ready, imminent death nestled in dark barrels. He moved continuously uphill, afraid that if he attempted to move along the mountainside he would stumble over one of those sheer cliffs.

Chris was starting to regret his decision to head up into the mists.

And at the back of his mind lay the fear of what would happen if he lost the hunters, and the Trail —

The phone in his pocket buzzed. For a second he panicked, slipping on wet rocks and going down hard. He'd assumed it was dead, waterlogged, the screen blank. He'd planned to wait until later, see if he could dry it out in any way. It seemed luck might have smiled. He looked around but saw no movement, then plucked the phone from his pocket and pressed the green button, saying nothing.

'They know where you are,' Rose said. 'They have a tracking chip on you somewhere, and the hunters will have GPS-equipped satphones.'

'What? Where is it?' Chris asked.

'Don't know, and it doesn't matter.'

Chris felt around his body, shoes, pockets, trying to think where the Trail might have planted something like that, when they'd have had the chance, how it displayed a level of planning and preparation he had not considered

217

until now, and how they must have hidden it to ensure —

Rose had given him the rucksack.

'You?' he asked.

'Huh? No, of course not me! But don't worry where it is. This is good, don't you see? You don't have to worry about staying ahead to keep alive, yet not far enough ahead that they lose you. They *can't* lose you. So surge ahead and get some rest. It'll lure them on, and the faster things go, the less out of control everything is.'

'And that's good?'

'For me, yes,' Rose said.

'What about for me?' Chris asked. 'What about for my family?' But she had already rung off.

He almost threw the phone into the darkness. He'd make himself alone, do his own thing, but if what she said was true, he could *never* be alone. They knew where he was, and even now those bastards might be huddled around a phone or a GPS unit, trying to work out which way they had to go to follow his signal.

They might even be close.

'Bitch!' Chris hissed. She must have known about this before but kept it from him. Maybe she even knew where the tracking chip was. He could take time to look for it, pick through the weatherproof jacket's seams and the rucksack's many pockets and stitching, even though Rose denied she had placed it.

But maybe it was better if he left it undisturbed. If the hunters could track him then so could the Trail, and if they realised that he'd found and discarded the chip, that might encourage them to end the hunt.

Chris almost lost whatever fragile control he possessed. Unfairness weighed down, exhaustion pressed in, and it would have been easy to find a rock to lie behind while exposure came to claim him. He'd often wondered what it would be like to die in the hills from the cold, and had read extensively about mountain expeditions that resulted in such tragedies. Everest was littered with bodies, and he'd had dreams about being one of them, a human statue sitting forever in the icy wilderness.

But he could not do that. His mantra was to *never* give in, and that outlook had got him through many tough moments in casual runs and races. During his toughest races he'd had to talk himself through dark patches. 'Never, ever, ever give up,' he'd said, again and again. There was always an easier time beyond those dark moments.

And the same would happen now. He would find an easier time. Escape these bastards, rescue his family, return to a normal life.

He cast aside the doubts and the whispering voice trying to suggest that there could *never* be normal again. It was his voice, but it spoke from years ago, before he'd pushed himself hard to find what he was capable of, both mentally and physically. He'd finished his first extreme Ironman race in a little over fourteen hours, just two years after losing forty pounds and running his first 5k race. *Anything is possible* was the Ironman slogan, and Chris believed that.

He had to hold on to that now.

He stood and started forward again, up into the mountains, away from the cliffs, deeper into the mists and the falling darkness. Movement would see away some of the cold that threatened to set his muscles shivering uncontrollably. He ate another energy gel and drank the last of his water, knowing he'd be able to lick moisture from rocks. There would be streams, too.

Even if the hunters did have night vision equipment, he was willing to bet that they'd be verging on exhaustion by now, and uncertain about moving by night. Chris paused and made a decision. Like a prehistoric man, the thought of light and warmth comforted him. At least he could give himself one out of two.

Head torch fixed and shining ahead of him, he broke from a walk into a steady, cautious run. His spirits were lifted.

An hour later, when true darkness had fallen and a strong breeze blew across the mountain's plateau summit, he saw the cabin.

★   ★   ★

It was a small stone hut with no windows and a rusted metal door. There were a few of these scattered throughout Snowdonia and the ranges stretching into mid-Wales, refuges for tired climbers or walkers that were sometimes stocked with tinned food and bottled water. It was expected that they'd be left as they were found, and that any mess was cleared out. Using them was a matter of trust.

Chris watched for a few minutes. As time ticked by and the wind grew more powerful, the horizontal rain cut into him like spears of ice, and the cold worked its way deep into his bones, the thought of the respite he'd find inside finally made him move.

He'd seen no signs of light or occupation. There was no way the hunters could have come this far ahead of him. In fact, he believed that they'd more likely be miles behind now, working through the unfamiliar landscape and probably, hopefully, hurting. He was hurting too, but it was a familiar pain. Lactic acid, cold, hunger, he'd experienced them all before, but worse. The animal, primeval part of him relished the discomfort, but it was time to give himself a rest.

He paused outside the hut for a moment, ear pressed to the cold metal door. There were no sounds from inside. He grabbed the rough handle and leaned on it, pushing the door open when the latch disengaged. It scraped over the stony ground, and he opened it just enough to squeeze through.

He slipped the rucksack from his shoulders, and as he was leaning back against the door to close it, he heard movement.

His thoughts raced. *Of course, stupid of me, idiot, the Trail will be up here to monitor the hunt, even though Rose changed the location they'll have quickly moved and planned ahead, and now I've walked right into them and they'll break my leg or hobble me to make it easier for —*

As a small light appeared close to the floor,

Chris flung his rucksack at it. He grabbed the handle behind him and pulled, but the door was stuck.

A shadow rose across the small hut, the weak light sending it dancing against the damp stone wall.

'Hey,' a voice said, and Chris shouted.

'Get the fuck away from me! I'll stab you, I have a knife, get *back*!'

The shadow seemed to flicker as it flinched away, then the light low down against the wall rose as another shadow stood.

'Take it easy, buddy,' an American voice said. 'No problem here, chill, we're just resting up for a bit.'

The door still would not open. Chris pressed back against it, not knowing what to do next. His knife was in the rucksack that he'd thrown at the standing man, and now he had little else on him that he could fight with. Only his fists and feet, and if they were Trail, they'd know how to fight.

'You look cold,' the first man said. He switched on a more powerful torch, aiming it at the ground so that it didn't blind any of them. 'Wet. Exhausted. We're not here to hurt you, we're just taking a break while the storm plays out. We can make you some sweet tea, if you like?'

'Sweet tea,' Chris said, and nothing had ever sounded so good. 'You got food?'

'Sure,' the American said. He sounded strange, uncertain. 'You, er . . . up here on your own?'

'Yeah,' Chris said. 'Mountain runner.'

'I'm Wes,' the American said. 'This is my brother-in-law, Scott.'

'Chris,' Chris said. *Can I trust them? Can I really?* They looked like experienced, well-equipped walkers, with all the right gear and the rugged, weather-worn faces of people used to being exposed to the elements. Could the Trail really have brought all this gear together on such short notice? He doubted it. He *needed* to doubt it, because he wanted nothing more than an hour's rest, some hot sweet tea, and food.

'Forgive me for saying,' Scott said, 'but you don't look equipped for a mountain run in these conditions.'

'No,' Chris said. He relaxed slightly and moved away from the cold metal door. He was shivering. 'I planned to be down by now, took longer than I thought. Dropped my fleece and the wind took it. Mobile doesn't work.' All lies, but he had to cover himself.

'Well, I've got reception on mine. You can use it to contact someone, if you like,' Wes said. 'Here. Do what you need while we make a brew.' It was strange hearing the American use a term like 'make a brew', and Chris couldn't help smiling. The men returned his smile, and when he saw the concerned, slightly troubled glance they shared, it cemented it in his mind. They weren't Trail. They were just ordinary guys on a mountain hike, and he'd been lucky to find them.

'Thanks,' he said, taking the phone Wes held out. 'And . . . I'm sorry about that. I was having a rough time out there. Found the hut, thought

223

it'd be empty. And when I saw you guys it shocked me. Sorry. Really.'

'No worries,' Scott said. 'Take it easy.' But he and Wes sat close together at the other end of the hut as they set up their Primus stove, and Chris couldn't really blame them.

He scrolled the phone's menu and accessed the internet. Even as he waited for the BBC News page to load he was doubting everything that had happened. *It's all a bad dream, none of this is real, nothing like this can actually be happening to me because —*

He stared at a picture of himself. It threw him for a while, because usually he saw this picture on the wall in his hallway. He was standing beside Terri on a beach holiday they'd taken in Turkey the year before, smiling broadly, and he could remember that day with a clarity that sometimes startled him. Swimming, a pizza in the poolside restaurant, drinks in the evening. It had been one of those Good Days that always seem to stick in the memory, even though as they're happening there is sometimes little to set them apart.

They'd blocked Terri from view, and now his smiling face stared from beneath a headline that read 'Man on Run From Murder House'. Chris glanced up at the two men sharing the hut with him. Scott was lighting the stove, Wes was filling a small saucepan with water, neither of them paying him much attention.

He scanned the news report. *At least three dead . . . police have identified no motive . . . suspect that he is holding his wife and two*

224

children captive . . . 'such a quiet, nice man, you wouldn't expect . . .'

Was that Jean? They'd gone to his elderly neighbour, who gave his kids chocolate over the garden fence and always gave Chris a bottle of wine when he cut her lawns for her, and now she thought he was a mass-murderer?

. . . armed and extremely dangerous . . . members of public warned against approaching . . .

'Jesus Christ,' Chris whispered, and Wes looked up from the kettle.

'You okay?'

Chris nodded, scanning the American's face for any signs of recognition. If they'd known his face, surely they would have given some sort of sign by now? Tried to run, or attack him?

'You contact anyone?' Wes asked.

'Yeah. Sent my wife an email.' He thought for a moment. 'You got GPS tracking in here?'

'Look in 'maps'.'

Chris quickly shut down the BBC News page and scrolled the browser menu until he could delete the search history. Then he accessed the 'maps' app and waited while the phone placed itself. He took the map from his rucksack — tattered, soaked, but still readable — and when the phone pinned his location, he placed it on the map.

Now he knew where he was. He saw the lake he'd swum across, and figured out which mountain he was currently almost sitting on top of. It didn't help him that much — south had been his aim, and still was. But the information might be useful in the future.

As of now, he was the main news headline. He'd be on TV too, that image of him from one of his happiest family times now slurred, tainted with blood. Family and friends would believe him to be a murderer. Terri's parents, his brother and sister, their friends in Cardiff and beyond, all of them. Whatever spin the Trail had put on the story — whatever they'd told Angie and Nick, and his friend Jake — he had no way to back out of it now. To clear his name he'd have to evade them and rescue his family.

Only then could he begin to rescue whatever might be left of his life. But he knew that once a story like this was out there, it would stick. His own story was fantastical, and even if he did by some miracle make it through with him and his family alive, most people would retain some doubt. His friends would never look at him the same again. His extended family would no longer trust him. And who would come to an architect whose face was forever associated with bloody murder?

Chris snorted laughter. He was worried about work!

'Tea's almost done,' Scott said.

'Right,' Chris said, nodding, laughing again. The situation was so ridiculous that he had to remind himself once more just how real it was. 'Sorry. Thanks. Just . . . glad to have made it here.'

'We've got a bit of spare kit,' Wes said. 'Waterproof jacket, dry socks. We'll wait out the storm, then in the morning you can come down with us.'

'No!' Chris said, and a sense of urgency bit in. But he closed his eyes and levelled his breathing, because there was nothing he could tell these men. He had to leave soon, but there was no reason for doing so that would stand up to scrutiny. As far as they were concerned he was almost delusional and close to death. There was no point in trying to state a case. He'd drink the tea, welcome their help, and then he'd be up and gone before they could stop him.

He had a long way to go.

Wes passed him a mug of hot tea, and Chris sighed and nodded his thanks. It burnt his lips but tasted wonderful, the sweet fluid coursing through his body and warming his chest and stomach. He actually felt the sugar hitting his muscles and bringing them alive again. *I should dry my clothes*, he thought. *Spend some time resting*. But he also knew that too long spent sitting down would allow his muscles to stiffen, his limbs to become heavy and weary. Keep moving forward, never give up.

'So, that coat,' he said.

Wes frowned, then opened the big rucksack propped against the wall beside him. In a zippered pocket was a rolled-up jacket, thin but wind- and waterproof. He tossed it to Chris.

'Thanks,' Chris said. 'Nice.'

'Bought it in Boulder last year.'

'I'll return it,' Chris said. 'I'll give you my email, drop me your address.'

'Sure,' Wes said. 'We have food.'

I need to eat. Chris looked back and forth between the two men. They were scared of him,

227

but their concern was greater. He could see that they were worried for his safety, and just for a moment he considered telling them everything. Would they believe him? He doubted it. Perhaps such a crazy story would only make him sound more delusional.

'That's very kind of you,' he said, and he slumped back against the wall.

Wes and Scott seemed to become suddenly more active. Scott ripped open three foil packets and Wes boiled more water. It was soon steaming, and when Wes poured the boiling fluid into the packets, the hut was suddenly filled with the gorgeous smells of hot food. Chris had eaten dehydrated meals before and knew they weren't the best, but his stomach rumbled and his mouth watered. A few minutes more spent here would pay off in the long run.

He glanced at the door. He'd been there maybe fifteen minutes. Same again, and then he should be gone.

'So where'd you run up from?' Scott asked.

'Oh, way down in the next valley. Left my car in a lay-by, figured I'd get up to the summit here by eight pm, then back down in the dark. Hadn't counted on the storm.'

'They do roll in without you knowing, sometimes,' Wes said. 'Lots of people get caught out by the weather.'

'I know what I'm doing,' Chris said. A stab of pride spiked him, and he couldn't keep it from his voice. He looked down at the mug of tea, swilled it around. 'Really. I've done loads of this stuff. Just . . . lost my jacket.'

'Almost lost your rucksack, too,' Scott said. Chris glanced up. Scott was holding his rucksack by one strap, looking at the tear in the material.

'Yeah, got caught on a rock.' Chris half-stood and leaned across the narrow space between them, handing the phone back and plucking the rucksack from Scott's hands. 'This is one run I'll never forget.' He tried to sound light-hearted. Scott and Wes both smiled and nodded, but then they swapped that glance again.

'Hey, Chris, listen,' Scott began, and then something banged against the metal door.

Chris stood, backing away.

The other two men looked startled, but then calm again. Why shouldn't they? They weren't expecting anyone with a gun.

Chris started rooting in his rucksack, his hands closed around the knife that had been deformed by the bullet, and then the door smashed open. It almost struck him across the face, and if he hadn't stumbled back half a step he might have been knocked out. Things would have turned out very differently.

The storm entered. Blondie followed. Seeing him close-up, Chris's first thought was, *I shouldn't have underestimated any of them*. He was a tall man, powerfully built, and even though he must have really pushed up the mountain through the storm to get here this quickly, he still looked fresh and strong.

Maybe that was the endorphin rush of knowing he almost had his kill. His rifle was half-raised, and it took only a split second for him to bring it up and aim at Chris's chest.

Blondie's own face was curiously expressionless. To him, Chris wasn't human. He was prey.

Time seemed to freeze. Chris saw every detail of the scene — an acne scar on Blondie's chin, a drip of rainwater forming on his nose, the ash-speckles of grey in his short goatee, the glimmer of a diamond in his left ear, rain hanging in the air around him like a spiked halo, the heavy darkness outside, swirled with mist, violence stilled by worse yet to come.

'What the fuck?' Wes said.

Blondie's eyes came alive. From dead, soulless things, a spark lit them as they went wide. His whole face seemed to elongate as his lips parted, and Chris was shocked at the whiteness of his teeth. Expensive teeth. Lots of dental work. Vanity and money on display.

The gun dipped slightly, and Blondie glanced to his right.

I've got seconds, Chris thought. *I've got the time it takes him to decide what to do. Shoot us all, make up some lie, or turn to run. I can't let him do any of those.*

Blondie looked confused, disorientated, as if stirred from an immersive video game he'd been playing for hours. He was waking to the world, and Chris took that moment of surprise to act.

He threw the heavy metal mug. It struck Blondie's nose and hot tea splashed across his face. His head tilted back and to the side. The gun fired.

It was shatteringly loud, but Chris's senses, though enhanced, were protecting him against danger. Everything became clear and sharp, slow

230

and considered, and as he stepped forward and grabbed the rifle's barrel his right hand swung around and struck Blondie in the chest.

He shoved the barrel up so that it was pointing at the hut's corrugated metal ceiling. As Blondie fell back he must have squeezed the trigger again, and Chris felt heat pulse from the barrel and into his hand. It was so hot that it felt cold.

Scott was by his side then, helping him shove Blondie away from the doorway and out into the storm. The gunman tripped over his own heels and fell back, and as he went Chris tugged the rifle from his grasp.

'Holy shit!' Scott said, stepping back, surprised at what he'd done. Chris moved to one side so that he wasn't silhouetted by the weak light coming from the hut.

Wes appeared in the doorway, breathing hard, rubbing at his ears. 'Motherfucker!' He stepped forward and kicked Blondie between the legs.

The downed man groaned and curled into a ball, hugging his wounded parts and rolling back and forth as the dull pain turned into a blazing agony.

Chris looked down at the rifle in his hands. He had never held a gun before, and he was surprised at how heavy it was. It had a small scope, looked expensive.

When he looked up again he saw Scott and Wes staring at him. Wes's eyes flickered from Chris's face, down to the gun, up again, as if sizing him up. Scott looked like a rabbit caught in headlights.

'They're hunting me,' Chris said. 'Five of

them. No idea who they are, but they're rich. They paid a lot of money to hunt and kill a person, and that's what's happening. The people who organised it, the Trail, they're holding my family somewhere. If I escape they'll kill my wife and daughters.'

Wes and Scott heard but didn't seem to register the outlandish story. The wind blew hard, rain slanting across the plateau and stinging exposed skin.

'I'm Special Forces,' Blondie said, voice sharp with pain. 'He's wanted for three murders, and I'm one of a few — '

'No, you're not,' Scott said. 'You're Mike Pinborough. The footballer. I saw you on *A Question of Sport* last month and . . . ' He drifted off, bemused.

Blondie actually smiled, as if pleased at being recognised.

'You fucking idiot!' Chris shouted. He stepped forward and pointed the gun down at the pathetic man, making sure he wasn't too close, and ensuring he could see Wes and Scott as well. They seemed like good, normal guys, lovers of the outdoors, and they'd surely try to help. But Chris didn't know who or what they thought was right. 'You think you're Special Forces? What fucking video game are you playing in your head? Who am I, when you get me in your sights and pull the trigger? My name's Chris Sheen. I have a wife and two beautiful daughters, I'm an architect, and you've paid someone so you can fucking hunt and kill me? What happens in your head when you do that? What do you . . . ?' He trailed off, because he saw how Blondie was staring at him.

He looked like a terrified kid. Confronted with the human reality of what he was doing, he'd started to shake, dribbling from his mouth.

A day ago, Chris might have felt sorry for him.

He turned the rifle around and smashed the stock down against the outside of Blondie's knee. The man cried out, Scott and Wes said things that Chris didn't let himself hear and understand, and he struck the downed man again in the ribs. Hard. He put every shred of frustration, fear and anger behind the strike, and he felt the breaking of bones transmitted up through the rifle.

'Son of a bitch!' Chris shouted. 'You know they have my family? You know they've got my two little girls tied up somewhere with a gun to their heads, you piece of shit?'

'N . . . no,' Blondie said, shaking his head, holding his hands up to ward off further blows. Chris hit him again, the rifle's stock striking his left hand and snapping fingers.

'Hey, friend, you need to calm down and — ' Wes said.

'Shut up!' Chris shouted. He didn't aim the gun, not really. But he turned it around again so that he was holding it properly.

He pointed the barrel at Blondie. The man squirmed on the wet ground, snot bubbling from his nose. He was groaning in pain, twisting as he tried to snake away from Chris and the dark, wide barrel of the gun.

'Who did you think I was?' Chris asked, voice

quieter now, barely audible above the rain. 'When you came out here to kill me. Just *who?*'

'I . . . ' Blondie said. 'I just thought . . . '

'No,' Chris said. 'You didn't think at all' For a second his finger closed around the trigger. But he was not a killer.

'They told us you were nobody,' Blondie said. 'An easy target. Someone who wouldn't be missed. A criminal. A loner, a drifter, and that — '

'And that made it okay to kill me,' Chris said.

Blondie seemed confused, frowning and shaking his head as he tried to process what Chris had said. 'Your family? I don't know anything about them, I had no idea — '

'Shut up.' Chris took a step closer and pushed the barrel down against the man's stomach. Blondie cried out but froze, hands clawed and held out as if to snatch life from the air. He was grimacing. He was probably a handsome man. Chris had seen his face in the media, Terri might have mentioned him, perhaps they'd even watched him on TV together once or twice, kicking a ball about and making sure his hairdo was the most talked-about of the match.

But today he was ugly.

'You bastard,' Chris whispered.

'No, please, no, I didn't mean to — '

Chris moved the rifle barrel down the man's legs, pressed it against the outside of his bent knee, pulled the trigger.

The loud gunshot, the man's scream, the other men's shouts of surprise and shock, all sounded around the plateau, echoing from rocks and from

234

the stone hut built to protect brave adventurers. A coward might hide in it now.

It was Scott who came for him. Chris had been expecting Wes. It only took a slight shift of the rifle barrel to halt the man's forward dash.

'You have no idea!' Chris shouted. Scott held his hands out placatingly, stepping back again. 'You really . . . no idea.'

Blondie continued to writhe, hands held either side of his ruined knee. He was too afraid to touch, in too much agony to remain still.

'In there,' Chris said, nodding at the hut. 'They'll find you.'

Blondie didn't look as though he heard, but Chris didn't care. He searched the man's pockets, found a satphone, slipped it into his own pocket.

'Don't follow me,' Chris said to Wes and Scott. 'Thanks for your help. Really. Nothing you see or hear about me is true, everything I'm saying is the reality. Just . . . believe me.' He shook his head. It didn't really matter what they believed. 'Patch him up if you like, but I wouldn't advise staying with him. I doubt the Trail likes loose ends.'

'What's the Trail?' Wes asked.

Blondie had stilled at the sound of the name, looking up at Chris as if for an answer. But there was nothing more to say.

He darted back inside the hut for the jacket Wes had lent him. He also picked up his rucksack and shoved a few packets of dehydrated food inside, and a full plastic water bladder. There was more he could take, he was sure. But the others might not be far behind Blondie, and though he now carried a rifle, he had no real wish to use it again.

Back outside, the two men were still standing where he'd left them. Scott looked just as shocked as before. They watched Blondie crawling towards the hut.

Chris paused for a moment, wondering what more he could gain from this. He tilted his head, smiled apologetically. 'Phone?'

'Sure,' Wes said. He pulled the phone from his pocket, lobbed it, and Chris caught it.

'Thanks. Sorry.' He shrugged, then set off away from the hut.

They were soon lost to sight behind him. He switched on his head torch, and before he'd moved far enough away for the storm to take him fully into its belly, he heard Blondie cry out. They were dragging him towards the stone hut.

More than anything, he hoped it hurt.

24

throats

There were families. Wives and children, brothers and mothers, sisters and fathers. And beyond there would be friends. Some would know of the Trail, but probably most did not.

Every action she took in these mountains had far-reaching consequences.

The fat bastard she'd killed had paid good money to hunt and murder someone, and yet she could not feel good about shooting him. In no way did it chip at her mountainous grief, because he'd had nothing to do with her family's murder. In a way he was as innocent as her, corrupted by the Trail simply because it had enabled his sick fantasies to come true. She didn't care about or mourn him, but the thought of his loved ones troubled her.

They'd hear about him shot dead on a remote mountain in Wales, and perhaps they'd never know why. He'd risen the day before, maybe preparing for a business trip to the City that might take a couple of days. Kissed his wife goodbye, if they had that sort of relationship. Ruffled his kids' hair. Then he'd left, always expecting to return, leaving unsaid things that could heal a wound or calm a troubled relationship. There were always things unsaid.

She and Adam had let many arguments fade

237

away rather than settling them. They were always minor things, but sometimes she thought about them, really analysed, and her heart raced and her thoughts drifted, making them monstrous blots on their marriage.

She was a new person, but she still retained the empathy that set her aside from the Trail. She had to. If she didn't remain human, she'd be just like them.

So just for a few moments, walking in the darkness, she forced herself to think about the families affected by this. And then she just as easily boxed them and set them aside in her mind. At least they could still draw breath, laugh, and cry. They were still alive.

In the darkness, the memory came again. Arriving at the quiet detached house on the outskirts of Birmingham, knowing it was the right place because she'd located Adam's phone using a 'find my phone' app on the new iPhone she'd bought, waiting outside to assess comings and goings. She didn't know then that the hunt had been called off almost a whole day before, soon after she'd dropped the tracking device into someone's pocket on a bus, given the hunters the slip, and literally gone to ground, hiding in the city's sewers for a day and night. She'd considered calling the police, but took the warning given to her by the woman she'd come to know as Grin seriously: *Call the police and your family die.* She knew little about who the hunters were, didn't even know if they were still alive. Right then she didn't care.

Creeping around the side of the house and

forcing the back door open using an old screwdriver rusting on a windowsill. Waiting for a barking dog and screaming occupant, but finding neither. Entering, and sensing something wrong the moment she crossed the silent kitchen. She didn't know then, and still had no idea, exactly what she had sensed. Maybe an unnatural silence, one honoured by the smallest creatures because this was a house for the dead. Maybe a stillness in the air, or the scent of something familiar. Family.

She found them downstairs in the basement.

On the Welsh mountainside, screwing her eyes against the unrelenting rain and wind starting to scream through the heavy darkness, nothing could make her not remember.

Adam was propped against a rack of shelving, both arms tied back to the framework at the elbows and wrists. They'd slit his throat and left him there to bleed out. His eyes were wide, head pressed back against a shelf containing a stack of *Empire* movie magazines. Ironic, because they'd loved going to the movies together. She'd spent long hours wondering what he'd seen as he died. Their children lying dead before him?

Or worse, their three beautiful children watching him die?

Molly was huddled against a damp wall, her long blonde hair covering her face. She'd liked animals and wanted to be a vet, just like her mum. They'd stabbed her behind the ear. Isaac, their youngest child at only five years old, was splayed in the middle of the floor with a halo of blood dried around his head. He had often made

239

up nonsensical songs and drove them mad singing them again and again. He was lying face-down. It looked like he'd been thrown there, and there was something so blase, so inhuman about that idea that it stuck with her more than the mess of his head. Alex was still holding his father's hand. He'd loved athletics and running, and his sports teacher in school had been pushing for him to enter some of the local club runs. Maybe he'd gone to him while he was bleeding, dying. Or perhaps Adam had to hold his son while they killed him.

Her whole past and future was dead in that basement. She stayed with her family for several hours, then when she climbed the staircase and emerged into daylight, the best of her remained down there with them, forever.

Rose breathed hard, drawing cold air into her lungs. She closed her eyes and turned towards the storm, relishing the stinging sensation of rain spearing her face. Whenever she thought of her family, alive or dead, returning to reality always felt like a dilution of life. The world was an emptier place for her now. Even revenge was a fleeting thing.

She glanced at the satphone that she'd taken from the dead pilot, hunched down over the screen to prevent it from being seen. After quickly appraising her position, she switched it off again. Chris had been motionless for almost half an hour. She wasn't letting that worry her just yet. He was probably resting, having put a good distance between himself and the hunters. Even if he *had* been injured or killed, the three

240

Trail men were still in the mountains with her. They were still hers.

But she hoped he hadn't. She liked Chris, and she found herself wanting him to get through this. Find his family, rescue them, make a life together with them again even after everything that had happened.

It was impossible, but she liked the crazy idea of a happy ending.

She swayed as dizziness hit her. Her whole arm and shoulder throbbed, heavy as a sack of coal, burning. She could barely open and close her right hand without searing pain pulsing through her whole limb. When it came to firing the rifle, she'd just have to grit her teeth.

That time had to be soon. She was weakening.

The storm had brought down an early darkness. The sun had almost set, and what little light it still provided was diffused and weakened by the heavy mists and driving rain. Her clothes were soaked through, even though she'd shrugged on her waterproof jacket. She shivered. The elements felt heavier than they were, urging her down to lie still and fade away. She would do neither.

But movement across the mountainside towards Chris was already dangerous, and very soon it would prove impossible. She'd taken a torch from the helicopter, but lighting herself up to become an easy target was a foolish idea. While Chris was still, perhaps she could afford to take a rest as well.

Find somewhere to hide away, take her time. Launch an ambush.

She shrugged the rifle from her left shoulder, knelt, rested it on her right forearm. And when she looked through the scope she cursed herself for not checking before.

Night sight! The hazy green view startled her for a second, then she swept the gun to the left and right and the landscape leaped into view. It was distorted by lancing rain, which looked like laser streaks across her field of vision, but she could make out rocks and slope, the darker shadow of emptiness to her left, and the green mass of the mountain above and to the right.

She could move.

Rose found herself lifted by this discovery, and she started moving faster through the storm. Doing so helped warm her tired muscles, and though she still shivered, the cold no longer seemed so bad. She considered taking the scope from the rifle and holding it to her eye, but she quickly discarded the idea. She needed it attached to the weapon. If she saw or heard anything of the Trail men closing on her, she'd need every advantage to beat them.

As she walked and climbed, the idea of an ambush grew. It was a good idea. Her plan was always simply to move forward and adapt to situations, and now she had the opportunity to take out at least three more Trail. Whether there would be more after that, she didn't know. She'd discovered that there were at least a dozen members of the UK cell, but there was nothing to say there weren't two or more cells at work in the same country. There was a good chance that reinforcements were already on their way, or they might even be here, closing on her from a different direction while the hunters continued to pursue Chris.

Taking the fight to them seemed to be the only logical way to go. She couldn't run very far in her current state, and the longer she left it, the weaker and more tired she became.

And she wanted Grin.

Holding the rifle up so she could see her way, she zig-zagged up the mountain. They'd know she was wounded — they would have seen blood at the helicopter site, and would probably find the scattered dressings and first aid kit she'd left behind — and hopefully they'd suspect that she would run, a wounded animal trying to escape her tormentors.

Even though not yet cornered, this wounded animal would turn and fight.

★ ★ ★

Fifteen minutes later she found the perfect site. Beneath an overhang, a huge boulder had tumbled and come to rest leaning against a sheer wall of rock. Water splashed down one side, covering any sounds she might make. Between the boulder and the wall, a narrow gap offered a wide field of vision down the hillside she had just climbed. She could see at least a hundred metres across and down the slope, with a scope of over ninety degrees.

Wishing for something warm to eat and drink, she huddled down to wait.

Chris was running with her, taking graceful, long steps while she struggled to keep up. He kept glancing back and smiling. It was as if his own family did not have a gun to their heads. He leapt a narrow gorge and did not even pause to make sure she made it over safely. She jumped, scrabbling at the far side, fingernails shearing off and knees smashing against rock as she tried to gain purchase. When she was up and running again, Chris was just ahead of her once more.

She was puffing beneath the weight of her dead family, all of them slung over her shoulders.

'They'll never catch me,' Chris said, and Rose thought, *But then your family will die.* 'Oh, no,' he said without turning around. 'If they never catch me and I keep running, my family will live forever.'

Adam's arm bumped against her side as she ran, and her daughter's blood-matted hair scraped her cheek.

They were in the basement again, only this time her family were no longer there. A dozen Trail members were tied and restrained, and Rose walked casually around the large room with a butcher's knife in one hand, slitting throats.

Grin was tied against the storage racking where Adam would have met his end. However many men and women Rose killed, she didn't seem able to reach her. Grin was always one death ahead, one slashed throat out of reach.

I need help, Rose thought.

'You need to do it on your own,' Holt said,

and his voice was so loud, so there, that everything else that Rose could feel and sense became unreal.

She opened her mouth to reply, but she could only cough.

★ ★ ★

She snapped awake. Another cough. Something hissed in the stormy darkness, perhaps a voice berating the cougher. Rose gathered herself and focused on the place, the moment, banishing any confusion. She'd drifted off, that was all.

She remained motionless. Her wounded arm was heavy and numb, and she was okay with that. When the time did come to move, she would compartmentalise the pain, give it to the wind and the darkness, while she did what needed to be done.

Her heart beat fast, but she was now calm and clear. She was doing it all on her own.

Through the rain and wind, she heard the unmistakable sound of stone on stone. Someone was walking across the slope before her.

She'd dropped off with the rifle resting on her legs, and now she eased it up and propped the barrel in the opening. She only had to lean to the side and edge forward to see through the scope. Her right arm sang a song of pain, but she shut it out.

There. Two of them, one less than twenty metres away, the other further downhill. She shifted slightly left and right, trying not to move too much. She couldn't see the third man.

It was definitely them. They both carried rifles in one hand. The one in front wore a casual leather jacket and jeans, and though she couldn't see what the other guy wore, she guessed it was something similar. She might be shivering and hurting, but they'd also be tired from dragging water-logged clothing with them, their muscles cold, dehydrated. They were as unprepared for these conditions as she was.

The lead man paused and raised something to his eyes. Night vision binoculars. Good. Though they had rifles, their weapons weren't as well-equipped as hers.

Her time was close. She had to be quick. The first, then while the shock bit in, she'd swing a few degrees and take the second. The second shot would not be easy — he was at least fifty metres away, the storm still raged, and she'd have maybe a second to aim. She'd be shooting left-handed, but she had spent plenty of time practising. She was good. Calm, ready, eager for the kill.

She wanted nothing more.

Breathing gently, Rose lifted her burning right arm and grasped the rifle, hissing softly as if to gasp away the pain. She readied herself, aimed, stroked the trigger. The man had drawn a few metres closer. He raised the binoculars, swept them left to right, paused.

Seen me, she thought, and she squeezed.

The gunshot was thunderous in the confined space, and her vision through the scope flashed bright green as rain and mist were stirred into violence. The rifle bucked and sent a shimmer of agony through her body, rippling from her wounded arm. She ignored it all, shifting the gun slightly down and to the left, sighting on the greenish shape that she hoped was the other man, squeezing, firing again.

Another recoil, another flash of green momentarily blinding her. She closed her eyes for a second, and when she looked again the scene had changed. The two men were down. The one close by was on his knees, bent over with his face pressed to the ground, motionless. The other was also on the ground, but crawling quickly towards cover. He was a blur, shielded partly by a hump in the terrain.

Two bullets left.

Still deafened, but now with a sort of glee surging through her, she aimed again and fired.

Either she missed, or the bullet barely grazed him. She saw his squirming outline for a couple of seconds more, then he found cover.

She turned back to the first man and he hadn't changed position. She briefly considered putting the last rifle round into him, but there was still one more Trail man out there somewhere, untouched, and now he'd be coming for her.

One shot left. She had to move.

As Rose stood, pins and needles tingled through her right leg. She tried to stamp it out but it weakened her muscles, turning a run into a crouching shamble. She kept the rifle to her shoulder, swinging it left and right so that she could see.

He'll be waiting and watching. If he has night

vision binoculars too, he'll hunker down until he sees me, watches where I go, gets a fix on me. Then he'll close in. And that gives me time to see him.

She paused right out in the open and did a slow, methodical sweep of the mountainside before and below her. The shift in position had altered her angle, and she could see the second man again now, huddled behind a rock and shifting slowly from left to right. She couldn't make out any detail, and didn't want to dwell on him for too long. It was enough to know that he was wounded and down. She would finish him soon, but the third man might be using his wounded colleague as bait, waiting for her to draw close.

A pistol shot from this distance would not be easy.

She moved on, passing close to the first man and taking a quick look. He was dead, head misshapen and wet. His rifle had fallen close by, but she had no time to gather weapons or ammunition. Her element of surprise blasted away, she now had to assume that she was in the third man's crosshairs.

Darting left and right, she headed across and up the slope to a position above the fallen boulder. She splashed through a stream, keeping the rifle to her shoulder, alternating looks ahead and around, and down at the terrain close by. If she tripped and he was watching her, it would take only a moment to settle his aim and —

She didn't trip. She slipped. The rain had formed new streams all across the mountainside, and the rocks beneath were slick with moss. Her left foot went out from under her and she held out her arm as she fell, doing her best to keep hold of the rifle.

As she struck the ground, breath *whoofing* from her and arm smacking hard against a jagged rock, the rifle slipped from her grasp. It hit the ground with a crack.

When the second crack sounded, she knew she was being fired on.

If she hadn't slipped, she would probably have been dead. She heard a bullet smack a rock behind her and ricochet into the storm, and she had to act quickly. No time to feel around for the rifle, especially in the chaos of the tumbling stream. No time to get to her feet with her wounded arm screaming at her once again.

She kicked at the ground and slid down the stream.

As she tumbled she tried to recall the area where she'd hidden away — the size of the boulder, the steepness and height of the rock wall it rested against, where the small waterfall had tumbled from. Then there was only water around her.

Before she had a chance to prepare, she struck the ground, slid, rolled, and fell again, this time down a gentler slope. She hit the ground again, and this time remained motionless.

Everything hurt. She'd banged her right arm, and the pain was all-consuming, a spreading flame that spread through her bones and muscles, setting her limbs twitching.

It's only pain! she thought, but mind over

matter had its limits. *Got to crawl . . . got to get . . .*

Another gunshot, but this time the bullet struck far away. He was shooting blind. Using his night vision binoculars to try to zero in, perhaps, but shooting and looking at the same time would be difficult.

Lost the fucking rifle! But she still had the pistol. She had to draw him close, lure him in to somewhere she could see his shape in the darkness, the storm, and put him down before he could bring the rifle to bear.

Her chances were slim, but she shoved away the doubt. She'd got two of them, and the third would now be in a panic, however hard he was, however well trained.

The wind howled, a wilder gust that seemed to feed on the violence. Rain splashed from the ground around her, distorting her meagre vision. She gathered herself, then stood and ran in a crouch, this time away from the leaning boulder and the men she had shot.

No gunfire followed her. Maybe he was moving as well, in which case she might have a few moments in which to hide. She tripped and almost fell, carried on, drew her pistol with her left hand. Each footfall brought a pulse of pain, but now she was almost feeding from it.

Ahead of her, the view was split into the darkness of the mountain and the softer, deeper grey of the stormy sky. If she could get to a place where she was not silhouetted against —

A shadow rose before her, and even as she thought of bringing her pistol up to fire, a blast

250

of blinding light erupted as the figure lit a flare. She squinted and fell, crying out as her damaged body was smashed and battered into the ground once again.

Gunfire cracked through the storm, five shots in rapid succession. She held her breath, but oblivion did not come. Gasping, there was no new pain to add to the old. She persisted in her wretched world.

Darkness had fallen once again, the flare cast aside. The shape had vanished from ahead and above. The stark line of the close horizon was as wild and inhospitable as ever.

Very close behind her, she heard a man groaning.

She was still clasping the pistol. It felt good in her grip, firm, something solid rooting her to the world. Everything else was fluid. Her pain seemed to project beyond her, affecting the black ground and the rain, the sweeping wind and the heavy mists that drifted across her vision, real or imaginary. She was shaking violently now, but unsure why; cold, pain, adrenalin?

Probably all three.

She tried to stand, not entirely sure that the threat was ended. Every movement jarred her arm, and every throb of pain pounded inside her skull, threatening to spill her onto the ground again. If she passed out she might die up here. And there was more left to do.

Looking behind her, she feared that a death had been taken from her. She felt lessened by that, as if her vengeance depended upon a certain quota of murders, a scale of spilled blood. Holt had told her that she needed to do all this for herself, and now she knew that he was right. He was a man who spoke with experience and history that she could never know. He was wise. She should have listened to him.

But who was that shadow that had intruded on the hunt? Just another perverted part of it?

The first man was less than twenty steps behind her. He'd been shot several times and now he was dead. She picked up his rifle, went through his pockets, found another handful of bullets. She checked her satphone. It was still functioning, so she stomped on his and left it. After picking up his night vision binoculars, she moved on.

The second man — the one she had shot — was still crouched down close to the boulder, also dead. She pocketed his spare ammunition.

Looking at the corpses she felt strangely empty, devoid of celebration or regret. Just blank. Perhaps pain was smothering all other emotions. Or maybe now that she was here, living her dreams, they could never quite reach the heights she'd hoped for.

It took her a while to find the third man. He'd crawled downhill, not far but far enough for her to have to search. She used the dead man's night vision binoculars, and finally found him slumped against an outcropping, both hands pressed to his stomach. Gut shot. Good. That would hurt, but he wouldn't die too quickly.

She moved in carefully, lifted his head, pulled off his 'I ♥ VNY' baseball cap. It was a woman.

Rose gasped, clenched the pistol tighter. Grin?

But no, this was someone younger and fitter, her build slim and lean. She coughed, looking at Rose with eyes that already knew her fate.

Rose crouched down beside her.

'Let's talk,' she said.

* * *

As Vey hustled her from the back of the van and through the converted barn's back door, Gemma did her best to look around and take in her surroundings. Holding her upper arm in a tight grip, Vey didn't seem to care.

'This is stupid,' Gemma said. 'You can't do this, it's not fair.'

'We're doing it.'

'If I run and you shoot at me, people will hear, and if that happens — '

Vey squeezed her arm so hard that Gemma cried out. Ahead of her, in the building's shadowy interior, she saw her mother take a step back towards her. Tom shoved her against a wall.

'I have a knife,' Vey said. 'There are rocks beside the driveway. A puddle deep enough to drown in. Don't think for a minute that there aren't thirty ways I could kill you, silently, if you give me cause to.'

'Bring her in,' Tom said. 'She'll see too much.'

Vey heard him, and answered, but she did not take her eyes from Gemma's face when she said, 'It doesn't matter what she sees.'

As she was shoved into the building's cool interior, Gemma felt the last touch of sunlight on the back of her neck.

25

fall

I could have killed him, Chris thought. *Maybe that would have been better. Safer for me. A statement of intent to the other three still out there, if they even find Blondie.*

He'd often put himself in an imaginary position — his wife or kids hurt, and him facing the bastard who'd hurt them. It had been a painful daydream, but the result was always the same. Though he hated violence, and always had, he recognised the need for it. Like that time years back in the pub, punching the man who'd assaulted Terri. Nice words would not have worked there.

But he had no regrets. If Blondie didn't die of exposure or blood loss, he'd have permanent injuries. Maybe internal damage from the broken ribs, and a knee that would never work properly again. If he really was a footballer, that was torture enough. The fact that the hunter had not hurt Chris — that the violence was all intent — didn't change things. He was part of the reason that Chris's family had guns to their heads, and that was as far as he needed to think.

If they're even still alive. But that was one thought too far.

Now that he was out on the mountain again, his energy restored from the food he'd been given, thirst quenched, and feeling warmer than he had for a while in the borrowed jacket, Chris felt a burst of optimism. He was running once more, albeit slowly, the beam from his head torch bobbing before him. The rain was just as heavy, the wind unforgiving, but he enjoyed the sense of isolation it gave him. For a moment he might have been all alone up here, master of his own fate instead of being steered and used by others.

He used that time to think.

He had a satphone now, and perhaps that would make it easier to call the police — Rose's and Scott's phones continued to have intermittent signals. But he could not see what that would achieve. If he told them who he was, all they'd want would be to talk him down. He could tell them about his family, but whether they believed him or not it would do no good. He suspected that they were being held in the greater Cardiff area, but it would take a lifetime to search that far.

Maybe they could track the signal from the satphone. He had no idea. He'd seen such things on TV and in movies, one policeman gesturing for the other to keep a killer or terrorist on the phone while they traced the call. But he had no concept of how something like that worked in reality. Perhaps the moment he connected with them, they'd have a real-time location for him. Then maybe they really would send the Special Forces up here to get him. If not military, then police. Hunted by sick and rich bastards as he was now, at least he had a chance. If anyone trained came to find him, he'd certainly be quickly caught or killed.

Knowing that the last three hunters could follow his position was useful. It would not be easy to escape them, but it also meant that he could push hard, giving himself a safety buffer and time to rest, refuel, warm up.

Nothing he'd done had improved the chances of him and his family getting out of this in one piece. He wondered whether Rose was faring any better.

His limbs soon grew used to running again. He watched the ground before him, leaping trip hazards, side-stepping holes, always alert for signs of a sheer drop or a rock wall to run into. As his feet came down and swept the ground behind him, he felt the connection with the land that he always loved. When he was running at his very best he always felt as if he were standing still, and it was the land itself being pushed behind him by his feet. A strange but satisfying feeling, and one that he experienced only on rare occasions.

Every fifteen minutes he surveyed the landscape, turned off the head torch, and crept a cautious twenty metres onwards. Then he paused and listened for any signs of pursuit. There was nothing but night sounds accompanying him. He enjoyed those brief moments when the head torch was off imagining that his presence here was no longer acknowledged and the natural world around him was back to its basic, primal self. Even the light from the torch changed things — the way rain completed its journey, the reactions of night animals, the feel of the place. He loved the wilderness most when it did not know he was there.

He glanced at the satphone screen every few minutes. He'd turned on a simple application on the tablet screen that provided a digital compass, and he made sure he headed southwards as much as possible. The time would come soon when he would encounter a road, and soon after that there might be signs, place names, and a deeper understanding of exactly where he was. The brief glance at his damaged map in the hut had located where he was, and what he thought was probably the lake he'd swum across. But he knew that any map could only describe landscape in an abstract way. Being on the ground was the only way to truly appreciate and understand a place.

He'd seen that he was probably in the wildest, most inhospitable, and least populated part of Wales. There were valleys here where only the hardiest walkers and adventure sportsmen came, and which were so remote that farming them was an unprofitable proposition. The best roads were dirt tracks. Most buildings were ruins. The perfect place for a hunt.

He thought again of the ultra-marathon in the Lake District. The race description had labelled it as a tough off-roader, but with the bulk of the trails definable, made up of compacted gravels and well-worn paths. The description had been misleading. At one part of the course the runners had to cross a high area of marshland, probably only two miles in total but out of sight of any manmade influence, and sparsely marked with a few windswept flags. This was thirty miles into the race, and by then the field had spread out so much that Chris had found himself alone up there. Those couple of miles had felt like the wildest, most remote miles he had ever run. Up to his shins in wet, sticky mud, he'd fought every step. The wind had risen, intermittent rain showers hammered down. A mist rolled in from nowhere. He'd wondered how many unwary walkers had died up here over the decades and centuries, and then he'd started imagining that, beneath the mud, the hard layers he felt under his shoes were the mummified corpses of the missing.

It had only lasted for half an hour, but that was the most frightened he'd ever been during a race. His tired mind had played tricks with him, and finally running down out of the hills towards the cheering masses at the finish had been akin to finding himself again.

This place felt ten times worse, and he was more tired than he'd ever been. But he could not allow himself to become distracted. This was still a race, but at the end there was so much more than a medal, a tee shirt and a burger. His family was his prize. His own life hung in the balance more than it ever had. He had to embrace the wilderness, not be intimidated by it. Rose had brought the hunt up here for a reason, and he had to cling to that — it was the most likely place where he could win.

The time would come soon to try to make contact with her again. Scott's phone had lost its signal, the hardy mobile Rose had given him was almost out of charge, but he had the satphone. All he had to do was discover her number on the mobile.

But first, he had to be safe.

Downhill, off the mountain, he followed rough paths worn into the landscape by cattle or wild ponies over the decades. Some had become streams in the torrential rain, and he skipped across these where he could, finding it safer to cover ground he could see. There could be rocks or holes hidden beneath the water.

As he followed one such stream, it disappeared. One moment it was tumbling beside him, the next its waters had vanished, and the torch reflected off nothing but a void of heavy raindrops.

Chris dropped, clasped his hands into claws, dug them into spiky heathers and wet ground. He slipped a little then came to a halt. He was panting hard, heart thudding. He turned and looked in the direction he'd been running. The light was swallowed by the night, the storm, and a million sparkling raindrops. The ground was gone.

He'd almost run off one of the cliffs.

He crawled uphill a little before regaining his feet and setting off again. He berated himself — he must have been running in a semi-daze, on auto-pilot, aware of the small circle of light before him and not thinking about what might lie beyond. He had almost made the Trail's job easy for them. Kill himself and they'd dispose of his family, gather in the hunters, and go about arranging a new hunt.

He had to keep his wits about him. Couldn't let his mind drift. But he'd been awake for almost twenty-four hours, and in that time he must have run thirty miles or more, including his early morning run for pleasure. That now seemed so long ago and a world away.

Chris had to tap into the endurance he had built over the years. He knew that he had a strong engine and a fit body, but as always he had to adapt. While his physical self drove forward, he had to remember at every moment that he and his family were in terrible danger. Endurance sport had a huge mental factor. Physical fitness was never enough, and now that had been complicated even more. But he could do it. Anything was possible, and he had to believe that now. Drive on, keep moving forward, keep planning, and save his family.

There were so many problems still to overcome — discover where his wife and girls were being kept, evade capture by the law, ensure that the hunt continued. But he would succeed. Failure was not an option. He *had* to believe that.

After moving forward for another half an hour he took a break. He needed a piss, and after that he hunched down in a small ravine and took out the phones. The one Scott had given him was blank. He pressed the button, kept his finger on it, waited for the screen to light up . . . but there was nothing.

'Damn it!' He almost threw the phone, then pocketed it instead. Out of charge, perhaps, but maybe he could try again later.

Rose's mobile still worked. It took him a while to discover her preprogrammed number, but as soon as he did he entered and saved it in the satphone. Then he called.

It went to voicemail. He almost laughed out loud. What, was she busy?

'Rose. We need to talk. One hunter's down, not dead but out of it. I'm moving onwards. Heading south, I'm going for my family, and . . . you have to help me. You *have* to. I'm on a satphone now, you'll see the number. Call'

He disconnected, then examined the satphone closer. It had an emergency button. He guessed it sent a signal, SOS, to mountain rescue, pinpointing his location and automatically calling for help. It was tempting . . . but no one could bring the sort of help he needed.

Chris ate a little, then ran on into the night, keeping thoughts of his family close.

★ ★ ★

It was while he was being most careful that he made the worst mistake.

Maybe it was the intense concentration. Focusing on his surroundings might have imposed a form of subtle hypnosis, his attention so sharp and forced that it began to drift and haze. He didn't even notice. He moved quickly forward, checked the terrain with his head torch, switched it off and moved again, and then the ground was gone, the cloudy sky and darkness switched and spun and changed positions, and he was falling.

His awareness of his surroundings vanished instantly, and darkness was the only solidity. Shock sharpened his reactions and he thought, *If I fall for more than —*

He struck ground hard on his left side. His outstretched arm took some of the impact, then his left leg and hip hit as well, smacking pain through his bones and joints. He didn't believe he could make an impact sound like that without breaking something, but his breath erupted from his chest in a loud cough, and he couldn't be sure whether or not he heard the snap or crack of bone.

He slid on something wet — not grass, something more slick — then slipped down a steep slope. Arms and legs waving, Chris tried to halt his movement.

Everything hurt.

He clawed his fingers and tried to dig in, but they scraped over rock, a white-hot pain kissing the fingertips of his right hand. The rifle over his right shoulder twisted hard against his back, stock pummelling his lower back and the strap pulled tight, burning against his shoulder.

The rucksack snagged on something and twisted him around, and for a moment he thought his fall had been arrested. Silence settled, the absence of scraping, shouting, grunting, and his panicked breathing faded in, shallow and hard. He was on his back looking up, and for the first time he thought the underside of the clouds glowed just a little brighter.

Then something tore and he was sliding again.

He hurt, but did not know from where. The pain seemed to shift around his body as he rolled and twisted, as if it too were attached to the ground and he was the only movable object.

He hit a rock hard and the breath was smacked from him. Movement ceased, and as he struggled to breathe — that terrible, winded sensation that he remembered from occasional childhood fights — the sound of loose stones tumbling around him seemed to snicker at his situation.

Chris gasped in a huge breath, uttering a groan of relief when he let it out again. He breathed in several more times, and then the pain began to sink in.

His left side felt battered from the knee right up to his shoulder. His left arm had been twisted and the forearm felt odd. Perhaps it was broken. His right hand felt like he'd dipped his fingers into hot water, and coolness touched them as they began to bleed. There were other aches and bruises, and his right shoulder also felt hot and damp where the rifle strap was twisted tight against the skin. The rifle and rucksack were beneath him, pressed between his back and the rock he'd come to rest propped against.

Fucking idiot! he thought, and panic began to bleed in around the shock. If he'd done some serious damage, broken something vital, then all this might be ended. He could not run with a broken leg. He could not climb with a snapped arm. Even fractured fingers would severely inhibit the ways he had to evade the hunters. Cracked ribs would slow him, bleeding wounds would weaken him.

263

Chris lay motionless for a while longer, trying to analyse the pains as they truly settled in. Nothing screamed at him. He'd fallen before, though not quite so far. A few tumbles from a mountain bike, one of them down a steep slope that luckily had been softened by heathers. A couple of falls from his road bike had given him severe road rash, a nicely stitch-laden scar, and dented pride, but little else. He felt like that now — abused, battered, bleeding here and there, his body finally screaming at the efforts he was asking of it.

He sat up gingerly, cautious not to disturb his position too much. He had to take stock, not only of himself but of his situation. Gingerly he reached up and flicked on his head torch. The beam diffused around him and, if anything, made him feel more enclosed.

It was misty again. Maybe he'd slipped down into a layer of mist, or perhaps it had formed again over the past moments. He knew how quickly it could descend this high in the mountains. The glimpse he'd caught of the lightening underside of grey clouds was no longer visible. He was on a steep slope. Darkness and the mist brought visibility in close, as if the landscape wanted him all for itself.

If he went back up he would risk slipping and falling again. The slope here was not sheer — he could climb on his hands and feet — though if he'd been here by choice he would likely have rope, crampons and proper climbing gear. But there had been that brief moment of weightlessness after he'd fallen and before he struck ground, which indicated a vertical drop of perhaps ten feet.

He was lucky he hadn't brained himself or broken a limb.

Several fingers on his right hand were bleeding. He went to suck the blood from them, then saw the smears of muck streaked with blood. He sniffed. It was foul and sickly, the stench of accumulations of bird shit. Instead, he wiped his hands on his running trousers.

Aiming the light downhill showed the slope continuing before disappearing into the mist. That was the way he needed to go. Down into the valley, then south towards his family.

He started moving that way, edging down on his backside, feet first with his hands propped behind him. The rifle stock snagged on a rock and he moved it aside, trying to sling it at a diagonal across the front of his body. He kept the head torch on.

The ground sloped so steeply that he constantly felt on the verge of losing his grip, and the fear of what he could not see below chilled him. It felt like lowering himself into an abyss that might never end.

The surface changed from bare, loose rock to a layer of tough heathers, and his fingers and heels dug in as he crawled downward. It felt safer, and he was also certain that the slope was lessening.

Maybe I'm almost down, he thought.

But then the slope ended at another sheer drop. He saw it several feet ahead and below him, a space where mist drifted and rolled with no sign of the mountainside below.

Chris made sure he was secure and switched off the head torch. It was a spooky experience. He felt so small and alone, a speck of insignificance in this huge landscape. The mist seemed so heavy that it was cloying, cooling his skin, settling on his tongue when he opened his mouth. Perhaps it was a little lighter than before, but it was so difficult to tell.

He now faced a choice, and neither option appealed to him. He could climb back the way he'd come and try to ascend back up to easier ground. He'd been descending for twenty minutes, and to climb up again would be three times slower. Or he could continue down, descend the sheer drop before him, and perhaps find himself below the mist when dawn came.

That would be soon. But he could not afford to stay in one place until it arrived. He had to keep moving, everything depended on that. The hunters would have seen that he was all but motionless and they'd be coming for him. Perhaps Blondie had another phone he had not found, and he might have told the others not to climb the mountain but wait for their target at the bottom. Chris could be climbing down towards them even now. They'd wait quietly, patiently, watching him moving on their tracking devices, fingers tight on triggers as he came closer, each of them wanting to be the one that made the kill. When daylight came and exposed him on the cliff, he would be in their sights.

Maybe they'd agree to all shoot at the same time, and all claim the kill.

And yet he could not believe they had moved this quickly. Blondie had been fast and fit. The others . . . he hoped they were still struggling across the dark and stormy landscape. If he descended quickly, while it was still dark, he could reach the valley floor and be away before they even arrived.

But Chris could know nothing for sure, and he could not afford to dwell on the situation.

He started climbing down.

★ ★ ★

He had discovered his fear of heights relatively late in life. On a family holiday several years before, Gemma had asked if she could do some high ropes. They were a network of ladders, bridges, and rope structures high in the trees, traversed from one end to the other. Anyone using them was clipped to a safety harness and it was impossible to fall. But Chris had almost frozen.

Even edging up the first ropes, set at an angle and in high tension, he'd not liked looking down. By the time they were almost thirty feet above the ground, his heart had been hammering, sweat slicked his hands, and the only thing that kept him moving was the sight of Gemma progressing confidently ahead of him.

Since then he'd happily look from an aircraft window at the ground far below, but he avoided ladders at all costs.

Head torch on, slipping over the cliff edge and feeling around for footholds, that same consuming fear settled over him. He remained in place for a couple of minutes, toes pressed tight on a narrow ledge, arms spread on the sloping ground before him, fingers clawed into the rugged soil. He'd secured the rifle and backpack, and now they both felt like weights seeking to pull him out and down. Maybe he should leave the rifle behind.

Chris closed his eyes and thought of his family. 'Get your fucking act together!' he said aloud. Then he started easing himself down the cliff face.

He focused. The slope was not quite vertical, but it was steep enough to necessitate care and consideration as to where he next placed his toes and fingers. He sought out each toe and hand hold, moving one limb at a time, testing his weight, shifting slowly. Sometimes the little ledges or cracks in the face were soft with soil and moss, other times they were cool wet rock. He hoped that every movement would be the last one, and that his foot would touch down onto a gentle slope, the beginning of the valley and the foot of the mountain. But the cliff continued.

He was breathing hard, heart hammering, yet he soon became immersed in his task. If he did think of the unknown drop below him his stomach turned, his bowels felt suddenly loose. What was he doing? How *stupid* could he have been? He was stuck out here on the face of a cliff, and if he froze now he might never get moving again. But it would only take a few seconds of searching, locating a ridge or crack, moving, before his mind was set to its task once more.

His left knee was stiff and felt swollen inside his running trousers. The ankle on the same leg was hot and painful. His fingers continued to bleed, wounds not given the chance to clot. The pain was rich and sickly, but he tried to shut it out. Pain was merely a warning that he chose to ignore.

The wind picked up. Gusts prised at him, attempting to tug him away from the cliff. Rain slanted in, running down the cliff face before him. The sudden change in conditions was shocking, yet painfully familiar. He pressed in tight and closed his eyes, trying to become part of the cliff, hoping that if he was still enough the storm would pass him by.

When he opened his eyes he realised that dawn had come, the wind had started to disperse the mist, and he could look down and see how far he had yet to descend.

Chris whined and hugged himself against the cliff as tightly as he could. He realised that he was going to die.

26

drowning puppies

For the first few hours they kept them restrained, seated on a leather sofa in a comfortable living room, wrists tied in front of them with itchy rope and ankles bound with zip ties. But then they let them visit the small downstairs bathroom. They also let them undress, and Gemma's mum swilled their piss-stinking clothes and hung them on a rack above the bath, and while they waited for them to dry they wore big, fluffy towels. Gemma had been worried about the nail — she didn't want anyone to know about it, including her sister or mum — but she managed to slip it into the space between sofa cushions before undressing.

Vey and Tom took it in turns watching them. Tom would sit in the window seat, leg swinging, gun in his belt, looking from the window. Vey would take the larger armchair and scan her phone. Neither of them said much, but they didn't seem to mind their captives chatting quietly.

From the minute they had arrived, Gemma had been storing away information about where they were being kept. Their mum chatted with them, told jokes, doing her best to keep her girls calm while she herself seemed ready to collapse at any moment. Gemma hated seeing her mother like that — shaking, pale, constantly swallowing as if verging on being sick — but she'd already decided that she was the one looking after them.

She didn't know how, or why. She'd never thought of herself as brave. But she was not about to question how she felt.

They'd had only a glimpse of their surroundings as they walked between the van and cottage. She'd seen a barren, wide landscape, mountains in the distance, steep, sweeping slopes closer by dotted with sheep and lined with old stone walls. Staggered fencing prickled one slope, turning it into a patch-work of fields. There were a few other buildings visible through hedges and past clumps of trees, and perhaps some were in shouting distance. Perhaps. She stored that knowledge in the box.

The cottage was large and well-maintained, with a simple garden of lawn and flower beds and a gravelled driveway. They entered through a side door into a big kitchen, passing through to a square hallway with a staircase and three other doors. One of them was the bathroom they'd been using, and another led into the living room. They had been there ever since.

It was a holiday home. She'd seen plenty of signs of that — small, tasteful notices; a folder of brochures of things to do in the area; a visitors' book in the living room — and she stored that away, too. She didn't think it was good news, because these people might have hired the place for a week or two.

They were somewhere in the wilds of Wales. Beyond that she knew nothing.

None of them knew *anything*.

She hugged Megs and tried to comfort her, and their mother held them both. They ate some bread and cheese, drank glasses of milk, and Gemma hated being so hungry. Eating what the bastards brought them implied some sort of gratitude, but she made them know for sure she wasn't grateful. When Vey told her to take the plates through to the kitchen, Gemma dropped them in the hallway and watched them shatter across the flagstone floor.

'You'll eat your next meal off your laps,' Vey said.

Gemma didn't reply. But she thought, *Stupid girl. Don't antagonise her. Don't make her think there's an inch of resistance in you. Put them at ease.*

Her mother asked what they wanted. So did Megs. Gemma asked too, with no need to feign the sudden tears that burned in her eyes. Vey said nothing, merely glanced up at their questions and then returned to surfing her phone. Once or twice Tom gave them obscure answers, which raised more questions than anything else. 'Ask your husband,' he said. 'Tomorrow will tell,' he said.

Gemma hated him. She hated both of them, and the hate helped her maintain the distance that kept at least some of the fear and panic at bay.

As dusk fell and Vey went around the living room closing curtains, Gemma probed down between the sofa cushions and tucked the nail back down the back of her washed and dried trousers. No one noticed. It was cold against her skin, and sharp. Her subterfuge made her feel that she was doing something positive.

★ ★ ★

'Should have had stitches in that,' her mother said later. Megs was asleep on the big leather sofa, head propped against the arm. Gemma sat at the other end, and their mother was between them, a hand on each of her daughter's legs. Gemma knew then that her mum was doing as much as she could. She was keeping control, fighting panic, and not doing a single thing that would risk her daughters' wellbeing.

Gemma was the one ready to take risks.

'It's okay,' she said. 'Doesn't really hurt any more.' She pulled her shirt collar aside and checked the cut on her shoulder. It was crispy and sore, and a bruise was forming around it. She would have a scar.

Vey watched them from the armchair. Several times now, Gemma had seen the woman's eyelids drooping, and she'd felt a flutter of excitement in her chest at the idea of grabbing the gun. It was stupid. Stuff like that only really happened in films. These people seemed slick and organised, they knew what they were doing — whatever the hell that was — and she had the impression this was far from the first time.

But the idea persisted. Vey relaxed in her chair. Her breathing came slower and deeper. Gemma didn't want to do anything to startle her into alertness.

'Good that she's asleep,' she whispered,

nodding at her little sister.

'Yeah,' her mum said. 'You okay?'

'I'm fine, Mum. It'll all be okay. If they were going to hurt us they'd have done it by now.' She knew that wasn't true, as did her mother.

'We should get some sleep,' her mum said. 'We'll be fine, Gemma. We'll know more tomorrow.'

'What do you think Dad's doing now?'

'Don't know.' Her mother turned away as if to dismiss the subject. Something about her changed. She became somehow softer, reduced.

'Mum?'

She was sobbing. Gemma leaned in and pressed her face to her mother's shoulder, reaching across her stomach to hug her, and she could hear the sobs coming from deep inside, feel them translated through her body. But she was trying to keep quiet. Probably so that she didn't wake Megs, Gemma knew, but she kept glancing at Vey, slowly nodding off in the armchair across the room by the large, curtained window. *That's it, keep it quiet, Mum*, she thought, *let's all keep it quiet.*

She thought she could remain strong. But hearing her mother's distress caused Gemma's resolve to slip, become more fluid and uncertain. Your mother was supposed to be the strong one, her warmth a place of safety, her smile a sign that all was well. As her sobs continued, fear threatened to overwhelm Gemma. It pressed in like the loaded shadows, heavy with dread, that she had once believed were trying to take her away.

She'd been eight years old then, and every night for a week she had dragged herself kicking and screaming from sleep, thrashing at sweat-soaked bedding and reaching for her troubled parents as they dashed into her room, arms held out ready to rescue her. The retreating shadows had glared from corners, on top of her wardrobe, and beside her bookcase, but between her parents she had always found a safe place. It was only when she was diagnosed with glandular fever that the cause of such night terrors had been revealed. Their hold over her had soon melted away.

This fear felt the same. An unstoppable force threatened her and her family, and the dread was heavy and slick. It pressed against her, constraining her breathing, dulling her senses. She blinked and the room grew darker. The overhead light had vanished, and a soft glow filtered through the open doorway from the hall. Her mother no longer sobbed, but her breathing was still uneven. Megs muttered in her sleep.

Gemma stood slowly from the sofa, and it felt like someone else. Her limbs were not her own, her body was alien, her intentions were unlikely and distant. She touched the nail down the back of her trousers, then let go and took three steps towards the sleeping woman and her gun.

'Sit down,' a man's voice said from behind her.

She froze. Breath caught in her throat. Fear winded her.

Vey stirred and then quickly stood, grasping the gun from her lap, smiling through sleep-swollen eyes. She pointed it casually at Gemma's face.

I've killed little girls tougher than you.

'Gemma!' her mother whispered, stirring behind her. Megs woke as well, mumbling.

'I could kill you and do just as well with the other two,' Vey said.

Gemma could not speak. No words came to her, and her throat convulsed, struggling to draw in a breath.

'Sit down,' Tom said, walking around the sofa and turning on the light. He'd been sitting at the small table in the corner of the room, keeping watch while Vey slept, and Gemma had not even looked for him.

Vey kept the gun aimed at her face.

Gemma drew in a long, ragged breath, afraid that it might be her last.

'Please,' her mother pleaded from behind her.

Vey grinned. 'Tom, tie them up again. Tight. And gag them.'

The light remained on for the rest of the night, and Vey stayed awake, looking at her phone. It buzzed once and she answered, hung up, and called out to Tom, who was making coffee in the kitchen, 'Still on!' From then until dawn she scanned the screen, chuckling now and then when something seemed to amuse her.

Pictures of drowning puppies, Gemma thought. And each time she closed her eyes to sleep, the promise of that dreadful gun's barrel kept her awake.

27

dawn

Rose popped another palmful of painkillers from the helicopter's first aid kit. Too many and she'd damage her liver. She almost laughed at the idea.

She welcomed the dawn. It came as she faced the Trail woman, casting light on their interaction and bringing stark colour to the situation. Mainly red.

'It's turned out a bit differently to how we'd expected. We knew you were still alive. And we always wanted you to be a challenge, a good hunt for us. But we didn't know if that would ever happen. And we didn't expect you to take control quite so comprehensively.'

'What do you mean, a hunt for you? The Trail?'

'Yeah. You're the one that got away, Rose. Of course we couldn't let it stay that way, and some of us have always wanted to sample what we sell. Believe me, it's always the same. Drug dealers become addicts, pimps screw their whores. I was Trail for only a year before I craved a kill, and I knew others who were thinking the same way.'

'What others?'

The woman coughed, groaning and curling around her stomach wound as if to hug it to sleep.

'What others?'

'Come on. Don't tell me you don't know something. You've been stalking us for years.'

'Not stalking. Hunting. A cold hunt.'

'And the war's just gone hot,' the woman said in a faux gruff voice. She even managed a laugh. 'Bit melodramatic, eh, Rose?'

'Melodramatic? You killed my family, you sit there with your guts squeezing out between your fingers, and you're taking the piss?'

'I didn't have anything to do with that,' the woman said, an element of fear creeping into her voice. Good. Rose didn't like to think that they were indestructible. Cool, calm, superior, almost always in control . . . but not immortal. *I'm sure they can bleed*, Holt had said, and she had proven that statement true. But Rose realised that he'd meant more than blood.

'So what were you doing when they were slitting my children's throats?' Her voice was flat and hollow. Any injection of emotion and she'd have broken down, taken up a rock and smashed in the dying woman's skull. And it still contained information she needed.

'Barely involved,' the woman said. 'I was logistics. Still learning the ropes. Just kicked out of the army for — '

'I don't give a shit about your history,' Rose cut in. 'You're just a voice to me. A source of information. So who killed my children?'

The woman's eyes flickered away from Rose, squeezed half-shut in pain.

'What's your name?' Rose asked. Even pretending to be familiar with this bitch left a stale taste in her mouth, like dried blood.

'Michelle.'

'Keep pressure on the wound, Michelle. Tell me a name and I'll call mountain rescue, they'll take you off to a hospital. I'll let you explain the bullet wound. I'm sure you bastards have failsafes in place for a situation like this. Just one name.'

She saw a flicker of hope in the wounded woman's face, a drifting of her harsh facade.

'You know only pseudonyms. This one you know as Margaret Vey.'

Grin! Rose thought. *It was Grin . . . she killed them . . . and I saw her, I was near her, I could have waited in her house and killed her there and then.*

She stood, whining in pain and grief reborn, pulling the pistol, aiming it at the woman's face.

The bitch who said her name was Michelle held up two bloody hands. In that last moment of her life she became a normal human being — not wanting to die, begging for mercy, mewling in terror and remorse.

'There's more!'

'I don't need more.'

'Holt.'

The name was like a blow to her gut. Rose blinked, trying to tie flailing ends of information together. She could not even grasp them. *Nobody knows him*, she thought. *Unless . . .*

'Go on,' she said.

The dying woman talked.

★ ★ ★

Chris was frozen. He'd had nightmares about situations exactly like this — caught halfway up a sheer cliff, exposed, his weak flesh and blood and bone body insignificant compared to the measureless weight of rock, the endless expanse of open sky. He *connected* rock and sky, both of them seeking to do him harm — the sky pulled, promising a quick fall; the rock pushed, its gravity drawing him down.

Climbing back up seemed impossible. Making his way down, looking between his feet, filled him with dread. Remaining where he was depended on the strength of his leg muscles, the clench of his fingers against sharp rock. Falling held a terrible allure.

He dared to look down again.

The cliff fell away below him. There were cracks and fissures, projections and dark areas, but the remaining descent was near-vertical. The base of the cliff was a litter of tumbled rocks and boulders. He tried to perceive distance, but it was difficult.

It's all scree, he thought. *They're all tiny pebbles, and I'm one step above the ground.* But even though there was little context to assess his height, he knew that was a vain hope. There were a few plants down there, and scatters of pale shapes that might have been a dead sheep's bones and tattered woollen remains. It was at least far enough to die if he fell, and that was plenty far enough.

He pressed his face to the rock and stuck out his tongue, feeling the rush of cool rainwater. He swallowed, grateful for the fluid. The rifle felt heavier than ever on his back, tugging him out and down. Perhaps its reason for being was to deal death in any way it could.

'It's always one step down,' he said. 'I'm close to the bottom. One step at a time. One step down.' But he could not fool himself. He prided himself on his mental strength, but this was nothing to do with strength, or endurance, or the levelling of pain. This was all about falling.

He was one movement and several seconds from death.

Terri, Megs and Gemma came to him then, not tied and terrified, but laughing and happy. That was how he would see them again. And he'd tell them about this, and Gemma would remind him how scared he'd been on the high ropes and how he'd vowed after that to confront his fears, face them and triumph. But after everything he'd done, dealing with that one terror was something that had slipped through the net.

'So this is it, Gemma,' he said. 'This is when it happens. For you and your sister, and your mother. This is me on the high ropes again, only this time I'm running, and you'll — '

A gust of wind roared across the cliff, driving water against his face and squeezing fingers between him and the rock.

'Fuck off!' he shouted. He clung on tighter than ever, waiting for the wind to lessen. Then he started down.

The worst of it was, he had to look. He couldn't risk locating toe holds simply through feel. But he did his best to blur his vision of anything below his feet, not planning the route of his descent, simply the next step. The boulder-strewn ground below was a grey mass, always only a step away. Rain poured down the rock face, and he used it to cleanse the wounds on his fingers, washing grit and blood away. Each time he touched something with his right hand it felt like pressing his fingers against blisteringly hot metal. He absorbed the sensation and cast it aside.

Rocks slipped beneath his right foot and fell away. He held his breath and gripped hard, scrabbling with his foot until he found a solid ledge. From below he heard a sharp *crack* as one rock hit another. It sounded like a gunshot.

Chris held his breath and froze. *I'm a sitting duck!* he thought. He turned his head to look north, out along the looming cliff face and across the lower landscape in that direction. There was no immediate movement, but he concentrated, shifting his gaze slowly left and right across the rugged terrain. If they were there and had already seen him, they'd be creeping forward. Wouldn't they?

'No,' he whispered. No, of course not. If they saw him climbing down the cliff they'd be racing each other to get close enough for a shot. All eager for the kill, there would be no need to conceal themselves from him any more. It would be about getting within range, taking time to aim, and then putting a bullet in him where he clung to the cliff. Then they'd cut off whatever trophy they desired from his broken body and wait for extraction. A posh hotel, perhaps. Nice hot bath, classy escorts to suckle their brave, manly hunters' cocks, bottles of expensive champagne, a dinner bill in the thousands.

He started down again, quicker than before, trying to translate fear into ease of movement.

Close to the bottom, confident that this really *was* the bottom and that the rocks he could see below were almost near enough to touch, he slipped. His left knee struck the rock wall and he cried out in pain, leaning out, arms pinwheeling as he fell backwards.

He hit the ground with a shattering thud, breath knocked from his body, limbs on fire. The only thing that stopped the back of his skull striking solid ground was the rifle across his back. The sky grew darker for a few moments then lightened again, and Chris lay where he'd fallen, twisted between rocks and waiting for the pain to roar in.

I've got the gun, he thought. *If my spine's snapped or my legs are screwed, I can try to shoot them when they get close, at least.*

It was a sickening thought. He didn't want to kill anybody.

The rain had reduced to a drizzle. He remained motionless for a moment longer, looking up at the sheer rock facade he'd just climbed down and marvelling at the gorgeous patterns of water flowing down its surface, touched by slanting dawn sunlight that drew hazy, oily rainbows in several places. He didn't think he had ever seen anything so beautiful.

Slowly, carefully, Chris stood. His left knee and ankle screamed at him to lie back down but he ignored them, stretching his leg past the pain and vowing that he would only feel it when this was all over.

He was not yet down in the valley, but the terrain was more familiar now, and dawn cast its gentle early light across this wild landscape as if to show the way.

It was time to start running again.

★　★　★

The storm had faded away, leaving sheets of rolling mists in its wake. The wind was a gentle breath, the rain had ceased, and the sound of running water rose and fell as Chris negotiated a rocky descent from the mountain. He was sliding down rocks, climbing down waterfalls, stepping and leaping towards the valley floor, none of it as difficult as the cliff he had faced and triumphed over. In pain from his wounded left leg, still he felt good. He was confident that he had a decent lead on the hunters, and now he was waiting to hear from Rose. That was pressing. He tried to bite down his panic, and his fear that either something had happened to her or she had abandoned him. But he knew that if he never heard from her again, he was finished. She was his only friendly link to what was happening. If she had gone, he might as well hand himself in.

He checked his watch, saw that it was just past six am. He had been on the move for almost eighteen hours, and on top of his long run the previous morning, his body was still holding on.

He paused on a relatively flat area of ground,

and as he ate the last of his energy bars the mists before him began to lift, revealing the shadowy spread of the valley before him. He was further down the mountain than he'd thought. Looking back and to the north he could see the dark, sheer cliffs, and further up the mountain was still shrouded in heavy mist. It was a beautiful scene, and it should have been tranquil. But not today.

He tried calling Rose again. Her phone was still off. He left another terse message, then moved on.

His limbs were heavy, left leg hot and stiff, and his clothing soaked in sweat, but he hoped that the sun's appearance over the mountains across the valley would go some way to warming and drying him. He still felt strong and confident. He still had purpose. He considered what his family were going through right now, and he almost screamed with frustration and rage.

If he had, he would have alerted the campers.

He saw the small tent as he mounted a shallow ridge, a bright orange splash on the otherwise bland, rain-washed landscape. It was a shock, although it shouldn't have been. He'd already met the two walkers, and he knew that even the remotest parts of Britain attracted sport and nature lovers. He rested for a few minutes, settling down so that he would not be seen if someone exited the tent. Maybe they were still asleep, or if not they might just be lying there, enjoying their warmth and waiting for the sun to fully rise. As yet, dawn was little more than a glow to the east and a gentle fading of the night.

He considered making himself known to them.

They might have food they'd be willing to share, anti-inflammatories, painkillers. He'd have to hide the rifle beforehand. But he'd been lucky with the first two men. They hadn't recognised him, even though his face seemed to be splashed all across the news. He might not be so fortunate a second time.

And something else also helped dissuade him from meeting these campers. Propped against a rock close to the tent were two mountain bikes. The thought of the rest he'd get travelling on one of those almost made him groan, and as if in response his legs tensed, muscles twisted. The first signs of severe cramping.

He didn't like stealing. So in his mind, he called it borrowing.

Chris had slept in a tent many times, and he knew what it was like hearing strange sounds from outside. Even if they did hear a footstep or a slip on slick vegetation, they'd lie there for a while, breaths held, listening harder and perhaps giggling as they made up some horror scenario. A mountain man, come to eat their hearts. An escaped, claw-handed killer. Anyone of a certain age knew the urban legends.

They'd never guess the truth.

He moved quickly and quietly, fearing that now he'd decided on his course of action, they would wake and unzip the tent, emerge to watch the sunrise. If they did that and saw him with the rifle, few explanations would make sense. He'd have to turn and run, or threaten them. Right then neither held any attraction.

Circling around the tent, keeping to high, soft

286

ground where he could, he made sure he didn't pass close enough to cast a shadow. And ten metres from the bikes, he heard a deep sigh. It was followed by a whisper and some giggles, a pause, and then a louder groan.

Chris froze. Looked at the bikes. Saw that one was a woman's mountain bike. As he listened to the tent's occupants making love like no one could hear them, he moved faster. He made a quick assessment. They were decent bikes, hardtails, still caked with yesterday's mud even though they showed signs of some half-hearted cleaning. They weren't locked up, and the man's bike carried a half-full water bottle, a tool kit beneath the seat, and a bar-mounted bag. He couldn't risk opening the Velcro fastener now, but he hoped there was food and other goodies inside.

He'd never done that much mountain biking, preferring the distances he could cover on the open roads. But he'd ridden some easy trails where he lived, and once or twice he'd been up into the local hills. He'd only fallen off a few times.

The sounds of lovemaking became more frenetic.

The satphone in his pocket rang.

You've got to be kidding me!

He grabbed at the man's mountain bike. The handlebars were wet and they slipped through his hands. The bike toppled, knocking the lady's bike over.

A surprised gasp, whispers, then louder voices.

He lifted the bike again and slung his leg over,

his left leg stiff and heavy. Pushing off, Chris aimed at the nearest slope, wanting to put as much distance between them as possible.

Behind him came the stark sound of the tent zip being whipped open.

He pedalled hard, pressing the shifters to change gear, then launched himself off a gentle rise. He landed heavily but remained upright, wheels spinning beneath him. They threw water up into his face.

'Hey, shithead!'

Chris did not dare turn around. He rode carefully but quickly. Now that he was lower down the mountain the terrain was easier, and his attention flickered further ahead and back to just in front of the bike, scouting his route and making sure he didn't hit a rock or a hole. He stood on the pedals, crouched back when slipping down a steeper slope, used his weight to shift the bike around obstacles.

The satphone had rung off.

Behind him he heard a woman cry out, 'But he has a gun!' Chris felt ashamed. He didn't want to scare anyone, and hated the idea that he'd be the bad guy in this couple's story.

He slammed on the brakes and turned around. He'd already made two hundred metres. The man was shamelessly naked, standing astride his wife's or girlfriend's bike and ready to give chase. She was standing outside the tent with a sleeping bag clutched around her.

'Sorry!' Chris called. The guy gave him the finger. He supposed it was fair enough.

He rode on, glancing back once or twice just

in case the man had decided to pursue him anyway. But he was alone on the mountainside, and within a few minutes the tent was out of sight.

Chris knew he shouldn't go too fast. The hunters must still be after him, and he had to keep things that way. He worried briefly about what they might do if they bumped into the mountain bikers, but there was little he could do about that. He couldn't really return to them and tell them to beware of men with guns, because he *was* one.

And it could be that they'd recognise him. If not now, then next time they checked the news on their smartphones.

He should have never turned around to show them his face. That was stupid.

The satphone rang again and this time he stopped, pulled it from the jacket pocket and answered.

'Rose, you have no idea — '

'We're close, fucker.' The man's voice was high and excited, and even through the crackly phone Chris could hear the impending loss of control. He'd run them through the night, and now they were hurting. But hearing the voice of a man intent on killing him was utterly chilling.

'What *are* you?' Chris asked.

'We see your little blue dot,' the voice said.

'Catch me if you can, you prick,' Chris said. Then he clicked the disconnect button. That was good, the hunt was still on, and it was in his interests to perpetuate that.

But could they really be that close?

He dialled Rose. This time she picked up.

'Chris, listen,' she said. 'I know where they're keeping your family.'

Chris's heart missed a beat. 'Where?'

'Closer than you think. I'm nearing you, but I'm hurt. Find somewhere safe, wait for me. I'll be . . . an hour, maybe less.'

'One of the hunters just called, he said he was close, too.'

'Doubt it, they're probably still up on the mountain. They must be frustrated, hoping you'll rush and make a mistake.'

'How can I believe you?'

'Wise up. You can't afford not to.'

'Where are you?'

'Almost down in the valley, closing on you. Now do as I say.'

'Why are you suddenly so keen to help me?' he asked. If she was the one who'd got away, he wondered how many hadn't. Could he really trust a woman who had brought hell into his life?

'I have my reasons,' she said.

'Screw you. Tell me more.'

'Not like this. We're using their phones, you think the Trail can't listen in, pinpoint calls? Wait and I'll find you.' And she cut the connection.

Chris almost threw the satphone. She was using him again, leading him on, teasing him with what she knew and feeding him just enough information to keep him under her control. He should make her lose control. Find the chip he carried, hide it somewhere — better still, attach it to a sheep or something else — then go out on his own. Find his family. Save them.

'Fuuuuuuck!' he shouted, so loud that his throat hurt. Several small birds took flight from a few metres to his right, startled into the dawn sky. They dipped and swooped down into the valley, and he so wished for their speed and ease of movement.

Maybe Rose had lied about where she was, and where the hunters might be. Perhaps they really were close. It was possible, he supposed. With the exception of Blondie, they hadn't looked like fit men. But perhaps the Trail had picked them up after they'd lost him at the lake, transported them through the night in 4x4s, depositing them close to him once the storm had died down and his location was pinpointed.

The more he thought about that, the more it made sense. These bastards wanted a hunt, but they also probably relished their home comforts. Would they *really* want to stalk him across a dark, storm-lashed landscape?

Uncertainty speeding his pulse, a sick feeling weighing heavy in his gut, Chris took a good look around before starting downhill on the bike once more. He couldn't see any sign of activity. He felt very much alone. But there were times when he could not trust his instincts. Dulled by tiredness, unused to such situations, he had to grasp on to whatever firm knowledge he had rather than feelings and fears that might haunt him.

However much he feared and hated Rose, it could be she was telling the truth, and his family came first.

It started to rain again.

As Rose found the first rough track leading down into the valley — little more than twin ruts on the hillside with hardy plants still growing on the hump in between — she thought of that dead woman's face, and wished she could kill her again. A handful of deaths wasn't enough. A hundred final moments of terror and understanding in Michelle's eyes could not soothe even a scrap of Rose's furious grief.

She glanced at the satphone every few minutes to ensure Chris was making good headway. He was ahead of her and moving fast, but she was moving quicker now, too. She had purpose. The kills she had already made were nestled in the back of her mind, not celebrated, yet propping her up and holding back the fear of failure. Pain was consistent, but she was managing it better.

Soon she would reach Chris, and together they could move on.

A misty rain had blown in while she was standing there staring, the gunshot still echoing in her ears. The moisture was cool, soothing. It diluted blood on the woman's face and washed it across her neck. The hole where her right eye had been still leaked, her left eye half-closed. If only a bullet could have negated all the wrongs those eyes had seen.

At least what she'd been told had stolen away some of Rose's pain.

Holt. A man of the Trail. It was a shock, an agony, the revelation a bullet to the head, the sense of betrayal like acid in her veins. And yet as the haze of shock had faded a little, it had started to make perfect, shattering, sickening sense.

She followed the track, splashing through muddy puddles. The rain fell heavier. Her wound was screaming again, but the agony only added to her determination. She'd been through so much pain, and Holt had taught her how to channel and use it, turn it to her advantage. He'd shown how it could make her more adept at running and hiding, and how it could feed her fury. He said it sharpened senses and focused the mind.

The bastard had been right.

Rose checked the satphone again and saw that Chris's tracking spot had come to a halt. It showed where she was in relation, and she reckoned she was maybe three hours behind him at the speed she was going. She hoped the hunters were further away, that their call to him had been a taunt, that they were still high up on the mountain, injured or exhausted. Because things had changed, and she so wanted to see Chris again.

She was convinced that Holt had already saved her once. News of his betrayal had given shape to the shadow on the mountain, and in her memory of it she saw his thin, gnarly silhouette. But she could not let that colour her judgement of him. She was confused, and she didn't like that. Though much of what Michelle had told her made sense, it had also screwed up her thinking.

It was a good bet that what Michelle had told her was true — she'd believed that she was

293

talking for her life, after all. As well as the information about Holt, she'd also revealed where Chris's family were being held by Grin, and that in seven hours they would be executed.

Rose needed focus and clarity, and with Chris she hoped to find just that.

⋆ ⋆ ⋆

He'd never really experienced the adrenalin buzz that true mountain biking could inspire. Aiming down the mountainside, much of the valley floor still obscured by driving sheets of fresh rain and drifting mists, Chris found himself enjoying some of the more technical descents. Standing on the pedals, hopping down steep drops, using his body weight to switch the bike left and right, feathering the brakes and sometimes coming to an almost complete standstill, he had to concentrate and prepare for a tumble at any moment. But finding a long spread of relatively smooth hillside where he could put on some speed ... that's what really got his heart pumping. The wind in his hair, rain striking his face, clothes flapping, bike bouncing smoothly beneath him as the suspension handled the shock and vibration, he howled like a wolf. It was less an expression of delight than a welcome release of tension, both from his mind and the knotted muscles of his body. Mud splashed, soaking him and the bike as he sped down the hillside, confident in his abilities and welcoming the tang of danger. He'd often looked at the small sign he had pinned above his desk: *Do one*

294

thing every day that scares you.

He'd certainly had his fill today.

At the base of one long slope he paused to look back and up the mountain. He thought he saw movement — a flicker of something bright, perhaps yellow, perhaps orange, slipping out of sight behind a rock. It might have been his imagination, or a trick of the light. The rain grew heavier, waves of it billowing across the mountainside like shaken sheets. It couldn't have been them, not if they'd pursued him up towards the mountaintop. And they must have, because they'd have been tracking his blue spot. It *couldn't* have been them.

But maybe Blondie had contacted them somehow, told them what had happened, and they'd continued along the lower slopes, just missing him at the cliff. If that were the case, they might be very close indeed.

Perhaps it was the mountain biker using his girlfriend's bike.

Or it could have been Rose.

But Chris would not stop, not now. He was close to the lowlands, heading into the valley and whatever might be down there. Trails, roads, maybe even hints at civilisation. Once he stopped, Rose would catch up with him. Then he'd have a chance to see whether she really had anything to say.

And he had the rifle. If for some reason she wanted him to halt for the hunters to finally catch up with him — if that suited her plan more — at least he might be able to protect himself.

The thought came again to call the police, and

at least try to let them know what was happening. The mountain bikers would have almost certainly made the call, and if they could describe him at least half accurately, the law would soon put the pieces together. The hunters would be joined by professionals, and the Trail would inevitably call off their hunt.

Maybe they'd kill him first, maybe not.

Time was compressing, and his future was a darker, closer place.

★ ★ ★

Topping a small rise half an hour later, Chris saw a slope leading down to the valley floor. It was crossed with rough tracks, and bounded a couple of hundred metres away by a tumbled stone wall.

A little way beyond that there was a farm. A sparse tree shaded one wall, a barn with a slumped roof was almost subsumed by bramble and heather, but a wisp of smoke rose from the chimney, soon washed away in the deluge. Sheep dotted the fields and hillsides. They'd have food, drink, and warmth, and if he hid his rifle — and if they didn't instantly recognise him — he could plead ignorance. Just a mountain biker who'd got himself lost.

It was a good place to wait for Rose.

28

rain

The old couple were only mildly suspicious. The fact that they seemed to speak only Welsh appeared not to hamper their understanding of his predicament.

'Thought I'd be off the mountain much quicker. Fell, bent a wheel and broke a few spokes, then a puncture straight after that. So . . . yeah, spent the night up there, cold and hungry. And now this rain, it's almost . . . biblical. Thank you. Thanks so much.'

The old man smiled, nodded, and gestured that he should enter. The woman had already retreated back into the house, and Chris could hear pots crashing and water flowing. He nodded his thanks, but took a moment to glance behind him one more time.

From down here in the valley, the mountains he had spent the night being hunted across loomed massive and imposing, a bulk of peaks and ridges behind the obscuring rain. The valley was still shadowed, the glow of the new day struggling against the clouds and barely pushing an unwilling darkness ahead of it. The sky seemed to reach the ground, as grey and heavy as the solid mountain it hid. For a moment he felt the sheer weight of it drawing on him, stirring his inner tides as if the landscape itself could steer his mood and fate. Perhaps that was true. He had always been aware of his relationship with the land around him, and even though he'd found civilisation he believed the mountains were still in charge. He suspected the old couple knew this. It certainly seemed to appear that they existed to the beat of the land's heart.

The farm could have been part of a rural life museum. Other than an old, mostly rusted tractor parked beside the slumped barn, there was no other technology on show. If the couple owned another vehicle, it was parked out of sight. The farmyard was a mess of mud churned into complex shapes by thousands of boot prints. A rough stone wall extended from behind the house and swung around the yard, linking the house and barn and ending at the head of a track that led along the valley. The track itself was rough, and probably impassable by anything other than a four-wheel-drive.

A scruffy dog hid beneath a lean-to shed at the far end of the yard, looking suspiciously at Chris and the bike he'd so recently stolen. Beyond, sheep dotted the land. There were stone walls here and there, but no real demarcation lines, no patterns of fields. He could hear chickens calling from somewhere behind the house, and he could see the edge of a large vegetable patch.

There was no sign of any power or phone cables leading to the house. He was willing to bet they even had an outside toilet and a spring-fed well as a water supply.

'Well?' the farmer said.

298

'So you do speak English.'

' 'Course. Don't find any use for it, usually.'

'Thank you,' Chris said, meaning it. He went to enter, then thought of the bike. He paused, looking at where he'd left it leaning against the house's stone wall.

'No one to steal it,' the old farmer said. His lip twitched, once, and Chris guessed that was a smile.

'I'll just . . . ' He grabbed the bike and wheeled it across to the dilapidated barn, limping alongside. The dog trotted across the yard and sat close by, staring at him, neither growling nor wagging its tail. The rain didn't bother it one bit.

'Hey, boy,' Chris said, but the mutt seemed not to hear. He slipped the bike behind a timber door hanging from its top hinge, then hobbled back to the house.

The farmer was still waiting by the door, and as Chris entered he closed it tight behind them.

Stepping inside the farmhouse was like taking a step back in history. The woman was fussing at a Rayburn, a huge wood-burning stove that threw out massive amounts of heat and which likely heated the rest of their house, as well as their water supply. Several oil lamps hung from the ceiling and sat on the table and dresser, throwing strange shadows that jiggered and danced as he entered. A large wooden table took up one side of the kitchen, and beyond, a darkened doorway led deeper into the house. Pots and pans hung above the Rayburn, the air was heavy with the smell of burning coal and cooking bacon, and two breakfast places were set at the table, with steaming mugs of tea, cutlery, and a loaf of knobbly bread.

Chris's mouth watered. He could smell the bread, and he suspected the farmer or his wife had baked it fresh that morning. Warm bread. Butter. And there was a jar of preserve, lid off and greaseproof paper slipped aside. Homemade. Probably everything here was homemade, and if they didn't keep pigs here then the bacon was probably from a neighbouring farm, or a farmers' market close by.

There were no photos on the walls of the large dresser that took up one wall, no sign of any children. This old couple had themselves and their farm, and Chris felt an immediate affection for them.

'Can you . . . ?' the man said. He nodded, and Chris realised what he was hinting at.

'Oh, yeah, sorry.' He shrugged off the dripping coat and hung it on a hook beside the door. His running trousers were also soaked. He touched them, looked at the farmer. 'Er . . . '

The farmer shook his head and nodded at one of the breakfast settings. 'Go on, then.'

Chris hesitated for a moment, then looked at the bread again and went to sit down. The chair's feet scraped across the flagstone floor, and the woman looked. She looked as old and grizzled as her husband, but there were laughter lines around her eyes and mouth which screwed up again now.

She turned back to the Rayburn and flipped bacon on its frying surface.

Chris started slicing into the loaf of bread.

The woman glanced back at him. Her face had changed. Not so wrinkled with laughter lines now, but her eyes were darker.

'Sorry, I . . . ' Chris said, pausing from cutting the bread.

The woman shook her head and returned to her frying.

'I'm Arfon,' the man said. 'This is my wife, Jean.'

'Chris,' Chris said automatically, then something jarred inside. *I'm all over the news,* he thought. And though he'd seen no power lines, and the room was lit with oil lamps, he couldn't believe that these people were totally cut off from the world. Maybe in the next room they had a laptop and a forty-two-inch TV, and they simply liked preserving the kitchen as it had been when they were kids.

'Christopher . . . Jones,' he continued. 'From Bristol. Came here two days ago for a bit of an adventure.'

'Well, you've had that,' Arfon said. He sat in the other chair and turned the loaf towards him, cutting a thick slice. 'Bacon?'

'Please,' Chris said. 'Thank you.'

Arfon waved the thanks aside and started buttering his bread. He scooped a huge dollop of jam on, spread it with a spoon, took a big bite. He didn't even look at Chris as he ate. It was almost as if he was no longer there.

I can't relax, Chris thought, listening to the sizzle of cooking pig. *Rose will see that I've stopped, she'll be here in a couple of hours. But* they'll *know that I've stopped too.* He was exhausted, and already the room's heat was tingling his cold skin, making him aware of the wetness of his clothing, and just how sore his legs and feet had become. His hands, too, worn red at the palms by the rough bike handles. He could *not* relax.

'Don't look set for mountain biking,' Arfon said.

'I had a fall, lost my helmet over a steep drop.'

'Mmm.' The farmer chewed, still not looking directly at Chris.

The woman said something in Welsh. Arfon stopped chewing. He glanced at Chris, only quickly, then up at his wife again, talking through a full mouth. They swapped a few more sentences in Welsh, the guttural, difficult language managing to sound both musical and threatening.

'Bacon's ready,' Arfon said, standing. 'You'll be wanting brown sauce.'

Chris looked over his shoulder at the man's wife. She was holding a plate piled with fried bacon, staring at him with wide eyes that now held only fear.

Oh shit oh fuck, Chris thought, and he went to push the chair back to stand, flee, grab the bike from the barn and the gun from where he'd hidden it behind the stone boundary wall, and his left leg seized, knee folding as he grabbed on to the table —

'Nope,' Arfon said. Chris turned, half crouched, and looked straight into the barrels of a shotgun. 'Nope,' the old farmer said again.

'Just stay there for a bit while I decide what to do with you.'

'Cellar,' Jean said, in English for Chris's benefit. 'Door's strong and secure, and you just fixed the lock.'

Arfon smiled, nodded, and said, 'That's why I love my wife.'

★ ★ ★

She was in too much pain to walk, so she ran. It was a headlong, desperate flight, but the speed and carelessness kept her senses alive. It defied logic. But the blood pumped faster, keeping her faint at bay, and the discomfort echoed through her body with each pounding footfall. She throbbed with it, and the pain needed to stay clear and strong. It was her driving force. However terrible, nothing physical could match her mental anguish.

Rose was pleased to see the new day, even though she knew she would not witness the dusk. She'd dreamed of her final day many times, and the chaos and vengeance it might see. Being there, it felt strangely sterile and blank. She hoped killing that bitch Grin would not come as an anticlimax.

Although she ran, injured arm tucked into her jacket, rifle slung over her shoulder, wallowing and almost drowning in a sea of pain, she had to be careful. She checked the landscape all around her for signs of movement. Paused every couple of minutes to listen for aircraft or vehicle engines. Doubled back once or twice to make sure she wasn't being tracked or rushing towards an ambush. There were three hunters still pursuing Chris, and in truth she had little idea of where they might be.

And there were most likely Trail people still after her. She didn't know how many, not for certain. Some would be with Chris's family. Others might have retreated back into their complex, real-life cover stories as soon as this hunt went wrong, severing ties and readying to move forward. But there would be some for whom killing her would remain their prime concern.

She checked the tracker to make sure that Chris's blue dot had not moved. It remained motionless. That could be a good thing, or bad. Maybe he was doing as she'd suggested and waiting for her, or perhaps he was dead. Or maybe he'd taken the time to find it and ditch it, thinking that might help. But she was too eager to reach him to call in and check, and either way she had to get there. She'd find out soon enough.

If you could see me now. The thought of her family shocked her and she moaned as she ran, remembering some aspect about each of them as one, single thought. It was an intense, shocking sensation. And she was right, they'd never know her as she was now. She was glad of that. A killer, perhaps a mad woman, she would not have wanted her children to see her shot and bleeding, nor Adam to look into her eyes and know that she had killed. Rose was a new person.

But she still held her family close. Though they would not know her, she had never for an instant forgotten them.

I'd always know you, bunny, Adam said, and Rose sobbed. She so wished it could be him saying that, and not her hearing it in his voice.

She saw the smoke first, a smudge of white in the vast wilderness. Attuned for danger, senses alight from conflict, the first thing she suspected was a burning vehicle or the trace of exploded ordnance. But as she leaned against a sparse tree and looked into the rainswept valley, she saw the small huddle of buildings.

Checking the satphone's screen, placing the blue glow of Chris's tracker, she knew that she'd found him.

They had a little under five hours left until Margaret Vey expected another call to confirm that the hunt was still live. That call would not come. A few minutes after that, she would murder Chris's wife and two young girls, then flee the scene and vanish. It might take Rose years to find the bitch again.

She took only a moment to survey the scene before starting down towards the farmhouse.

★　★　★

There was a rifle at the base of one of the stone walls. It wasn't hidden very well, but Rose could see that it was one of the hunters' weapons.

Must be the one Chris took. But why leave it? Then she realised why. He was a normal guy, and he'd never have considered taking over the

305

farmhouse by force. Which was stupid.

They might have already called the police.

Hunched down, Rose approached the building across a muddy field. It looked old, ramshackle. No sign of a phone line, but that didn't mean they had no means to call out. The smoke indicated the place was occupied; surely Chris wouldn't have been stupid enough to light a fire in an empty house?

As Rose slumped against the farmhouse's stone wall, dizziness threatened. Her vision faded and senses receded, dulling her surroundings. *Come on*, she thought. *You've only been shot!*

She moved along the wall to the doorway. It was inset slightly, shadowed, the small porch containing two pairs of upturned boots.

Something growled. Rose froze, hand going slowly towards her pistol. Across the yard, close to the dilapidated barn, a black and white shape emerged. The sheepdog growled again, hackles rising. It stepped out into the downpour, unfazed by the rain. All of its attention was on her.

'Good boy,' Rose whispered.

The dog barked.

Rose knocked on the door. It was the only thing to do. She stood slightly aside from the door, and sideways on so she could see across the farmyard as well. The dog was not moving forward, but it remained crouched low to the mud, growling, teeth showing. If it sprang, it would be on her in a few seconds.

Could she have the pistol out by then?

The door opened. There was no cautious shout, no hesitation. An old man stared out at

306

her. In his face she saw years of hard experience, a man well versed with this land and all the dangers it could throw at those who tried to tame it. He was carrying a shotgun, barrel aimed down at the ground in a non-threatening way. His eyes flickered from her face to the rifle on her shoulder, back again.

Rose thought quickly.

'We got your call,' she said quietly, urgently. 'I'm with the police, I'm here to take him into custody. Where is he?'

The man nodded slowly, then looked over her shoulder into the yard.

She glanced right, saw no movement, turned to face the man.

'Got no phone,' he said. He started to raise the shotgun. 'I sent my — '

Rose moved quickly and calmly, seeing that she had time and not wanting to panic. She pushed the gun aside and stepped in close. 'Let go,' she said.

The farmer struggled, trying to step back so that he could free up the shotgun. But she followed him, pressed close to keep the business-end of the weapon facing away from her. She trapped the shotgun between her and the door frame and slipped the pistol from her pocket. She showed it to him. He dropped the gun. It was that simple.

'Please,' the old man breathed, and Rose kicked the door shut behind her and held up her hand. She pulled her wounded arm from her coat. It hung heavy.

'Listen to me. I'm not going to hurt you. You

hear? We're the good guys.'

The man suddenly looked old and terrified, all his years of experience and living off the land clouded by something else. 'Did you hurt Jean?'

'Jean?'

'I sent her for the police. We don't have a phone, and those mobile things don't work up here.'

'How long ago?' Rose asked.

'Two hours.'

'No, I haven't seen her. So where is he?'

'In here.' She heard Chris's voice, muffled by a door. It was across the room, beside the big dining table that took up most of the space. A low door, almost comically small, she guessed it led to a small store cupboard or basement.

Rose felt a flood of relief, unexpected but welcome. She hated putting her trust in anyone else — she'd only done so with Holt since her family had been killed, and his betrayal had planted a cold seed of fury in her heart — but she and Chris had business to finish. Wounded, she would need his help.

'Open it,' she said to the farmer.

He glanced at her gun again. She lowered it, but not all the way.

'I told you, I won't hurt you,' she said. 'But I will ask you for some help. Now hurry. We don't have much time.'

The farmer took a key from his pocket and approached the door. As he unlocked it and it swung inwards, he mumbled something to himself that she couldn't make out.

'What?' Rose demanded.

'Wasn't talking to you, girl,' he said.

Chris emerged, wincing against subdued daylight leaking through the rain-lashed windows. He took in Rose's condition quickly, saw the guns, nodded his thanks at the farmer.

'I'm not what they say,' he said.

'Don't care,' the old man replied.

'Chris, come on. And you, we need some food and your vehicle.'

'Jean took our car.' The farmer shrugged. 'Welcome to the tractor if you can get her started. Damned if I can, more than one time in three.'

'Fuck it!' Rose said.

He raised an eyebrow. 'You have to use such language?'

She laughed, almost manic.

'So where are they?' Chris asked. 'And how long do we have?'

'I'll have to tell you while we're moving.'

'You *can* move?' he asked, glancing at her arm.

'I have to.' She saw the bread and pot of jam on the table. 'You bag that for us?' she asked the farmer. He grumbled something under his breath, opened a drawer in the dresser, pulled out a plastic bag.

While he was doing that, Rose nudged the shotgun with her foot and told Chris to pick it up. Her heart was racing, pulse hammering in her head. She needed water, food, a rest, and medical attention. But there was something she needed more, and she'd not stop for anything.

She swayed on the spot, taking the bag when the farmer held it out, then nodded her thanks to him. She supposed she could have apologised, too. But every word was an effort, and all her effort had to be focused.

'I can't stop moving,' she said. Chris followed her to the door, shotgun held in both hands. He shrugged on his soaked coat.

Rose opened the door onto the storm. The rain was so heavy now that it splashed mud up from the ground, stirring the farmyard into new shapes.

As they moved from the shadow of the house and the door clicked shut behind them, the gunfire began.

29

trust

Rose dropped so quickly that Chris thought she'd been shot. He rushed to the barn and crouched down, then turned around and scanned the farmyard and countryside beyond. The barn protected him only from certain angles of fire. If the hunters had reached them, spread out, taken ambush positions . . .

Rose grabbed his foot. She was down low, crawling in the mud. 'Into the barn!'

'Where's it coming from?'

'In!'

Chris did as he was told, slipping through the gap between leaning door and barn wall. Inside it was musty, puddled with dripping water, scattered with rusting machinery and piles of mouldering bags, split with shards of daylight penetrating the holed roof and cracks in the walls. The perfect place to defend.

'Trapped in here,' Rose said. 'We'll have to break out or we're sitting ducks.'

'But we're under cover!'

'Until they close in. Three of them, two of us, remember. And you with just a shotgun, two shots. We can't cover every angle.' She moved to the far wall and took a look through a dusty window. She was moving awkwardly. She must have smashed her injured arm when she dropped to take cover.

311

The window shattered inwards and another shot rang out.

'They're not close,' Rose said, frowning. 'Whoever it is they're a good shot.'

'How long do we have?'

'Few hours. Maybe less.' Chris blinked, trying not to let desperation get the better of him. He felt faint. He felt sick.

'Is there time to — ?'

'Plenty of time, but we have to get away from here *now*! If that old bastard's wife really has gone for the law, it might all end here.'

'End?' Chris asked, but he didn't need an answer. He knew what that end would entail. He could not think about it, would not allow it. He had to go on. Filled with energy, determination, hope, he was ready to run forever.

'Got to draw them closer,' Rose muttered.

'Get ready,' Chris said. He moved to a narrow, open doorway that would emerge close to the track leading away from the farm.

'What are you — ?'

'Watch for them to break cover!' He didn't wait for a response. There was no time to argue. He ran through the gap, shotgun held across his chest, sprinting past the opening in the low boundary wall where the track left the farm. Halfway across he stepped in a mud-filled hole and tripped, slipped, holding the shotgun out with one hand as he tried to keep his balance. Something hissed past his head, flicking his hair, and the shot sounded a moment later. He found his footing again and dived behind the far wall. Two more shots came from much closer by. The shotgun banged against his chest. He scanned the yard, the farm buildings, the other stretches of boundary wall, expecting to see camouflaged shapes sliding over them at any moment. If he did, he'd open up with both barrels.

He hadn't even checked to see if the shotgun was loaded.

'Chris!' Rose called.

'Yeah.' He was panting, heart hammering in fright. His knee screamed. If he'd fallen, he'd have been a sitting duck.

Rose appeared low at the doorway he'd just run from. 'It's not them.' Her eyes were wide and wild, he couldn't tell whether it was fear or excitement. Both, perhaps.

'What?'

'There's a vehicle across the fields. It's the Trail. Hopefully just one of them.'

'How?'

'They've been tracking you too, remember? I've already killed three of them up there.' She frowned, looked aside. 'Four, I guess. One of them told me the tracking chip's in your running shoes. So they'll be coming for me, too.'

'My family?' he asked.

'The hunt's still on.'

'You know that for sure? You've killed seven people, and you know for sure they're not just pulling out, abandoning the whole thing?'

'Eight. I bagged one of the hunters. And yeah. I know'

'How?'

'Because while those fat bastards are trying to kill you, the Trail are supposed to be hunting me.'

Chris frowned, trying to process things.

Rose shook her head. 'Doesn't matter! Not now. I know where your family are, and we have to get there.'

'Yes!' he said. But he could see that Rose had her own reasons. Of course she did. This had always been about her.

'I'm getting back into the house,' Rose said. 'Give me two minutes. Upstairs, I'll be able to see a lot further, should get a good shot. Watch for me. When I signal . . . ' She gestured with her head.

She wanted him to make himself a target once more.

Chris nodded. Rose disappeared back into the barn, and a moment later she exited the main door. He watched her crawl quickly across the muddy yard, rifle over her shoulder, and could barely imagine the pain she was putting herself through.

From somewhere away from the farm, someone whistled, high and sharp.

They were signalling. Which meant there was more than one.

Chris waited for more gunshots but none came. But there was *something*. A rapid, pattering sound, like heavy rain hitting muddy ground, yet audible even above the deluge. Chris shifted where he crouched, tilting his head to try to make out exactly what he was hearing. He blinked rain and sweat from his eyes.

The farm dog appeared from around the far corner of the house. It slunk forward a few steps then settled in the mud, growling.

Dogs! Chris thought. The pattering was footsteps, and they were growing rapidly closer. It sounded like more than one.

'Rose, I can hear — !'

A shape leapt over the stone wall in the farm's rear garden, slamming into a lush green bean frame, knocking it over, thrashing around and then emerging. Growling. Running.

Rose had seen it. She rolled onto her side and dropped the rifle, rolling back to pick it up and aim it at the running animal.

It was a huge dog. Chris wasn't sure of its breed, but it looked as mean as murder. Saliva flicked around its head as it ran. It passed the house and skidded on the muddy yard, front legs splaying in opposite angles as it slid towards Rose.

She fired her rifle and tried to roll, crying out when her weight landed on her injured arm.

The dog barked, a surprisingly high yelp from such a big beast. It slid to a standstill and did not get up, but continued squirming, legs kicking as if to move itself away from the pain.

Rose glanced back at him, then stood in a crouch and ran for the farmhouse. She hit the door with her good shoulder and disappeared inside.

Behind him, Chris sensed movement. He turned in a crouch, trying not to raise his head above the stone wall.

The Alsatian stood with front paws on the wall twenty feet past the open gateway, surveying the farmyard with a startling, chilling intelligence.

It saw Chris, growled, lowered itself slightly,

then jumped completely onto the wall, dropping down into a clump of nettles and brambles without hesitation.

Chris lifted the shotgun. It was like a dream, a nightmare, the situation so unreal that he felt like someone else performing these movements and thinking these thoughts. He could smell the wet mud, hear the dog's companion whining and kicking across the yard, feel the white-hot stiffness in his knee and the swelling in his left ankle, but this might as well have been a game on Megs' Xbox. He saw blood splash his vision and a starry crack across the screen of this nightmare, heard Megs saying, *Aww, Dad, you're crap at this*, but this was a game he could not lose.

The dog leapt free from the plants and ran at him.

He had no time to aim. Still seated, he pointed the gun and tried pulling the trigger. Nothing happened.

Barking, the little farm dog skittered across the yard towards the big Alsatian. The Alsatian stopped, turned, growled.

The sheepdog paused a dozen feet from the bigger animal and barked, jumping left and right.

The Alsatian did not hesitate. It ran at the sheepdog, snapping out when the farm dog tried to scamper away. They became a storm of twisting, barking, snapping, and yelping, difficult to discern which was which. Flashes of white from the sheepdog, brown and black from the Alsatian, and then a shocking splash of red, accompanied by a high, pained yelp.

Still keeping below the top of the wall, Chris turned and readied himself to dash to the barn. He glanced at the farmhouse but saw no sign of Rose at the windows. He wasn't going to wait for her, not when he risked getting his throat ripped out when the Alsatian had finished with the other wretched creature.

The animal Rose had shot had stopped kicking and now lay motionless, its chest rising and falling rapidly as it panted itself towards death.

A shot sounded. He heard no bullet, no impact or ricochet. Another two shots close together, and these sounded like they were from a different weapon.

Screw this, Chris thought, glancing at the farmhouse windows once more. He took in a breath, prepared to ignore the molten pain in his left knee and ankle —

Someone slipped over the stone boundary wall close to the farmhouse. A man, short and lean and carrying a rifle, dressed in jeans and a white tee shirt, soaked to the skin and looking completely out of place. His eyes were wide as if in shock. He saw the dead dog and paused. Then he looked directly at Chris.

Chris raised the shotgun, aimed, and pulled the trigger. Nothing happened again. 'Rose!' he shouted. He tried to find a safety switch, something else. Tried pulling the trigger again. '*Rose!*'

There was a second of complete, unreal silence.

The shooting had stopped, the dogfight

behind him was over, the breeze was stilled to a held breath.

The man brought the rifle to his shoulder and sighted at Chris.

Chris ran for the barn as a fusillade of shots rang out, explosions that echoed around the yard and slammed into his ears.

He smashed into the barn door and fell inside, splintered wood falling around him, one shard smacking him on the head and drawing blood. It gushed into his eyes. He waited for the pain to kick in from a bullet's impact, the darkness to come. But he felt and saw neither.

Outside, someone screamed, 'Motherfucker!' It was a horrible sound, high and wretched. Two more gunshots echoed into silence.

What the hell was that? Chris thought, and the dog entered the barn. It was big, surprisingly silent, standing amongst the remains of the door he'd crashed through. When it bared its teeth both they and its muzzle were bloody.

Chris wiped blood from his eyes and felt around the shotgun for a safety catch, sure that he'd missed something simple, and then the Alsatian jumped at him. Holding it in a shooting grasp he brought the gun up, its barrel meeting the underside of the animal's jaw with a solid thunk. He took a step back and stumbled, the Alsatian landing on its back legs and coming for him again. As he fell, Chris swung out with the shotgun's stock, catching the dog across the shoulder.

Its teeth snapped shut so close to his face that he could smell its breath, meaty and foul. Its claws scrabbled to drive it closer to his throat, ripping down his stomach, crotch and thighs, and he cried out as he felt and heard his running trousers being shredded.

Chris rolled and threw the dog from him. It landed in a jumble of loose gardening tools and several of them fell across its back.

It was a natural reaction when the dog crouched down away from the falling implements, and equally natural when Chris knelt and brought the shotgun up over his shoulder, both hands around the barrel, stock smashing down on the back of the Alsatian's head.

The impact was so hard that the stock snapped from the gun and clattered across the barn's wet floor. The dog whimpered, eyes rolling in its head, tongue lolling. Chris felt a flash of pity.

He paused and listened, trying not to breathe too hard. He was shaking from the confrontation. Blood blurred his vision and ran down his stomach and legs. The dog scratched weakly at the concrete floor.

He had no idea what was happening outside. Maybe he should go out through the broken door, climb the wall, creep along to where he'd hidden his own rifle a couple of hours before. What if Rose had emerged and been shot? What if he was left alone, without knowing where his family were being kept or exactly how long he had left?

Then he heard Rose's voice, and he knew that she was still with him. As the enraged shouting began, he went to see who else had arrived.

'You complete bastard.' Rose was too angry to shout. She aimed the rifle at him and he let her. Her finger stroked the trigger, keeping an even pressure close to firing, just a gentle squeeze to change her life. This death might not be so clear and easy to handle. Everything was becoming more complicated, and she didn't like or need that. Revenge was simple, but this was something different.

'Don't shoot me,' Holt said. Of course, he knew that she would not.

'What am I supposed to do with that?' The farmer stood framed in his doorway, a big man who'd led a harsh life, but now looking scared. He stared at the Trail man slumped against the wall. Blood glimmered darkly on the man's white shirt, and his head bobbed with each desperate breath.

'Go inside,' Holt said. The old man did as he was told, and the gentle click of the door closing seemed to silence them all.

Holt raised an eyebrow at Rose, then shrugged.

'What, so you're sorry?' Rose asked. He wouldn't care about her anger, or what he'd done, or how he'd lied to her. And neither should she. What she *should* care about was why he hadn't finished what he'd begun.

Maybe he was here to do just that.

'I can say that if you want to hear it,' he said.

'Rose?' Chris asked, but she ignored him. She wished he'd go inside with the farmer and stay there, let her get on with what she had to do. He'd only inconvenience her. But then the pain in her arm pulsed, seeming to clutch her bones and crush, melt, twist them, and she realised that she could no longer do this on her own.

But she'd rather be dead than do it with Holt now.

'You're one of them,' Rose said.

Holt actually laughed. 'What, one of the people I've been killing? I've saved your life once already, and I just saved his, too.' He nodded at Chris.

'And if he'd been killed, I'd have taken that fucker out when he went to check on him.' She pointed at the shot man. He'd grown still, chin touching his chest. She could see no movement. He'd died while they were talking. She didn't think she recognised him, but that meant little. He was Trail, that was all that mattered.

It still should have been her that killed him.

Chris looked stunned at what she'd said, but she didn't care.

'You called me, remember?' Holt said. 'Asked me for help.'

'A long time ago. You refused me, told me I had to do all this alone. And you were right.'

'I usually am,' Holt said, a mild attempt at humour.

'So did Michelle tell me the truth?' Rose asked, though she was already certain. It was no surprise that Holt knew exactly who she was talking about.

'She could only know their side of things.'

'So what's your side?'

'What does it matter?'

She frowned, considering that. Really, what *did* it matter? But she found herself thinking of the reasons for his change, more than what he'd been and what he had become.

'I just want to hear why you lied to me.'

Holt carefully slipped his pistol into a belt holster. He looked around, constantly alert. He barely seemed to notice Chris standing there. 'Didn't you learn even a shred of what I told you? Trust no one, Rose. Only yourself, and only then if your motivations are clear.'

'You were teaching me all that for a hunt.'

'And now you're hunting.'

'But it was meant to be the other way around. I was the one that got away, so the Trail thought it would be fun to hunt me down. But they wanted me worth the effort.'

'Yes. I was supposed to make you proficient at shooting, running, fighting. And I was then supposed to hand you over to them. They'd have kept you on ice, locked up somewhere until they could set up their own hunt. Then they'd let you go, maybe even give you a head start. But I taught you more than I should have — how to hide and live below the radar, for one. And I did that because I grew to like you. Admire you.'

'Bullshit.'

He sighed, looked around again. 'We need to move.'

'We?' she almost spat. 'No fucking way. You're Trail, and there's no way — '

'Not any more.' He waved the idea aside like an irritating insect.

'How many people did you kidnap and kill?'

'For the Trail, none. They didn't care about anything, and I severed my ties with them the minute I left you in that restaurant.'

'And you do care?'

He raised his eyebrows as if offended and surprised that she even had to ask.

'Me,' Rose said, suddenly understanding. 'You care about me.'

The Frenchman turned away. 'After you left, I made myself vanish. I knew I could look after myself, keep off their radar, and I was confident you'd manage that too. I'm pleased you did. They've got no honour. One of you is worth a hundred of them, and I — '

Rose dropped the rifle, stepped forward and struck him across the back of the head, a clumsy hit. He stumbled forward.

'Don't follow me any more!' she shouted. She hit him again, more force behind this one. His head flipped forward, her knuckles sang. He almost slipped in the mud and she barged into him, shoving him down, falling onto his back and hitting his shoulder, his head, with her one good hand.

'Rose,' Chris said behind her, but she ignored him.

Holt took the blows. She felt no weakness in him, only strength. No submission, only a calmness. She wasn't hurting him at all.

Not physically.

Rose pushed on his back to stand again, staggering back from where he lay splayed in the mud and shit. 'Don't track me, or try to be my guardian fucking angel!' she said. 'If I ever see

323

you again, I'll kill you.'

He stood slowly, wiping mud from his face, running a hand through his greying hair and flicking muck at the ground. He remained facing away from them, looking up at the mountain looming to the east, and for a moment Rose thought he was going to turn around and strike her back. But then he said, 'No you won't.'

She glanced at Chris and nodded towards the track. Chris hesitated, then darted to the wall, climbed over, and came back with his rifle. All the time Holt stood with his back to her, and Rose stared at the back of his head. There was no way she could even pretend to understand what was going on in there, but she thought she had an inkling. She'd come closer to knowing him than anyone else in a long, long time.

'There'll be at least two of them,' he said at last. He paused, as if expecting her to shout at him to shut up. When she didn't, he continued. 'Wherever the family are being held, one will be close to the prisoners, the others further away, keeping watch. They'll communicate with each other, but the only outside contact will be the regular calls to say the hunt is still on. They won't receive those calls any more. This Trail cell is denuded, and this hunt effectively over. You have a few hours before that call fails to arrive and they kill your friend's family. Then you'll both be ones who got away, and they won't stop looking until you're both dead. Unless their hunter clients reach you first, of course.' He laughed quietly. 'Though I've no pity for them if they do.'

If he expected thanks, Rose disappointed him. She kicked the dead Trail man onto his side and searched his pockets. She found some loose change, a takeaway menu, a wad of tissues, a credit card, a condom wrapper, but no keys. The barn obscured his vehicle from view, but she thought it was a Jeep. They could use it, get where they were going much quicker.

Holt had taken a few steps and now sat against the farmyard wall, ankles crossed. Rose did not catch his eye.

'Come on,' she said to Chris. She picked up her rifle and slung it across her back, then climbed on the bike he'd found somewhere. He frowned, then started jogging along the track and away from the farm. She gripped the handlebars with her left hand. It was years since she'd ridden a bike, but it came back quickly.

The wheels made a constant wet whisper as they rolled through the mud.

After a minute she paused and put her left foot down, turned, looking for Holt. But he had disappeared. Of course. He was a shadow.

★ ★ ★

'Who was that?' Chris asked.

'Someone who helped me after my family was killed.'

'He was Trail?'

'Seems so, for a while.'

'And you didn't kill him.'

'No.'

He was confused. But it didn't matter right

325

now. The man had helped them, then melted away into the landscape once again. Whatever history there was between him and Rose, its telling would last until later.

'Wait here,' she said. 'Hold the bike. If I find the keys I'll wave you over.'

Chris took the bike and watched Rose crossing the uneven ground towards where the Trail man had left his vehicle. Even wounded she moved with an economy of effort that would have made a distance runner proud. He took the opportunity to assess his own wounds. The knee and ankle were both swollen, hot, stiffer than ever. He could run with them and ignore the discomfort, but he knew that he was doing more and more long-term damage. That didn't matter. The fingertips of his right hand were still raw and burning, the wounds clogged with muck and clotted blood. He'd need antibiotics and a tetanus jab.

The dog had scratched him across his stomach and groin and down his right thigh. He lifted his shirt to check the wounds and groaned when he saw the rich red scrapes, pearls of blood blooming all along their length from his chest to his belt line. Holding his breath he pulled his running trousers and underwear out and checked his groin. The scratches continued, just missing his most valuable parts but scoring his right thigh in two vivid lines.

'Put your cock away,' Rose said. She was back already, breathing hard.

'No keys?' Chris asked, looking past her. The Jeep was parked almost out of sight behind a small hillock, but even the glimpse of white bodywork looked so welcoming.

'Nope, it's locked up tight. Maybe he hid them.'

'Or maybe Holt has them.'

'Maybe. Come on, let's go.'

He almost suggested going back to ask Holt for the keys. But the man had already vanished, and Chris knew that time was ticking. The police would undoubtedly be on their way. And now that they had a firm destination in mind, every minute counted.

They moved out.

Rose had said the now dead Trail woman told her that his family had been taken out of Cardiff and were being held in the small village of Llwybr south of here. They'd been moved when Rose had interrupted the Trail's plans, bringing them, the hunters, and the Trail cell sent to kill Rose closer together. The Trail had a converted barn in the area where they entertained rich clients. Feeding them well, drinking good wine, laughing and joking as they planned to kidnap, hunt and kill an innocent man or woman. They'd talk about what trophies to take — ear, nose, cock. Then open another bottle of wine.

The rain started hammering down again, turning the rough track into a quagmire. It was so heavy at times that it almost crushed him down, weighing on his head and shoulders, pushing him towards the ground. It washed sweat from his head into his eyes. It soaked him to the skin, weighing down his clothing, its coolness soothing his many aches and wounds.

He usually loved running in the rain, but not today.

Exhausted, Chris ran faster. Rose called out for him to slow down, she wasn't used to riding a bike, especially one-handed, and especially in such weather. But he could not slow down, only speed up. Accelerate towards the future.

Because now he *knew* how this could end. They had time to get there, just. And perhaps they still had the advantage.

30

big ears

When she was a kid, Gemma's dad sometimes called her Big Ears. She'd drift around the house, not *trying* to be silent but doing so anyway. She liked to huddle down in the strangest of places to read — under the stairs, beneath her bed, behind the sofa — and more than once she had revealed knowledge of a conversation her parents had assumed was between the two of them.

'Dad, what's a fucking prick?' had elicited howls of pained laughter and red faces from her mum and dad.

'None of your business, Big Ears,' he'd replied.

She was Big Ears again now. Leaning across the arm of the sofa as far as she could, ignoring her mother elbowing her foot in an attempt to urge her back into a seated position, hands once again tied behind her back, she tried to calm her breathing and swallowed to make her ears more sensitive.

A new person had arrived moments before and Tom, Vey and she were having an urgent, whispered conversation in the kitchen.

Gemma caught parts of it. Every part sounded bad.

' . . . killed Michelle and Javier and . . . fucking unbelievable,' the new woman said.

329

A mumbled question.

'No, someone else is . . . from out of nowhere. A guy . . . '

'And the target?' That was Vey asking that. Her voice, though quiet, seemed filled with concern.

' . . . yet, but . . . today.'

'Today, one way or another.' That was Tom.

Her mum nudged her foot, harder. Gemma kicked back at her mum's leg, shook her head. This was important. They sounded unsettled. Something was wrong.

More mumbling, then a pause.

'In there, tied up and gagged,' Vey said.

Gemma heard the footsteps and squirmed, struggling to sit upright before Tom swung the door open. He saw her. She opened her eyes wide and he knew that she'd been snooping. *Big Ears*, she heard her dad saying.

What's today, one way or another? she wanted to ask.

Tom stared at her, his eyes cold and dead.

Gemma struggled upright and turned away from him, looking across the room to the window along with her mum and Megs. Vey had opened the curtains, and they could see past the simply maintained garden and stone wall to the wild landscape beyond.

Tom clicked the door closed and the mumble of voices continued, words now unknown.

Gemma wished she could talk. She looked at her mum, eyes wide, but there was no way to communicate everything she was thinking, not even a part of it.

Someone's been killed, names I don't

recognise. *I heard them say. We've got to try something. This is serious, Mum. They haven't said what they want, or why, so I don't think this is really about us but . . . it's serious. They're serious. They don't carry guns for nothing.*

Her mother smiled and leaned sideways, pressing her forehead to Gemma's.

Over the next few minutes, Gemma drew the nail from the back of her trousers, manoeuvred it so that the tip point was upwards, and started plucking at the rope around her wrists. She pricked herself several times, and the blood started to lubricate between the rope and her skin. Her hands turned easier. The binds felt looser.

It's only pain, she remembered her dad saying when she asked him how he could run so far, and how he kept going when it started to hurt. *It's there to tell you something's wrong, but if you know something's wrong and are prepared to accept it, you can make it go away. And you never remember what pain feels like.*

Feeling the welcoming pain, and then instantly forgetting it, then doing it all again, she gripped the nail in her right fist and started twisting her arms back and forth against the rope.

31

tracks

'Stop!' Rose shouted.

'No, there's no time, we have to — '

'Fucking stop if you don't want to get shot!'

Chris came to a standstill and looked back. He seemed relieved when he saw that she wasn't actually aiming a gun at him. Then he must have seen the look on her face.

'The old coot's wife really did go to the law,' she said. 'Come on. We don't have long.'

Chris came back and helped her off the bike, following her away from the farm track and across the sodden moorland. He wheeled the bike with him, trying not to snag the pedals on ferns.

He pointed towards a copse of gnarly trees, and Rose followed.

The sound of a car engine was still distant, but the mountains kept the motor's growl contained, echoing it back and forth. The track was in very poor condition, and even if it was a four-wheel-drive it would take a while to get here. They had to find cover close to the road, so that as soon as the vehicle had passed they could move on again. It wouldn't take long for the police to make it to the farm and find Chris and Rose gone.

They reached the trees and the small hollow they grew around, a stream twisting along the bottom. The stream was wide, boiling, and Rose could see grasses swaying just beneath the surface. Before today this must have been a calm spot, but now the stream was in flood. It was a perfect place to hide. The trees would shade them, enabling them to look out towards the rough road.

But they had very little time to rest.

'Don't get comfortable,' she said as they crouched down, and Chris stared as if she was a fool.

'You think I want or need to rest?' he asked. He looked at her supported arm and bloodied clothing. 'I'll have to leave you behind.'

'No you won't.' She'd seen him hobbling, and his clothing was torn by the dog's claws. He carried his own wounds, she knew.

'If you slow me down, I will. I'm not waiting for anything or anybody. If I run as fast as I ever have before, I'll reach the village in maybe three hours, without disruption. Then find the place, figure out how to get in . . . ' He stared at the ground before him, frowning intensely as if he could find the solution in heather and mud.

'It'll be fine,' Rose said. 'I'll be with you, and I can help. Take this moment to catch your breath. They're coming.'

It was a police Land Rover. It was too far away to be sure, but she thought the vehicle contained three people; the one in the back had grey hair. She wondered whether the officers were brave or stupid, driving up here on their own to confront an armed man wanted for multiple murders. But it was likely that they knew the farmers, and after

333

calling in armed response, their first reaction would have been to go to help the old man. Stupid, then. But she could not help admire their bravery.

'The track,' Chris said.

'What?'

'Look!'

She looked. The long, snaking line of the wheel trail, filled with silvery water, was obvious. Beside it, Chris's spaced footprints.

'They won't see them,' she said.

'You sure?'

No, she wasn't sure. Rose touched the gun in her belt. She couldn't do it, she wouldn't — not police officers, or an old lady — but as far as they were concerned, they were facing at least one murderer. The fear would be enough.

'Rose . . . ' Chris said, looking at her hand resting on the gun.

'Of course not!' she said. The fear in his eyes, and the doubt, almost shamed her.

As the vehicle passed them and bounced up the track, Rose nudged him. 'Come on. No time to waste. Soon as they know we're not there they'll turn around. They'll have put the call out. Won't be long until this place is crawling with police helicopters and armed response units.'

'And then?'

'Doesn't matter. We won't be here.' She struggled to push the bike up out of the hollow, thankful for his help when he grabbed the saddle and heaved.

'You're faster than me, even on this,' she said. 'So you set the pace. I'll keep up.'

'You sure you're not going to — ?'

'I'll keep up!'

Chris nodded and started jogging across the rough ground back towards the farm track.

She *had* to keep up. There was no alternative, no way she could do anything else. Grin was at the end of this, and Rose would use a knife to cut it from her face.

A few minutes later she heard a distant crack. She braked gently and tilted her head to one side. Another shot, from back the way they'd come. She didn't want Holt's help, but she could do nothing to reject it now.

At least if the police thought the shooter at the farmhouse was Chris, it would keep them there. She only hoped that he wouldn't be shooting to kill.

'What?' Chris called from up ahead. He was panting, but he cut an imposing figure of determination and fitness. She'd barely noticed it before.

'Nothing,' she said. 'Keep on running.'

They followed the farm track for another half an hour, and as each moment went by, Chris impressed her more. He'd always been a means to an end. A way to get to the Trail, draw them into the open, damage their plans and then hurt them. She'd done that, and would do so some more, for as long as she possibly could. But as she watched him running ahead of her, she saw him as a human being as well. A man desperate to help his family, and so close to ending up like her. All it would take was three gunshots, three slices of a knife, and he *would* be like her. Bereft,

335

grief-stricken, lost. She couldn't imagine any-thing worse.

Rose decided then that she would not let them ruin another life. This was now as much about helping Chris as satisfying her own need for revenge.

He'd been running for a day and a night, and looked as if he'd only just begun.

★ ★ ★

Chris was beyond exhausted. He'd moved into that zone where it was almost entirely mental attitude keeping him going. He'd been there before — during his first marathon, then his first ultra-marathon through the Lake District moun-tains, and then his Ironman race — and in some ways that made it a little easier. He knew he could run through the exhaustion and pain. He knew that a strong mental approach could defeat physical exhaustion, for a time at least. He was lost in the running, existing in a world where one step in front of the other was all that mattered. Each step took him closer to his wife's smile, his daughters' giggles. Against them, the pain in his knee was nothing, the dog scratches and hot-spots of blisters forming on his feet meaningless.

He felt time closing in, and the faster he ran, the better chance he had of beating it to the line. If that meant leaving the woman behind, so be it. If she fell off the bike and broke a leg, fainted because of her gunshot wound, or aimed a gun at him and ordered him to halt, he'd just keep moving forward. He was an unstoppable force, and the only immovable object that would stop him would be death.

Rose didn't care about his fate or wellbeing. Everything was on his shoulders, and Chris discovered that he was strong. He'd developed a solid can-do attitude with his fitness and challenges, and he fed on that now more than ever before. Not finishing this race had never been an option.

His family drew him on. They were closer than they had been since he gave his dozing wife a kiss before leaving for his morning run. Closer than that last glance he'd given his sleeping daughters. He'd felt happy leaving them all, knowing that they still slept and dreamed, looking forward to his long jaunt through the hills and countryside that set him up for the day, made him feel alive.

He would never be happy leaving them again.

At last they came to the end of the farm track. It had been rough going, probably more so for Rose than him. But running out onto the potholed tarmac road, leaving the mud and puddles behind, felt good on his feet.

It also meant that they were getting nearer to civilisation.

He couldn't be seen. The risk of being recognised was too great. He pulled his running cap from his pocket and slipped it on, then chuckled to himself as they started off again. He and Rose were carrying fucking rifles over their shoulders. Hiding his hairdo would do little to protect him from discovery.

The road followed the widening stream at the valley bottom, twisting left and right and crossing over low stone bridges when the terrain necessitated it. They passed several junctions, always heading south. He guessed the other directions led towards other remote farmsteads. It felt like they were really moving now. His left foot grew more painful, his knee stiffer, but he fed on the pain. It made him angry.

The bike wheels whirred behind him as Rose free-wheeled down a long slope. Then the road veered upwards again, and he heard her heavy breathing and grunting as she pedalled hard. She had to change gears partly by crossing her left hand over to the right. He didn't slow down. Maybe she'd have been happier running, but he doubted it. Once she gave him the bike, he'd be gone.

He thought of shoving her off and just taking it. But he knew that he'd need her. The violence yet to come was her game.

As the road started to climb out of the valley, heading for a ridge that looked a long, long way up, they saw a car heading down towards them.

'Off the road!' Rose shouted. Chris was already jumping the narrow ditch and leaping from rock to rock, and he heard her gasp as the bike went over.

He turned around. She was down in the flooded ditch, bike on top of her with the back wheel still spinning. She struggled to keep her head above the water, groaning as it washed through her wounds, left hand slapping at the ground as she tried to haul herself out. They locked eyes.

338

Chris went to help, hauling the bike from her and slinging it over his shoulder. He held out his left hand and she grabbed on, squeezing, nodding her thanks as he pulled her upright.

'Food,' she said. 'And water. Just until they go by, we can have a minute's rest.'

Chris wanted to object but knew that she was right.

The car was an old VW van. It sped past without slowing, and there were no signs that Chris and Rose had been seen. They drank some water and ate the farmer's bread and jam, crouched down behind a tumble of boulders. As soon as the van was out of sight, Chris stood to move on.

'Can't we just . . . ' Rose said, not even finishing the sentence. She could barely speak. Blood soaked her shirt and jacket arm again from the reopened wound.

'No time,' Chris said.

She glanced at her watch, nodded, and stood up.

Shooting shattered the silence. Whoever it was, they were close, and there was more than one gun. But they were also bad shots.

Chris dropped. Rose was already down, twisting to bring the rifle from her shoulder.

'Trail?' he asked.

'No. This is scatter shot, and we were sitting pretty. If it was them they'd have made sure they hit us the first time.'

'The hunters? They can't have found us, how could . . . '

'Fuck,' Rose whispered.

'Tracker.' Chris looked down at his shoes. He should have ripped them apart, changed them, but with everything that had happened he'd forgotten. And honestly, he had never believed that these men could have caught up with them, not now, not this far away. He'd been trapped in the basement for over two hours, true. But had they really run through the night like him?

It didn't matter.

'Wait here,' Rose said.

'Don't kill them!' he said.

'What?' She sounded dumbfounded.

'Just . . . shoot to injure, or something.'

'That's harder than shooting to kill!'

'Please!' So much killing. He felt sick at the thought of more.

Rose shook her head. More shots sounded, wide and wild. She peered around the rocks and looked for some time.

'They're coming down off the slopes,' she said. 'All three of them. Give me your shoes.'

'Why?'

'I'm going to lead them off. I know what I'm doing. Remember, they don't know that we know about the chip. If we did, we'd have got rid of it by now.' She shook her head. 'Fuck sake.'

'Hey, I'm not like you, I just didn't think of it.'

'I was swearing at myself. Come on. Shoes.'

He slipped off his trainers. It felt divine, but he knew it would be torture putting them back on again. Rose kicked off her own boots — they'd be too small for him — and pulled his trainers on.

'Euch. Warm and wet.'

340

'You should be honoured.' He tried to smile, but his weak attempt at humour didn't go that far.

'I won't be long.'

'Don't,' he said. 'I'm going to take the bike.'

'No. Wait.'

'Tell me where the Trail's barn is.'

'So you can go on without me?' She shook her head. 'No way. I've got as much business there as you. If you get there before me you'll mess things up.'

'But what if they kill you?'

'They won't.' She nodded at the bike. 'Take it, but wait for me. Couple of miles along the road, find a safe place and give me . . . an hour.'

'Half an hour,' Chris said. 'Then I'm gone and I'll find the place on my own. I mean it.'

'Chris, we've got to shake these bastards from our tail, you know that.'

'So hurry.'

Rose pursed her lips, and he thought she was going to argue some more. But she could see his determination.

'Wait here for ten minutes, then go.' And she was gone, creeping away from the road and across the countryside. Chris watched her until she disappeared, hidden by folds in the land.

He crouched down and waited behind the rocks, rifle resting on the ground before him. After a couple of minutes he risked a glance, looking across the road and up the gentle slope opposite. He saw two men lumbering down the hill, heading for a point several hundred yards along the road. One was the fat one, and he

341

couldn't help admire his resilience. The other had gone almost completely Rambo, stripping off his shirt to reveal a fleshy, pale torso, mud smeared across him, running in the rain. He could not see the third man.

He watched them struggling to run, obviously close to exhaustion. They remained close together, and every now and then the fat one consulted something in his hand. He pointed ahead and they continued, reaching the road and crossing quickly, guns held at the ready.

Chris readied himself to move, then heard a soft, low voice.

'Here we go. This is it. This is it!'

He closed his eyes, breathed softly, and started to turn around.

'Wait . . . wait, keep still . . . ' the voice whispered, panicked, excited. 'Gun down. Now!'

Chris continued turning around, gun held pointed down, and made eye contact as quickly as he could. 'My name's Chris Sheen,' he said. 'My daughters are called Megs and Gemma. I'm their dad. My wife is Terri, and she's beautiful. I have a family like yours.'

The hunter's eyes were wide, glinting with shreds of madness. His camouflage gear was heavy with rainwater and mud. He was breathing hard. He gave no sign of hearing, or processing what he heard, and Chris knew then that appealing to the man's humanity would be useless. This had gone way beyond that.

'Here we go . . . ' the man said, and his whole body tensed as his rifle ceased wavering.

'Safety catch,' Chris said.

The man frowned, glanced down at his weapon, and tilted it slightly to the right.

Chris fired from the hip. The blast was deafening, the recoil jarring, and as the man flipped back onto the ground Chris brought the gun up to his shoulder and aimed at his torso. His finger remained tight on the trigger, ready to fire again.

The man had dropped his gun and clasped both hands to the left side of his stomach. Blood bloomed. He groaned, then started to whine as he rocked gently from side to side. He might have been crying, but his tears were lost in the rain. Chris felt a surge of fury. How *dare* this bastard cry?

Gunfire came from along the road. Chris glanced that way but could see nothing, and he had to assume Rose could deal with them herself. Two quick shots echoed across the landscape, then after a few seconds, two more.

'You fucking shot me!' the man on the ground said through gritted teeth.

'You'll live,' Chris said. The disgust he felt, the rage, the smothering sense of unfairness, all pressed down to suffocate and crush him. But he could not allow that. He was better than them. 'Can you walk?' he asked.

The man sat up slowly, both hands pressed to his side. The bullet must have barely touched him, passing straight through the overly fleshy part of his hip. He took his hands away, examined the wound, and said, 'Yeah, think so.'

Chris took one step closer and shot him in the right shin.

This time he screamed. His leg smacked against the ground and settled out of shape, the unnatural angle making Chris gag. He kicked the hunter onto his back and picked up his rifle, slinging the weapon he'd just used over his shoulder.

'Chris!' Rose was calling from a long way off. There was a side to her voice that he didn't like, so he crouched down and listened again.

The man he'd shot was still shouting. Chris prodded him in the chest with the rifle and held a finger to his lips. The man, eyes wide and face now pale as snow, bit down on his lip until it bled.

'Chris!' she called again.

He heard footsteps running along the road, growing rapidly closer. *Heavy* footsteps. He was shielded from the road, but once the man drew level he'd be able to see them both. He decided not to wait that long.

Taking a deep breath, Chris braced the gun against his shoulder and stood.

The man was barely ten metres away, running with his rifle held across his bare chest. He wore a camouflage head-scarf and had mud smeared across his body. Sweat and rain had washed it into streaked patterns. It was the Rambo character, lost in his own fantasy. The image should have been comical but wasn't. He was a fat, stinking pig of a man, and Chris came so close to shooting.

'Stop!' he shouted instead. The man skidded to a halt and looked around, still not seeing him. 'Gun down . . . slowly.'

'He means it!' the shot man shouted.

For a split second, Chris thought the fat man was going to try to bring his own rifle up to shoot. *I won't hesitate*, he thought, finger tightening on the trigger. 'You want to die?' he asked.

Rose appeared along the road, running a few steps before shouldering her own rifle.

'You've got one second,' Chris said.

The man threw the gun aside and fell onto his front, arms and legs held out in a star shape.

Rose lowered her rifle and ran. Chris expected to see a fresh wound, pale face, glimmering blood, but she reached him quickly and nodded once.

'The other one?' he asked.

'Dead.' Whether she'd done it on purpose or not didn't matter to Chris right then. All that mattered was that they were wasting time.

'You, fat fuck. Down there.' He nodded across the ditch and behind the rocky pile to where the other man still writhed in pain. The fat man crawled from the road, leaning across the ditch and scrambling up the other side.

'Can't just leave him,' Rose said. 'He'll run, get help.'

The fat man was not helping his hunting companion. He sat apart from him, staring at Chris and fearing his own fate. He was barely human. Chris wondered if he had kids and a wife, but he didn't want to know. All this was making him feel sick to the core, despairing of the humanity that he'd had such faith in. These men were the minority, he knew that. But knowing that even a small minority like this existed tainted everything.

'Have fun explaining this,' he said.

The fat man's eyes went wide. Chris aimed. The man shuffled backwards, back pressed against a rock, grew still. Chris fired and missed.

'No, no!' the man shouted, and he turned to scramble away.

'Chris —' Rose began, but he shouted over her.

'Keep still or I'll just shoot into your gut!'

The man settled again, resting on his side, shivering.

Chris aimed and fired again.

The man's right knee exploded. He was so shocked, the pain clearly so intense, that it took him almost a minute to start screaming. In that time Chris and Rose stripped both men's trousers and underwear down their wounded legs, smashed their satphones, took their remaining food and ammunition. Neither had any water left.

Chris took a pair of walking boots. Rose kicked his running shoes into the ferns and slipped her own boots back on, and he felt a curious pang as they went. He'd run hundreds of happy miles in them before all this, and discarding them was like casting aside part of his history.

They left without a backward glance. Chris saw Rose giving him an admiring appraisal, and he almost shot her as well. She had made herself into a killer, and he did not crave her admiration for what he had done. He was not like her. He still had a life, if only he could save it.

32

safety

They dodged two more police cars before they reached the point where the road passed over the high ridge. The cars were travelling quickly, and Rose hoped that they would pass by the dead man and two survivors without spotting them. With luck, the wounded and humiliated hunters would have hidden away, waiting for the Trail to come and extract them.

They didn't know that most of this Trail cell was already dead.

Chris had watched as she'd dragged the man she'd shot further from the road, not offering to help. Fair enough. He'd already seen more violent death than any normal person ever should.

Looking down into the next valley they saw civilisation at last. Walls and hedges criss-crossed the landscape, road surfaces glimmered silver with rain, and a couple of miles away the small village of Llwybr huddled low, dwarfed by the expansive landscape. Weak daylight reflected from windows and car windscreens.

'Close,' Chris said. She heard the hope in his voice and it cut deep, surprising her, reminding her that her own life was now without hope. They might yet save his family, but whatever rage-filled revenge she continued to exact on the

Trail, her own was still dust. Nothing could bring them back. Tears mixed with the rain to cloud her vision. Death and murder had tainted her, and yet in the purity of Chris and his family, perhaps she could find some peace.

'There'll be at least two of them,' she said. 'One or two keeping watch, another close to your family.'

'With a gun at their heads.'

'Yeah.' She pulled a smartphone from her pocket and accessed the screen, relieved to see reception. She opened an app, entered the name she'd been given, and Goytre Barn appeared on a map. Touching the screen brought up a small compass in the corner, and she turned until the map shown lined up with the wide vista before them.

'Plan?' Chris asked.

'We've got just under an hour until the call's due,' she said. 'They'll know I'm here, and some of what I've done. But hopefully, they still think the hunt is on.'

'So?' He was panting, sweating, determined.

'So we don't have long. And we need to hit the barn quickly and without warning. We waste time looking for the one who's on watch, that might warn whoever's at the barn.'

'You know them, don't you?'

She didn't answer. Her arm was numb now, but she could feel the damage that had been done. She was past exhausted; her eyes burned with tiredness, her muscles were weak and watery. But Margaret Vey smiled in her mind's eye, drawing a knife across her husband's throat

348

while her children watched.

'I call her Grin,' Rose said. 'She's the woman who killed my family, and the one guarding yours.'

'She's done it before.' Chris's voice sounded flat.

'She won't do it again.'

He nodded, looking down into the valley. They could not quite see Goytre Barn from here — it was too far away, hidden in the wrinkles of the land — but he was close to his family, close to winning. She didn't dare tell him how unlikely it was that he'd ever see them again.

'We'll go in from two directions,' she said. 'If one of us runs into the guards, the other one will get through.'

He looked at her, doubtful. He didn't trust her, and she could hardly blame him. Selfishness had been her driving force, and perhaps it still was. But now she could see that his own triumph might be hers as well.

'Really, Chris. I'll do everything I can.'

'And your guy won't help us again?'

'Holt? No.' She shook her head, although she wasn't sure. He'd have escaped from the farm, she was quite convinced of that. And he'd come this far to protect her because . . . he'd fallen in love with her? She hated even considering that because it felt like such a betrayal of Adam and her dead children. But the truth was there before her — in his abandonment of the Trail, the ease with which he'd let her go in Italy, and the fact that he was here now. Confronting it, she wasn't quite sure how she felt. And that confusion troubled her even more. 'No, we're on our own.'

'Okay,' Chris said. 'The guard will be close to the barn, he'll want to stay in touch. And as soon as he hears any trouble . . . ' He shook his head. 'Got to be a better way. Come on. We don't have long, let's think while we've moving.' He started running again, the hunter's walking boots slapping hard at the road surface.

Rose pushed off on the bike and rolled downhill after him.

★ ★ ★

We're so close, Chris thought. *Nothing can go wrong now. I can't let it. I* won't.

Running in the stranger's boots felt unnatural. His feet were heavy, legs fluid, muscles hot and aching. Blisters burned on his feet, and his groin felt chafed, nipples sore and bleeding from where they'd rubbed back and forth across his breathable top. His left knee was stiff and hot. He'd suffer for weeks, but he'd suffer for so much longer if he didn't push himself onward with every shred of determination he could muster.

The barn was across the valley on the eastern slopes of another, smaller mountain. The looming bulk was harsh and steep, great swathes of rock having broken away and tumbled down over the aeons. People didn't think about that when they built their villages and dwellings. They didn't consider the vastness of time, and the chance of another huge chunk of mountain breaking away and burying them all. Time would wear away the whole mountain, but it was an order of time that did not affect a human lifespan. Chris often thought about this, how a human's life was nothing. And yet the lives of those he loved were everything, and he'd tear away at the mountain with his bare hands for every remaining second of his life if he thought it would save them.

The road veered south, away from the location of the barn, so he climbed over the stone wall and started across the fields. Rose called for him to slow down, let her catch up, but he didn't listen. If he stopped now he might not start again. After all he'd been through, the idea of getting there a minute too late was too terrible to contemplate.

He yearned to see his family again. Hold them to him, hug them tight, tell them that everything was going to be all right. What came after . . . he could not think about that right now. That assumed survival, and beyond that was a whole different world. He would open the door to that new existence only when the time came, and not an instant before. Chris was not a superstitious man, but he would not tempt fate.

The field became marshy and he had to pick his feet higher, lifting his knees to wade as much as run. Behind him, Rose was struggling with the bike. He could hear her grunting and cursing, and then there came a single shout and she cast the bike aside. She was running after him now, and he admired her determination. She'd kept going all through the afternoon and night before, and she was pushing on now. Even with a wound in her arm. There was something special about her, or perhaps her quest for revenge was really a form of madness. Would he go mad if he reached the barn only to find his family . . . ?

He tried to shove the images away, but the more he pushed the more insistent they became. Terri, the girls, and blood. His eyes watered. *No!* He ran faster. The rifle strap had rubbed his shoulder raw and the stock bashed against his lower back with every step. Everywhere was pain. The few parts of him that didn't hurt felt numb and strange, as if they had no part here.

He climbed into another field, paused to locate himself in the landscape, glanced back to Rose. She was close, struggling across the field but no longer urging him to slow down. Her face was grim, pale but resolute. She caught his eye and nodded for him to go on.

How long? She'd said an hour, but maybe it was less. Maybe it was half an hour, or twenty minutes. Perhaps Rose was starting to believe they were minutes too late, and they'd close in on the barn in time to see the two Trail members leaving in a Land Rover, the building behind them still echoing to his family's dying screams.

Chris ran. He had always run, but it had never been towards anything so important.

The end of this run meant his whole world.

He crossed a wider spread of marshy land, aiming for the areas where sharp marsh reeds grew, hoping that meant drier land. The ongoing deluge drowned out the splashing and his groans of effort. Sometimes he went up to his knees in mud, but he was still strong. He pulled through.

Rose was almost keeping up with him. He

352

wondered at the boundaries she was crossing. Pain, exhaustion.

They reached another road, and looking slightly uphill towards the mountain he saw the barn at last. It sat on a flat area of land on the gently sloping hillside, several outbuildings surrounding it. Smoke rose from the chimney. That almost stopped him in his path, because it was such a homely sight. Someone wanted heat, and comfort, and warm water. He wondered whether the two Trail gave a shit about his family's comfort, and knew that they did not.

Whatever the outcome of this hunt, surely his family were doomed from the beginning. Even if the hunters had found and killed Chris, how could his family ever be released? They'd have a story to tell, if only a small part of the whole truth. And the Trail could not afford that.

But this was not his world, he had no idea how these things worked. He was just a fucking architect.

Maybe they'd been dead since yesterday morning.

The thought was sickening, but he could not let it influence him. He shoved it aside.

Rose reached him and grabbed his arm. He pulled away and went to set off again, but she kicked his foot from under him, tripped him, fell across his body and pinned her arm across his throat. She was panting so much that she could barely talk, but she screeched out in pain from her injuries. Chris had to respect her force of will in carrying on. He tried to buck her off, but she increased the pressure. The gun was pressing painfully into his back.

'Wait,' she gasped at last.

Chris shook his head beneath her arm.

'*Wait!*'

Chris relaxed a little.

'Vehicle.'

Chris listened and heard a distant motor.

'How long?'

'We've got half an hour. Long enough. But we can't be seen.'

He struggled again, but Rose was stretching to look over the tall reeds, up towards the barn and its approach road. When she saw the vehicle she let Chris up at last, but kept one hand on his shoulder to make sure he stayed out of sight.

'Saved by the post office,' she said. 'We'll see where the guard is now.'

The red postal van bounced along the barn's approach road, moving faster than it should have. Even from several hundred metres away Chris could hear the van's chassis bouncing from the uneven road surface, suspension groaning, metal screeching.

'Too fast,' he said.

'Yeah.' Rose knelt up and slipped the rifle from her shoulder.

Chris crouched, watched the van, scanned the barn's surroundings, saw no one. He wanted to start running again, to get there as soon as he could. But getting himself shot in these final moments would serve no purpose at all.

'Can you shoot from this far?' he asked.

'Long shot.' That was all she offered.

As the van neared the barn its brakes slammed

on. It slewed to the side and struck a stone wall, throwing up a fan of mud. The driver's door opened.

Holt, Chris thought, *it's him, and he's come to help me save my family.*

But the man who emerged was much taller than Holt, and definitely not a postman. He wore casual clothes and carried a machine gun slung over one shoulder.

'Fiona!' the man called.

Closer to Rose and Chris — much closer, maybe only two hundred metres away — a woman emerged from behind a rusted cattle feeder. She was short and lithe, wearing a heavy waterproof jacket and carrying a Kalashnikov.

'What's up, Tom?'

Tom walked from the van and leaned against the stone wall. 'It's definitely all gone to shit,' he shouted. 'Fucker had help, that Rose woman from a few years back. And she's still out there somewhere. We're compromised, cell's wasted.'

'No shit?' Did this new Trail woman care? Chris wasn't sure. Perhaps only for herself.

'Rose!' he whispered urgently. She touched his mouth with her hand, never taking her eyes from the exchange.

'Margaret inside?' Tom asked.

'Yeah.'

Tom seemed to sigh. He looked up at the mountains around them, and for a moment Chris thought the Trail man was smiling. He muttered something then, shaking his head.

'What?' Fiona asked.

'I said it's a damn shame,' Tom called. 'Come

on. Let's help Margaret clear up.'

'Clear up?' Chris muttered. He went to stand. Crouching down here, hiding, waiting, could do nothing. He had to keep moving forward, one step in front of the other.

'We'll give them one minute — ' Rose said. But Chris was done giving them time, and done listening to her.

Rifle held at the ready, he shoved with both feet, launching himself away from Rose and out into the open.

He ran.

Tom saw him first, eyes going wide, right hand fumbling for the machine gun hanging from his shoulder.

Then Fiona turned around.

★ ★ ★

Fucking idiot! Rose thought, but she couldn't blame him. If she'd heard that fucker Tom right — and over this rain, that wasn't guaranteed — it sounded like they'd already killed Chris's family. Now there was nothing left to fight for but revenge.

It had kept her alive for so long. She let it guide her now.

She brought the rifle up to her shoulder, aimed, and fired in one motion. Chris was between her and the woman, Fiona, but Rose could not let that stay her finger. His only chance was her first shot.

Fiona's head flipped back as the bullet struck her in her face. She stiffened, then hit the ground like a fallen mannequin.

Chris ran on, shooting at Tom as he went. It was pointless.

Tom crouched behind the wall and let loose a burst of machine-gun fire. The range was long for such a weapon to be accurate, but Chris dropped and sought cover. It was what Tom wanted. He sprinted for the barn.

Rose fired at him three times before he reached one of the outbuildings. If she hit him it didn't seem to slow him one bit.

'Chris, circle around!' she called, hoping the instruction reached Chris but not the Trail man. She started moving forward, eyes on the barn and outbuildings.

Chris stood, swaying. His face was splashed red, but he was beyond caution. He started running again, limping badly, veering slightly to the left to bypass a dip in the ground.

Tom darted for the barn's front door. If it had been open, maybe he'd have got inside.

As he stood struggling with the handle, Rose braced herself into a shooting position, shutting out the pain, aimed, fired.

The bullet smacked Tom against the door. He slid down, leaving a smear of blood on the old oak.

Rose readied to fire again but the barn door opened and Tom slumped to the ground. There was movement inside. She eased her finger from the trigger.

She wanted to see Margaret Vey's face as she killed her. Wanted to kill her slowly, make her feel every moment of it. A bullet through the skull was much too kind.

The door slammed closed again, and Rose felt an instant of regret. If Chris's family were still alive, maybe that one shot would have saved them.

But the moment was past.

Rose followed Chris towards the converted barn, alert for movement at the windows. Grin would certainly be watching.

Chris reached one of the outbuildings but did not pause. He ran across the tended lawn and pressed up against the barn's wall.

Rose passed the woman she'd just shot. Half her face was missing. The other half was pale and attractive, and she wondered what made a young woman like this do the things she'd done.

Money, of course. But that was the least of it. The Trail were as bloodthirsty as the clients they served.

A window smashed and Rose ducked down. But no gunfire came.

'I'm leaving here!' a voice called, and Rose felt a wave of nausea. Margaret Vey. The woman she'd dreamed of killing for so long, and who now was less than a rifle shot away. 'I'm coming out, and you both need to step back and drop your weapons. Both of you!'

'No way!' Rose called. She was close to the edge of the barn's garden, hidden in a field of ferns. She lifted her head a little, saw Chris. There was blood on his face and neck. His eyes were wide. He was in the same place, gun across his chest, not knowing what to do. If he dropped the gun and walked into view, she'd likely shoot him. Rose didn't think he could see her, but she still held up her hand — *Stay there!*

'I have three of them in here,' Grin shouted. 'I'll kill the first two quickly! He'll not want them all dead, I'm sure. Not all of them. Three seconds and I send the first one out to die.'

'No, don't!' Chris shouted, and then there were squeals from inside, and then a gunshot.

'No!' Chris ran for the door, passed it, ducked around the smashed window.

Rose readied herself to hear the gunshot that would take Chris's life.

★ ★ ★

He saw them.

Terri, his dear wife, in her jogging bottoms and tee shirt. And his girls, Megs still wearing her pyjamas, Gemma in wrinkled school clothes, dried blood on one shoulder. They were sitting on a sofa, Terri in the middle. Their arms were tied behind their backs. Their ankles were bound. They wore gags, but their whines could not be constrained when they saw him.

The woman from the van was crouched behind the sofa, gun pointing at the window.

Chris went to lift his rifle, but she was turning slightly towards him, and he saw not an instant of doubt or hesitation in her face.

He dropped down and back as she fired, and the bullet whispered by close to his face. He'd already been shot in the cheek by the machine gun. He didn't know how bad it was, his entire face burned and blood flowed, but he didn't

359

care. As long as he could still see, stand, shoot, he didn't care.

Rose was running across the garden. She signalled that he should stay down as she headed for the front door.

Where was the guy she'd shot, Tom? Chris didn't know. Badly injured, at least, but that didn't mean that he couldn't fire a gun.

'Last chance!' the woman shouted. 'I'm sending Megs out the window now, and if I can't see you both standing there with guns on the ground, I'll blow her brains all over you!'

No no no! Chris thought, but he could see no other way. He hated the bitch using his daughter's name. The woman meant to escape, and she'd happily kill them all to do so. If she had only one hostage, it would be easier for her.

As she'd said, killing the first two would be quick.

'Okay!' he said. 'I'm backing away, dropping my gun!' His jaw and face hurt when he spoke. He sounded desperate.

Rose frowned at him from by the front door. He raised his hands — *What else can we do?*

Rose tried the front door, and from deeper in the house Tom called out, words lost but his alarm obvious.

'You try the front door again and I'll start shooting them in here!'

Chris stared at Rose. Desperate. Hopeless. To have come so far . . .

She lifted her jacket and showed him the pistol in her belt. He signalled for it. She shook her head.

Chris scurried along the barn's wall to Rose, whispered, 'She'll be watching you, not me.'

Rose shook her head again. The woman was the one she'd come here to kill, and to hand over that task to Chris —

Chris grabbed her shoulders, ignoring her wince of pain. 'It's not all about you,' he whispered.

'Yes it is,' she said. But he could already see that she was wavering.

Chris reached for the pistol.

Rose tensed. Then let him take it. 'You'll have to be very quick,' she whispered.

Chris nodded as he tucked the pistol into the waistband of his running trousers. Everything was moving very slowly. He wished he was still running and could run on forever, but sometimes things had to stop. Every race came to an end.

'I'm coming out!' the woman shouted.

Chris and Rose threw the rifles onto the grass and backed away, but not too far.

Megs appeared at the window.

★ ★ ★

Gemma had thought they were fireworks. But only for a minute. Vey's reaction made her hear and see the truth. Their captor dashed from the room, more shooting sounded, and the heavy front door opened and slammed again. She returned a few seconds later carrying a big gun. She moved quickly and calmly, but her eyes were wide and Gemma heard her fast breathing.

There was blood on her hands.

Gemma, her mum and sister pressed in close. Megs whined behind her gag. Gemma looked at her mum, wishing she could communicate something about what she was doing, what she had in her hand. But through the sudden sting of tears, all she could do was smile with her eyes.

Vey scooped up a potted plant and threw it at the window. The glass was single glazed, and it smashed, the pot cracking and spilling soil and roots across the carpet and windowsill. Gemma had a flashing, crazy vision of her own body doing the same. Breaking, falling, spilling —

Vey came at them with a knife. Megs squealed, their mother writhed against her restraints, Gemma tensed. But Vey said nothing as she knelt and slashed the ties binding their ankles.

And now she'll go for our wrists and she'll see what I've been doing and I'll have to try to get her, because everything's happening now and I might not get another chance.

Panic hovered at the periphery of her senses, sharpening them. But that curious distance also remained, and while events moved quickly, Gemma was able to observe and absorb, slowing things down and settling her thoughts as much as possible. If she looked at her mum and sister again she might lose it, so she breathed deeply, feeling the warm nail in her right hand and the bloody, burning pain where she'd been working her wrists against the rope.

Vey disappeared behind the sofa, but she didn't cut their ropes. Instead, she knelt and rested the rifle across the sofa's back. Its barrel

362

touched Gemma's neck briefly, shockingly cold.

Vey started shouting.

Gemma closed her eyes. She heard the hated woman's voice but it was only volume, a song of hatred, and she ignored the meaning of the words. It aided her concentration. Her right hand slid from the loop of rope, and it felt like someone was pouring acid on her hand, stripping skin and scouring exposed nerves. She shivered with pain.

But that's okay, she thought. *She'll think I'm scared. And that's good.*

And then she heard her dad's voice and everything changed. All the coolness, the concentration, were swept away by a terrible sense of dread and hopelessness, and though she wanted to remain quiet Gemma squealed loud and long against her gag.

A gunshot smashed into her ears, her head, thumping at the centre of her. Dust rained down around them, and all sound receded. It faded back in slowly; Megs crying, coming in from a distance to Gemma's ringing ears.

Her dad appeared at the window. There was something wrong with his face. He was bleeding. But he saw them, and Gemma saw him.

He fell back just as Vey fired the rifle.

The noise slammed Gemma's hearing to nothing, and she realised that the previous warning shot must have been from the smaller gun. It was like the whole world had exploded. The impact was a physical thing, seeming to bruise her ears and head. It sent a wave of pain through her whole body, and Gemma grabbed hold of this.

The pain, the nail. She clasped them both, because she knew they might both help her.

The pain, the nail. The rage.

★   ★   ★

Rose felt curiously distant. No longer armed, she was not part of this any more. She was an observer, and whether Chris killed Grin, or Grin killed both of them, was now out of her hands.

She had spent so long trying to maintain control that it felt terrifying to be helpless.

But Chris had been right. Grin would be watching her, not him, because she was the greater threat. And the only slim chance they had of stopping her killing them all — because she would try, Rose had very little doubt about that — was now all on Chris's shoulders.

She heard his gasp as the gagged little girl appeared at the ground-floor window. A rifle barrel smashed away more glass, then a bloodstained hand dropped a small rug over the sill. The kid sat up on the windowsill and was shoved through. Her arms were tied. She fell to the ground and hit hard, but it was a flower bed, and she rolled and sat up. Her eyes were wide with terror as she struggled to her feet. She stared at her father.

Rose couldn't help thinking of Molly, sitting up dead with blood in her ear, and she resolved to do anything to avoid seeing this girl become the same.

Another shape appeared, the older girl. She followed Megs through, swinging her legs out first and managing to land on her feet.

'If you run I'll shoot your mummy!' Grin shouted.

Bitch. She was going to shoot them anyway. She wanted a clear shot at Chris and Rose, then the others — the innocents, those who were not a threat — would fall last. Rose glanced sidelong at Chris and hoped he knew that. He'd been shot in the face, the wound pouting, fleshy. He was shaking slightly, difficult to read. Yet staring at his daughters, his eyes seemed clear, his expression neutral. *Trying to stay calm*, Rose thought, but she didn't really know this man at all.

A woman came through next, Chris's wife, hands also tied behind her. And then Grin. She kept the woman close to the window as she climbed out, rifle barrel pressed into her back. Then she stood behind the woman and two children.

The older girl backed up against her mother. There was something about the girl's expression. She was scared, but also tensed. Eyes wide.

'Hello, Rose,' Grin said.

Rose did not answer. She watched Grin appraising the situation — the rifles on the lawn, Rose's injured arm, Chris's face, their empty hands. She seemed almost satisfied.

Rose took a small step to the right, just enough to attract Grin's attention, make her alert. The bitch watched her intently.

As she stepped out from behind her hostages and lifted her rifle towards Rose, Grin tried to put them at ease. 'Okay then, now we can all — '

'Safety catch,' Chris said.

Grin paused, smiled. She didn't look down at her weapon, because she was too much of a professional for that, and knew that the catch was not on.

But she did lift her head just slightly as she laughed.

Chris's eldest daughter pivoted on her left foot, swung her right arm around, and slammed her bloodied fist into the side of Grin's head. It wasn't a hard impact. But Grin's eyes went wide, and even from twenty feet away Rose saw the woman's eye flood red.

The girl pushed her mother and sister to the ground.

Rose fell to the side as Chris reached into his waistband, pulled out the pistol, and fired.

Grin's rifle fired as well. Rose gasped, ready for the impact, ready for the shock of white-hot pain to rush in. Perhaps there would simply be darkness.

Another shot from the pistol, someone hit the ground, then another impact from closer by. She rolled, cried out as her arm was trapped beneath her, then knelt up.

Chris was on his side, arm stretched out, hand still clasping the pistol. He was bleeding from somewhere else, but Rose couldn't see where.

Grin was down. Squirming, trying to sit up and lift the rifle again.

Chris's family ran to him. They dropped to their knees, the wife leaning over and pressing her face to his chest, hands still tied behind her back. The older girl pulled their gags off and the sisters fell upon their parents, seeking succour and an escape from this hell. She glanced across at Rose. Rose tried to smile, but the girl looked away, burying her face against the side of her father's neck. Perhaps she was telling him how much she loved him.

Rose struggled to her feet. She'd been shot through the hip, but her leg still supported her weight. The pain was remote, belonging to someone she'd left behind.

Because *this* Rose now had Grin.

The Trail woman had been shot once in the right shoulder. She also had a nail protruding from her face an inch behind her left eye, and the orbit leaked blood and viscous fluid. Chris's daughter had done that. Good girl.

Grin's arm was useless, flapping around like a dead fish as she tried to lift the rifle, protect herself. But Rose got there first.

She stood on Grin's shoulder and pressed down. Grin screamed. Rose smiled.

Then her smile slipped. She looked back at the family crying and bleeding into the soil. They had already seen enough. *Done* enough. More than anyone, she knew how events like this could change people.

She snatched the rifle from Grin and smashed her around the head. The temptation to strike the nail, and complete its journey, was great. But she struck her across the right temple. The woman moaned woozily, head lolling to one side, and Rose hit her again.

And then she walked away.

She took a moment to hobble into the house and find Tom. He was slouched in the hallway, still conscious but bleeding out. Maybe he'd survive, maybe not, but he was no immediate threat. She aimed the gun at his face and he blinked slowly. Rose felt sick, tired, and something stayed her trigger finger. She searched through his pockets until she found the keys to the postal van and a flick-knife, then staggered from the converted barn.

Grin was still down and out cold.

Rose took a moment, breathing deeply, left hand seeking her new wound. It throbbed with each beat of her heart, and blood was making her jeans heavy. But she didn't think there was any serious damage.

Time would tell.

She limped towards Chris, hoping against hope that she would not find something worse.

★　★　★

Chris was crying. His family's tears merged with his own, diluted by rain, and somewhere there was blood. But he could not tell the difference, and one pain seemed to merge with another so that it was also impossible to tell where else he'd been shot. His sweet girls clung to him, Terri buried her face against his chest and sobbed. There were tooth fragments in his mouth and his face felt out of shape, burning and pulsing with every heartbeat. But he could still tell his family that he loved them.

'Hey,' a voice said. He spun round, still sensing danger. Rose. She leaned down, groaning, and slit the ropes still tying Terri's and Megs' wrists.

Chris tried to sit up. Terri helped, her touch firm but caring. Then she gasped when she saw the blood.

Rose crouched close to him, wincing, and appraised the wound. The bullet had glanced from his knee, scoring a bloody path through muscle and skin.

'Be a nice scar,' she said.

'As long as I can run again,' he said. He looked at her hip.

Rose shrugged, then nodded at the house. 'The other guy's in there, not quite dead. He stays alive, maybe it'll make things easier for you with the police. He knows the Trail, and hopefully they'll get him to talk.'

Chris was still not ready to think that far ahead. A few seconds, a few minutes with his family were all he wanted right now. This hunt was over, and whatever came next was the future.

The investigation would be an endurance test all of its own.

'You?' he asked, but he already knew. He looked past Rose at the woman lying on the ground with a nail in her head. 'You should turn her in.'

'After everything I've done?' Rose sounded suddenly colder and emptier than she ever had before. Chris's family winced away from the voice as if it could touch and hurt them.

He had no answer for her. She'd known the course she wanted to take, and he supposed she'd achieved more than she had ever believed possible.

With a little help from him. And from Holt.

'Okay,' he said.

'Good luck,' she said. Then she stood and limped away. With her one good arm, and with all her weight on her uninjured leg, she dragged the unconscious woman towards the postal van and sat her against the open passenger doorway. From the driver's side she hauled her inside. Then she stripped off her own belt, leaned the woman forward and bound her arms tightly behind her. Sweating, pale, groaning with every movement, the effort was staggering.

She only looked back when she was almost ready to go.

After a long pause she said, 'Have a good life.' She was looking at all of them, not just Chris, and sounded like she meant it.

He watched as Rose reversed the van around and drove back down the rough road. The gunfire would have been heard by surrounding properties and down in the town itself, and the police would be coming.

He hoped she made it away before they arrived.

Alone at last with his family, Chris allowed himself to believe that he had won.

33

coup de grâce

Each jolt of the post office van sent spears of pain through her hip and into her pelvis. Blood flowed and soaked the seat beneath her backside. But she did not care. She had already won, and yet she felt strangely resistant to delivering the coup de grâce. She tried to convince herself it was because Grin was still unconscious and she wanted the bitch awake when she killed her. But in truth, Rose realised that she was terrified of this being over.

The thought of revenge had given her something to live for.

The long, rough driveway gave way to a narrow country lane, its surface almost as uneven and potholed. Stone walls lined both sides, broken here and there by farm gates and stretches fallen into disrepair. She passed occasional grey stone houses, homes where families lived. There would be pets asleep inside, waiting for adults to return home from work and children from school. Perhaps a stew in the slow cooker. After dinner they'd take a walk in the fields, maybe aiming for the darker spread of forest that lined the foothills in the distance. Then they'd have family time in the evening, watching TV or playing a game, making sandwiches in readiness for their next, normal day. She envied them their normality.

She drove sitting in a pool of her own blood, a pistol warming between her thighs, and an unconscious woman breathing away her final minutes in the passenger seat.

An elderly couple walked along the road, and Rose accelerated past them. Glancing in the side mirror she saw the old woman raise a hand in greeting, and Rose switched on the hazard lights for a couple of flashes in response. Of all the vehicles she could have hoped for, this probably gave her the best cover.

So long as nobody wanted their mail.

'Postman Rose,' Grin groaned from the seat beside her, even managing a pained chuckle.

Rose picked up the gun and struck Grin across her wounded shoulder. The woman cried out. Rose grimaced against her own agonies, pleased that she made no noise.

'Don't speak,' Rose said. 'Don't say a thing. I don't want a conversation with you. There's nothing you can say to me, so sit there and shut up if you want to live a while longer.'

'They'll hunt you down and kill you,' Grin said.

'Really? What, those three arseholes up on the mountain? The birds have already taken their eyes. The helicopter pilot? The skinny runt with the dogs?' She glanced across just in time to see a dark look cross Grin's features. Then the Trail woman put on a pained smile once more.

'You really think — ' she began.

'Just shut up,' Rose cut in. 'Maybe I'll let you live. Give you to the police, a nice big public trial. Face splashed all over the papers, pictures

372

of your wounds, that fancy tattoo on your thigh. That nail sticking out of your head. You'll become notorious, infamous, and everyone everywhere will know your face. Do you have a family? I know you don't have a husband, or if you do that doesn't stop you spending time picking up young men to fuck. But you must have an extended family out there. Siblings, nephews and nieces, people you care about. Maybe your parents are even still alive, though Christ knows what they did wrong with you. So the Trail, or whatever's left of it, what will they think of you dishing the dirt on them?'

'They know I won't.'

'But I reckon they'll do everything they can to make sure, don't you?' Rose shifted the rearview mirror so she could see the woman's face.

Blood pooled and dribbled from her left eye, its lid drooping half-shut. Grin squirmed a little, arms trapped and bound behind her. She continued trying to smile through the pain. A sickly grimace.

'Beaten by a young girl,' Rose said. She laughed.

Grin did not respond.

They came to a junction and Rose had to pause, letting a car and a tractor pass from right to left. The farmer in the tractor glanced down at the postal van, and the smile slipped from his face. He shielded his eyes to see better, and Rose moved off the way he'd come, squeezing past the tractor and the stone wall. She lost the wing mirror on her side. Stone screeched against metal.

I've dreamed of this for years, she thought,

and now I have no idea what I'm going to do. Maybe it was blood loss and pain, tiredness and fear over what was to come next. She'd imagined having Grin at her mercy a thousand times. She'd use a knife on her, slowly, painfully. Garden implements, covered with dirt and dead worms, pressing into the bitch's soft belly and exposed throat. Electrical wires taped to her sensitive parts and wired to several car batteries. Bricks to crush her limbs, ground glass fed to her in yoghurt, metal filings pressed into her eyes. Rose had sickened herself by imagining the things she wanted to do to Grin, but never in those daydreams did she see Adam and her children smile. *They don't know me now,* she thought, that familiar idea. But she had come to realise a long time ago that she was doing this for herself.

For now she was just driving. She had no destination in mind. The idea of delivering Grin to the police *had* crossed her mind, but only briefly. So much would remain unfinished if she did that, so much left to chance, that it was not an option. It never had been. For now, she was simply looking for a suitable place for an execution.

She heard a sound that brought her instantly back to the moment — sirens. Sliding her window down a couple of inches, the sound came in clearer and grew rapidly louder.

Grin shifted in her seat. Rose smacked the pistol against her injured shoulder again, twice, three times, feeling the wet give in the woman's body where bone had been broken and blood flooded the flesh. Grin screamed.

Rose leaned over, hooked her arm around the woman's shoulders, and pulled her down into her lap. She pressed the pistol against her temple, nudging the nail protruding there. Grin whined.

The police car appeared around a bend in the road and roared uphill towards them. Rose slowed but did not stop, tried on a smile, then when the car drew closer she let go of the steering wheel and waved, spreading her fingers in an attempt to obscure her face.

The police car powered past without slowing. Rose breathed a sigh of relief and shoved the woman away, steering with one hand and using the other to push Grin back into an upright position. She did not fight or resist.

Rose glanced at her, back to the road, at the woman again. *She's hurting. Hands still bound, numb, probably useless by now. And she's barely conscious.* It didn't seem to Rose that she was feigning. But she had to decide what to do, and soon. The further she drove with Grin trussed up beside her — with *both* of them bleeding and suffering — the more chances there were of something going wrong.

The road dipped down a steep hill, turned a sharp bend, and they were in a small huddle of houses and buildings. A shop stood on one corner, displays of fruit and vegetables on a rack outside, windows filled with posters advertising local events. A little chapel sat further along the road. Several cars were parked on either side, and a few people milled around, some on their own, a small group chatting outside the shop.

Rose slowed. They'd expect to see someone they knew driving this van. One woman raised a hand, a man smiled, and then the hand and smile dropped away.

'I killed the kids first so your husband could watch,' Grin said. 'The girl, knife behind the ear, slowly. Then the whimpering little shit. Last kid, he'd crawled to your husband for help, so I grabbed his hair and — '

Rose plucked the pistol from between her legs and slammed it into Grin's mouth. Teeth broke and the litany of horror ended. *Goading me teasing me trying to force me to make a mistake . . .*

She almost pulled the trigger.

The woman and man still watched aghast, shocked, terrified, and they didn't deserve to see anything like this. That was part of the reason why Rose's finger eased from the trigger. But the main reason was that she was still in control. This moment was always going to be hers, and she would not let Grin dictate the time and manner of her own death.

As Rose drove quickly from the village, the woman beside her groaned, spitting teeth and blood. The police would be looking for them now, and the van that had proved such a convenient disguise would stand out, a bright red flag on the landscape.

A mile from the village she took a lane to the left, leading past a huddle of derelict farm buildings and down towards the valley floor. It was overgrown and unused, and several times Rose thought the van might become stuck. But then she reached a wider area beside the river, shielded by heavy trees and with a beautiful view across the valley to the hills beyond. She stopped the van, lowered the windows, killed the engine, and sat listening to the sounds of nature.

For a moment she turned away from Grin and pretended that she was alone, but then the woman snorted. Rose looked at her again. The woman was staring at her, smiling through gashed lips and shattered teeth, her tongue shifting like a swollen slug in the mess of her face. Perhaps she was trying to talk, but Rose no longer cared. She looked hard into her eyes, one clear, one bloodied, searching for a reason for all of this. But there was no regret there, no sign of weakness. Grin was already resigned to her fate.

Rose pressed her gun against Grin's right eye and pulled the trigger.

The woman's head flipped back against the door frame.

Rose fired again to make sure, and one more time just because she could.

She leaned back and closed her eyes for a few seconds. She no longer felt any pain in her hip or arm. She felt very little.

She considered simply leaving the corpse in the van and fleeing on foot, but whoever discovered it would be traumatised for life. So she took a good, long look at what was left of Grin, then went to search for somewhere to hide a body.

34

thirteen days

'Mummy, when are we going home?' It was Megs' usual question when they woke up, but today the answer was different.

'Today,' their mother said.

'Mum?' Gemma asked. 'Really?'

Her mum nodded. She was already dressed, and she looked exhausted. Earlier, Gemma had listened to the low mumble of voices as she spoke with someone in the adjoining bedroom. For the thirteen days they had been there that had happened most mornings, and most afternoons and evenings too. Some of them were police, some social workers. Health workers, too, who would come in and sit with them all, ask questions, talk about a variety of things which were, she knew, all about what had happened.

Her dad's brother and sister had been there, seeing them in the Cardiff hotel after visiting him in hospital. They told her mum that they'd been helping the police with their inquiries. Both of them had looked scared, as if this had all happened to them.

What she struggled to get over to everyone was that she was fine. Her mum and Megs were alive and well, and sharing the hotel suite with her. Her dad was alive, still in hospital being treated for his wounds under police protection.

Under arrest, in fact, although no one had told her that outright, and none of them really knew what came next for him.

So she was fine.

Because it could have been so much worse.

'What about our house?' Gemma asked. They'd been told that it was a crime scene.

'They've finished there,' her mum said. 'We've had people doing work while we've been away, too. New carpets, fresh paint. It'll be nice.' She frowned, voice going quieter as she said, 'We'll have some policemen staying with us, for a while.'

'How long?' Gemma asked.

'I'm not really sure,' her mum said, the uncertainty etched on her face.

'Will we have to move?'

Her mother didn't reply.

'I broke the shower curtain,' Gemma said.

'I'm sure that's been fixed too, sweetie.' Her mum hugged her, then slipped across to Megs' bed and lay down beside her. Gemma's little sister had been unnaturally quiet since those bad days, and their mum spent a lot of time with her, talking, playing games, sometimes just lying there hugging.

'Can I go for a last swim, Mum?' The hotel had a pool and sauna area, and Gemma had been twice every day they'd been staying there. She thought it was thirteen days. She'd lost count.

'Just don't be too long. They're sending a car for us at one o'clock, and I thought it'd be nice to have lunch in the restaurant first.'

'Will Daddy be coming home with us?' Megs asked, and Gemma turned away and started packing her swimming things. No one knew the answer to that for sure, her mum had recently revealed. Their solicitors were working on it, but the police were eager to continue questioning, and it could be that he'd be held in custody while they did that. Gemma hated the idea of their dad being held anywhere against his will. She knew what that was like.

She heard her mother's calming, soft voice as she whispered to her sister, and then Gemma said goodbye and left the room.

A man was sitting outside. His name was Dave, and he was a policeman. He was friendly enough, but she could not bring herself to trust or like him. His being outside their room was just another indication of how big a deal this was. And she didn't want anything about this to be a big deal — not that they were taken, not that her dad had been hunted like a bloody fox, not that a strange woman had come along to help him and killed people up in the mountains, and more around the farmhouse where they'd been kept prisoner. And not that she, Gemma, had stabbed a woman in the side of the face with a nail.

She slept well, but sometimes upon waking, Gemma knew that she'd been dreaming of Vey.

No one knew where their kidnapper was now. She'd spoken to her mum about it, during their fourth or fifth night here. They'd all just returned from the hospital, leaving her dad in a fitful sleep, and Megs had gone straight to bed.

Her mother opened a bottle of wine, and after a glass she'd had a sudden, explosive fit of sobbing. Gemma had cuddled her, rocking her back and forth on the double bed.

'Don't be scared,' she'd said. 'The police will find her. She can't have gone far. I banged a nail in her head.' The weak attempt at humour had seemed to bring her mum around. She'd wiped her eyes and laughed softly.

'Oh, I'm not worried about her. She'll be dead by now.'

Gemma's blood ran cold at the memory of what her mum had said. It had come from her dad. Such knowledge to carry.

Everything had changed. They were all together again, but she feared that her old family was gone forever, and nothing would ever be the same again. Gemma was starting to understand that, and the reporters who hassled them whenever they left the hotel made that clear. Sometimes she wasn't sure just who the police were guarding them against. She was too afraid to ask.

'Going for a swim,' she said to the policeman.

'Don't be too long. Your mum tell you?'

'That we're going home today?'

Dave smiled and nodded. 'That's nice news for you, kid.'

Gemma couldn't help smiling back. Maybe he wasn't so bad after all.

★ ★ ★

There were three other people in the pool. She recognised two of them, older women who had been staying at the hotel for the past four days. They might have been sisters. They swam side by side, but Gemma had never heard them speak a word to each other. The third person was a young boy, maybe her age. When she entered the pool room he glanced at her, then did a double-take. He smiled. Gemma turned away, aloof, and walked to the deep end.

The cold embrace when she dived in was welcome, and she glided underwater for a few metres. When she broke the surface she fell into a smooth, economical front crawl, pulling herself towards the shallow end, performing a perfect tumble roll, then settling into a comfortable rhythm. She was a good swimmer. Though she'd had lessons when she was younger, it was her dad who'd really taught her how to swim properly. He'd said that one day maybe they'd do a triathlon together, and the idea excited her.

Gemma had no idea whether that could happen now. Her dad had been shot. *Shot!* And though he was recovering well from his wounds and ordeal, the doctors had said he faced a long rehabilitation, with physical and psychological therapy.

She swam, and tried to let her worries drift away. The rhythm, the stroke, the regular movements, were all calming and almost hypnotic. Ten lengths, twenty, thirty, and she paused in the deep end and held on to the side of the pool.

The two women had gone. So had the boy. She hadn't noticed any of them getting out, but she was glad to have the pool to herself. Soft music played. Machinery hummed. She swam ten more lengths, then hauled herself out, showered, and entered the sauna.

Her mum said she needed to open up and let out her emotions about what had happened. She said Gemma had grown cold, distant, and she was afraid that things had affected her far more deeply than anyone else. Sometimes she said these things directly to Gemma, but she'd also heard her mum talking about her in the next room, to the social and health workers who paid regular visits. Big Ears strikes again.

'I'm fine,' Gemma whispered in the sauna. She threw water onto the rocks and welcomed the loud hiss.

And she really thought she was. Soon she'd be home, and then she'd be able to talk to her friends again. She'd been allowed a few calls, but they hadn't permitted any of them access to a phone or iPad. That had troubled Gemma more than what had happened; being out of the loop was hell. She could go to school, catch up, and start putting things behind her. Pull forward, like she did in the pool. She'd have to help her family, too, especially little Megs.

And her dad. When they visited, sometimes he looked at her and cried.

'I'm fine,' she said again, and the sauna door opened.

'Hi,' the boy said.

'Hey.'

He entered and sat in the opposite corner, rubbing sweat from his face, sighing at the heat.

'You here alone?'

'Just stay the fuck away from me!' Gemma

snapped up the water bucket, wielding it in one hand, jumped to her feet, and kicked the door open.

'Woah!' the boy said, hands held out.

'Touch me and I'll smash this across your face. There are police here, everywhere, and they're just waiting for someone to try anything!'

'Wait! Gemma, I'm sorry, I — '

'How the *fuck* do you know my name?'

He didn't answer. He just stared at her, hands still held out as if to ward off violence.

She stood in the open doorway, half warm, half cold, feeling slightly ridiculous holding the bucket raised in one hand. *I'm fine!* Lowering it slowly, she raised her eyebrows.

'Well?'

'Some woman gave me something to give to you.'

'What woman? What something?'

'Dunno.'

'What did she say?'

'She said to tell you, *Nailed her.*'

Gemma blinked sweat from her eyes and dropped the bucket. It rolled on the tiles and came to rest. 'Okay. Then give it to me.'

She followed him across the pool room and entered the male changing area with him. There was no one else there, but it still felt weird. Gemma focused on the boy, and what he'd said. It must have been her. *Must* have been. But what did she want?

'Here,' the boy said, handing her something from the kit bag in his locker. It was an A5 envelope, sealed.

'You didn't want to open it?' she asked. 'You know who I am, right?'

'I do now. Don't care. She gave me some money, and . . . ' He shrugged, almost embarrassed.

'She scared you.'

'Just a bit.'

'Thanks,' Gemma said. She left the boy, and the changing room, and ten minutes later she was dried and changed and back in their hotel suite. Her mum and Megs were dressed, cases packed.

'You were quick.'

'Yeah, I'm excited to get home,' Gemma said. 'It'll be good to get back to normal.'

Her mum's expression hardened, her smile slipped. Gemma looked away.

In the bathroom, she looked again at what Rose had given her. There were two objects. The first was a memory stick, unlabelled. Gemma knew that in truth, *nothing* would ever be normal again. But perhaps whatever information the stick contained might take them halfway back.

The second object was a small square of thin paper. It carried a simple message.

'If you or your dad ever need help, Tweet: *Jane Doe was born in Sorrento.*'

The memory stick she would hand over to her mum's solicitors. The message she would keep to herself. After reading it three more times she tore up the paper and flushed it down the toilet.

Gemma stared into the mirror, and the girl looking back smiled.

35

moving

'Is this the one that got away again?'

'I thought you might call. So who am I talking to?'

'You can call me John. How's the arm?'

'It's doing okay, thanks. I can still shoot a gun.'

'You showed that quite well in Wales.'

'Yeah. Enjoyed that.'

'And the hip?'

'I can still run.'

There was silence for a moment, broken only by a crackle of static on the line.

'You did a lot of damage.' He had an accent that Rose couldn't quite place. Probably European, though she wasn't even sure of that. 'Most of the British cell wiped out, and the survivors mopped up with the info the girl passed to police. And they were one of the oldest, active for . . . a long time. So you know we can't just let you go.'

'I thought you might say that, too.' Rose was nervous, but she didn't let it show. Her voice was firm, and she was in control. She had to believe that. 'So I've just got to tell you this, 'John'. Or maybe you're Hans Kluge. Or the husband of Chrissie Pinn. I could name quite a few more people you might be, because I know

386

so much more about the Trail cells in other countries than you can imagine. Everything I know about the Trail beyond the UK is recorded, placed in safe keeping in several places around the world. And I learned a trick from you guys, here — if I don't check in every week, that information is released to police and made public on the internet.'

John was silent for a while. Then he started giggling. It made Rose shiver, because it sounded so out of control. But really, she should know better.

'What do you know? A few names? Some websites, email addresses?'

'More.'

'Addresses, maybe. A few bank account details, some of our suppliers, photographs. Details of some of our friends. If you reveal that, do you really believe it'll do anything we can't undo?'

'Yes.'

'Our clients have included businessmen, actors, drug dealers, models. Several politicians, mostly from Eastern European countries. Mostly. Also one high-ranking army officer, close to retirement and mourning the fact he'd never killed. We've used our network to rid your country of several undesirables. The UK cell was as good as state sanctioned! And we have fingers in industries, governments, and business organisations around the world, and no one finger knows what any of the others are doing. I'm in telecommunications. We have lawyers, financiers, doctors. We've been around for a *very* long time.' He laughed again, but all the humour had gone. 'So even if something *did* happen to you, do you really think you could hurt us?'

'I'd do my very best.'

John fell silent again, for much longer than before. Finally he said, 'We want to see you try.' The line went dead.

Shaking, skin tingling, Rose placed the satphone on the floor of the Jeep and stamped on it, again and again until it was in bits. Then she drove for a mile until she reached a bridge and dropped it into the river below.

Driving. She'd done a lot of that recently. There was nowhere she wanted to settle.

Dragging Grin's corpse from the postal van, wedging it deep between rocks where hopefully it would remain undiscovered for a long time . . . there had been no epiphany there, no release, and no sense that anything like this could ever be over. Really, she'd felt nothing at all.

That frightened her.

She'd driven the van three miles further before dumping it and stealing a more nondescript vehicle. Then after leaving Wales she'd gone to ground for a couple of weeks and watched Chris regain some of his life. But only some of it. The infamy was instant, with the news full of his capture and the trail of bodies that led to it. His family's incarceration was also reported, and as the details of where and why they had been held — and Chris's role in their release — began to leak out, the whole tale became much more complex. He became notorious, and feted.

The media revelled in the story. Naked survivors shot and left in the mountains — one of them a minor reality TV character, another a retired football player — were not as innocent as they might seem. A couple of lovers who'd had their mountain bike stolen by the man at the centre of the story appeared on talk shows and signed a book deal. And several historical murder cases were being linked. A man on the Underground, tongue cut out; a woman in Cornwall, stabbed to death in an old tin mine, her corpse missing its hands; a body found in Liverpool minus its head.

The public loved it. Rose didn't. Chris had found his family again, but she knew that he'd be changed in ways that could not be undone. She went through a series of feelings for him — jealousy, respect, pity. She hoped that the simple fact of his brief celebrity would protect him from any desire for revenge from the wider Trail organisation; if he and his family were harmed, that would be seen as final proof of his whole wild tale. In truth, she was quite certain that the overseas Trail cells would hardly be concerned at what had happened to their British counterparts.

Her, though. She had rattled their cage.

She hoped that the information she'd passed to Gemma would help ensure the family were treated fairly. It would also guarantee at least a dozen high-profile arrests for older murders, and the scandals would keep the press occupied for weeks, or months. Perhaps with so much going on, Chris and his family might eventually be left alone.

In the end, though, she became ambivalent to

Chris's story. It seemed that was the final tragic tale of her own life. They'd taken her family, and in doing so had stripped away most of what made her human.

So she drove.

★ ★ ★

Thirty-seven days later she looked out at an ocean far from where home had once been, and felt the sun burning her skin. She'd cut her long hair short and dyed what was left to a blazing blond. Her arm and hip had been treated by a friendly doctor she knew and were healing well. It had been amusing to take on a French accent. She dressed in floral dresses, very feminine, very not her. She used a variety of names.

She was lost.

The breeze brought the smell of the sea, and she remembered Adam once telling her that it was the taint of death. The scent of the coast that so many people loved was actually produced by countless dead bodies, brought in by the ocean and deposited on the beach, rotting. Rose smiled and breathed in. It seemed quite fitting.

She walked along the beach for some time before she saw him. He was sitting in an old plastic chair with his crossed legs resting on a sea-smoothed log. He nursed a clear drink in a glass in his lap. His hat was tilted over his face and his greying hair was dark again, but she knew who he was.

Rose found another chair waiting outside the small beach hut, almost as if it had been placed

390

there for her. She dropped her backpack in the doorway and dragged the chair down the beach, leaving lines and footprints in the sand.

Sitting beside him, feeling the chair's legs sink in, she came to rest. Neither of them spoke.

Perhaps for a while she could stop moving.

Other titles published by Ulverscroft:

KILLING KATE

Alex Lake

Kate returns from a post-break-up holiday with her girlfriends to news of a serial killer in her home town — and his victims all look like her. It could, of course, be a simple coincidence. Or maybe not. She becomes convinced she is being watched; followed, even. Is she next? And could her mild-mannered ex-boyfriend really be a deranged murderer? Or is the truth something far more sinister?

CROSS THE LINE

James Patterson

Shots ring out in the early morning hours in the suburbs of Washington, DC. When the smoke clears, a high-ranking cop lies dead. Under pressure from the mayor, Detective Alex Cross steps into the leadership vacuum to investigate the audacious killing. But before Cross can make any headway, a wave of murders erupts across the city. The victims have one thing in common — they are all criminals. And the only thing more danger-ous than a murderer without a conscience is a killer who thinks he has justice on his side.

NO TURNING BACK

Tracy Buchanan

When radio presenter Anna Graves and her daughter are attacked on the beach by a crazed teenager, Anna reacts instinctively to protect her baby. But her life falls apart when the schoolboy dies from his injuries. The police believe Anna's story, until the autopsy reveals something more sinister. The evidence seems to connect Anna to a decades-old serial murder case. Is she really as innocent as she claims? And is killing ever justified, if it saves a child's life?

THE LONG COUNT

J. M. Gulvin

Marion County, 1967: Texas Ranger John Quarrie is called to the scene of an apparent suicide by a fellow war veteran. Although the local police want the case shut down, John Q is convinced that events aren't quite so straightforward. When his theory is backed up by the man's son, Isaac — just back from Vietnam — they start to look into a series of other violent incidents in the area, including a recent fire at the local Trinity Asylum and the disappearance of Isaac's twin brother, Ishmael. In a desperate race against time, John Q must try to unravel the dark secrets at the heart of this family, and get to the truth before the count is up . . .

UNDERTOW

Elizabeth Heathcote

My husband's lover. They said her death was a tragic accident. And I believed them . . . until now. Carmen is happily married to Tom, a successful London lawyer and divorcé with three children. She is content to absorb the stresses of being a stepmother to teenagers and the stain of 'second wife'. She knows she'll always live in the shadow of another woman — not Tom's first wife Laura, who is resolutely polite and determinedly respectable, but the lover who ended his first marriage: Zena. Zena, who was shockingly beautiful. Zena, who drowned swimming late one night. But Carmen can overlook her husband's dead mistress . . . until she starts to suspect that he might have been the person who killed her.

THE LAST ONE

Alexandra Oliva

When Zoo agrees to take part in a new reality TV show, *In the Dark*, she knows that she will be tested to the limits of her endurance. Beating eleven competitors in a series of survival tasks deep in the forest, while living on camera at the extremes of her comfort zone, will be the ultimate challenge before she returns home to start a family. As the contestants are overcome by hunger, injury and psychological breakdown, the mind games, tricks and hazards to which Zoo is subjected grow ever darker. This isn't what she signed up for: the deserted towns and gruesome props; the empty loneliness. Is this a game with no end? And what is happening away from the camera's gaze? Discovering the truth will be just the beginning . . .